THEM OR US

DAVID MOODY

GOLLANCZ
LONDON

The right of David Moody to be identified as the author of
this work has been asserted by him in accordance with the
Copyright, Designs and Patents Act 1988.

First published in Great Britain in 2011
by Gollancz
An imprint of the Orion Publishing Group
Orion House, 5 Upper St Martin's Lane,
London WC2H 9EA
An Hachette UK Company

A CIP catalogue record for this book
is available from the British Library

ISBN 978 0 575 08471 1 (Cased)
ISBN 978 0 575 08472 8 (Trade Paperback)

1 3 5 7 9 10 8 6 4 2

Typeset at the Spartan Press Ltd,
Lymington, Hants

Printed in Great Britain by CPI Group (UK) Ltd,
Croydon, CRO 4YY

The Orion Publishing Group's policy is to use papers
that are natural, renewable and recyclable products and
made from wood grown in sustainable forests. The logging
and manufacturing processes are expected to conform to
the environmental regulations of the country of origin.

www.davidmoody.net
www.orionbooks.co.uk

For Mum, Dad and Pete.

THE LAST ENGLISH SUMMER

At the height of the last English summer, the skies turned black as coal and never cleared. Backed into an inevitable corner by an enemy which had remained elusive until the last possible moment, the Unchanged military were left with only one remaining card to deal. And they dealt it, unleashing hell and killing millions. Or had they – had that final, decisive strike been delivered by those who coordinated the so-called Haters? Had they pushed the button? Whoever was ultimately responsible, the end result was the same. The vast, city-centre refugee camps all imploded, and over the space of a few short days virtually every major city in the country was destroyed in a white-hot nuclear haze.

A 'limited nuclear exchange' was an overused misnomer, but though it had been limited in duration, perhaps, it was not in effect. Although the weapons which had been used (mainly tactical field-based missiles) had relatively low yields in the overall scheme of things, their combined after-effects were catastrophic. Many thousands of people, predominantly the tightly packed, panicking Unchanged, perished immediately in the initial blasts (collateral damage, they used to call it). Those who had survived the maelstrom were forced out into the wastelands where their enemies waited for them impatiently: relentless, determined, and with an insatiable bloodlust.

The numerical advantage originally believed to have been held by the Unchanged proved to be another crucial miscalculation based on misguided and outdated assumptions. There may well have originally been an average of three Unchanged for each one of *the others*, but the typical

Unchanged was too slow, too fearful to kill even one Hater, while a single Hater was so full of brutal hostility that even the weakest of them was capable of killing hundreds. That initial statistical advantage was swiftly reversed.

The Unchanged became a vanishing breed: millions were slashed to thousands by the war; thousands were reduced to hundreds by radiation sickness and starvation. Those remaining hundreds were steadily hunted out and killed.

FIVE MONTHS, FOUR DAYS AGO

Before the burns on his back and his busted right leg had even begun to heal, they made Danny McCoyne fight again.

He waited deep in the forest of yellow-leaved trees, one of a group of more than forty fighters, huddled in twos and threes, trying to shelter from the dirty black rain while they waited for the next kill. Johannson, the hard bitch who'd ousted the last leader of this pack when she'd hacked him down in the middle of another battle a week ago, knew exactly how to hunt down the enemy. That was why so many people stayed with her now. The hunt and the kill were all they had left.

McCoyne sat with his back against a rock next to a man whose name he didn't know, sheltering under a limp canopy of bracken and drooping branches. He stared deep into the forest, eyes struggling to stay focused, looking for signs of movement. Times past he would have been desperate to fight, to tear those fuckers apart, but not any more. Those days were gone, and now he didn't give a damn; he did it because he had to. The war had taken its toll and left him a hollow man, little more than a shell. He was just a shadow of who and what he'd once been, his body broken, his spirit crushed.

There was a time, not long ago, when Danny McCoyne fought without question. When all the Unchanged have been hunted out and destroyed, he used to tell himself again and again, then things will start to change. When the enemy are extinct, the rebuilding will begin. The longer the war continued and the more intense the fighting became, however, the less likely that began to look. The level of damage inflicted on everyone and everything was severe, the scars indelible. So why did he bother? Why not just turn his back on the rest of them and walk away? The answer was disappointingly simple: his body had been badly damaged and the reality was that, right now, he couldn't survive on his own. For the moment, McCoyne's options were stark: if he wanted to stay alive, he'd have to stay with these people, and if he wanted to stay with these people, he would have to keep killing with them.

They'd been waiting out here in the dying forest since before dawn. It was lighter now, but McCoyne struggled to estimate the time, or even how long they'd been here in the undergrowth. The heavy, smoke-filled sky was dark; it had been that way since the bombs. He'd barely seen the sun since the morning he'd lost the last thing that mattered to him, his final tangible connection with the man he used to be.

Johannson's tactics were uncomplicated and effective. Most of the Unchanged survivors who had survived the blast had gradually returned to the city, taking cover in those few buildings still standing after the shockwave and firestorm. For some reason they figured slow death from starvation and radiation poisoning would somehow be preferable to an equally inevitable yet immeasurably more violent death at the hands of their enemy. Johannson had other plans. She had at her disposal a core of dedicated fighters, desperate for action and almost Brute-like in their passion for Unchanged blood. They'd do anything she demanded just to kill again. She sent a squad of them into the city to flush the enemy into the open, rounding them up and herding them towards the waiting Hater hordes.

Was this it? McCoyne sensed a sudden murmur of activity around him and caught a glimpse of movement up ahead. His heart began to pound hard, beating too fast, making him feel dizzy with nervous anticipation. He remembered the excitement and exhilaration he used to feel at moments like this, but now he just felt sickness and dread. *Can't do it,* he told himself, trying to picture the moment when the Unchanged finally came into view and he had to attack, *I can't fight any more.*

Then they came.

Rustling undergrowth and snapping branches heralded the arrival of the fittest. Two relatively strong Unchanged were stumbling through the forest, too terrified of what they were running from to think about what they might be running towards. They zigzagged through the trees, looking behind them twice as often as they looked ahead. Johannson's fighters waited, listening to them approach, fighting against their basic instincts, swallowing down the hate and desire to kill until their leader gave the signal. They'd learned to obey her, safe in the knowledge that if they didn't, they'd be dead too. Do what she says and you'll get to kill. Fuck with Johannson and she'll break you in two.

Johannson stood up and revealed herself, just yards ahead of the nearest Unchanged who, unable to stop in time, ran into her suddenly outstretched arm at speed. It caught him across the windpipe and he dropped hard onto his back, too stunned to react.

'Kill 'em!' she screamed, her deep, hoarse voice echoing through the trees.

There were eight Unchanged in view now, and still more following, and now they started splitting off in random directions, like a herd of panicked deer. They were attacked from all sides as fighters emerged from their hiding places to drag their enemy down, tearing each one of them apart.

As usual, McCoyne lagged behind, but in spite of the frenzy of the ambush and the chaos all around, his reticence hadn't gone unnoticed. There were others with worse injuries who were moving faster.

'You don't kill, you don't eat,' cried a ruthless man called Bennett as he barged McCoyne out of the way to get to another Unchanged, a young woman who was creeping back through the trees, thinking she hadn't been noticed and trying to get away again before it was too late. McCoyne forced himself to follow, his legs heavy as lead, his body aching, his head pounding.

But before Bennett had got anywhere near the lone woman, a Brute appeared, charging through the undergrowth. McCoyne pressed himself back up against a tree to get out of the way as the powerful, barely human killer approached. He looked briefly at the Unchanged the three of them were converging upon: Christ, she looked bad, so pitifully weak that even in his own miserable state he knew he'd have no problem taking her down. Her skin was blackened – she'd obviously been badly burned in the bombings – and her face was a haunted mask of scar tissue, the whites of her eyes the only remaining visible features. She was aware of the danger ahead now, but she looked resigned to her fate, knowing there was nothing she could do about it. She glanced back over her shoulder – every movement required a massive effort – then faltered. McCoyne could see more killers approaching now, at least three more of them, but before any of the fighters could react, the Brute struck. It leapt through the air with a grace which belied its stature, its powerful body naked and lean, still man-like in appearance but its movements more animal than human now.

The creature covered the girl's entire face with one large hand, then slammed her head against a rock, caving in the back of her skull. With a flash of awe-inspiring violence and speed, it stamped on her chest, crushing her ribs, then yanked her right arm from its socket with a single powerful tug. It ran deeper into the woods, carrying the dripping limb like a trophy, leaving its dying enemy spurting blood into the leaf litter. One of the fighters booted the woman's disfigured face, then the rest of the fighters moved on, each of them desperate to be the one who made the next kill.

McCoyne stopped and waited for them to disappear. Johannson was close. He could see her beginning to move towards him as she finished killing another. She stumbled momentarily, tripping over the trailing legs of her victim, then steadied herself as she crashed through a brittle-branched bush into the clearing where McCoyne was hiding. He quickly grabbed the woman's collar, lifted her head inches off the ground, and punched her jaw before dropping her back down. He hoped he'd made sure Johannson had seen him; he'd been trying to give the impression that he was the one who'd struck the killer blow. Johannson made momentary eye contact with him and he relaxed, relieved that the boss had seen him at work, satisfied that she'd fallen for his pathetic improvised deception.

'Keep fighting,' she grunted. 'More coming.'

She grabbed his shoulder, hauled him up onto his feet and dragged him back into battle.

Many hours later, in an empty warehouse on a hillside near a long-deserted factory, the group took shelter from the heavy, polluted rain which had been driving down all day and all night. It was cold, more like February than August. Some heat and light came from a pyre of Unchanged corpses, but ringside seats were reserved for Johannson and her most prized fighters. McCoyne and the rest of the hangers-on – the weak, the injured, the old, the indifferent – sat on the edges and took what they could, begging scraps, trading anything they'd managed to scavenge during the course of the day for meagre mouthfuls of food.

Soaked through, shivering with cold and unable to sleep, McCoyne stared into the darkness outside. Another endless night. The fear of being attacked kept him awake, but when he did manage to lose consciousness, nightmares would inevitably wake him again. He dreamed about the bombs every night, remembering the heat and the light and the impossibly huge mushroom cloud of smoke and ash rising up over the vaporised city; horrific images for ever burned into his mind. For a few days immediately after the attack, the bombs had given him a misplaced sense of relief, comfort, almost. He'd sought solace in the fact that such unspeakable horror had been unleashed and he'd survived. The bombs were the ultimate symbol of the Hate – how could things possibly get any worse?

As the night dragged on, McCoyne remembered a conversation he'd had, many weeks ago, with a long-dead friend. They'd talked about vampires and werewolves and other fictional creatures from the past, and had come to the conclusion that although they were still alive, the monsters he and the rest of his kind had come to resemble most of all were zombies. Back then he'd tried to imagine what would happen to the undead once the last of their prey had been hunted down and destroyed. Today he decided he'd found the answer. *This* was all that remained: this constant, never-ending purgatory. They would continue dragging themselves through what was left of their world until their physical bodies finally failed them, all of them desperate to satisfy an insatiable craving which would never be silenced. Nothing else mattered any more. Their lives were empty, but for the hunt and the kill. It was an inescapable paradox: by destroying their enemy they were also removing their own reason to live.

He curled up in the darkness on the outside edge of the group and tried to rest, knowing that somehow he had to build up his strength for tomorrow. The hunting and fighting would begin again at daybreak. *Who I used to be, and everything I've done before today, counts for nothing*, he thought to himself as he tried to shut out the noise of the animals around the fire. *If I don't kill tomorrow, I'm dead.*

THREE MONTHS, THREE WEEKS AGO

Johannson was gone, killed in a battle over hunting grounds several weeks back. In the days preceding her death, her growing army had slowly drifted east towards the coast until it reached the edge of territory controlled by a man called Thacker. Although nowhere near as ruthless a warrior as Johannson, Thacker had other qualities which inspired hordes of fighters to follow him; their numbers ultimately gave him a crucial edge. Much of the population had become nomadic, but Thacker was different. He ran his operations from an easily defended location, which provided shelter as well as storage for food, weapons and other vital supplies. Seeing Thacker's set-up, Johannson's own people turned against her when she challenged him, quickly realising they'd be better off with this new lord and master. Thacker was not just aware of the importance of hunting and killing the Unchanged, he was also thinking of the future: about what might happen tomorrow, or the next day, or the day after that. Unlike just about everyone else, Thacker had started to plan ahead.

Thacker had occupied the coastal town of Lowestoft, populating it with his fighters, several hundred of them, and an ever-increasing horde of accompanying scavengers. Before the war it had been a curious mix of industrial port and seaside resort, and its relative remoteness – it was the most easterly point on the map – had shielded it from the worst of the fighting. It had been stripped of pretty much everything of value, but unlike most of the country's towns and cities, its basic physical infrastructure was sound.

Though there were few unbroken windows or secure doors, most of Lowestoft's buildings were still standing.

Thacker was a sensible man (in his pre-war life he'd been national operations manager for a large and successful chain of hotels), and he immediately recognised the potential value of a place like Lowestoft in this new post-war world. Its coastal location was important, and easy to defend. It was an ideal size: large enough to cope with a decent-sized population, but sufficiently compact to be managed effectively by him and his small army.

First light. McCoyne reported for duty and joined the back of the queue of volunteers, as he did every morning. He'd been picked up off the road after the bombs and forced to join the hunting parties, but they had gradually begun to change in purpose over the last few weeks. The Unchanged were becoming harder to find, and the competition to be the one who actually made the precious kills was intensifying. Like an increasing number of people (Switchbacks, Thacker liked to call them – *Christ*, McCoyne thought, *why does everyone have to have a label these days?*), McCoyne had volunteered to be a scavenger, working alongside the hunting parties. Those who weren't particularly capable fighters but who had retained useful skills from their pre-war vocations – builders, mechanics, medics and the like – found some useful employment in the town. They were paid in food by Thacker to repair and rebuild as best they could with the limited resources. But there was no call for a useless half-rate desk jockey like the man McCoyne used to be, so his career options had been reduced overnight to a simple choice: scavenge or beg – and at least scavenging meant he'd sometimes find the odd extra scrap which he could shove in his pocket when no one was looking to either eat himself or trade with later.

Lowestoft might not be much, but it was as good as it was going to get, and it was his best chance of survival. He wasn't stupid – tired, maybe, apathetic, and sick of constantly fighting, perhaps, but not stupid.

A fleet of battered vans left Lowestoft each morning at daybreak. Each had a couple of fighters sitting up front and a handful of scavengers crammed into the back behind them. Thacker's generals (those few fighters who were able to exert any real influence over the rest of them) dispatched the vehicles out towards villages and towns in a steadily widening arc. Once they'd arrived at their destinations, the teams were under orders to split up. They were looking for Unchanged, first of all, then food, water and fuel, and then anything else they could find.

McCoyne stood behind the van in the middle of a dead village he didn't even know the name of and looked around dejectedly. The hissing grey rain had stopped momentarily and now all he could hear was the water dripping off roofs and trees and trickling down drains. It was already obvious that this place was hopeless, and he silently cursed whoever it was who had decided to send them here. There were obvious signs that numerous other scouting parties had been here before them. *Mind you*, he thought, *it probably won't make any difference where we go. Everywhere is like this now.*

Hook, the lead fighter who'd driven the van this morning, shoved McCoyne towards a row of buildings on the other side of the road, grunting at him to check them out. McCoyne stumbled forward, but managed to keep his balance. A quick scowl over his shoulder was as defiant as he dared to be; any more of a protest might provoke an unwanted reaction. Grumbling under his breath, he wrapped his arms around himself and limped towards the buildings, chest rattling with the cold.

He peered through a grubby, cobweb-covered window into the first house in the row of five narrow, terraced cottages. He couldn't see anything inside and moved on, more interested in the takeaway place next door, and the newsagent's next to that. The newsagent's seemed the most sensible place to start. The door was stuck but he managed to shove it open, the unexpected noise of an old-fashioned entrance bell ringing out and announcing his success at gaining entry. He stood still in the middle of the shop and waited for a moment, wondering if anyone was going to come to the counter, a dumb, instinctive reaction. The owners of this place were almost certainly long gone or dead. Judging by the stench in this gloomy, icy-cold building, he was betting on the latter.

Once his eyes had become accustomed to the low light, he swung his empty rucksack off his shoulders and started picking his way through the waste scattered all around the musty room. He took everything he could find, no matter how insignificant: newspapers and magazines to help light fires, a couple of paperback books, some string, scissors and other bits of stationery . . . Around the back of the counter he found some sweets – several bars of chocolate and a handful of lollipops, which he split unequally between Thacker and himself, shoving what he designated as his own personal hoard into the pockets of the trousers he wore under his baggy over-trousers, where Hook and the others wouldn't find them. He checked the rest of the building and found some garden tools in an outhouse, some bedding, and a few pieces of cutlery. He briefly checked inside a storeroom but didn't waste much time there: it was almost empty anyway, and he could tell from the droppings which covered the floor and the holes which had been gnawed in the sides of the few cardboard boxes which remained on the shelves that he wasn't the first scavenger to have been there. There was a body slumped against the back wall and he could see the flesh of the corpse had been picked clean by rodents' teeth. Yellow bone was visible beneath flaps of heavily stained clothing.

McCoyne returned to the road outside to dump his stash.

The rest of the party had busied themselves clearing out a service station and a small hotel, and by the looks of things they'd already found a damn sight more than he had.

Hook just happened to be looking up at the wrong moment. He stormed out to meet him and snatched his rucksack. 'This it?'

'There's nothing left. What am I supposed to do if there's nothing left? I can't magic stuff out of thin air,' McCoyne growled.

Hook shoved McCoyne angrily in the chest, and he tripped and fell on his backside, landing in the gutter. He was soaked with dirty rainwater. Hook grabbed another empty bag from the back of the van and threw it at him.

'Keep looking,' he ordered, 'find more.'

McCoyne wearily picked himself up again and trudged towards the takeaway, praying he'd find enough stuff inside to avoid the inevitable beating he'd get from Hook if he came back empty-handed. His body ached and he felt permanently tired; he didn't know how much more of this he could take.

Inside the shop, a waist-high counter separated the public area from the rest of the building. He fumbled with an awkward brass latch, then lifted up the hinged section of counter and went through to the back. *Please let me find food*, he thought to himself, and found himself making desperate contingency plans just in case – could he creep back to the van, steal some of what the others had already found? Then he could hand it back in again as his own and try to make it look like it was newly discovered stash . . .

The kitchen was disappointingly, if not unexpectedly, empty. It had obviously been ransacked, like the shop next door, and subject to the same ferocious vermin infestation. He checked every cupboard and shelf, desperate to find something that might appease Hook, but there was nothing left. He walked along a hallway into a compact living area behind the kitchens and stared out into the overgrown back garden. He was trying to decide whether he had enough strength (or desire) to try and get back to Lowestoft by himself, and avoid facing that bastard Hook altogether, when he heard something – footsteps – and they were directly above his head, in a room upstairs.

He quietly lay down his bag, unsheathed one of his knives and crept slowly towards the bottom of the staircase. Whoever or whatever was up there, it might be enough to get him out of a battering. There was silence now, but he hadn't imagined the footsteps, he was certain. With his pulse racing and his mouth dry, he climbed the steep steps to the first floor. It was dark, but he didn't need to see to know that there was someone up here with him; the pungent whiff of sweat and fresh human waste gave it away. He needed to take his time and not screw this up. It was either someone like him, who'd turned their back on what was left of society (and he'd come across several people like that before now), or it was one of *them*.

The room above the kitchen was empty. There was a bed, which looked like it had been recently slept in, and a pathetically small store of supplies. Whoever had been staying here had shown some initiative; they'd been living off the vermin who were living off the food downstairs and next door. Three dead rats were hanging by their tails from a clothes drier, and next to them was the deflated husk of something he didn't recognise, a cat or a small dog, maybe. And no matter what else turned out to be here, this was *meat*, and that meant that McCoyne now had *something* to give to Hook. He opened the threadbare curtains, filling the room with dull morning light, and looked around for something to carry his booty in.

As he walked back towards the top of the stairs to check the other rooms, he caught himself on a wooden chest of drawers, which was sticking out from the wall at an awkward angle. Curious, he leant over the top of it, and saw that there was a small hole in the wall, just wide enough for someone to crawl through from this building to the next. Clever little fucker, he thought to himself as he carefully pushed the chest of drawers out of the way. Whoever he'd disturbed had a nice little escape route, and that was no doubt how they'd survived here undetected for so long. By now they'd probably have disappeared out through the back of the building next door, or secreted themselves away in some other equally devious hidden hiding place. He crouched down and looked through the gap, but he couldn't see anything other than complete darkness on the other side. He leant further in, and was considering crawling right through when he heard scurrying footsteps running up fast behind him. He tried to reverse out, but he couldn't move quickly enough in the confined space and a grunt of effort was followed almost immediately by sudden blinding pain as he was cracked across the back with something. He screamed in agony, and managed to roll over just in time to see a scrawny figure chucking away the plank he'd been hit with and sprinting out through the bedroom door.

'Up here!' he yelled, hoping that someone outside would hear him and help. 'Unchanged!'

He limped out of the room, his legs weak and his back throbbing, and staggered downstairs. By the time he'd got outside, Hook and another fighter had already caught and killed the Unchanged man and his body was lying in front of the takeaway. Bright blood-red splashes of dribbling colour stood out on the dust-covered grey concrete surface. Hook was standing on the pavement outside, the euphoria on his face clear even from a distance.

'Bastard was hiding,' McCoyne said, groaning and stretching for effect. 'Came up behind me and—'

Hook grabbed him by the scruff of the neck and threw him against the side of the van, leaving McCoyne half-stunned. 'You're fucking useless, McCoyne,' Hook sneered. 'Couldn't even kill one starving Unchanged. You need to watch yourself, sunshine. Fuck up like that again on my watch and you'll be the next one I kill.'

'I won't,' McCoyne tried to say, his strangled voice barely audible.

'That Unchanged,' Hook continued, 'he'd got more back-bone than you, you prick – at least he made an effort. You, you're just a fucking waste of oxygen. Completely fucking useless.'

SEVEN WEEKS AGO

McCoyne stood outside the recently built cordon which had been erected around the centre of Lowestoft, jostling for position. None of the crowd of fifty or so wanted to be there, but needs must. They all kept themselves to themselves, barely acknowledging each other, though the unseasonably low temperature and biting wind meant the warmth provided by people in close proximity was welcome.

If anyone had asked Danny McCoyne if he thought things could possibly get any harder in the days immediately after the bombs, he'd have said no; how could life possibly get any worse? But that was before he'd reached Lowestoft. He was sick and malnourished, and he'd spent every day since then hunting and scavenging for little return. Anything he did manage to find was immediately taken and added to Thacker's 'central store'. But that was then, and Thacker, for all his forethought, was now no more; he'd been usurped and disposed of in a very public manner by one of his prize fighters, an evil fucker called Hinchcliffe. The people on the streets called him KC, King Cunt. McCoyne had had his doubts about Thacker, and before him Johannson, wondering if they were really bloodyminded and ruthless enough to cling onto power in this screwed-up new world disorder. There were no such questions over Hinchcliffe's suitability for the role. In the short time since he'd assumed power, Lowestoft had been transformed, and McCoyne's position, like that of every other non-fighter, had deteriorated rapidly. The strongest had, by default, assumed positions of authority: they ruled the place, attacking first and asking questions later, and they weren't about to give that up.

Hinchcliffe's first move had been to build a blockade around a square quarter-mile in the very heart of the town, where he and his army, now several hundred strong, based themselves, together with all their stores, supplies and vehicles. It was bounded by the ocean on one side, on the other, the main road, the A12, which ran through the centre of Lowestoft. High metal barriers had been erected across the A1144 and A12 at the northern end of town and, at the south, a single checkpoint, now stretched across the full width of the road bridge where the A12 crossed the narrow channel of water at the mouth of Lake Lothing. All other access points had been sealed: Hinchcliffe had ordered row upon row of empty houses to be boarded up along the remaining edges of the compound, and every minor road had been rendered impassable with piles of rubble, abandoned cars and the like. Once the area had been completely sealed off from the rest of the town, no one came in or out without the KC's approval. Those Switchbacks who were useful, who could fulfil a particular function, were allowed inside. The rest of them could go to hell as far as Hinchcliffe was concerned, and Danny McCoyne, with no discernible talent or incentive, was one of them. He had become one of a thousand-strong underclass, living in the empty ruins.

Outside the blockade what was left of Lowestoft had turned into a shanty town. There was neither sanitation nor clean water, and people occupied broken houses or camped out in makeshift shelters. It reminded McCoyne of the squalid Unchanged refugee camps before they'd been nuked: the people here were different, but many of the problems they were experiencing were the same. Violence frequently erupted, and disease was becoming an issue. Food was in desperately short supply – Hinchcliffe only provided essential rations to a fortunate few – and a short-lived black market had collapsed quickly in the face of no actual goods to supply. Things were looking increasingly grim.

Those who were in the best position outside Hinchcliffe's compound were those who continued to scavenge the wastelands. They were paid for their efforts with a meagre cut of whatever they found – grossly unfair, but better than being beaten to death, which was the other alternative.

So the non-fighting underclass, with nowhere else to go (and no means of going, even if they wanted to), increased daily as people stumbled into the town, drawn by rumours of Hinchcliffe's 'new society'. KC tolerated them, and used them when it suited him. He controlled the food supplies, carefully coordinating storage across numerous sites and ensuring that he was the only one who knew where everything was, and he controlled the fighters. He had done better than his predecessors, worming himself into an apparently unassailable position. His foot-soldiers were rewarded for their loyalty with a life which was more comfortable than many would have ever believed possible when the war had been at its bloody peak. On the right side of the compound wall there was a supply of (fairly) clean water, enough food for all and, occasionally, heat and power. On the other side there was nothing.

The crowd which McCoyne had joined this morning was gathered in front of the larger of the two gates, at the northern edge of the compound. Word had spread that a scavenging party was heading out west today, into an area which had, until now, remained relatively untouched. Over the last couple of months it had been established that at least six cities (or more precisely, six refugee camps) had been destroyed by the nuclear strikes last summer: London in the south, Edinburgh in the north and Manchester and Birmingham, among others, to the west. Without the means to measure pollution and radiation levels, it had been assumed that the bottom third of the country and a wide strip running the length of the land, from the south coast right up into Scotland, was most probably uninhabitable. But now, almost six months after the bombs, necessity was forcing the foragers to start looking further afield for supplies.

Hinchcliffe had ordered a Switchback, a woman who'd once been a school science teacher, to research the situation, using the reference books in what was left of Lowestoft Library. She'd also found books documenting what had happened in Hiroshima and Nagasaki, and while they weren't necessarily scientifically accurate, there was enough useful information for her to conclude that although the actual targets were still nowhere near safe, it was probably okay to scavenge a little closer to the bomb sites. Hinchcliffe was happy with that – he wasn't the one going out there.

The huge metal gate across the road was pushed open and two lorries drove out of the compound, quickly parting the waiting crowd. Once the gate had been closed behind them, the lorries stopped and a shaven-headed fighter jumped down from the cab of the second lorry. People scurried out of his way, leaving a bubble of empty space around him, their sudden distance a mark of fear, not respect. Llewellyn, Hinchcliffe's right-hand man, was one of the few fighters known by name to virtually everyone left in and around Lowestoft. He had a genuine military background, combined with both strength and aggression; and a reputation second only to that of his boss. He was older and quieter, but no less deadly.

'I'm looking for about fifteen of you,' he said, and McCoyne squirmed forward, trying to squeeze through a gap that wasn't there. The person on his right pushed him back the other way, and he tripped over someone's boot and landed on all fours at Llewellyn's feet.

Llewellyn grabbed his collar and pulled him up. 'What the fuck are you doing?'

'Volunteering,' McCoyne said quickly.

Llewellyn looked him up and down. 'Suppose you'll do,' he said, throwing him towards the back of his lorry before reaching out and grabbing someone else, 'and you, and you—'

McCoyne climbed into the empty lorry and found himself a dark spot at the very back of the vehicle from where he could watch the others. He unsheathed one of the knives attached to his belt, just in case, and pulled his knees up tight to his chest, trying to get warm. *Get out there*, he told himself, *get what you can, then get back.*

The drive away from town was long, slow and disorientating. Conversation in the back of the windowless lorry was sparse, and the time dragged painfully. It reminded McCoyne of another journey he'd taken, almost a year ago, back when his eventual destination had been a gas chamber. He'd barely managed to escape from that trip with his life; what the hell was he going to see when they opened up the back of the lorry today? He felt bad – an uncomfortable mix of travel sickness and nerves – or was it more than that? Every mile they drove in this direction was taking them deeper into the deadlands, with its poisoned, radiation-filled air.

The engine stopped abruptly, and there were sudden murmurs from the people all around McCoyne. Some got up and started moving about, but he stayed where he was, fingering the hilt of the knife that he'd left unsheathed, just in case. Then the roller-shutter at the back of the lorry was thrown open, flooding the inside of the vehicle with unexpectedly bright light.

'Out,' one of the fighters ordered, and the 'volunteers' did exactly as they were told. McCoyne, the last to move, jumped down onto gravel then looked around and grinned, caught off-guard by his unexpectedly bizarre surroundings.

'What the hell's this?'

In front of him was a picnic area and an iced-over, duck-free duck pond, to his right a children's playground.

'I came here with the family once,' a stooping, painfully

thin man next to him whispered, grinning wryly. 'Place has gone downhill since then . . .'

The group of volunteers and their fighter escort were standing in the first of several immense, interconnected car parks. McCoyne shielded his eyes from the hazy sun and looked up at a huge advertising hoarding covered with faded pictures of smiling kids' faces, cartoon characters, roller-coasters and rides, things he'd hadn't thought about in what felt like an eternity. A theme park. He'd heard of this one – he'd even talked about bringing the kids here once with Lizzie, but he'd managed to talk her out of it because, as he'd told her at the time, it was too long a drive from home, and the entrance prices were obscene, and then he'd have had to pay to feed them all, then the kids would have wanted to go to the gift shop and . . .

'Oi, you!' an angry voice shouted in his direction. McCoyne spun around and realised he was on his own; the others were already shuffling along an overgrown path which led through a copse of bare trees, deeper into the park. 'Stop fucking daydreaming,' the fighter yelled at him. 'You're here to hunt, not to fucking sightsee.'

McCoyne ran after the others, his legs already aching as he struggled to catch up. He had to focus on the job at hand, even in these unexpectedly surreal surroundings. He crossed an artificially rickety wooden bridge over a murky stream, catching his breath in surprise when he looked down and saw a frozen figure standing ankle-deep in the water. But it was only a mannequin, a caricature of a old-time gold prospector. The paint was fading from the exaggerated, cartoon-like features, but the plastic man still looked in better shape than he felt.

Ahead of the group, the silent heart of the theme park began to appear through the trees, first the tops of the tallest, long-since silent rides, the occasional scaffolding tower or the curving arc of a stretch of roller-coaster track. McCoyne was finding being here unexpectedly painful – not because it made him think about who and what he'd lost; rather it made him realise what he'd never get back again. Finding the basic necessities to survive each day was such a struggle; he couldn't even imagine a time when places like this fulfilled a useful function again. Playing, laughing, time-wasting . . . it had been a long time since anyone had done anything even remotely pleasurable, and it would most likely be another age before any of them did again.

The group gathered in an open courtyard at the start of the theme park proper, crowding dutifully around Llewellyn as if he was their tour guide. The buildings scattered between the rides looked small and insignificant beneath the erstwhile attractions. They were all made to look like they'd been built for the gold rush; somehow the prospecting theme felt strangely appropriate. Directly in front of them was a large, odd-shaped concrete building with a faux-rock fascia. A large sign across its frontage said: *The Mine*. The door had been roughly boarded up, like the windows of the house in a zombie movie where the survivors were hiding, with gaps between the overlapping planks perfect for undead arms to reach through. McCoyne couldn't tell whether the boards were real, or just there for effect.

Llewellyn, now wearing a face-mask and with a rifle slung over his shoulder, appeared, flanked by similarly masked fighters on either side. He addressed the volunteers: 'Hinchcliffe reckons we'll find good pickings here. Places like this have been overlooked, not looted over and over again like the towns have. If you don't bring me back as much stuff as you can carry, then you will be officially designated as "fucking useless", and I will leave you here to rot. Understand?' No response, but no arguments either. He continued, 'There's probably all kinds of nasty shit still hanging around in the air here, so the quicker you lot move, the less chance there is you'll get sick.'

His second comment got more of a reaction than the first – even the vaguest mention of radiation poisoning was enough to cause concern in the underclass ranks. McCoyne couldn't understand it. Why were they so bloody stupid? Hinchcliffe was certainly was no fool; he'd hardly send them here to collect poisoned food from a poisoned place, would he? This was just scare tactics, designed to increase the tightness of the stranglehold grip he already had on the rest of the population. Was he really the only person who could see him for what he was? Maybe the others all realised but, like him, they chose to keep their mouths shut rather than risk incurring Llewellyn's wrath . . .

As the group split up, McCoyne deliberately kept his distance from everyone else. If he didn't collect enough stuff today, he knew he was a dead man.

'You have one hour,' Llewellyn shouted, his voice echoing eerily across the empty theme park. 'Tear this place apart, then let's get out of here.'

More than three-quarters of the allotted hour was gone and McCoyne knew he was in trouble. His bag was only slightly less empty than when he'd started hunting. He'd wasted time mooching around an abandoned zoo, trying to work out what each of the various piles of odd-shaped, oversized bones and scraps of fur had once been. Hinchcliffe had been right about one thing: the theme park hadn't been trashed and torn apart like everywhere else – but his assumption that there'd be rich pickings had been way off. There was hardly anything here. It was as if the food and supplies had simply disappeared.

Use your brain, he told himself, *try to stay calm and not panic. Think logically.* He walked under a dried-up log flume towards a long, narrow wooden hut which spanned the space between the entrance and the exit for the ride: this was the place they'd have been slowly channelled through to buy low-quality, overpriced souvenir photographs of themselves screaming, presented in cheap cardboard frames or printed onto mouse mats, key-rings, hats and mugs. None of this was helping. *Put yourself in their shoes*, he thought, *try and remember what it used to be like. I'd have got off this ride and I'd have been cold and wet and hungry* . . . He looked around, and noticed the side wall of another shack facing out onto an almost black lake. That, he presumed, would have supplied the flume. So was this a café, maybe? There was no one else scavenging around here, and it was his last chance. *Christ*, he thought; *I hope I'll open the door and find a previously undiscovered stock of food in this hut*. Anything would do. Just something for him to hand in to Llewellyn . . .

McCoyne was about to force the door of the building when he stopped. He could smell something. It stank like raw sewage. Was it just the stagnant lake? He leant over an ornamental wall and peered down. It took him a moment, then he spotted the source of the stench: a glistening heap of shit on the muddy bank below him, which was being slowly washed away by the lapping water. The smell was noxious, and it made his stomach churn, but he swallowed his nausea and kept control. He couldn't throw up, not here. He looked at the bank again: this didn't make any sense. It looked like human waste, and there was far too much of it to be from just one person. Was this from an emptied-out slop bucket? That was the only logical explanation. Would one person have repeatedly used the same bucket? Wouldn't they have just come here to shit and saved themselves the hassle of lugging it anywhere? *So*, he said to himself, *unless Llewellyn has passed around a communal bucket for everyone to crap in while I've been out here alone, this is probably from another group of people. And if they're hiding in a place like this, then there's every chance they're Unchanged.*

'Ten minutes,' Llewellyn bellowed from the courtyard.

McCoyne had to move fast.

'Found anything?' a voice asked, startling him. He turned around and saw it was the stooping man he'd spoken to earlier.

'Nothing,' he answered.

'Anything in there?' the man said, gesturing at the shack McCoyne had been about to investigate.

'Empty,' he answered quickly, lying to protect his potential find. 'Look, do me a favour will you, go and tell Llewellyn that I think there have been Unchanged here.'

'Unchanged? Are you out of your fucking mind? Don't you think we'd have found them by now?'

'Don't bother then. Suit yourself.'

The other man turned his back on McCoyne and walked away, shaking his head and mumbling under his breath, 'Fucking idiot . . .'

Whether he told Llewellyn or not wasn't important. As soon as he'd gone, McCoyne opened the door of the small wooden building and disappeared inside. He'd been right: it was some sort of café, and it was as empty as everywhere else – in fact, it had been stripped clean. A deep-fat fryer in the small kitchen was filled with rancid oil, but the chiller cabinets and vending machines were empty. Even the sachets of sauce and other condiments had been taken. In a corner on the floor he found one small sachet of ketchup which he ripped open and sucked clean while he continued to investigate. There was another door at the back of the kitchen which opened outwards just a few inches, but no further. It was chained shut from the other side. He quickly took off his pack and left the strap hanging through the gap, then he dropped to his hands and knees and lay down on his side. It was a tight fit, but he was desperately thin now, and once his shoulders were through, the rest of him followed easily. Once on the other side he pulled his rucksack through, then picked himself up and looked around. He was in a triangular-shaped patch of open space, with the shack behind him and another similar-sized building adjacent. On the third side was a wire-mesh fence, and beyond that, forest – probably the same part of the forest they'd walked through to get here. He headed for the other hut, stopping when he reached it. He listened carefully, sure he could hear movement. Probably another one of the scavengers, he told himself. He lifted his hand to pull open the door, but found himself staggering back with surprise as it was kicked open from the other side. An emaciated man came at him with a knife.

McCoyne knew immediately that he was Unchanged and he felt himself tensing up inside. He reached for the knife at his belt, then stopped. *Hold the Hate*, he silently ordered himself. *There might be more of them.* He lifted his hands in mock-surrender, and the Unchanged man, obviously terrified, took a couple of steps back. It occurred to McCoyne that the longer this unexpected stand-off continued, the less obvious it would be that he was going to rip the fucker's head from his shoulders any second now. He could almost see the man's mind working behind his frightened, constantly moving eyes. If he hasn't killed me yet, he was thinking, then he can't be one of *them*.

Turn this around, McCoyne told himself, *play the victim.*

'Help me,' he said quietly. 'They're here. If we don't get out of sight they'll kill us.'

'Who are you?' the man croaked, his voice barely audible. 'How did you get here?'

McCoyne was struggling to come up with a plausible response when he heard Llewellyn shouting again, calling them back to the lorries. He didn't have long.

'They're coming,' he said, 'loads of them – there are two lorries full. They followed me here. We need to get under cover.'

The man stood his ground for what felt like an eternity, eyeing McCoyne up and down, trying to make sense of the situation. McCoyne forced himself to stay still, not to react, all the time knowing that he should finish off this Unchanged bastard, right here and now – if anyone ever found out he'd stood here talking to one of them like this, they'd probably kill him as fast as they'd kill the Unchanged.

'This way,' the man said suddenly, turning around and

gesturing for McCoyne to follow him inside. He led him into the hut, which turned out to be a gift shop, its shelves still well stocked with teddy bears, toys and other assorted rubbish, through an interconnecting door and into yet another, similar building, then finally out through another rear exit and across a narrow strip of tarmac. Hidden behind waste-bins and a mud-streaked golf buggy emblazoned with the theme park's logo was a door in the side of a large, brick building. McCoyne followed him through, making sure to shut the door again behind him. He threw the latch, just in case the Unchanged realised and tried doubling back and getting away, and followed him down a steep staircase, then along a narrow, twisting corridor before emerging into a huge, dimly lit space. McCoyne struggled to make sense of what he was seeing for a moment. The room was a vast, clearly artificial cave, with fake stalagmites and stalactites bolted to the floor and ceiling, and pools of foul-smelling, dripping water. Light came from a number of lanterns dotted around the room, just enough illumination for him to see at least another eight Unchanged, all wide-eyed and mole-like. He shuffled back until he reached the nearest wall, and his foot kicked against a heap of dummies like the one he'd seen standing out in the stream. And then it dawned on him that this was The Mine, the huge building he'd stood outside earlier.

He could hear the man who'd led him down here saying, 'He was outside by the kitchens.'

'For Christ's sake, Jeff, *they're* outside. Are you fucking stupid? He's with *them*!'

'He's not, I swear – he's like us. Would I be standing here now if he was one of *them*?'

McCoyne slid along the wall, watching the small group beginning to splinter, listening to the arguments develop and the volume of their voices increase.

No time for this. Got to act.

He ran forward, into an unexpectedly deep puddle, his

boots sinking into several inches of silt. Off-balance, almost blind, he tripped over a rocky mound and fell. He could hear the Unchanged, panicking in response to the sudden noise, and as he picked himself up several of them ran after him. They were close behind, he could hear their footsteps echoing. He kept moving, unable to see much more than shadows.

Llewellyn and the others were about to leave, so he had to do something . . . The ground beneath his feet began to slope upwards and he found himself running up what might have been a long access ramp. He hit a wall, bounced off, and noticed, over to his right, the faintest chink of light. It had to be the way out. One of the Unchanged dived for his legs and caught hold of one of his boots. McCoyne kicked out at him, and managed to get free. He pulled himself to his feet again and kept moving, running now with arms outstretched. Another sharp bend, and up ahead he could see the boards across the entrance that he'd seen earlier, and shards of brightness pouring through the gaps between them. He slammed against the wood, but the planks were nailed solid. He peered through, and could see the others were leaving, walking back to the lorries dragging half-filled bags of supplies behind them.

'Llewellyn!' McCoyne yelled, as loudly as he could. 'Back here!'

Someone lagging behind turned around and looked for him, but when he couldn't see anything he turned back and continued walking towards the lorries. One of the Unchanged reached McCoyne, and tried to pull him away from the door, but McCoyne kicked him in the crotch and he fell to the ground, sobbing in pain as McCoyne turned his attention back to the boarded-up door. This time he managed to force one of the smaller boards free. He shoved his arm through and started working at another plank.

'Unchanged!' he screamed, at the top of his voice, hanging onto the boards for dear life as two Unchanged tried to drag him away from the entrance. The Unchanged were desperate, but, incredibly, they were even weaker than him and they couldn't break his grip. Now a third one was hanging onto his back, tugging at his shoulders . . . weak as they were, there were too many of them, and he could feel the fingers of his right hand starting to slip off the wood.

McCoyne tried to stand his ground, but it was impossible. He was wrenched from the entrance and dragged down onto his back. One of the Unchanged came at him with a knife, its blade glinting in a narrow shaft of light, but the man was obviously terrified, and had no idea how to use the weapon effectively. As he dropped down and lunged for him, McCoyne managed to roll away, but he was quickly rolled back, and the Unchanged started grabbing for his kicking feet and thrashing arms.

Everyone stopped dead as a new sound permeated their grunts: the splintering of the wooden boards across the door. Someone outside was striking at them repeatedly. Realising their danger, the Unchanged dropped McCoyne and scattered, and McCoyne scrambled up onto his feet and pressed himself flat against the wall as a flood of fighters and scavengers alike began to pour through the gap in the entrance. He crawled out into the open and sat on the dusty ground, panting hard, listening to the screams coming from The Mine, and waiting.

All talk of radiation levels and other such threats had been forgotten in the sudden euphoria of the kill. Three-quarters of an hour later, the theme park courtyard was still a hive of activity. Scavengers searched the den and collected up the piles of supplies the Unchanged had been hoarding. Fighters dragged the bodies of their enemy out into the open and stripped the corpses of anything of value. Eleven kills. More than the last ten days combined.

Llewellyn marched over to where McCoyne was lifting

food into the back of one of the lorries. 'What's your name?' he asked.

'Danny McCoyne.'

'Lucky find, McCoyne.'

'Suppose.'

'So what happened? Did you just stumble into their nest? Take a wrong turn and find yourself surrounded?'

'Something like that.'

'Talk me through it.'

'Why?'

'Because if you don't I'll break your fucking legs.'

McCoyne sighed and threw the bag of food he'd been carrying into the lorry. 'I found one of them while I was scavenging. I made him think I was like him and that you lot were looking for me, then I got him to take me to the rest of them.'

'And it was that easy?'

'Yep, that easy.'

'So how'd you manage that then?'

'Just something I picked up.'

'Is that right?'

'Yep.'

Llewellyn grinned at him. 'You devious little bastard. You can hold the Hate, can't you?'

McCoyne looked away and picked up another bag. Did he really want anyone to know? Bit late now. 'So what if I can,' he said nonchalantly. 'Not a lot of call for it these days, is there? Hardly any of them left.'

'When we get back to Lowestoft,' Llewellyn said, leaning over him until their faces were just inches apart, 'you're coming with me to see Hinchcliffe. He'll be interested to know we've got a freak like you in town.'

TODAY

The two men skulked silently through the filthy streets like starving rats, skin deathly pale, eyes blinking wide, both of them looking from side to side in constant, never-ending fear of attack. When they reached the collapsed ruins at the edge of the town they ran frantically, trying not to drop the food they'd managed to scavenge. Fear and adrenalin drove them on, temporarily masking their physical pain. Their bodies were wrecked; they were exhausted and underfed. It was the first time either of them had been out in the open in more than two weeks but weak as they were, Fisher and Winston were still the strongest members of the last remaining group of Unchanged in the area. They'd had no choice but to do this. There were only thirteen of them left now, including the straggler who'd found them a few days back. They both knew that none of them would last much longer if they didn't have food.

Fisher froze. 'Up ahead. Top of the road. Two hundred yards.'

Winston grabbed his arm and pulled him back against the wall of the nearest building. He watched the Hater in the distance. Was it alone or part of a pack? His eyes were failing, making it hard to tell anything from here, but it looked like a young boy, probably one of those feral kids like the one that had killed his dad last summer. It paused on the dotted white line in the middle of the road, sniffing at the air like a hunting animal trying to catch a scent. Winston forced himself to remain completely motionless and prayed that Fisher would do the same. Even the slightest movement or noise might give them away and that'd be it – months of constantly struggling to survive ended in a heartbeat (though maybe that wouldn't be such a bad thing, he thought). He watched the figure up ahead as it began to move again, very slowly at first, then sprinting away at speed when something in the distance caught its eye. Winston didn't move until he was completely sure it had gone. In those unbearably long moments, he asked himself again (as he did at least once every hour) why he was even bothering to try and stay alive. Why not just give up and get it over with? A few seconds of agony and it would all be over and he could stop at last. The fear of death had been enough to keep driving him on until now, but life was rapidly losing its appeal. Imagine the relief, he thought. No more running. No more hiding. No more crying. No more sitting in silence in the dark with the others, freezing cold, doubled up with hunger pains, feeling himself draining away, just waiting for the inevitable . . .

'We're clear,' Fisher said, his voice just a whisper against the icy wind. Winston pushed himself away from the wall and ran forward again, just managing to keep his balance as he tripped down the kerb. He narrowly avoided the crumbling edge of a huge, egg-shaped crater in the road, where the skeletal body of someone who had once been like him was lying face down in several inches of dirty rainwater.

Another few minutes of breathless, stop-start running and hiding, and they were almost there. Winston dropped the supplies he'd been carrying in front of the wooden fence then with fingers numb with cold he quickly lifted up the third panel along from the right. Fisher hurriedly climbed through the gap then reached back for the tins and boxes they'd collected. He stood up again and took the weight of the panel so the other man could follow him through. Winston paused to snatch up a can of fruit that Fisher had missed, and to check they hadn't been seen. Behind them, everything appeared reassuringly silent and still. A flurry of grey, ash-like snow drifted down, each flake settling on the ground for just a fraction of a second before melting away to nothing. The remains of the town where he used to live looked as lifeless as Winston felt. The gaping doors and broken windows of battle-damaged houses offered unwanted glimpses into a world he used to belong to, but which he was no longer a part of. A dead world. *Their* world.

'Get a bloody move on,' Fisher said anxiously, his teeth chattering. Winston pulled his head back and Fisher quickly dropped the panel down with a welcome thud, blocking his view. They snatched up the food and scrambled down a steep, grassy bank towards what once used to be a permanently busy road but which was now just a desolate, wide grey scar lined with rusting wrecks.

In their pitiful condition, the two men struggled to control their descent down the muddy incline, and Fisher found himself slipping. He fell nearly to the bottom of the slope, dropping most of the tins and packets he'd been carrying and filling the silent world with ugly, *dangerous* noise. He frantically scooped everything back up again, still constantly checking his surroundings for movement, before racing after Winston, who was too scared to stop and wait for him.

Beneath a bridge, in the middle of an otherwise featureless concrete wall, was a corrugated steel roller-shutter and, another couple of yards further along, a metal door. The door was dirty grey, and with the once-important warning signs now purposely obscured by a layer of black grime, it was well camouflaged. A few smudged handprints around the handle and on the edges of the frame were the only indications that it had been used recently. Precariously balancing his supplies in one arm, Winston hammered on the door to be let inside. Several seconds passed – several seconds too long for his liking – before it finally swung open inwards, revealing an emaciated man brandishing a nail-spiked baseball bat. He ushered Winston and Fisher indoors, then peered down the road in either direction before shutting the door again.

Stumbling in the sudden darkness, Fisher and Winston followed the short access corridor down towards a pool of dull yellow light: the main room of the Highways Agency storage depot, where the others were waiting. They dumped their hoard in the middle of the room and the other survivors – those who were conscious and still sane – all looked on in disbelief.

Sally Marks said what everyone else was thinking. 'Where the fuck did you get all that?'

Fisher dropped to his knees and began examining the treasure they'd found, holding each can in turn up to the weak light emitting from the single battery-powered lantern, struggling to read the labels. Around him, stomachs started to growl with hunger, and mouths began to water at the prospect of food. Corned beef, tinned vegetables, soup . . . how long had it been?

'Where did you find it?' Sally asked again.

'Exactly where he said,' Winston answered, pointing at the man in the corner. He'd only recently arrived – and thank God he'd found them. He'd told them he'd been following the road for days, ever since his last hiding place had been discovered by the enemy, and he'd tried to take shelter in their hideout, not realising it was already occupied.

'And how did you find it?' Sally asked him, unable to make out his face in the shadows.

'I already told you,' the man answered, 'I saw it just before I found you lot. There was no way I could carry it all myself.'

'Does it really matter?' Winston sighed.

'Yes it does,' Sally said grimly.

'Remember that corner shop, next to where the coach station used to be?' Fisher volunteered.

'On Marlbrook Road?' Sally asked.

'That's the one.'

'But we've been there before,' she said. 'Christ, we've been there *hundreds* of times before.'

'So?'

'So did we just walk past this stuff all those other times? Did you find a hidden store room we hadn't found before? Open a door you hadn't seen? *Someone* put this stuff there for us to find, you dumb bastards. It was one of *them*! It's a trap, you fucking idiots, and you walked right into it!'

'What the hell does it matter?' Winston spat angrily, struggling with the ringpull on a can of pineapple chunks. His fingers were numb with cold and he didn't have the strength. 'No one followed us back, we made sure of that. We only saw one of them in all the time we were out there, and that was just a kid, way off in the distance. If this was a trap, then it didn't work. This place is dead – even *they* don't come here any more.'

'*He* found us,' she said, pointing at the man in the corner again.

'That was just luck,' Winston argued. 'He's like us, Sally – he found this place the same way we did.'

Sally shook her head in despair and walked into the shadows, where no one could see her. She leant against the wall and massaged her temples. Maybe Winston was right and she had overreacted. It wouldn't be the first time either. Every day the pressure of being cooped up in here was getting harder and harder to handle. A year ago, all she'd had to worry about was getting the kids to and from school and getting herself to work on time. Now here she was, hiding in a storage depot with strangers, eating cold food from a can, shitting in a bucket in full view of the others, fearing for her safety every second of every minute of every hour of every day . . . if she'd known what her life was going to become, she'd probably have ended it when the troubles first began.

*

36

They tried to ration the food, but they were starving, and more than half of it was gone within an hour: desperate hunger temporarily silenced with a decent amount of food after weeks of being drip-fed scraps. It didn't matter. Eating was a distraction which helped reduce the tension in the shelter for a precious few minutes. Sally looked around at the few faces she could see in the low light. Eight-year-old Charlotte stared back at her from the corner where she always sat, surrounded by the barricade of traffic cones she'd built around herself, her face as pale as ever. The two other children sat close by, Chloë fast asleep, eleven-year-old Jake dutifully sitting beside her, drawing shapes in the dirt with a stick. On the opposite side of the room, Jean Walker and Kerry Hayes spoke together in hushed whispers about nothing of any importance. Sally had thought Kerry beautiful when she'd first met her, but her full figure had wasted away to nothing since they'd barricaded themselves in here. She looked anorexic now: all protruding bones, stretched skin and straw-like hair. In the opposite corner, Brian Greene did his best to disguise the fact that he was crying again . . .

A packet of stale biscuits (what luxury, Sally thought to herself dejectedly) was being passed around. She took one, but stopped before she ate it, distracted suddenly by a low rumbling in the distance.

'Did anyone hear that?'

'Hear what?' Kerry asked, immediately concerned.

'I thought I heard something,' she said, already beginning to doubt herself. 'It sounded like an engine.'

'There's nothing,' Fisher said quickly, scowling at her. 'Just *them* moving around up there. Either that or your imagination . . .'

He was probably right. She couldn't hear anything now. Sally passed the packet on to the man sitting next to her – the new arrival. He'd hardly spoken since he'd got here, but it was pretty obvious he was as desperate as the rest of them:

he was a scrawny bag of skin and bone, and he had a haunted expression etched permanently onto his weary face. He took the biscuits from Sally and passed them on without saying a word.

He waited for a few minutes longer before quietly getting up and slipping further back into the shadows. He stepped over a couple of bodies – one sleeping, one dying – and made his way through to the part of the cramped storage depot which they used as a toilet.

Sally tried to block out the foul noise of the man pissing from a height into a metal bucket. She'd never get used to such indignities, she thought to herself, and heaved a silent sigh of relief when it finally stopped. She waited for him to come back, but when he didn't immediately return she started to worry. Inside the shelter it was almost pitch-black, but she got up and felt her way along the cold, damp walls until she found him by almost falling over him. He was lying on his back on the ground, and he was trying to force open the roller-shutter. A chink of light spilled across the floor where he'd managed to get his fingers under the shutter. With a grunt of effort he lifted it up another six inches.

'What the fuck are you doing?' Sally asked, standing directly behind him, but the man didn't answer her – he didn't even look at her. He just kept working, shoving his hands further under the shutter, forcing it up a couple of inches at a time until the gap was wide enough for him to slide through. He rolled over onto his front and was about to work his way through the gap when she grabbed him by the heel of his boot and yanked him back.

'Don't panic,' she pleaded with him, keeping her voice low so the others didn't hear. 'Please don't do anything stupid. I know it's hard, being trapped in here, but we're—'

Catching Sally's extended hand he pulled himself to his feet and then, catching her off-guard, he spun around and pushed her up against the wall. He covered her mouth with his left hand and sank a knife deep into her belly. He was barely panting; the whole episode had taken a matter of seconds and she'd put up no fight at all.

'I'm sorry,' Danny McCoyne said, keeping her mouth covered to stifle any noise she might still make. 'It's better for all of us this way. Trust me.'

He laid Sally's body down and after making sure she was dead wiped his bloodied hand clean on her jacket before sliding out under the roller-shutter.

In stark contrast to the desolate emptiness of an hour ago, the road outside was now full of movement. Several battered vehicles and a group of armed figures had gathered a short distance from the storage depot doors. McCoyne picked himself up off the ground, brushed himself down and wearily walked over to talk to Llewellyn, who was marshalling the fighters from the back of a pick-up.

'Had fun in there, McCoyne?'

'They're fucked,' he grunted. 'They won't give you any trouble.'

'How many?'

'Eleven of them left, three kids. They've got a few basic weapons, but all of them are pretty weak. A couple of them are virtually dead already.' .

Llewellyn gestured for his soldiers to take up their positions. Five men, armed with blades, bludgeons and guns, stood on either side of the roller-shuttered entrance and waited as a Transit van reversed into the gap.

'Wilson,' Llewellyn bellowed, 'let them go.'

On his command the driver, Kevin Wilson, Llewellyn's chief kid-wrangler, got out and moved around to the back. He yanked the doors open and two small children came tumbling out. They were both naked and filthy, and they were struggling furiously to escape their leads, but when a terrified Unchanged face appeared under the roller-shutter for a split second, both children lunged forward and threw themselves at the man with furious speed. It was all Wilson

39

could do to untangle himself from the leather straps and let go before he was dragged inside with them.

Exhausted, McCoyne leant back against Llewellyn's pick-up and waited for the inevitable. It took barely half a minute for the other door into the shelter to fly open as the terrified Unchanged were flushed out. He watched as they came running out, straight into the arms of the waiting Haters, and fighters starved of enemy kills for too long vented all their anger and frustration on the helpless refugees blinking their way into daylight. One of them, the once-pretty girl he thought was called Kerry, somehow managed to escape, weaving around the two fighters who went for her at the same time and ended up knocking each other over. But she'd barely made it twenty yards before they'd picked themselves up and were after her again, this time working together. She was halfway up the grassy bank when one of them grabbed hold of her thrashing feet and the other thumped an axe into the small of her back, severing her spine. She died almost immediately, but they continued to brutalise her body, over-come with the euphoria of the kill. They continued hacking at the girl until the remains of her body had been splattered across an area several yards wide: a bloody swathe of violent red marring the wet yellow grass.

1

The bonfire outside the ransacked Unchanged shelter is burning out of control. The morons who were supposed to be watching it got distracted and started squabbling over food. There's a momentary flash of flame and a sudden loud explosion and they scatter, running for cover like frightened kids on Bonfire Night. Probably just an aerosol can, lying too close to the heat, but whatever it was, Llewellyn's not happy. He grabs hold of one of them and kicks his legs out from under him, then he drags the scrawny little bastard over to the fire and pushes his face into it. He's screaming and shouting at him, and the little man's sobbing and reaching into the flames, attempting to salvage some of the meat that'd been roasting, but Llewellyn's not pacified. He yells at him again and kicks him in the side of the head, knocking him out cold. The way the fighters treat the others makes me sick to my stomach. I look at the man lying flat on his back and I think, *that used to be me.*

I'd rather keep my distance, but my feet and hands are numb with cold, so I walk towards the bonfire to try and warm up. In a year that's so far been filled with hundreds of fucking miserable days, this must be the worst yet. The gusting wind cuts through me like a knife, making the already sub-zero temperature colder still, and blows the sleet that's filling the air into my face like a constant hail of tiny needles. I'm less than a yard from the fire now, but I can still hardly feel it.

Wilson, the kid-wrangler, is still struggling. He's managed to get one of them back into the van, but the other one's causing him problems. The kid doesn't want to go back

41

inside. He's constantly straining on his lead, desperate to break free and escape out into the wild where he belongs. Three men have got him cornered, but he's refusing to give up. As I watch, he drops to the ground and scuttles away at high speed, nipping between the legs of one particularly slow, clumsy bastard. It'd be laughable if it wasn't so pathetic. The feral boy gets to his feet and makes a bolt for freedom, but he's forgotten he's still on the lead. The force of his sudden movement almost yanks Wilson over, but he manages to stand his ground. The kid starts running in my direction, but finds the way suddenly blocked by me and the bonfire. He stares up at me, and that moment of hesitation is time enough for Wilson and two others to grab hold of him and manhandle him to the ground. They wrap the long leash around him several times, binding his arms and legs tight to his body, then he's screaming with rage and frustration as they carry him over to the van and throw him in the back.

I feel increasingly disconnected from all this bullshit. In some ways it was easier when I was just another face in the crowd. I guess I should feel something – pity for the kid, maybe, or the guy Llewellyn knocked out, or even the Unchanged – but I don't. I feel hollow, like every nerve in my body has been cauterised, and I don't give a shit about anyone or anything. I watched Llewellyn's men clear out the Unchanged hideout with ferocious speed and brutality just now, and I felt nothing. Some poor sod was dragged out and thrown on the fire still screaming. Others were just left on the ground where they'd been killed – and still I don't give a damn.

It's been a long time since we found an Unchanged nest like this, and the effect it's had on these fighters is frightening. It's been a release for them, a chance to get rid of some of the pent-up anger and aggression they've been forced to keep bottled in since the rest of the Unchanged were wiped out. There's an empty void in these miserable people's miserable lives now. Before, when the war was at its height, the hunt and the kill kept them occupied, but now there's nothing. Bickering among themselves and abusing the non-fighters alleviates some of their frustrations, but it's no substitute. *Oh for the days when there were still plenty of Unchanged to kill*, I've heard them say – those who are able to construct such considered sentences, that is. For most of them, their conversations amount to little more than a series of increasingly aggressive nods and grunts.

'Food,' someone next to me says, jabbing me in the gut with a bony finger. It's a woman, my height, with dirty, pockmarked skin. Clumps of lank, yellow-white hair have been torn away from her scalp, leaving scarred gaps. I take the chunk of greasy meat from her – half a leg of something or other, not sure what – and take a deep breath before I force myself to bite down and chew. It's tough and barely cooked, and it tastes pretty much as bad as I expect. Grease dribbles down my chin as I force myself to swallow, then bite again, and again, and again, until the whole damn thing is finished. I throw the bone onto the fire and it's only then that I allow myself to look at what it is I've just eaten. I'm not surprised when I see the rest of Llewellyn's men tearing strips of flesh off what's left of a dog's carcase. Dog is one of the easiest meats to find these days. And rats and birds – they all feed off the scraps of the world, and we feed off them. Three of the fighters are arguing over what's left of the food. The woman who gave me my share is hanging back deject-edly, licking the grease off her fingers while she waits for scraps. After a while she sits on the ground, next to the guy Llewellyn laid into. He still hasn't moved.

My stomach's already churning in reaction to what I've just forced into it. I don't have the same capacity for food I used to, but I don't refuse it. I guess I'm fortunate that Hinchcliffe likes to make sure I'm well fed (being in with the man in charge has its advantages), but eating isn't some-thing I derive enjoyment from any more. The taste isn't important; it's a necessity now, and I've learned not to ask questions. I eat what I'm given and deal with the consequences afterwards. And after what I've just swallowed, I know there will be consequences . . .

I help myself to a mug of coffee (is it coffee, or just lukewarm dirty water?) which helps take the edge off the overpowering aftertaste of dead dog. The bitter liquid provides some welcome heat for a couple of seconds but it fades quickly. Doesn't matter how many layers of clothing I wear these days, I never seem to get any warmer. I'm so thin I sometimes think I might snap in two. Sometimes when I look down at my body or catch sight of myself in a window or mirror I have to look twice to be sure it's me. There was more meat on that dog leg I just ate than there is on my whole body. If they shoved a skewer up my arse and roasted me over the fire, there'd be a lot of disappointed people going hungry.

It's quieter out on the street now, with most of the fighters either busy eating or clearing out the Unchanged hideout. Apart from the 'cook' (who's now trying unsuccessfully to pick a scrap of burned dog flesh out of the embers of the fire) and her unconscious mate, there's an ocean of space between me and everyone else. It doesn't bother me; I'm used to it. If it wasn't for Hinchcliffe, they'd have probably got rid of me by now, but the fact is, I've been damn useful to him, and he knows it. I can't match the violence of the people he surrounds himself with, but I can do things they can't, and that, as he regularly tells me, makes me valuable.

I guess he's right. Days like today help me secure my place in Hinchcliffe's empire. If it wasn't for me, they'd never have found this nest of Unchanged. His dumb fuckers couldn't work out why the stuff they'd been stockpiling kept disappearing; it was me who set the traps and left the bait and tracked the Unchanged back to this place. It was me who told Hinchcliffe and Llewellyn where this shelter was, and how best to attack it. I'm the one who spent the last couple of days underground with those foul fuckers, sitting on my hands, swallowing down the Hate like bile and forcing myself not to kill them until Hinchcliffe's men were in place. If it wasn't for me, none of this would have happened.

I have to stay focused on my own self-preservation. That is all that matters now, and if that means playing Hinchcliffe's games for a while longer, keeping him onside, then so be it. The sooner every single last Unchanged is completely dead and buried, the sooner the war will be over.

There's a sudden flurry of activity around the entrance to the Unchanged hideout again as the door flies open and Patterson, an enormously powerful man, drags a small Unchanged kid out by its long blonde hair. The kid is only five or six years old, screaming in panic and pain. Patterson is visibly struggling to stay calm and not kill her, though he could snap her neck in an instant, but he's under orders not to. His fear of Hinchcliffe and Llewellyn is even greater than his desire to kill the kid, so he picks the girl up and throws her into the back of a van.

Hinchcliffe says that Unchanged kids are important. He says we need to understand them.

'Good result,' Llewellyn says, startling me. 'I was starting to think this "holding the Hate" business was just bullshit you were using to get out of work and get yourself more food. I've just spoken to Hinchcliffe. He's pleased.'

'Good.'

'How long's it been since we last found any of them?'

'More than three weeks,' I tell him. 'Three of them in the basement of that church, remember?'

'Whatever,' he grunts, obviously not really interested. 'Anyway, get your stuff together. We're heading back.'

He walks away and I watch as the last Unchanged bodies are dragged out of the shelter and dumped on the fire beside me. The noise and smell of burning flesh is making my stomach churn again. The scavengers are rifling through what's left of the Unchangeds' possessions, though they've already been ransacked by the fighters. They're emptying rucksacks, going through crates and boxes, looking for anything of value but finding next to nothing.

All that time those miserable bastards spent hiding in that godforsaken shelter . . . all those hours and all that effort, and for what? Why did they bother? Did they really think they'd be able to survive here indefinitely? They might have stayed hidden for another couple of days, maybe as long as a few months, but they must have known that sooner or later they'd be forced out into the open, into the waiting arms of someone like Hinchcliffe or Llewellyn. I guess that's the one thing we all still have in common, them or us: we just keep going, even when common sense says it's time to stop struggling and roll over and play dead. We all keep fighting to survive, whatever the cost. It would have been easier if these people had just given up a long time back. Same result, much less pain and effort.

2

None of the bastards I'm out here with today trust me, and the feeling's entirely mutual. Typically, the only space left in the convoy of vehicles returning to town is in the back of the van with the captured Unchanged kids. There are three of them in the padlocked, wire-mesh cage that's bolted to the inside wall of the van. Outside, there's only me, and they cower away from me, even though there's an ocean of space and the metal barrier between us. The lad keeps the two girls behind him as they huddle together in the furthest corner of the cage, their backs pressed against the wall. He watches my every move, flinching whenever I change position, occasionally spitting and swearing at me when I get too close. He's too scared to look away. One of the girls is completely motionless. She's staring vacantly into space over the boy's shoulder. I do all I can not to look at any of them, partly because I don't know what Hinchcliffe's planning to do with them, but also because looking at the children makes me remember the things I try hardest to forget.

The van driver treats me with as much contempt as the children. I'm literally stuck in the middle here, not belonging on either side. I can't help but wonder what's going to happen to me when the Unchanged have finally been eradicated and I've served my purpose. Until we found this group, there hadn't been any sightings in three weeks. For all I know these kids might well be the last three left alive, and my 'talent' for holding the Hate could soon be redundant. I've no doubt Hinchcliffe will chuck me back onto the underclass scrapheap just as quickly as he plucked me from it.

The van slows unexpectedly. The engine is sounding like it's on its last legs, and I'm immediately on guard. I get up fast, and my sudden movements are met with another volley of spitting and swearing from the boy in the cage. I look out of the back window, but I can't see anything – the days are short and the nights long now, and the light's fading rapidly. I'm guessing we're well into January by now but the days, weeks and months seem to have all melted into one another and become a single dragging blur. No one even mentioned Christmas or New Year – I didn't think about them until long after they'd gone.

The engine's still threatening to stall, but with much cursing the driver just about manages to keep it ticking over. He over-accelerates and steers up on the kerb and I brace myself against the side, trying to keep my balance as the van lurches across the pavement. Now I can see there's a body lying in the middle of the road behind us. Even in the low light I can see it was a Brute – although I haven't seen any of them in a while. They're a dying breed. The war was all they had, and my guess is most of them ended up back in the irradiated remains of the refugee camps. Those few that survived are roaming what's left of the countryside, looking for Unchanged that are long gone. This guy I know, Rufus, he says the Brutes are a warning, that there's a lesson to be learned from what's happened to them. For what it's worth, I think he's right. I'm not sure what the lesson is, though.

We're nearly back at Lowestoft. It's an almost bearable place to live (in comparison to everywhere else), but from time to time I wonder if I'd be better off elsewhere. I'm sure there are other places like this around the country. I can't bring myself to call it a community, because that word conjures up all kinds of nostalgic, old-fashioned images of people actually getting along and working together for the common good. Lowestoft is just a place where people with nowhere else to go have drifted together. The most aggressive fighters, those who can hit the hardest, they rule the roost now, like some kind of prehistoric élite, propped up by the subservient underclasses, who live off the scraps they discard. These days, no one has bigger fists than Hinchcliffe. And so Lowestoft limps along from day to day, for now at least.

There's definitely a problem with this van. No doubt it'll be dumped as soon as we get back to town. No sense wasting time trying to repair it, they'll say. Just find another. The rest of the convoy has long since left us behind and the driver is constantly cursing and over-revving the engine to keep it from dying. We swerve again, weaving between the wreck of a car and a pile of crumbling masonry from a battle-damaged building like we're on a racetrack chicane. The Unchanged kids are safe in their cage, but I'm thrown around the back with every sudden change of direction. Eventually I wedge myself into position between the side of the van and the cage and stare out of the window, trying to stay focused on the barely visible glow of the moon behind the dense cloud layer. My guts feel like someone's mixing them in a blender. If I don't get out of here soon we'll all be seeing more of the dog I ate earlier.

We reach the gate across the bridge spanning the A12 at the bottom end of town. It's little more than a pair of tall metal doors removed from a building, their hinges welded to the back of two lorries parked facing away from each other. These gates don't need to be particularly strong – there are enough guards around to prevent anyone getting inside Hinchcliffe's compound without his permission. Having visible guards positioned at these key points helps the population to remember who's in charge here, and the underclass maintain a cautious distance. Even if any of them did get inside, they wouldn't last long. Pity the poor fuckers who are stationed out here in the cold, though.

We have a delivery of Unchanged kids to make. We're through the gate now, and I can see the drop-off point looming up ahead. Silhouetted against the purple-black sky is the distinctive angular outline of 'the factory'. It's an ugly, sprawling mess of industrial buildings, protected from the ocean on one side by a strong seawall. It used to be a seafood-processing plant – probably a major local employer, churning out tonnes of food every day to be shipped around the world. Even now, though it's been dormant for the best part of a year, the stench of rotting fish still hangs over it like a poisonous cloud.

This is where the Unchanged kids Hinchcliffe has collected end up. I don't know what they do to them, and I don't want to know, either. A long time back I heard rumours that they could be 'turned' to be like us, but I don't know if that's true. More to the point, does it even matter, now the Unchanged are all but extinct? I look at the children in the cage – still cowering, still crying – and I wonder whether I should do them a favour and kill them now? Put them out of their misery? I must be getting soft. I don't think I'd be able to do it.

We come to an abrupt halt in the middle of the road which runs parallel with the seawall, well short of the factory. The wind is fierce tonight, and immense waves are battering against the sides of the wall, sending huge plumes of spray shooting up into the air then crashing back down again. The noise and the water and the constant rocking of the van in the swirling breeze makes me feel like I'm trapped in the eye of a hurricane, the full might of which is, for some reason, focused on me alone.

'Out,' the driver shouts, and it takes a couple of seconds before I realise he's talking to me. I get up and move towards the back of the van. The kids panic again because they think I'm coming for them, but I'm the least of their problems tonight.

I jump out of the van and land hard on my weak right leg. My feet have barely touched the ground before the driver accelerates away again, the back door still swinging open.

He swerves around to the right onto a narrow access road that disappears away into the bowels of the factory complex.

And suddenly I'm alone, soaking wet and freezing cold, just me and the sea and no one else. I haul my backpack up onto my shoulders and start walking along the seawall, heading out of town. I welcome the isolation.

An enormous wind turbine towers above everything in this part of Lowestoft, and I gaze up at it as I pass. It's not working – Hinchcliffe reckons he's going to get it operational again one day soon, so the town will have a steady power supply rather than having to rely on generators and the like. I hope he's right. For now it just stands here useless: one of its massive blades broken, its internal mechanics and wiring no doubt completely fucked. It's a huge white elephant: a constant reminder of what this place used to be.

I pull my coat tight around me, put my head down and press on: the house is still more than a mile away. I could live in Hinchcliffe's compound if I wanted to, one of the chosen few, but I'd rather not. I prefer to remain at a cautious distance on the very outskirts of town, well away from everyone else. Out there I'm close enough to Lowestoft to be able to get in and take what I need, but still far enough to stay out of sight and out of mind of everyone else.

3

Out of habit I follow the same route each day, using the footbridge to cross the empty road into the estate. I'm out of shape: the steep steps are always that much steeper than I remember, and every day I have to stop halfway across to catch my breath.

The world is dark tonight – no street lamps or house lights or queues of traffic to produce that ambient glow of old – and the centre of Lowestoft behind me is easy to make out. In the midst of the darkness is a clutch of blinking lights and burning fires, Hinchcliffe's compound. It's hard to believe that this is what passes for a major centre of population now. The same thing has no doubt happened around the country, minor towns becoming major towns by default, because they're the only habitable places left. It reminds me of a medieval settlement. I remember watching TV documentaries when I was a kid about a social experiment, where people tried to live like they did in the past, in Iron Age settlements or Tudor houses. This place feels like that, but in reverse: it's as if people from the past have moved in and taken over the ruins of the present. I have a hard time believing all those places I remember are gone, destroyed or abandoned: London, Birmingham, Manchester, Cardiff, all reduced to piles of toxic ash. If all those places really are as dead as I've heard, then way out here on the east coast is probably as safe a place as any to be. I'm guessing it's only the extremities of this odd-shaped little island – Wales, Scotland, Cornwall, here – which are still liveable.

I'm off the bridge now and within a couple of minutes I've been swallowed up by the darkness of the deserted housing estate where I've based myself this last month or so. This maze of interconnecting roads was probably a perfectly decent middle-class area before everything went to hell last year, the kind of place Lizzie always said she wanted us to end up in. Now it's just like everywhere else, and the ruins are welcome camouflage.

I've got a system of landmarks to guide me, things no one else would give a second glance. I walk across the deserted children's playground, catching my breath when the wind rattles the chains of an empty swing, turn left at the road where three of the houses have collapsed on each other like dominoes, then turn right by the blasted oak – it's probably not an oak, but it's a dead tree and that'll do me – and right again by the old corner shop to reach the road block. I wonder who built it? They were obviously determined to defend themselves: there are four cars wedged across the full width of the mouth of a cul-de-sac, nose to tail, almost like they were picked up and dropped into place. When I'm on foot I have to climb over the cars to get through, and I always cringe at the noise I make, even though there's never anyone else here. Was this the site of the desperate last stand of a hapless group of Unchanged survivors? Were they cowering here together in terror, like the Unchanged I helped flush out of their hideout today, doomed to inevitable failure but unable to do anything else but keep trying to survive? I've freaked myself out before now, convincing myself that they might still be here, watching me from an upstairs window, just like I watched the military advancing ever closer towards my flat all those months ago.

I slip through a narrow alleyway, cross another road, push through the side gate of yet another empty house and down the path I've trampled along the overgrown garden to a hole in the back fence, and I'm there. Home sweet fucking home.

I check around, making sure I haven't been seen. I deliberately chose the most inconspicuous house I could find so I wouldn't draw attention to myself, but it hasn't always worked.

And something's not right tonight.

I can see from here that the kitchen door of the house is open slightly. I draw my favourite knife from its sheath and creep across the road. It's bound to be bloody scavengers again – thieving bastards. I really can't be bothered with this. I feel sick, and I just want to sleep. I hope they've already gone. I'm not in the mood to fight, but I suppose I'll have to if I don't have any choice.

It's hard keeping the house secure without blatantly advertising the fact that I've got stuff worth nicking, so I keep most of my things hidden or locked away. Right now I need to take my time. If the thieves are still here I'll have to deal with them before they can get away with any of my stuff. I can afford to lose the house, but not what's in it.

Keeping low, I limp across the driveway and press myself up against the wall beside the partially open door. The lock's been forced, but it's nothing I can't fix. Someone's moving around in the kitchen. There are no voices, so there's probably only one of them. The chances are they're looking for food. I guess it's easier to steal than to work for it. When I peer through the gap I can see a single figure, trying to prise open a cupboard door with a knife. Whoever it is, they're so preoccupied that they don't notice me creeping up behind them. Now I'm close I can see that it's a woman, wrapped up in so many layers of grubby clothing to keep warm that her movements are restricted. She's bent *my* breadknife trying to get in. When I'm close enough I wrap my arm around her neck and hold my own blade up to her face where she can see it. She drops my breadknife in surprise and I spin her around and slam her back against the wall. Every bone in her body rattles as she tries to fight me off, but she gives up quickly. Even in my miserable condition I still have the advantage of weight and strength.

'Don't hurt me,' she begs, moaning pathetically.

I slam her back against the wall again and she whimpers with pain. Lowestoft is full of useless fuckers like this: definitely not Unchanged, but nowhere near strong enough to fight, or to be of much use to anyone. They're really only one step up from our defeated enemy, the old, the crippled, the unskilled, those who are naturally just shysters or cowards – the people who would previously have been propped up by the welfare state. There are far too many of them out there, and if they're not careful they'll end up taking the place of the Unchanged in the eyes of the fighters. I'm sure I've seen this particular one hanging around here before, and she'll probably come back again if I don't do something to deter her. I push the blade of my knife into her wrinkled cheek, just deep enough to draw blood – it probably feels worse than it is – and she starts sobbing with fear now. Her neck's all scrawny. I reckon she must be in her late sixties – just a little old lady, reminds me of an old bird who used to live down the road from me and Lizzie. She yelps again, and for a second I find myself pitying her. She's not Unchanged, just desperate.

'What the fuck do you think you're doing here?'

'I need some food,' she starts. 'I'm starving—'

'There's nothing here for you – go back to town.'

'But I—' She starts struggling again.

She should count herself lucky she chose my house to break into; anyone else would have killed her by now. I should hurt her, but I can't bring myself to do it. She doesn't need to know that, though. I lift the tip of my knife up until it's just inches from her right eye and she freezes with fear.

'If I see you back here again, I'll kill you, understand?'

She nods and mumbles something indistinct. I throw her out of the door and she collapses in a heap, but when I start forward she scrambles to her feet and backs away from me. I keep watching her until I'm sure she's gone.

I bolt and bar the damaged door, using a padlock and chain to replace the broken lock for now. Once the house is secure I take my keys from my pocket and unlock the cupboard the woman was trying to break into. She'd have been disappointed if she had managed to get the door open; there's no food there; just a gas-ring. It's tedious having to be so careful, but it's important. The value of everything has changed immeasurably in the last year. I could leave a bloody Rolex watch in the middle of the street and it would probably still be there a week later. Drop a scrap of food, though, and there'll be a crowd fighting for it before the fastest of the few remaining seagulls have had a chance to swoop.

I double-check to make sure the vagrant woman really has gone before unlocking another cupboard and getting out my kettle, a mug and a spoon. Then I peel back the linoleum in the corner of the kitchen and lift up one of the loose floor-boards underneath. I've stashed a torch there, and now I use it to search for a jar of coffee. I know I've got at least two down here somewhere – Christ, there's enough food stored under my kitchen floorboards to feed half of Lowestoft. I've been stashing small amounts away for as long as I've been working for Hinchcliffe – I'm not eating much and I hold on to every scrap I'm given, so my stocks are building up. If I opened a shop I could make a fortune selling what I've got hoarded away in here – except there's no one left who could afford my prices, and food's probably the only viable currency left anyway, so there'd be no point. At least I'll be able to bargain with some of it if I need to. There's a cruel irony about many aspects of life these days: all that woman wanted was a little bit of food. I've got all this and I don't want any of it – but if I'd fed her, then she'd only be back again tomorrow, begging for more, bringing others like her to my door. Things don't work like they used to any more: you have to be ruthless if you want to survive. There's no room for compassion here.

I fetch water from the bathtub upstairs (I collect it in buckets, pots and jars out back), then let down the blinds and pull the curtains to hide the light from the gas-ring. The hiss of the burning gas is welcome, taking the faintest edge off the otherwise all-consuming silence. I try to warm my hands around the pale blue flame, but it doesn't have any effect tonight.

I've made my coffee and I'm about to start locking every thing away again when my stomach suddenly starts cramping. My mouth watering, I unlock the door, struggling to free the chains and get it open in time, then run outside, lean over next door's low fence and finally say goodbye to a gut-full of semi-cooked dog. For a couple of minutes I just stand still and breathe in deeply. The air is ice-cold, but I'm soaked with sweat and feeling worryingly unsteady on my feet, I wipe my mouth on my sleeve and stagger back indoors.

My coffee's gone cold by the time I've pulled myself together again and locked everything away, but it's still strong enough to disguise the bilious aftertaste of puke. In the living room I zip myself into my sleeping bag and collapse into my chair, pathetically out of breath.

The pile of books beside the chair is taller than the coffee table. Books can still be found relatively easily, although they're used to fuel fires more than to fuel minds these days. I switch on my headband torch – like a miner's lamp – and pick up the book on top of the pile. I can't help laughing to myself: I'd never have been caught dead reading something like this before the war. Not that I used to read much anyway, but this – this is the kind of book bored pensioners used to read, lonely spinsters still dreaming of the moment their knight in shining armour would arrive to whisk them away from their loveless lives. It's a trashy thriller-cum-romance novel, and as clichéd as it sounds, this sort of book has become something of a release. They help me to forget where I am and who I am, and what I have to deal with each day. They almost make me feel human again.

I look again at the beautiful painted woman on the front cover. Something about the shape of her face reminds me of the Unchanged woman I killed in the shelter earlier today. She was my first kill in weeks, and I didn't want to do it – I don't have the same burning desire I used to – but I knew I didn't have any choice. She'd have suffered more if I'd let her live.

I've just got to the part in the book where the female lead first meets the guy who'll change her life for ever on his way to saving the world. Christ, what's wrong with me? I can already feel myself welling up. By the time they inevitably end up in bed together, I'll be crying like a fucking baby.

4

Some fucker's banging on the door. My eyes are still screwed shut. I'm nowhere near ready to start another day. If I don't react, maybe whoever it is will give up and go away. I half open one eye and look around. It's light outside, not long after dawn. My book's on the floor. My tired body aches more than it did when I went to sleep.

The hammering on the door continues and I know who it is now. He lifts the flap of the letter box and shouts at me. I know he's not going anywhere, but I make him wait a little longer.

'Come on, Danny, I know you're in there!'

'Piss off, Rufus,' I yell back.

He starts knocking on the window, rapping on the glass with his knuckles, and the sound hurts my head. I'll go and see what he wants, then get rid of him. Rufus has this annoying habit of coming here when he's got nowhere else to go. He's always wanting to talk for hours, about nothing in particular. Normally I can tolerate him, but I don't feel so good this morning and I'm not in the mood. Sometimes he stays all day and we play cards together and put the world to rights (although that particular problem's bigger than both of us), but I'm not up for that, not today.

But he's not going anywhere. Admitting defeat, I start to get up, but fall back down again when the morning cough hits me. I've smoked less than a handful of cigarettes in my whole life, but these days I sound like a chain-smoker on a fifty-a-day habit for the last twenty years. The cough comes in wrenching waves and I know there's nothing I can do to fight it. I steady myself on the back of the chair as another hacking burst overtakes me. My sleeping bag drops down around my feet like a used condom, leaving me exposed and freezing cold. One more tearing retch that makes me feel like I'm being turned inside out, and the coughing finally starts to subside. I spit out a sticky lump of bloody green phlegm into my empty coffee cup, step out of the sleeping bag and stagger over to open the door.

'What?'

'You took your time,' he says, not impressed.

'What do you want?'

Rufus glares up at me (he's a good few inches shorter than I am), then ducks under my outstretched arm and pushes his way into the house. 'You're a pain in the backside, Danny. Why didn't you just let me in?'

'*I'm* a pain in the backside? You're the one banging on the window like a bloody idiot.'

'Did you not hear me knocking? Bloody hell, I've been out there for ages. It's freezing outside.'

'It's winter, what do you expect? Anyway, it's no better in here.'

I climb back into my sleeping bag, pull it up over me and sit down again. He stands in front of me in the middle of the living room, flapping his arms around himself to try and get warm.

'You should light a fire or something,' he says, blowing into his hands.

'Can't be bothered. Too much effort.'

'You need to start taking more care of yourself. You're not looking so good.'

'Thanks.'

'You know what I mean.' He picks my book up off the floor and starts flicking through the pages. He has to hold it right up to his face to be able to read anything. Poor bugger's eyesight is bad. He was a voracious reader, but he's been reduced to reading children's editions because the print's larger. He used to wear strong glasses but the lenses were broken when he got caught up in the middle of a fight he had nothing to do with. Rufus doesn't handle conflict well – makes me wonder how he's lasted this long. He has another fresh bruise on his face this morning. He's probably wound someone up again; half the time he doesn't even realise when he's doing it.

'Don't know how you can read this crap.'

'It's simple, shallow and predictable. Just what I need.'

'Yes, but there's a whole load of literature out there, Dan. Read some classics. Broaden your horizons.'

'I don't want to broaden my horizons. In fact, I want to start limiting my horizons to the four walls of this house and screw everything else.'

'Don't be so narrow. Listen, have you read *1984*? I managed to salvage a pile of post-apocalyptic books from the library before Hinchcliffe's morons burned them. You should read it. And *Earth Abides*, that's another. It's really interesting to see how people thought things were going to pan out. I mean, they were all miles off the mark, but don't let that—'

'Rufus,' I interrupt, 'what is it you want? You didn't come here this early just to make reading recommendations.'

He doesn't immediately answer my question, distracted by his own thoughts. Then he says, 'Breaks my heart, it does.' He sounds genuinely emotional.

'What does?'

'What's happening to this place . . . the way it's all falling apart. Burning books for fuel! Jesus, I never thought I'd see the day.'

'Half of Hinchcliffe's fighters probably can't read anyway.'

'I know, but that's not the point. No one's learning anything any more. How can we move forward if no one's learning anything?'

'Who said anything about moving forward? Most of Hinchcliffe's lot are happy as pigs in shit.'

'For now, maybe. They won't be so happy when the food

stores are empty. For crying out loud, I doubt we could even summon up the brainpower or ingredients in the whole of Lowestoft to make a single bloody loaf of bread! The war's only lasted a year, but it'll take decades to put everything back together again.'

'Rufus, shut up. I've got better things to do than listen to you moaning.'

'Have you?'

'You didn't answer my question,' I answer, avoiding answering his. 'What do you want?'

'Come on, Danny,' he sighs. 'You know I only disturb you when I absolutely have to.'

I know he's right. He always does exactly what he's told (he's too scared not to) and he wouldn't be here at this hour if he had any choice. Rufus is an ex-civil servant working as a gopher for Hinchcliffe and his cronies, running errands and carrying messages. His intelligence and natural ability to talk rings around everyone else elevate him above the rest of the underclass, but he's not a natural fighter and every day is a struggle for him to survive. Rufus calls me his friend, and although I think he needs me far more than I need him, I guess I do to. I spit into my cup again and wipe my mouth on my sleeve.

'You really do need to start taking more care of yourself, Danny,' he says again, looking me up and down.

'I'm tired, that's all. I spent the last few days hunting.'

'I heard – most of the people in the compound heard. The beer was certainly flowing last night. They were toasting your success. Hate to think what's going to happen when they run out of booze.'

'Whatever. So why exactly are you here? Is that all you came to tell me?'

Rufus doesn't answer straight away. He's distracted by the picture on the cover of another of my trashy novels. I whistle at him to get his attention and he finally looks up.

'He wants to see you. He's got another job for you.'

My heart sinks. 'He' is Hinchcliffe, and I don't need any more detail. If he wants to see me, then I don't have any choice but to go and find him. And when I get there and he tells me what it is he wants me to do, I'll have no choice but to do it.

'Christ, Rufus, what is it this time?'

'I'm just the messenger, Danny, you know he doesn't tell me anything.'

'Bloody hell. I swear, it's like being back at work sometimes, the amount of stuff he has me doing. Is it more Unchanged or—?'

'I told you, I don't know. He's not a happy bunny though.'

'Great.'

Despite the fact that Hinchcliffe genuinely seems to value me (as much as anyone values anyone else these days), and the fact that whatever he asks me to do, I've probably already had to do much worse, I immediately feel nervous. I can try and hide it, bullshit and make light of the situation until I'm blue in the face but the fact remains: Hinchcliffe scares the shit out of me. I think our collective fear of good old KC is the glue which holds this fragile place together.

5

Rufus is on his pushbike, riding alongside me as I walk into town. I'm glad of the company, even though he never shuts up.

'Of course, I saw all this coming before the Hate.'

'All what coming?'

'This chaos. We've been on a sticky slope for years. We were over-reliant on technology – how ironic is that? The easier it was for people to communicate, the worse at communicating they became.'

'I don't have a clue what you're on about.'

'Did you ever try phoning a teenager's mobile?'

'Not that often, why?'

'I did. Buggers would never answer. I worked with a lot of students, and they always had their phones in their hands, so how come they never answered?'

'You tell me,' I mumble, knowing full well that he's about to.

'Either they were being selective, only talking to who they wanted to, or they were too busy using the phones for something else – all that "social networking" and stuff. *Anti*-social networking, I used to call it.'

'I wouldn't know about that. We didn't even have a computer at home – couldn't afford the Internet.'

He gives me a sideways glance, then continues, 'People started using technology instead of thinking, letting machines do all the work, and now where are we?'

'Suffolk,' I answer glibly.

'You know what I mean,' he says. 'I knew this lad once, he had one of those sat navs, remember them? Bloody thing stopped working when he was driving up for a meeting, and you know what happened?'

'He got lost?'

'Worse than that: the bloody idiot just kept driving in a straight line until he got a signal again. Didn't think to look at road signs or get himself a map, did he? It took him almost fifty miles to get back on track. And there was another time I had a girl in tears because she couldn't unlock her car because the battery had gone in the key fob. The key fob, for Christ's sake! I had to march her down to the car park and put the key in the bloody door for her myself!'

Rufus continues to witter as we approach the centre of town. I don't interrupt; I know this is his therapy: his chance to vent his many frustrations without fear of taking a beating. Me, I'm too nervous to give a damn.

'The other day I saw that Curtis fellow, and do you know what he was doing? He was kicking in the door of one of the buildings next to the courthouse and using it for firewood. Where's the sense in that when there's so much they could use outside the compound? They're just too blinkered. They don't look any further than—'

'Rufus, shut up.' I stop walking and he stops pedalling. We're deep among the underclass now, and something's happening up ahead. I gesture for him to hold back and we wait by the side of a partially collapsed garage. There are other people all around us, most of them doing the same, keeping their distance. There's a lorry waiting at the barricade, just back from a scavenging mission, by the looks of things, and it's surrounded. One of the fighters in the front gets out and starts swinging a bludgeon at the people who are closest, forcing them back, but the crowd is large and volatile, and when he lunges for one section, people elsewhere surge forward. A couple of them manage to scramble up onto the back of the lorry and help themselves, only to be kicked back down by another savage bastard hidden under the canopy. No sooner have they hit the ground than other vagrants are swarming around them, trying to 're-steal' what they've just stolen. The situation deteriorates with frightening speed until two more fighters appear from the back and wade into the crowd. One of them is brandishing a sub-machine gun, which starts firing into the air, and the people scatter. As soon as there's sufficient space around the lorry, the gate opens and it drives through.

'Lovely,' Rufus says. 'I think this is where I'll leave you.'

He pushes off and pedals away. I don't know where he's going, but I do know he has as little desire to head into Hinchcliffe's compound as I do. At least he has a choice.

The closer I get to the gate around the compound, the more human detritus there is to wade through. This so-called society has divided itself into its own bizarre class structure. It's like a pyramid now, with Hinchcliffe perched alone at the top. Below him are his generals, Llewellyn and a couple of others – they're all fighters, of course, but more than that, they understand how this new world order works. They're ruthless enough to hold their own in any conflict, and they know how to deal with Hinchcliffe. Beneath them are the rest of the fighters, their position in the overall scheme of things depending entirely on their individual strength and aggression, and beneath them are the Switchbacks, those who've desperately tried to regain something resembling their old lives, finding new routines and responsibilities to fill the void where now-defunct jobs and dead families used to be. At the bottom of the heap are the hundreds of useless vagrants like these. Hinchcliffe has a simple way of evaluating each person's worth: does he need them? If they weren't there, he asks, would it matter? With resources so limited, he's not about to waste time and effort on useless people who are only ever going to take.

I pass by the crowds of underclass. Some are begging for food they know I won't give them, some are scavenging, picking through a huge mountain of waste like a landfill site, some are hunting the rats which others have disturbed. And as I look at all those people who are just sitting and staring into space, I wonder where I stand in the overall scheme of things today. I quickly come to my normal conclusion: *I don't.* I don't fit in anywhere – and I don't think I want to. Even before the war I felt out of step with everyone else; now I struggle to believe we're all part of the same species.

I reach the cordon and hammer on the gate with my fist.

'Who is it?' someone shouts.

'Danny McCoyne,' I answer. 'Hinchcliffe wants to see me.'

A narrow hatch is opened and a fighter stares out at me, then the gate starts to open and I'm pulled through as soon as the gap's wide enough. There's never any delay when I mention the big man's name. It's slammed again the moment I'm inside.

I head up what used to be Lowestoft's main shopping street, avoiding the foul-smelling piles of rubbish on either side, towards the courthouse building which Hinchcliffe has taken for his own. The atmosphere is different on this side of the barriers. There are fewer people out in the open, and those I can see are moving with purpose. In here the Switchbacks compete to stay in favour with the fighters. They remind me of the little birds which used to risk their lives to clean crocodiles' razor-sharp teeth, or the parasitic fish that lived off sharks. But this is a more symbiotic relationship, because they all need each other. The fighters are a uniformly foul breed – a mix of the physically strong, the instinctively aggressive, and those who are both. They're a deadly combination of hard bastards who look like they've been fighting all their lives and younger vigilantes on the cusp of adulthood, and they're always ready for battle. They float like pond scum on top of everyone else, relying on the subservient Switchbacks to fix their cars, fetch their food and do most of the other menial tasks in return for a minuscule amount of water and food. It all feels precariously balanced.

I should go straight inside when I reach Hinchcliffe's

place, but instead I pace up and down the pavement for a couple of minutes to compose myself first, trying not to start coughing again. The hazy sun peeks unexpectedly through a gap in the heavy clouds and I cover my eyes. Even the sun seems to have changed since the bombs. It's never as clear as it used to be, and the light looks like a layer of colour has been stripped away. But then again, maybe it's just my eyes.

I feel sick, and the smell here's not helping. Sanitation is pretty basic – people have taken to crapping in the gutters to get their waste into the sewers, and the stench is inescapable. It's not going to be long before we're reduced to slopping out again, and people'll be emptying buckets of shit into the street from their upstairs windows.

A sudden gust of wind clears the air momentarily, and I stop and breathe in the cold breeze. No one pays me any attention and that's good, that's the way I like it. I can see a crowd around the entrance to the shopping mall which Hinchcliffe uses as a food store and, occasionally, a distribution point. These queues never completely disappear: there are always more people than there is food, but no one dares to steal. Just a little way up the road is what's left of Hook, the last thief Hinchcliffe caught. Once the bane of my life, his corpse now hangs from a lamp post by its feet like a grotesque piece of street decoration. When Hinchcliffe found out what he'd been up to, he strung Hook up and gutted him like a pig. There's a rumour that someone else was pulling his strings . . .

The courthouse looks squat and small from street level, but its size is deceptive; the building goes back a long way. Hinchcliffe has occupied a large part of the surrounding area and most of the neighbouring buildings have been taken by his army of fighters. There's usually power and water in this part of town; you can hear the huge oil-fired generators thumping away continually in the background like a monotonous, mechanical call to the faithful. Hinchcliffe is no fool: this place is a less-than-subtle symbol of his unquestioned authority here. No matter what the people here have become, everyone is still conditioned, to a certain extent: they look at places like this and they see people in charge, whether they admit it or not. I certainly do.

The sooner I get this over with, the sooner I can head back home again. I take a deep breath, trying not to gag, and go inside, heading unchallenged for Hinchcliffe's room. Many of the rooms in the courthouse are filled with boxes of supplies, piled so high that in places they're blocking the corridors, though it's not so much that there's a vast amount of stuff here, more that it's incredibly disorganised. And dirty, too. Every surface I touch is covered in dust, or sticky with a layer of grime. The windows are opaque.

Hinchcliffe's empire is based on a few core principles. Central to his control (both of the fighters and the underclass) is the provision (or at least the *promise*) of food and water, backed up with the threat of brutal force if anyone steps out of line. He drip-feeds the people here to keep them sweet: *do what I say and you might get what you need; fuck with me and I'll kill you.* Today he hoards whatever he can find, stockpiling everything at various locations within the compound. I know where one stash is kept, and I have an idea about two others, but I don't know any more than that – no one knows where everything is except for Hinchcliffe. He manipulates the situation to consciously generate an air of mutual distrust between his fighters, encouraging them to grass on anyone who doesn't play ball and rewarding loyalty with increased rations.

Hinchcliffe is the worst of the worst because he is physically *and* mentally stronger than anyone else. He's the closest thing I've ever seen to a Brute with a brain.

I pause outside the tall double doors to his office to compose myself, trying to make myself look more confident than I feel. I go through, and thankfully my entrance goes largely unnoticed, even though the heat in the room stops me in my tracks. There are more electric and oil-fired heaters around the edges of the room than in the rest of the town combined. Recycling, energy efficiency . . . they're all consigned to history now. The amount of waste in here alone is astonishing. Hinchcliffe and his posse get through food as if there's no tomorrow, as if they're expecting fresh supplies to turn up any day now, delivered in a bloody supermarket lorry.

This used to be the main county courtroom, but today it's stripped of all gravitas, barely recognisable as a seat of justice. Boxes and crates are stacked in haphazard piles, and the floor and desks are covered with rubbish – food wrappers and general litter, and a lot of discarded, paperwork too. This is supposed to be the administrative hub of the town – the beating heart of Hinchcliffe's empire – but it doesn't look like anyone's doing very much. I pick up a map from the desk next to where I'm standing. Black crosses have been scrawled over every town and village within thirty miles of this place. There's a sudden noise behind me and as I spin around I see Llewellyn hurtling towards me. I try to put the map down, but it's too late; he's snatched it from my hand and pushed me back against the wall. He hits me harder than I was expecting and my skull cracks against the plaster.

'What the *fuck* are you doing?'

'Hinchcliffe wants to see me,' I say as firmly as I can manage.

'Does he? And did he say you could come in here and start looking through my stuff?'

'No, I—'

'You nosy fucker, I'll break your fucking legs if I catch you at it again. He shouldn't be letting a freak like you just wander around.'

'You tell him then,' I stupidly say, and I've barely finished the sentence before Llewellyn has his hand wrapped around my neck.

'You cheeky bastard! You watch yourself, McCoyne, because I'm going to—'

'He's coming,' another fighter cries as he bursts into the

room. 'I've just seen him – he'll be here in a sec.' The fighter is Curtis, Llewellyn's deputy – half his age, but just as vicious. He always wears full body armour, taken from his first ever kill, he tells anyone who'll listen.

Llewellyn snarls at me and lets me go. He brandishes the crumpled map and Curtis follows him out of the room. I rub the back of my head and perch on the edge of the nearest desk. Llewellyn's got a real problem with me, but I don't much care: if he touches me, Hinchcliffe will kill him, and he knows it. Maybe that's why he hates me – he doesn't like the fact that Hinchcliffe seems to trust me, if trust is the right word. His jealously is thinly veiled, almost childish, and it's pitiful.

As I wait for Hinchcliffe to arrive I watch three fighters I don't recognise crowding around a thin slip of a man in the far corner. He's trying to repair a radio and even from here I can see his shaking hands. Sitting at a desk facing me, working on a battered old laptop, is Anderson, Hinchcliffe's 'stock-keeper'. He's a gopher, like Rufus. He used to be an accountant. Now he's the man who keeps tally of everything that Hinchcliffe controls: the land, food, weapons, vehicles, people . . . I walk past him, but he doesn't even look up. As I glance back at the screen I see that he's playing Solitaire, not working at all.

The man trying to fix the radio makes a mistake and there's a bright spark, accompanied by a sudden loud cracking noise, a wisp of smoke and the smell of burning. He yelps in surprise and pain, and one of the fighters, obviously not impressed, cuffs him around the back of the head then picks him up and shoves him face first into the wall. Dazed, he reels away, blood dripping from his nose. After a moment he wipes his face clean and returns to the radio again to avoid another slap, though his hands are trembling worse than ever and it looks like he's barely able to focus. He keeps stopping to wipe away the blood which is still dripping from his swollen nose.

Hinchcliffe appears through the doors in the back of the room, which swing shut in the face of a woman I don't immediately recognise. She's straightening her clothes as she walks, and it's obvious why she's here. It's unusual to see any female around here unless they've been brought in for sex – another sad indictment of the 'new society'. The days of women's lib and equality are long gone. Women fighters may be easily as aggressive as men but they're less physically strong, so fewer of them rise up through the ranks. It's ironic; the arrival of the Hate wiped out all the prejudices which used to split society – but now the war's ending, they've all flooded back, and they're even more divisive than before. Hinchcliffe gave me his typically blinkered view on this a while back. He said it was tough shit, because that's just the way it is now. There are no human rights groups to help you any more; we're each of us on our own. He said, 'I don't care if you're a black lesbian one-legged Jew,' labouring the point, 'if it comes down to a straight choice between you and me surviving, you're fucked.'

When he finally notices I'm here, Hinchcliffe says something to the woman and she slopes away.

'Danny,' he grins, his voice full of obviously false enthusiasm, 'how are you this fine morning?'

My head aches from being slammed against the wall, my body aches and my guts are still churning after last night's gourmet dinner, but I spare him the details. 'Shit.'

'Excellent!' he says sarcastically. 'Come here. I need to talk to you.'

He leads the way back through the swinging doors, down a short corridor and up a flight of stairs into the first of his private rooms. Though I've been in here before it still takes me by surprise, because it's more like a teenager's bedroom than anything else, like a house where the parents have gone away and left the kids to run riot. There's a flatscreen TV fixed to the wall – possibly the last unbroken TV left in the whole town – and lots of different games consoles lying around. The recently vacated double bed is unmade, and the air is heavy with cigarette smoke and other equally unpleasant smells. We continue through to his office, a slightly more businesslike room. The large oval table is covered in just as much shit as everywhere else and the once cream-coloured carpet is stained heavily in several places, no doubt bloodied by those unfortunate people who pissed KC off.

Hinchcliffe sits at the head of the table in his wing-backed leather swivel chair that's way bigger than the rest. He gestures for me to sit next to him and I do, still trying to disguise my nerves. Despite his inner circle of fighters, he is the only person at this table who really matters. He is the law-maker, the judge, prosecutor and defence, the jury and the executioner, all rolled into one terrifying being. I try not to let him see quite how much he intimidates me, but though I act casual and do my best to maintain eye contact, the fucker just grins and of course I'm the one who looks away first. Is he really such a threat, or am I blowing things out of proportion? He reminds me of the senior managers I used to work for at the council, except he's far, far more intense and, unlike them, he has a personality. He's no stronger than many of the people he surrounds himself with, but he's clever and witty and smart, and that's the real danger. When he looks at me like this it's as if he's trying to get into my head and take me apart so he can understand what makes me tick. Most people have shed pretty much every aspect of their former selves, but Hinchcliffe is different. He used to be an investment banker – he'd probably have sold his own mother to turn a profit – but now he trades for much higher stakes. According to Rufus, when the Change took him, Hinchcliffe single-handedly wiped out an entire floor of more than forty traders.

Take it easy, I tell myself, *don't let him see you're nervous.*

'You really don't look so good,' he says, viewing me up and down.

'You're the second person who's said that to me today.'

'How many people have you seen?'

'Just two.'

'Well we both must be right then,' he says, continuing to stare at me. His face is an unreadable mix of fascination and disgust. Then his expression suddenly changes and he ducks down and pulls out a four-pack of beer which he slides over to me.

'For helping us get rid of those Unchanged fuckers yesterday. Good job.'

'Thanks.' I take the beers and quickly remove them from the plastic rings holding them together. I shove the individual cans into different pockets of my long coat. I might drink one later, but the rest will be going under the floorboards when I get back to the house.

'I was really pleased with what you did. Biggest Unchanged haul in ages.'

'Six weeks.'

'I thought we'd seen the last of them – thought we'd finally got rid of them all.'

'Me too. Maybe we have now?'

'And we got a few kids too – that was a bonus! Wasn't expecting that.'

'Neither were they.'

There's another long, awkward (for me, anyway) silence.

'I've got another job for you,' he finally announces. 'Ever heard of a place called Southwold?'

Southwold is a village a few miles further down the coast. I've never been there, and I know very little about it other than its name. I shake my head. The more Hinchcliffe thinks I know, the more he'll expect from me.

'It's about ten miles from here,' he says. 'It used to be a nice little spot – couple of people I knew in the City had second homes down there, back in the day.'

Ten miles. It doesn't sound far, but distances aren't what they used to be. People tend to stay put in Lowestoft now, unless they're out scavenging. We rarely venture more than

74

a couple of miles in any direction. Most travelling's done on foot now, and that puts Southwold the best part of a day away.

Hinchcliffe lights up a cigarette, leans back, takes a long draw and slowly blows out a cloud of blue-grey smoke. The only people who smoke these days are those who've got the connections to get their hands on a steady supply of fags. Most people are struggling to find food, never mind anything else. Of course, Hinchcliffe can have any damn thing he wants, and that includes the wherewithal to fuel his pointless habit. Cocky bastard.

'Want one?'

'No thanks,' I say. 'I don't smoke. It's bad for you.'

He laughs and shakes the cigarette box in front of me. 'You sure? These are the real thing,' he says. 'Word to the wise: if you do decide to start, come and see me first. There are some dirty fuckers making their own fags from scrag-ends and dried leaves and whatever else they can get their hands on. Bit of a black market starting to spring up around here . . .'

'You were talking about Southwold,' I remind him, keen to get the conversation back on track and this audience over with.

He leans forward secretively. 'I might have a problem,' he whispers.

'Unchanged?'

'Not this time.'

'What then?'

'Settlers. I need you to check them out for me.'

'Why me?'

'Christ, Danny, why do you always ask the same bloody questions? You know why: you're forgettable. No one notices you – no one even gives you a second glance.'

'Thanks.'

'You know what I mean. You can handle yourself. It doesn't matter who or what you come across, you treat

75

them all the same. You don't rush in there with your fists flying like everyone else I've got who could go.'

Bit of a back-handed compliment, but that's as good as it gets with Hinchcliffe. 'So what's your problem?' I ask. I've obviously got no choice, not if I want to see tomorrow.

'Bit of an issue with the neighbours,' he says, grinning again. 'There's something going on down there, I'm sure of it. I've been talking to them for a while, trying to get them to pack up and come here. Thing is, they wanted to stay where they were, so I figured I'd keep them onside and let them get the place sorted out for me, then go in there and annex them.'

'And I take it things aren't going to plan?'

He screws up his face and takes another drag of his cigarette. 'It's not so much that,' he says, 'I'm just starting to get a little uneasy. There are about thirty of them, and they're not being as cooperative as I'd like. I think they're stockpiling and digging in, and I need to get a handle on things.'

'Before someone else does?' I suggest.

He pauses, and for a fraction of a second I think I might have overstepped the mark. Then he grins again and points at me. 'You got it! See, you don't miss a trick, Dan. That's why I like you!'

He doesn't like me and we both know it. Fucking idiot.

'So what do you want me to do?'

'There's a guy called Warner running things down there. John Warner. He's a local, came with the territory.'

'And you don't trust him?'

'I don't trust anyone,' he answers quickly. 'Do you know Neil Casey?'

I struggle for a few seconds to picture the man. I know he's one of Hinchcliffe's top cronies but to tell the truth, they're all pretty much the same to me. Rufus says they've been deindividualised, and I know what he means: it's easy to lose track of which one's which. The only way I can tell them apart is by comparing their scars and their level of aggression.

After a moment, I think I know who Casey is. 'Tall guy, nasty scar on the back of his head?'

'That's him. I sent him down there a few days ago and he's not reported back to me yet. You know the deal, Dan: if you're working for me and I send you outside Lowestoft, you make contact at least once every twenty-four hours.'

'And you think they've got rid of him? Is Warner planning something?'

'I don't know what I think, and that's why I want you to go there. Try and get a feel for what's going on and let me know if there's anything I should be worried about, okay?'

Not okay, I don't want to go anywhere, but what else can I say? Hinchcliffe doesn't ask, he tells. 'Okay,' I say.

'Good man. Take a car from the pool, pick yourself up a radio and get down there as soon as you can.'

'Now?'

'Why? You got something better to do?'

'No, it's just that I don't feel—'

'Get down there now and report back to me tonight. The sooner you go, the sooner you get back, and the happier I'll be.'

Bastard. I can't stand being used like this, but it's do the job or risk a beating, maybe worse. There's no point arguing and delaying the inevitable. I get up to leave, but I'm not even halfway across the room when the coughing starts again, exacerbated no doubt by Hinchcliffe's smoking and the arid heat in here, and I'm doubled over before I know what's happening.

'You've got to start taking better care of yourself, Danny,' Hinchcliffe shouts at me, 'you're a key member of my team.'

I glance up at him but I don't say anything. Is he being genuine or sarcastic? I can't tell the difference any more.

6

Hinchcliffe has a vast collection of vehicles, in varying states of disrepair. Cars are just another commodity, and he's gradually stockpiled them, like he has everything else. He has several mechanics working for him, but their skills are seriously lacking and the stock of vehicles is relatively good, so if engines break down for anything other than the most basic reasons, the cars are generally stripped down for spares, then dumped (much the same as everything else these days). Hinchcliffe's vast car pools are starting to look more like scrapyards than garages, with heaps of discarded body parts all over the place. Seeing them today makes me remember Rufus grumbling about bread first thing this morning. He has a point though, and the exact same thing's true of transport: for now there are still plenty of cars and lorries around, but the lack of spares and available fuel is seriously beginning to limit their usefulness. Soon the knowledge to maintain them will be lost. Only a year and we're not far from that stage already. Today a burst tyre is stupidly close to a total write-off.

Most of the better vehicles are kept in a car park behind the police station, and the rest are parked on a guarded patch of wasteland next to the railway station. I always try to get the same car. Hinchcliffe's men look at me as if I'm crazy when I ask for the same little silver box-shaped car every time. It's a nice, safe, reliable, old man's car – it may not have the biggest engine, or the strongest body, or the most space inside, but it does have a working CD player.

It was generally too dangerous to travel anywhere by road in the weeks leading up to the nuclear bombings, when the

Unchanged still outnumbered us and before they squandered their military advantage in desperation. Now, though, the lack of people and fuel have combined to make the roads – what's left of them – quieter than ever. For me, getting into a car is a way of shutting out everything and everyone, at least for as long as the journey lasts. And when you have music, it's even better . . .

I leave the railway station with music blasting out, ignoring the fighter guards, who are looking at me like I've gone insane. I never used to listen to this kind of music before, but I don't care any more. The name of the piece, the composer, the conductor, the orchestra – none of that matters now. All that's important is the effect: the sound takes me back to a time when people sang and laughed and played instruments and made CDs and listened to the radio and went to gigs, a time when people didn't kill each other (that often), and when having a bad day meant you'd missed something on TV or you'd had a run-in with someone at work.

Checkpoint. There are two guards on duty at the gate which closes off the bridge. The stretch of water below is called Lake Lothing, although it's not much of a lake at this point, more a narrow channel running into the sea. One of the guards mans the gate; the other stands at the side of the road and flags me down. This guy's always around here. He lost the bottom part of his left leg in the war, but he still keeps fighting. Right now he's standing upright, his stump, wrapped up in layers of crusted brown dressings, resting on a pile of sandbags as high as his other knee. That's probably the closest he's ever going to get to a false leg. I stop a short distance away (far enough that he can't reach out to hit me without hopping over first) and wind down the window. I refuse to turn off the music.

'This one of Hinchcliffe's cars?' He shouts to make himself heard.

'I'm doing a job for him,' I shout back. 'Check with him if you want.'

'What?'

'I said check with him.'

He still can't hear me. 'Turn that shit down, you fucking idiot.'

'What?' I yell, feigning deafness. He starts to repeat his request, but I'm just playing with him. I hold up the radio – one of Hinchcliffe's standard-issue handsets – and he immediately nods his head, signals to the other man and waves me through. Having a radio is as good as having an ID card – there's no access to these things without Hinchcliffe's express permission, and he controls them himself. It's not the danger of having communications interrupted that makes him so anal about this radio equipment, it's the fact that he's rapidly running out of batteries and spares.

The other fighter opens the gate, and as soon as the gap's wide enough I accelerate through it, past the underclass crowds and on towards Southwold, trying not to think too much about what I might find there.

7

The road is empty. I drive along the A12 until I reach the village of Wrentham, a strangely skeletal place. Everything of value has long since been removed and taken back to Lowestoft. In the silent centre of the village there's a junction. The road sign directly opposite is bent over double like a drunk throwing up, and it's hard to make out what it says. I think it's around a mile and a half to Southwold. Fortunately the road names here are pretty self-explanatory: Lowestoft Road, London Road (note to self: don't go down that one), Southwold Road . . . I follow the Southwold Road, looking out for somewhere safe to leave the car. I'll finish the last mile or so on foot – I'll draw less attention to myself and have more chance of avoiding trouble that way. Damn Hinchcliffe. I *really* don't want to do this. If there was more fuel in this car I could make a break for it, try to find another place like Lowestoft – but then again, what's the point? Every surviving town will probably have its own KC.

After another mile or so I reach a business park which looks to be as quiet as everywhere else. I drive as deep into the estate as I dare, until I come across a large warehouse. I check it out, but it doesn't look like anyone's been here for months – there's an undisturbed layer of dust everywhere, which is reassuring. I need to be careful with the car. Not only will Hinchcliffe hit the roof if I don't get it back to him in one piece, but it's also my ticket out of here. I take my CD with me, just in case, shoving it into my rucksack alongside my clothes, weapons, two books, some scraps of food I've brought along to trade and Hinchcliffe's radio.

*

I have a dog-eared tourist street map of Southwold which Hinchcliffe gave me and I find myself checking it repeatedly as I follow the main road which runs right through the centre of the town. I don't feel like a tourist today. For some reason I'm nervous as hell.

There's not much to this place. I'm assuming that as in Lowestoft, any settlers will have gravitated towards the centre, where the shops, pubs, offices and everything else used to be. And if there are only thirty or so people here, they probably haven't spread out that far. I don't know anything about this guy John Warner, but it's probably safe to assume he's a nasty bastard. He must be pretty sure of himself to have turned down Hinchcliffe's 'invitation' to relocate to Lowestoft. He's either dumb, or he's got balls of steel.

This place is like a ghost town. I can see plenty of superficial damage, but most of the buildings still look structurally sound. The once carefully tended verges are overgrown now, although the grass is brown and mushy, and weeds are breaking through the cracks in the pavements. I stare through a dusty window into the deceptively normal living room of an abandoned house, then catch my breath when I hear voices nearby, carried on the winter wind. *Focus!* I tell myself. I can't afford to take chances. There's a reason these people are defying Hinchcliffe, and if they're prepared to piss him off, they'll have no qualms in getting rid of me.

There's a lighthouse up ahead. It's marked on the tourist map, but unlike most lighthouses I've come across, this one is nestled deep in the centre of the town, rather than out on the rocks, or at the edge of the water. I edge closer and peer around the corner of a row of modest-looking houses. Circling the very top of the lighthouse is a metal gantry, and there's someone pacing around it, presumably keeping watch – and though I can't see much from this distance, there's a better than fair chance that he's armed. I decide to work my way around the centre of the town in a wide circle; I might avoid getting shot at that way.

Through a narrow gap between two rows of houses I can see a small group of people working in a field next to a church and I change direction again. Anything to avoid any confrontation. I'm keeping close to the fronts of the buildings I pass, trying to minimise the chance of being seen by the lighthouse lookout, and I find I'm walking down towards the ocean. The steadily increasing noise of the waves crashing against the shingle shore is welcome. The wind coming up off the water is bracing, almost too cold to stand. The morning sun, briefly visible in Lowestoft, has disappeared now and the sky is again clogged with heavy dirty grey cloud. It's raining – I'm not sure if it's sea spray or sleet – and I ask myself again, *what the hell am I doing here?*

An empty road runs parallel with the shingle beach below, stretching the full length of the town, all the way towards a crumbling pier reaching out into the sea. I'm struck suddenly by the fact that there's something very different about this place in comparison with everywhere else I've been; it's just taken me a while to realise. All the roads in this part of town have been cleared. There are the usual burned-out cars and occasional piles of rubble lying around but here, unlike in Lowestoft, they appear to have been moved out of the way. This is *weird*. No one cleans anything any more, there's no point – there's barely anything left to clean *with*. The whole country is covered in a layer of radioactive grime which no one ever touches. People climb *over* obstructions, they don't *remove* them. Elsewhere, near to the pier, a small car park appears surprisingly full, virtually every space occupied and every vehicle parked properly. Is this John Warner's equivalent of Hinchcliffe's scrapyard car pools?

A sudden gust of wind catches a loose window somewhere behind me, slamming it shut, and my heart leaps into my mouth. My body immediately tenses up, ready for confrontation, and I grab my knife and look around in all directions, but I can't see anyone and I curse myself for getting so easily distracted. Next to the house with the open window is a corner shop, with an estate agent's 'To Let' board still hanging above the door. Its bare shelves look to have long since been stripped of anything of value but, feeling exposed, I go inside.

The shop was probably cleared out before the fighting began in earnest. If this had been Lowestoft, or anywhere else, the floor would be covered in crap, the furniture broken into pieces for firewood, the windows smashed, a couple of bodies left rotting in the corner . . . But here there's a pile of papers neatly stacked on the end of a counter, next to an empty display unit, looking for all the world like the outgoing owners just left them there on their way out. There's a local newspaper on top of the pile, dated last February, and I casually flick through it, this time happy to be distracted. The yellowing pages immediately take me back to a world that's long gone. There are a few mentions of the beginning of the Troubles which eventually consumed everything and everyone, but generally the paper's filled with the kind of stories that used to be so typical – which used to *matter* in places like this – local traders protesting about increased parking charges, the proposed merger of two secondary schools, an amateur dramatics group desperately trying to hawk tickets for their production of *Our Town*, a new car dealership opening . . . For a while I'm hypnotised, reading through the TV and local cinema listings, looking at programme titles I thought I'd forgotten and the names of films I never got to see, but at last I remember where I am and what I'm supposed to be doing and I make myself move.

On the floor by my feet, wedged under the counter, is a postcard, lying face down. I pick it up and flip it over. On the front is a picture of Southwold beach and the pier, taken on a gloriously sunny summer's day, way back when. The colours of the postcard are still remarkably bright and vivid. 'Greetings from Southwold' it says at the bottom, in large orange and yellow text. Maybe I should send it to Hinch-cliffe? I don't think he'd appreciate the joke.

I take the postcard outside with me and compare it to the real world. The original photograph must have been taken from somewhere very close, because the view of the pier is virtually identical. I cross the parade and lean against the metal railings. Holding the postcard up, I can clearly see the contrast between the past and the present. Apart from the weather and the lack of colour (everything today is disappointingly monochrome), the other major difference is the pier itself. There's now a large chasm about two-thirds of the way along, where part of the structure has collapsed and fallen into the sea. It looks like something impossibly heavy crashed down into the pier from on high, leaving bent girders and buckled supporting struts. A plane perhaps? I start to walk towards the pier, curious as to how it came to be so badly damaged. Was there a bomb, or did something hit it from below? At the entrance to the pier is a large pale yellow art deco building which probably housed the usual seaside distractions: an amusement arcade, cafés and gift shops. Running up the centre are wooden shacks – yet more cafés and shops, I presume. I know I'm wasting time, so I resist the temptation to get any closer, but the normality of what I see has taken me by surprise. The waves crashing against the shore, the breakwaters jutting up through the spray, the long line of small wooden beach huts, they've filled me with unexpected nostalgia, made me remember long-gone family holidays. This whole town must've run on tourism – summer holidays, ice creams, buckets and spades . . . and all gone for ever now. Christ, the very idea of a holiday seems out of—

'What the fuck are you doing here?'

The unexpected voice catches me completely by surprise and I spin around to find myself face to face with a tall man carrying a rifle. He's dressed in mud-splattered fatigues and his head is wrapped up in this bizarre, checked hat-scarf combination. He looks like a cross between a farmer and a freedom fighter, like he should divide his time between milking cows and hiding in Middle Eastern caverns. A bushy grey beard hides his mouth and makes his expression frustratingly hard to read. Christ, I'm a dumb prick. He could have killed me several times over, and I don't even have my knife ready to defend myself. All I've got in my hand is a bloody picture postcard. I drop it fast, hoping he hasn't noticed.

'Sorry, mate . . . I was just looking. I didn't know if—'

'I don't know you. Where you from?' he interrupts. He doesn't sound like he's going to stand for any bullshit. Whether he'd use his rifle on me is debatable, but I'm not about to take any chances. I try to clear my head and remember the story I'd thought up for myself on the way here from Lowestoft. *Act dumb. Pretend you're lost. You're not here to fight.* I make myself remember I'm just here to observe.

'I've been working my way up the coast,' I lie.

'Doing what?' he sneers. 'Taking in the sights?'

'Scavenging. Honest, mate, I didn't know anyone was here – I thought the place was dead, like everywhere else. Just let me go and I'll get out of your way.'

'Found much?'

'What?'

'On your travels . . . have you found much?'

'Not a lot. Not a lot left anywhere, to be honest.'

'You on your own?'

'Best way to be. What about you?'

'Nope. Plenty more of us in the village.'

'You *live* here?'

'Yep, if you call this living.'

He seems reasonably calm, although appearances can be deceptive. I don't get the impression he's looking for trouble, but I can't risk making assumptions. For all I know, he could

86

be the head honcho of a family of cannibals, or something equally unpleasant. Stranger things have happened.

'Listen, I'm starving. You got any food? I'll trade for it.'

'You'll need to talk to Warner,' he says, gesturing with his rifle back towards the town. 'He makes the decisions around here.'

8

He doesn't say another word as he leads me back towards the centre of town, all the way along the parade, passing the lighthouse, until we reach a pub where we turn right and walk up a narrow road lined with odd-shaped, brightly painted cottages packed tightly together. The blues and yellows might have faded a bit, but they still stand out amidst the muted greys and browns of everything else. This place is in such good condition that I keep getting distracted, and I don't realise we've reached the boss's place until we're there. It's a large, rather grubby white-fronted hotel right in the very centre of the town, overlooking a junction where one road merges with another to form an open arrowhead-shaped space. The roads are completely devoid of any moving traffic. It looks like this place has become the new village square. There are several vehicles parked, not abandoned, and stacks of equipment in neat piles. The frontages of some of the buildings have been fortified with wood and barbed wire. There are two men standing next to a glowing brazier a short distance away, but it's otherwise quiet, and I can't see anyone else about. It's still relatively early; no doubt I'll see more activity later – always providing I survive my meeting with Warner, that is.

'Is this it?'

The man disappears inside the hotel, both avoiding my question and answering it at the same time. I stand and wait in the middle of the street, feeling vulnerable, but doing all I can to keep up the illusion that I'm just a scavenger who happens to have stumbled across this place, not a spy sent here by the local neighbourhood despot. I can see movement through the ground-floor window of the hotel, but I can't make out who it is, or what's happening inside. I feel for the reassuring shapes of my knives as I try to prepare myself mentally for the quick getaway I'll have to make if things turn nasty. I try not to look too conspicuous as a group of people emerge from around the side of a building behind me, dragging a trailer between them, but thankfully they pass by quickly, barely giving me a second glance. Already this place is a world apart from Lowestoft – there you often can't move along the pavement for the loitering swarms of useless underclass. But I can disappear into the crowds when I don't want to be found; here I have no cover whatsoever . . . or protection.

The tall man appears from a passageway running down the side of the hotel and beckons, and I've little option but to follow. The short alley between the buildings almost immediately opens out into a large cobblestone courtyard, and he gestures for me to go through a doorway into the building adjacent to the hotel. I'm reluctant – am I walking into a trap? – but why should he be trying to trap me? Unless he really does want to kill and eat me, of course, and if that's the case I'm as good as dead already. Apart from turning up here unannounced, I don't think I've done anything to arouse suspicions.

Judging from the decor, which includes a load of almost undamaged oak panelling, I think this must have been some kind of town hall, although it's the smallest town hall I've ever seen. I'm ushered through another door into a large, high-ceilinged room which is empty save for a gaunt, white-haired man sitting at a table writing figures in a book. He doesn't even look up when we enter. He looks like a country squire, but appearances can be deceptive, I keep reminding myself. First impressions don't count like they used to.

'You Warner?' I ask.

He doesn't react at first, but finishes writing, then puts down his pen, takes off his glasses and carefully lays them on the desk. Finally he looks up at me. 'Yep,' he answers, 'and who might you be?'

'My name's Rufus,' I tell him, picking the first name that comes into my head, then immediately wishing I'd chosen something less conspicuous.

'And what can I do for you, Rufus?'

His simple question is stupidly hard to answer, probably because of the ominous way he asks it, staring straight at me. Is he trying to catch me out?

'Says he's been scavenging down south,' the man who brought me here says from the doorway behind me.

'Has he now?'

'That's right,' I tell him, my mouth dry with nerves.

'Not been too close to what's left of London, I hope.' He grins knowingly at the other man. 'Don't want our little town contaminated.'

I shake my head. 'Nowhere near it. Look, I don't want any trouble. I didn't know there was anyone here, I swear. I'm just looking for something to eat and somewhere to shelter. I'll be gone again tomorrow.'

'You look like you need feeding up. The road not been kind to you?'

I shrug my shoulders. 'No harder on me than anyone else.'

'Why are you here so early, then? Couldn't you sleep?'

Warner's strange question throws me so much that I instinctively slide my hand into my pocket and feel for the hilt of my knife again.

'What?'

'You been walking through the night?'

'I don't understand—'

'Common sense says,' he begins, leaning across the table, eyes burning into me, 'that most people rest at night and move during daylight hours, when it's safer – especially with it being the middle of winter and all, and with the world being such a fucking horrible place all of a sudden. So why

90

are you turning up in front of me now, before we've even got to mid-morning?'

Stay calm, I tell myself, feeling my body tensing in anticipation of an attack. There could be any one of a hundred plausible explanations why someone might have chosen to walk through the night. *Just don't panic* . . . I grip the handle of the blade in my pocket.

'Go for that knife and I'll have you killed before you've even drawn it,' he says calmly.

I let it go and lift my hands. 'I set out at sunrise,' I tell him, swallowing hard, plumping for the simplest, most logical explanation I can come up with. 'I knew I wasn't far from this place, but I must have lost my bearings somewhere along the way, because it turned out I was a few hours further down the road than I'd thought. I'd got it into my head I had another half-day's walk ahead of me.'

He nods slowly. Is he deciding whether he believes my story, or working out how he's going to get rid of me? Warner's obviously no fool. I see flashes of the arrogance of a fighter in his eyes, but there's clearly much more to him than that. I stand my ground, hold my nerve and keep quiet.

'But I found him up by the pier,' the man behind me says.

'So?' Warner asks.

'So that's north of town, John. He said he came here from the south.'

Warner's silence demands an answer.

'I did come from the south,' I tell them both, trying not to be noticed as I reach for a different knife inside my long coat. 'I didn't see anyone when I first got here. I just kept walking out along the seafront, and that's where you found me.'

'I'm not sure about this. There are enough people out in the fields – surely he'd have—'

'I saw them. By the church . . .'

'So why didn't you ask them for food? You said you didn't know there was anyone here.'

Warner raises his hand to silence the other man. He sits in front of me, impassive, like a judge about to pass sentence, and I realise I'm waiting for him to give the order, and for a pack of previously hidden fighters to emerge from the woodwork and take me out. I'm woefully out of shape and I haven't fought seriously for weeks. I'd struggle to defend myself against these two today, never mind anyone else they might draft in to help them. Fucking Hinchcliffe and his stupid fucking empire-building – why do I let him manoeuvre me into situations like this? The answer's disappointingly obvious: he'd kill me if I didn't do what he said.

'Let it go, Ben,' Warner says, still surprisingly calm. 'Does it really matter? Fact is, he's here now, and he's got a simple choice to make. He can play ball and follow our rules, or he can fuck off and keep walking. And if he's as cold, hungry and miserable as he looks, I think he'll do what he's told.'

'I will,' I say quickly, sounding deliberately pathetic, 'I don't want any trouble.'

'Fair enough then,' Warner says, picking up his pen again and chewing thoughtfully on the end of it. 'The first rule is: it's one day's work here for one meal and one night's shelter. You work hard and you keep working until you're told to stop and you'll get fed. Any slacking and you'll get fuck-all.'

I thought people only made threats now, not deals.

'Sounds fair,' I say, trying not to sound so surprised.

'I wouldn't go that far, but you get the idea.'

'Okay.'

'Second rule: any problems here, you come and see me. Understand?'

'Understand.'

'You don't try and sort things out yourself, right?'

'Right.'

Warner leans back in his chair and continues to watch me for a few uncomfortable seconds longer. 'You don't look like you'll last the day,' he says. Cheeky bastard.

'I'm fine.'

'Right then,' he announces, 'get him out to the others, Ben, and find him something to do.'

9

Bloody Hinchcliffe. This was never supposed to be part of the deal. The light's poor and I have no way of telling the time, but I feel like I've been working here for bloody hours now. The time is dragging and I'm fucked, but I don't dare stop. I'm not interested in the promise of a meal (I'll take their food, but I'm not hungry – I'll probably end up adding it to my stock back at the house), but there's no other way to find out what Hinchcliffe needs to know.

He's got good reason to be suspicious; something's not right here. All this 'one meal for one day's work' bullshit just doesn't ring true. They're definitely playing from a different rule book here in Southwold, but I don't know what they're hoping to achieve. Maybe John Warner's got Lowestoft in his sights? Perhaps he's trying to build a platform here, a stepping stone to taking over? Whatever's going on, he must be personally benefiting from it somehow – no one does anything 'for the greater good' any more.

Hinchcliffe is expecting a report from me before nightfall, but days like today confirm that his faith in me is badly misplaced. I'm not cut out for all this subterfuge bullshit. He sent me here to uncover what's going on in Southwold, but so far all I've done is dig a pit in a field. I've been kept well away from everything and everyone else. There are a handful of other people in the field – some look like fighters, others are acting more like underclass – but conversation is sparse, everyone's keeping themselves to themselves. Ben didn't say much, but I managed to get that there are several work parties today, some just outside the town. They're trying to prepare fields for planting crops next year – which is bloody optimistic. There's been so much smoke, radiation and Christ knows what else thrown into the atmosphere that I doubt anything will grow again for a long time. Before Hinchcliffe plucked me from the crowds, back when I was just another member of his scavenging pack, I saw the full extent of the damage the war has done: huge swathes of countryside completely dead, forests full of bleached, bare-branched trees, corpses of thousands of birds littering the ground . . .

'You asleep?'

I shake my head and look around quickly. Not asleep, just daydreaming. 'Sorry,' I say to the short, nervous-looking man who's standing next to me with a shovel. He's just finished filling a barrow with soil, and I'm supposed to be emptying it. He stares at me through glasses held together with tape and long strands of greasy black hair blow wildly in the wind – the comb-over from hell is whipping back and forth across his otherwise bald pate.

'Focus on the job,' he whispers to me. 'They won't feed you otherwise.'

He makes it sound like they're fattening us up so they can eat us. I've got to get this sudden cannibal fixation out of my head, but where else is Warner getting all this food I keep hearing about, and why is he so keen to share it? I push the barrow over to the mound of earth and empty it out. I'm exhausted, even though I've not moved far, and I take my time so I can get my breath back. Across a low stone wall I can see another working party in the distance. Looks like the people there really drew the short straw: they're ploughing a huge, odd-shaped field by hand, and all they've got to help them is a single horse, but even from here I can see it's painfully thin, hardly able to support its own weight, let alone do anything else. It's the first time I've seen a horse in as long as I can remember. I watch as it bends down, its legs shaking, and begins nibbling at the weeds on the edge of a sandy pit. It takes me a moment, then I realise that I'm looking at what's left of a golf course. The people don't appear to have made much progress, and I'm not surprised. Even though it's approaching the warmest part of the day, the soil here is still frozen hard.

When I return to the others, almost everyone else is taking a break, but as I was late to the party (and also because my lack of effort has been noticed), I'm told in no uncertain terms to keep working. One other man is left working with me, a strong, thickset fighter who's digging at the bottom of the pit. His head glistens with sweat through his thinning silver hair. He's got a solid, muscular body, if not particularly athletic, and he looks like he's been doing this kind of work all his life. He's hardly said two words since I've been here, but as the others are a safe distance away and I've got my back to them, I risk trying to make conversation. It's not easy: he's buried chest-deep in the six-foot-square pit and he digs constantly, only pausing to either swap his shovel for a pick or to pass up another bucket of soil for me to dump into the barrow.

'You been here long?' I ask.

'Couple of weeks,' he says, barely acknowledging me.

Maybe if I offer information I can get him to talk. 'I just got in this morning. Looks like a pretty well-organised place.'

'Warner does okay,' he says, grunting with effort as he shifts another bucketful of dirt.

'You get much trouble here?'

'Only from people who ask too many questions.'

'Sorry.'

A handful of sheep, looking as hungry as the horse, have wandered into the field and are milling around. Their fleeces are patchy with mange. They're trying to graze, but the poor grass is obviously unsatisfying. They barely look up when I wheel the barrow past them to empty it.

When I return to the pit I take a chance and try again.

'Look, I heard what you said about asking questions, but what exactly are we doing out here?'

'Digging a bloody big hole,' he answers, no hint of sarcasm in his voice.

'I know that, but what's it for?'

He stops working momentarily and looks over the lip of the pit, back across the field. No one's looking at us, and they're pretty far away. It's enough for him to feel comfortable enough to talk. 'You won't do yourself any favours if you keep asking questions like that, I already told you.'

'I know. I'm sorry.'

He glances around again. 'We lost a few people over the last couple of weeks,' he finally explains. 'We would have burned them like usual, but Warner's got this idea that things here have gone too far the wrong way. He said he wants them buried, like we used to. Says if someone doesn't start making a stand, we'll be living like savages again before we know it. We'll all end up going the way of the Brutes.'

'So what happened?'

'A few of them got sick . . .'

'And the others?'

'An accident,' he tells me reluctantly. 'A handful of people got hurt, two were killed.'

'What kind of accident?'

I know instantly from the expression on his face that I've pushed too hard.

'You really need to stop talking and get working. I've told you all I'm going to.'

10

The sun has set by the time I am finally allowed to stop. I'm exhausted; weak with the unaccustomed effort and numb with cold.

The pit was finished a while back. Warner, his right-hand man Ben, and a crowd of others pulled a trailer loaded with corpses into the field. I counted at least five bodies, but they were wrapped up in blankets and black plastic so it was impossible to tell who they were, or how they'd died. I'm sure one of them must have been Casey, Hinchcliffe's missing soldier. I even volunteered to help fill in the grave so I could get a better look, but that was a bloody mistake: a load more unnecessary effort and I didn't manage to see a damn thing.

But something's *definitely* not right here. Warner and several others stood silently around the edge of the pit, watching the dead being buried and muttering and whispering to each other. I can't make up my mind whether Warner is genuinely hankering back to pre-war values of respect and dignity, or whether this was a mock burial to throw people off the scent. Is all of Southwold just an elaborate façade? Were they burying evidence, trying to hide their crimes?

After they'd buried the bodies, a couple of us were sent into a copse of trees to fetch firewood, which we loaded onto the back of the trailer. Virtually everything's dead, so it took less time than I'd expected to gather up a large enough load. Some more people arrived a while back to collect the firewood.

Now I've been summoned to a nearby house, together with the rest of the group I was working with, but the house turns out to be just a shell. There are a couple of faded photographs hanging drunkenly on the wall, but that's the only trace I can see of the people who used to live here. Everything else – the furniture, all their personal belongings – has gone. A fire has been built in the hearth, and most of the others are already sitting around in its orange glow, trying to get warm, staring silently into the flames and waiting for a dented billycan of water to boil. I find myself a space on the muddy, threadbare carpet and lean back against the wall. The floor's cold, but I'm too tired to care. What heat the fire provides is completely negated by the icy draughts blasting in through the broken windows and the gaps beneath the doors. I wrap my arms around myself, trying to keep warm, and look around.

There are six other people here with me. A large, straw-haired woman called Jill, I think, one of the work-gang leaders, eventually gets up and makes hot drinks, which she hands around in chipped mugs. The wood on the fire crackles and pops as it burns. The chimney's blocked and the house is filling with smoke.

'There'll be food in the square outside the hotel later,' she says. 'It won't be much, but it should help keep the cold out.'

'What about tomorrow?' the man with the tape-repaired specs and the comb-over asks. He's sitting opposite me, leaning back against the wall.

'No work here,' she answers, 'but Warner will find you something. There's always the fields.'

'This place is well organised,' I say to her, taking advantage of a natural gap in the conversation to try and push for information again.

'You just arrived?'

'Got here this morning.'

'Then you might want to think about staying. You'll not find anything better around here. You'll probably not find anything better *anywhere*.'

'Why's that?'

'Because John Warner's a good man. Because the things he's planning are going to give people like us our lives back.'

'People like us?'

'People who don't want to keep fighting for everything,' she explains. 'The war's over, and it's time to start picking up the pieces again. Time to stop all the killing and start remembering what it's like to be human again.'

She's obviously never been to Lowestoft, I think to myself, trying not to smirk at the thought. I suddenly feel like I've wandered into a hippy commune from the sixties. Thing is, all that peace and love bullshit never really counted for much then, and from where I'm sitting, they count for absolutely nothing now. Remorse, compassion, regret . . . publicly demonstrate any of those emotions and you're likely to get torn apart. Give someone an inch, and they'll take ten miles. Hold your hand out to help someone, and some nasty bastard will tear your arm off and beat you to death with the bloody stump. That's how it is in the rest of the world outside Southwold, anyway. Everyone I've so far seen is stuck in a rut: no one wants to go back to the lives they had before, but there are no new roles for people instead. The violence which brought us all to this point has become the norm.

'So how's Warner planning to change things then?' I ask, genuinely curious. 'By making you bury bodies? By getting people to plough fields where nothing's ever gonna grow?'

She shakes her head angrily. 'If you don't like it, just fuck off.'

'It's not that,' the silver-haired pit-digger I spoke to earlier says from another corner of the room. 'Warner's just trying to pick the pieces up again and restore some order. It's not so much *what* we're doing; the important thing is the fact we're doing it at all.'

'Sorry,' I say quickly, back-pedalling fast. Publicly bad-mouthing Warner was a *stupid* move. 'I didn't mean to sound so critical – it's just that it's been a long time since

I've seen anything like this. This is the first place I've been in weeks where people aren't constantly at each other's throats.'

'We've all done more than our fair share of that,' Jill says quietly, swilling the dregs of her drink around in the bottom of her mug then knocking it back, 'and chances are we'll all have to fight again someday.'

'You don't always have a choice,' someone else says, their face hidden by the darkness.

'There's *always* a choice,' Jill says. 'That's what John'll tell you.'

There's an underlying tension, real emotion, in this woman's voice that I didn't expect. Am I the only one who's picking up on it? She sounds like she genuinely supports Warner, like she believes in what he's doing, whatever that might be. I guess the fact she's here at all is proof that Warner's chosen not to echo Hinchcliffe's 'management model'. If she were in Lowestoft she'd most likely have been swallowed up with the rest of the underclass, unless she was a particularly strong fighter or had a particular skill which Hinchcliffe needed. Even then she'd certainly not be assuming any position of authority or worth. Could this place and its leader actually be for real? I'm still not convinced: how is Warner managing to find enough food to feed thirty people regularly when most people can't even feed themselves?

'Someone I passed on the road said something about another settlement? A little further up the coast from here?'

'That'll be Lowestoft.'

'And what's it like there?'

'Don't rightly know,' she answers quickly, 'and I don't want to know either. Warner talks to the people in charge up there when he has to, but he ain't got a lot of time for them. We keep our distance. He says they're going about things the wrong way.'

'How so?'

'What's your name, mate?'

'Rufus,' I reply, remembering at the last second that I used a false name when I arrived this morning.

'You ask a lot of questions, Rufus,' she says.

That's the second time I've been warned today. I need to make it the last time too. 'Sorry – I've been on my own for too long. I'm just looking for somewhere to stop for a while, and if I'll get a better deal here than in Lowestoft, then—'

'It's not about deals,' she interrupts angrily. 'That's the difference between us here and them up there. We're small enough and sensible enough to work together. Up in Lowestoft, their leader, this guy called Hinchcliffe, he keeps people dangling on pieces of string. He uses them, tempts them with promises and stuff, then gets rid of them when they don't do what he says. He's the only one who benefits. It might work for him, but he's a bastard and we don't want that here.'

'Sounds bad.'

'It is bad. Fighting has replaced thinking, if you hadn't already noticed. And until people start thinking again, we're all in trouble.'

I drink more coffee to stop myself from speaking, because right now I've pushed as far as I dare. She's absolutely right about Hinchcliffe, and I'm precisely the kind of person she's talking about, sitting here in the cold, being manipulated by him from a distance while he sits back there in the comfort of his courthouse throne room. But what choice do I have? Are things really any better here? Is Warner as honest and decent as she's making him out to be? I doubt it; I don't think anyone really gives a damn about anyone else any more. I certainly don't. My gut feeling is that Warner is profiting from this somehow, and whatever he's doing, he's playing with fire. I wouldn't want to risk doing anything that might piss Hinchcliffe off, not unless I'd got a foolproof contingency plan and an untraceable escape route mapped out first.

'I'm off,' Jill says suddenly, getting up and walking towards the door. 'I've got things to do. See you all later.'

And now my paranoia is going into overdrive. Have I said too much? Is she going to see Warner, to grass me out? Is it time to get out of here? I wait for a moment longer, staring into the embers of the fire, then I glance up. The man with the comb-over and broken glasses is watching me from across the room, but he looks away as soon as we make eye contact and I know that I've aroused suspicions. They'll be watching me now, so I'll shut up and keep myself to myself from now on. Despite all the bullshit I've just heard, I know that like everywhere else, no one here trusts anyone else.

11

The woman – Jill – was right about the food – it was warm, and it was limited, both in taste and volume. I forced myself to eat, knowing that I needed to build up my energy after the unexpected exertion of the day. I never expected to have to do a full day's physical graft here and now every muscle in my body hurts and I feel half-dead, even worse than usual.

I've been trying to walk off the food, which is lying heavy on my stomach. I'm determined not to spend another night throwing up. I walk slowly around the perimeter of the village square, trying to observe as much as I can without drawing attention to myself. There's a very different atmosphere here, much less immediate tension in the air. In Lowestoft everyone's constantly on edge – fights break out at any moment, for any reason, and just as often for no reason at all. Here there really does seem to be more tolerance and cooperation. They must know something about Warner and his regime that I don't, either that or this place *is* genuine and these people are trying to rebuild.

I do my best to avoid the crowds – considering there are only around thirty people here (if I believe Hinchcliffe), it's harder than I expected. They're much more spread out than in Lowestoft, and I can see candles and lamps visible in many of the buildings around the square; it feels like there are eyes watching me constantly. I know that's just paranoia, because no one gives a shit about me, and that's one of the reasons Hinchcliffe sent me here. If anyone asks, I'll just tell them I was looking for a place to kip.

There's a lorry parked across the full width of a road up

ahead, blocking it off. It's an ex-army vehicle, I think. It's painted matte green, and some kind of crude emblem has been daubed on one side and on the bonnet. It looks like a target, red and white concentric circles with more red at the bull's-eye. I can hear voices in the street behind it and as I walk past the mouth of the road I glance around the back of the lorry, but I can't see much. There's a small crowd of people there, but I can't tell how many, or what they're doing. I keep walking, then take the next right turn, hoping that the side-street I've just entered will somehow connect with the road which runs parallel. It doesn't, but the houses I'm now walking past back on to those on the other road. I carry on a little further until I'm sure that there's no one else around, then climb over the gate at the side of the house nearest to me. It's quiet, and as I walk the length of the overgrown back garden I can hear the voices in the blocked-off street. I squeeze through a gap in the end fence – I'd never have got through it if I wasn't so thin – and make my way up to the house. To my relief it's dark; it looks empty. The back door is missing, the frame badly damaged. I go inside, checking all around that there's no one's there, and slowly creep up the stairs. From an echoing room at the front of the house I look down onto the street below.

There are five figures waiting in the road. I can't tell who any of them are from this distance, but I can see that they're armed, although their weapons are held casually and they don't seem to be expecting trouble. One of them sits down on the kerb, another takes a swig of drink from a hip flask.

It's a while before anything happens and I'm almost falling asleep when the man sitting down gets up quickly and the posture of the others changes. They stand ready as a group in the middle of the street. Then I hear an approaching engine, and I see headlamps coming closer. It's another ex-army vehicle, like the one that's blocking the other end of the road, and it stops a short distance away with a sudden hissing of brakes.

The driver and two other men get out, moving fast. One opens the back of the lorry and climbs up into it, then he starts passing stuff down to the others, who start carting the boxes and crates down the road to another house which has a garage, near the blocked mouth of the road. They're working steadily for a good few minutes, unloading a stack of food, some weapons and other, less easily identifiable, supplies. It's a decent-sized hoard – suspiciously large, in fact. They won't have got their hands on that much stuff anywhere around here. Within a few minutes the unloading is complete, and as quickly as they arrived, the second lorry, its driver and passengers all disappear. I catch a glimpse of that same circular red and white insignia as the lorry reverses down the street.

Smugglers! Christ, that's it – no wonder Warner's so cocky. The wily bastard is stealing to keep Southwold running just the way he wants it, and he's obviously building up a decent support structure too. So the next question is, where's he actually nicking the stuff from? This is all very well organised, and whoever he's stealing from must have enough stuff in storage not to notice the occasional lorry-load disappearing. There's only one person who controls enough around here likely to be in that position, and that's Hinchcliffe . . .

But this wasn't an opportunistic raid; everything I just witnessed looked carefully planned, and that can only mean that Warner has people on the inside. Maybe Neil Casey wasn't killed; perhaps he'd been working for Warner all along? Fuck me, this is getting complicated. I feel a strange sense of relief that I've actually found something to go back to Hinchcliffe with. It means I should be out of here before long.

Once the road outside is completely empty I leave the house the way I came, slipping quietly back through the hole in the fence, down the side of the house and out onto the other street.

'So where d'you think that lot came from?' a voice asks suddenly from somewhere behind me. I spin around anxiously, clumsily dropping my knife as I reach for it in a hurry. The owner of the voice switches on a torch and shines it at me and I try to rush him, but he steps out of the way then angles the torch directly into my face, blinding me. 'Don't panic,' he says, 'I don't want any trouble.'

The man shines the light back at himself for a second and it reflects off his thick glasses. I recognise him immediately: it's the guy from the working party this afternoon, the one with the bad comb-over who was watching me so closely in the house. This is all I fucking need. Is he on to me? What am I supposed to do now, kill him? I pick up my knife, just in case.

'I don't know what you're talking about,' I mutter.

'The delivery,' he says. 'I heard it, so you must have seen it. Same thing happens every few days, always around this time.'

'I saw nothing,' I tell him.

'So why are you here?'

'I was just looking for somewhere to sleep,' I lie.

'Bullshit. I've been watching you. You've walked past more than two dozen empty houses.'

'You've been watching me? Why?'

'Because I want to talk to you. Look, can we go somewhere less public—?'

'The middle of the street's fine – anyway, why would you need to talk to me? Are you some kind of stalker?'

He ignores my jibe. 'It's Rufus, isn't it?'

'Yes,' I answer, after a brief but noticeable delay.

'So what do you think?'

'About what?'

'About what they're doing here? About the lorry you just saw? About the way Warner's trying to get these people organised?'

'Did he send you to find me?'

'Not at all. I'm just trying to work out what's happening here, same as you are. So I'll ask you again, what do you think?'

'I think I'm bloody tired after working all day and I really don't care about Warner or any mysterious lorries,' I answer. 'I'm grateful for the food, and now I just want to find somewhere I can crash for the night, like I told you. I took a wrong turn, and that's why I'm here. I'm really not interested in anything else.'

'I don't buy that.'

'I don't care.'

This guy is some kind of deluded little idiot. Maybe he gets a kick out of causing trouble – is he a masochist looking for a beating, perhaps? Whoever he is and whatever he wants, I'm not getting involved. Things are complicated enough already. I try to sidestep him, but he stands his ground and blocks my way through.

'I'm sorry,' he says, 'but I don't get it. You've just seen a lorry full of supplies being unloaded, and you're telling me you don't want to know where it came from?'

'I'm not telling you anything.'

'Why are you really here?'

'What's it to you?'

'I know you're lying to me, Rufus,' he says. 'I can read you like a book. My name's Peter Sutton, and I want answers, same as you. Things aren't what they seem around here.'

12

My mind's racing, and I do all I can not to show it. Who is this person? I need to be bloody careful here; I must keep up my act. If he's working for Warner, then I could be in real trouble – likewise, if he's discovered I'm here spying for Hinchcliffe, there's every chance I won't get out of Southwold alive. I need to find out which it is.

'So talk.'

He looks around anxiously, despite the fact he already knows the street's clear, then speaks. 'I don't think we're seeing the full picture here.'

'Tell me something I don't know.'

'We're only seeing what Warner wants us to see.'

'Isn't that usually the way with leaders?'

'Yes, but this is different.'

'How?'

'I can't quite put my finger on it yet, but those lorries are the key. If we knew where they were coming from, then things might start making sense.'

'Nothing's made sense for the best part of the last twelve months. Anyway, why are you so interested in Warner? As long as he provides food, does it matter where it comes from?'

'Yes, but—'

'You make it sound like you think he has an ulterior motive.'

'Maybe he does. Someone's supporting him, that much is obvious.'

What's equally obvious is that Peter Sutton doesn't have any useful information. He sounds as unsure about what's happening here as I am. I start to walk back towards town. I'm tired, and I'm desperate not to screw up my 'mission' by saying something I'll regret, let alone getting caught talking out on the street so close to Warner's food and weapons cache. I need to find somewhere quiet where I can report back to Hinchcliffe, then get some rest in case I end up working another full day tomorrow.

'I should go . . .'

'Wait. Just give me a few more minutes.' Sutton is obviously anxious about something.

'Why?'

'I need your help.'

'You need my help?' Now alarm bells are beginning to sound.

'Just stop and listen to me, Rufus. I'm like you.'

'The only thing we have in common is that we're both still alive.'

He stands in front of me, blocking my way past. 'There's more to it than that. I know what you can do,' he says. 'I know you can hold the Hate.'

For a second I'm floored, although I try not to show it. I push past him and keep moving. How the hell did he know that? Someone must have told him – although I don't know who, because no one here knows anything about me. Maybe he came here from Lowestoft too? Oh fuck – is that sick bastard Hinchcliffe playing mind-games with me?

Finally I say, 'You're talking crap. You know nothing about me.'

'Yes I do,' he says. 'I know what you can do because I'm the same. I can hold it too—'

Do I believe him? Does it even matter any more? The Unchanged are extinct, so holding the Hate has become as irrelevant a skill as being able to speak Russian. I'm gripping my knife tightly and psyching myself up to use it if Sutton doesn't piss off. Could I kill him? He might not look like much, but I don't know what he's capable of, and it's all about aggression levels now, not size. The screwiest are often the most unpredictable. I've seen people half his height kill others twice their weight. Nope, whatever trouble he's got himself into, I'm not getting involved. I've already got enough on my plate – correction, I've got *nothing* on my plate – and that's how I intend keeping it.

I'm about to tell him as much when he starts talking again.

'When I found out what I could do,' he says, 'I tried to stop fighting, to pull away from the war, but there was nowhere to go and I got tangled up in things I couldn't get out of. When I learned how to hold the Hate, I started to look at things differently again. I started to question what I'd been told, and why things were happening. All they wanted me to do was hunt and kill—'

'Wait, who is "they"?' I ask cautiously.

'Simon Penkridge, Selena, Chris Ankin . . .'

Two of the three names mean nothing to me, and I try not to react, but it's impossible when he mentions Chris Ankin, And I find my self repeating, 'Ankin?'

'I never saw him, but the others said they were working for him. They were sending people into refugee camps like bloody suicide bombers.'

'And you refused?'

'You don't say no to people like that. I went along with it for a time, then I managed to get lost in the crowds. That's how I got away from them.'

'Wise move,' I'm forced to admit, reflecting for a second on my own experiences. The things he's saying are interesting, but the fact remains: why should I care? All of that is history now, and I need to focus on today. But he might know something that could be useful to Hinchcliffe, so, against my better judgement, I ask, 'So what's your connection with this place?'

'Just passing through, same as you.'

'And these lorries. You've been watching them for a while?'

'I've seen them coming and going, but I don't know anything about them.'

'So you don't know where this stuff's coming in from?'

'No idea, but I'm trying to find out. Fact is, I need all the food I can get my hands on right now, so I'll take whatever's going.'

'You don't look like a big eater.'

'I'm not. Look, where are you heading?'

'How many times do I have to tell you? To find somewhere to crash for the night.'

'I know a place. Come with me. There's something I want to show you.'

What the hell could he possibly want to show me? 'No thanks,' I tell him. 'I think you've got the wrong man.'

'No, I haven't,' he insists, walking alongside me again. 'You're the only one who can help. I can't do this on my own any more.'

'Do *what*, exactly?'

'Not here,' he says, looking nervously at the small crowd gathered up ahead in the area where the food was distributed earlier. I decide to try and get deeper into the crowd, where I can give him the slip. Whatever his motives, I get the distinct impression this guy's a liability. I'll keep him talking for a few seconds longer, try to hide my intention of doing a runner.

'We're not the only ones who can hold the Hate, Sutton,' I tell him. 'I've met plenty of others.'

'And where are they now?'

'Dead,' I'm forced to admit, remembering the misguided kamikaze freedom fighters I managed to get myself briefly mixed up with.

'Exactly. See, I knew you'd say that. You're the first person like me I've come across since the bombs.'

'I'm *not* like you – stop saying that. I'm not like *anyone*.'

'Yes, you are, and I knew it as soon as I saw you out in the field earlier. The questions you were asking just confirmed it. You're no scavenger – that's not why you're here.'

Shit, somehow I have managed to blow my cover, though I don't know what I did. 'So how could you tell?' I ask. 'I didn't sense that you were any different – in fact, for all I know you could be lying to me, feeding me bullshit just so you can—'

'No bullshit, I swear,' he interrupts me, holding his hands up. 'You didn't see that we're the same because you weren't looking for it. It's not about what you do; it's what you *don't* do that really gives you away.'

'What?'

'I don't know what really brought you here to Southwold today, but I'm damn sure it wasn't the promise of a meal and a bed for the night. You didn't pick up on me because you were preoccupied with something else. It was obvious – the way you asked so many questions, of different people, the way you avoided eye contact. We're not like the rest of them—'

Just keep the conversation going for a few more seconds, I tell myself. I'm close to the edge of the crowd now.

'I ask questions because I don't want to fuck up. I've been on the road for weeks, and this is the best place I've found in a long time.'

'You've no more been on the road than I have – I *know* you're lying, Rufus, but I understand. We all have things we need to keep hidden. But the point I'm trying to make is that I'm on your side.'

'On *my* side? Who said anything about taking sides?'

'It's all about taking sides now.'

'Is that right?'

'Okay then, tell me the name of the last place you passed through before this one? How long were you there for? And the place before that?'

I don't bother answering. This guy's a fucking crank –

probably had one too many bangs on the head on the battlefield and now he's finally lost the plot. No matter; he's not my problem. We've reached the crowd and when Jill, the woman from the working party, appears in front of me, I grab hold of her arm and pull her closer.

'Jill,' I start, 'this guy wants to talk to you.'

I push her and Peter Sutton together and before either of them can react I shove my way through the rest of the bodies and slip away into the darkness.

13

I spend another half-hour walking the streets in the sub-zero dark, looking for somewhere I'll feel safe while I report back to Hinchcliffe and then grab some sleep. I eventually come across an empty bank, and make my way upstairs. From my position at the top of the building I look down onto the entire square below through a window covered with strong iron bars, like a prison cell. The place is virtually deserted, with just a couple of people left standing guard, warming their hands over a fire burning in a metal dustbin near the hotel.

I watch for ages, but nothing else happens and after a while my curiosity is overtaken by my exhaustion. I try to read my book for a while, but I'm too tired. I make a pillow from a pile of papers and spare clothes from my rucksack, lie back on the hard floor, cover myself with my coat and close my eyes. There's time to get a little rest before reporting back to Lowestoft.

But a little rest has turned into a lot of sleep – I've been completely out of it for hours, and I sit up quickly when I realise it's late and I still haven't called in. Hinchcliffe's going to be fucking furious. I grab the radio from my bag.

'It's me,' I whisper, trying to keeping my voice low. I cringe and fumble for the volume control when a sudden burst of loud static deafens me. It sounds like it's filling the entire building.

'Jesus Christ, Danny,' his distorted but distinctive voice immediately answers back. 'Where the hell have you been? I was starting to think they'd done you in. Either that or you'd defected.'

Defected? Is he just trying to be funny? I wouldn't fucking dare . . . His voice sounds slurred, like he's been drinking. He probably has.

'Nothing like that,' I tell him, wiping the sleep from my eyes and trying to sound more awake and alert than I actually am. 'I wanted to find out as much as I could before I got back to you.'

'And?' he asks.

I hesitate, and then say, 'And I don't know what's going on here. Warner's got these people well and truly onside. He makes it look like all he's trying to do is organise them according to his rules, and to get them to—'

'And that's half the problem,' Hinchcliffe angrily interrupts. I'm surprised by the strength of the alcohol-fuelled venom in his voice.

'What is?'

'*His* rules. Don't you see, Danny? Warner's rules aren't my rules.'

'Suppose not,' I quietly agree, suddenly feeling like I'm walking on eggshells. I'm beginning to wish I hadn't bothered calling in.

'You've heard the old story about the two boats in the harbour, haven't you?'

I don't have a clue what he's talking about. 'Remind me.'

'They start out next to each other. They're both supposed to be following the same course, but one gets it wrong, just by a *fraction* of a degree. They set off together but the longer they're at sea . . .'

'The bigger the gap between them.'

'Exactly. You see what I'm saying? That can't happen, Danny, not when Southwold is so close.'

'Well if it's any consolation, I can't speak for Warner but I don't think the people here are looking to pick a fight. They think he's just—'

'Don't get me wrong, that's not what I'm looking for either,' he continues, not listening, 'but everybody there needs to understand that things run the way *I* want them to around here. You play ball or you fuck off, that's your choice.'

'And have you tried telling them?' I ask, only feeling brave enough to confront Hinchcliffe because he's ten miles further up the coast. 'You could come down here, try a little diplomacy first and then—'

'Yeah, yeah, yeah . . . Fuck, Danny, it seems to me there's only ever two options these days, full-on or fuck-all. Why can't these people just do what I tell them?'

'I know, but—'

'What happens in Southwold is important,' he interrupts again, his voice sounding even angrier now. 'I can't risk having a rebellion on my doorstep, you know what I mean?'

'But are you sure Warner's a threat?'

'*Everyone* is a potential threat. I thought you'd have worked that out by now.'

'I still think you should talk to him. Try and find out why—'

'What's the state of the place like?' he interrupts.

'What?'

'What kind of condition is Southwold in?'

'I don't know. It's pretty much like everywhere else. A little less damaged than most places but—'

'And what about supplies?'

'Now that's the thing. Warner's got them getting the fields around here ready for planting. On the face of it he seems to be planning for the future. I've been working all bloody day digging bloody holes . . .'

'Nothing's going to grow. Everything's fucked.'

'We don't know that for sure. It might be that—'

'I asked you about supplies, Danny. I'm not interested in next year; what are they eating *today*?'

Hinchcliffe's going to hit the roof when I tell him about the delivery. 'I saw a lorry arrive,' I say eventually.

'A lorry?'

'Great big army thing. It wasn't one I'd seen before. They unloaded a stack of stuff out of the back.'

'What kind of stuff?'

'Couldn't tell. Food, weapons . . . I couldn't see what they—'

'Fuckers! Those will have come from *my* stores. Fucking Neil Casey, I bet he's got something to do with this – bastard's told them where I keep my supplies. Cunt's sold me out.'

'I haven't seen Casey – he wasn't with the lorry. They buried a few bodies this afternoon and I thought he might have been one of them, but I don't know if—'

'You said weapons?'

'A few rifles, that's all, nothing any bigger than that. Look, Hinchcliffe, I really don't think that—'

'I'm not interested in what you think. All I want to know is what you've seen.'

'And I've told you everything. I'll find work again tomorrow and see what else I can find out.'

'I don't think you understand the importance of this, Danny. There are implications for all of us if Warner begins getting support for what he's doing. People here will start hearing about him, and the grass is always greener on the other side, remember that expression?'

'But the grass is yellow *everywhere* now,' I tell him. 'What's happening here is on a very small scale, Hinchcliffe. If Warner's stealing from you, that's one thing, but I don't think it's worth . . .' I stop talking when I realise he's not there any more. The radio's dead.

14

The sound of engines wakes me up. The floor is icy cold as I scramble across the room to the window and look down onto the square. As usual I start coughing the moment I begin to move, but I try to muffle the sound in my sleeve. All around the edges of the large, triangle-shaped area, people are emerging from buildings and spilling out onto the street, and as I watch, several of them dive for cover as a fleet of vehicles powers into the centre of Southwold, filling the air with black fumes and noise. I recognise some of these lorries and vans; they're from Lowestoft. Hinchcliffe's obviously thought about our conversation last night and has decided to flex his muscles, remind everyone who's boss around here. So much for fucking diplomacy and negotiation – not that I ever expected anything different from him.

The convoy stops, filling almost the entire square now, and an army of fighters floods out into the open and begins rounding people up. For the most part they do exactly what they're told, shuffling towards the centre of the square. One woman refuses and tries to run the other way, but she's chased down by one of Hinchcliffe's thugs and clubbed to the ground. She lies on the tarmac screaming, blood pouring down her face, and everyone else is too scared to help. The fighter drags her over to the others. Christ, I need to get out of here.

The arrival of Hinchcliffe's troops means my time here is up. I begin to gather my stuff and pack everything back into my rucksack as quickly as I can, but I start coughing again and for a few seconds it's like I've lost control of my body. I try to clear my throat by drinking from a bottle of stale water, but the first gulp I take ends up sprayed across the floor before I can swallow it down. Eventually the coughing subsides. Panting with effort, I spit a lump of sticky, foul-tasting muck into the corner of the room, then lean against the window, trying to pull myself together.

Down on the street below, directly outside the hotel, there's an uncomfortable-looking stand-off taking place. Several of Hinchcliffe's vehicles have been parked in an arc around the entrance to the building and as I watch, his fighters are advancing. I recognise a couple of the more notorious faces. Patterson is moving closer, and Llewellyn is loitering ominously somewhere at the back of the assembled troops, no doubt there to coordinate them and to keep Hinchcliffe updated. Getting out of the lead lorry now is his protégé, Curtis, wearing his usual uniform of full body armour. He's a nasty bastard, not known for his negotiation skills. These discussions won't last long.

I finish collecting up my gear and swing my rucksack onto my shoulders. I'm keen to get the hell out of Southwold, fast. I glance out of the window again, and now John Warner is emerging from the hotel. He's barely dressed. He's walking towards Curtis with arms outstretched, palms up, showing that he's unarmed and ready to talk, gesturing for Curtis to follow him into the hotel. Curtis marches towards him – *oh fuck!* – what the hell's he doing? He doesn't even *try* talking to Warner; the bastard's just lifted his machete and taken a vicious swipe at the white-haired leader of Southwold, chopping down into his neck with such violent force that Warner's taken by surprise. He drops to his knees, the blade wedged deep into his flesh. Curtis grips Warner's shoulders and yanks him up, then wrenches his machete free. Still holding the old man, he plunges the blade deep into War-ner's chest, and as he pulls it out again he swipes it through the air as if to get rid of the excess blood. Warner staggers back, his body soaked in glistening red, then his legs give way and he crumbles to the ground like a marionette with severed strings.

There's a brief moment of silent, stunned disbelief, then all hell breaks loose.

The powerful pit-digger I met yesterday is the first person to react. He charges at Curtis, but he's killed as quickly and as easily as Warner as another of Hinchcliffe's fighters comes up behind him and cracks him around the side of the head with a baseball bat, thwacking the skull so hard he almost decapitates him. Perhaps it's because I wasn't expecting it, but even after all I've seen and done myself, this sudden brutal violence shocks me to such an extent that I can hardly move.

'Round them up,' Curtis yells to the rest of the fighters. 'Take anything worth having and burn the rest. Kill anyone who gets in the way.'

Is this my fault? Even though I'm starting to think that Hinchcliffe sent me here just to find an excuse for him to demonstrate his obvious strength and superiority, I can't help wondering if it could have been avoided if I'd handled him differently – maybe if I'd told him everything was okay and that Warner was one hundred per cent onside, would he have let Southwold be? Who the hell am I kidding? The more I think about it, the more I realise that yet again I've been Hinchcliffe's patsy; he's played me like a pawn on a chessboard. *Screw the fucking lot of them*, I tell myself as I run downstairs and look for a way out of the back of the bank. *This is* not *my problem*.

I can hear the fighting outside, even through the heavy wooden front door, as I head for the back, squeezing down a narrow corridor past the open door of an unlocked vault, cursing myself for picking such an impregnable hiding place. It seemed sensible last night, and the security was welcome, but every window here is either barred or heavily shuttered, and the only other exit I can find is a solid-looking metal-clad fire door that I'll never be able to get open. I've no choice but to go back out onto the street.

I slip out through the front door and press myself tightly against the outside wall, doing all I can to fade into the background. The village square is in utter chaos now, the remaining population of Southwold panicking as Hinchcliffe's troops turn on them. I see Jill, the work party leader from yesterday, struggling to load and fire a rifle. She lifts it up but I can see her hands are shaking and before she can even get her finger on the trigger a fighter chops into her side with an axe. I stand there like an idiot as Hinchcliffe's men grapple the locals to the ground, then force those still alive into the lorries which will ferry them back to Lowestoft. Our inglorious leader has obviously decided that having people living here outside his direct jurisdiction is an unacceptable risk – but Christ, did he really need to react like this? A woman is hit with a riot baton when she won't cooperate, first in the ribs, which leaves her winded, then bludgeoned around the side of the head. She's left on the ground close to Warner's body, blood pooling around her face, her cheekbone shattered. Her eyes are moving, but nothing else is. She looks straight at me . . .

Spencer, one of Hinchcliffe's men, comes at me with a crowbar but I'm stunned, and too slow to move. He's a tall, sinewy black kid in his early twenties, and the sick bastard grins with excitement as he sprints towards me, high on the thrill of the fight. He swings out wildly and at the last possible second I manage to react. I lean over to one side and I feel the rush of wind as the crowbar whooshes through the air, whistling just inches past my ear. He lunges at me again, all fired up with the adrenalin-rush of battle, intoxicated by the sudden release of long-suppressed frustrations.

'Wait!' I shout at him, 'Spencer, *don't*! I'm on your side – Hinchcliffe sent me here.'

He doesn't recognise me, probably doesn't even hear me, and as he swings the crowbar through the air again he catches me hard on my right shoulder. My padded rucksack strap absorbs some of the impact and I drop to my knees, landing close to the dismembered remains of another poor dead Southwold resident. I scramble back to my feet and now I start running for cover, Spencer in close pursuit. He's gaining fast as I weave around the bonnet of a reversing van; and I break right, desperate to shake him but knowing I can't keep this speed up for long—

—and run straight into another one of them, who blocks my path. Now I'm really fucked. I drop to the ground and cover my head, anticipating a barrage of strikes.

'Not this one,' a familiar voice says.

After a moment I cautiously look up, still expecting to be clubbed, and see that it's Llewellyn. He reaches down and pulls me up onto my feet like I'm a half-stuffed rag doll.

'What's going on?' I ask him, gasping for breath, desperately trying not to start coughing again.

'What do you think's going on? Just carrying out the boss's orders,' he answers abruptly.

'But this is fucking madness—'

'You tell him,' Llewellyn says, looking me straight in the eye. 'I'm just doing what I'm told,' he says again. 'Now get in the lorry, or I'll personally beat seven shades of shit out of you.'

Relieved, I start to do as he says, but then I stop.

'Wait – Hinchcliffe's car. I left it just outside town. He'll want it back.'

Llewellyn looks at me for a second, then nods his head. 'Go and get it, then get yourself straight back to Lowestoft. Any fucking around and you'll have me to answer to. Right?'

I don't need to be told twice. I start running, though I'm not sure which direction I need to take; I'm just desperate to get away. I glance back once. Southwold has quickly degenerated into a depressingly familiar sight, with broken bodies scattered across the tarmac, the dead and the dying side by side. People are fighting, or running in all directions like a scene from any one of a hundred battles I've seen before . . . except this battle is different, because there are no Unchanged here. It makes me feel ashamed, responsible almost. I'm ashamed because of my connection with the man behind this bloodshed, and equally ashamed because all they're doing is the same thing I've done countless times before. It's just a different class of target, that's all.

There's the sudden crash of smashing glass and when I turn again I see a flash of bright yellow flame lighting up the early morning gloom. Hinchcliffe's men are firebombing the hotel. So that's his tactic this morning: eliminate the figurehead, publicly and violently, take anything and any*one* of value, then do enough damage to render the village uninhabitable, leaving the survivors of the massacre with only one remaining option: it's Lowestoft or nothing.

15

I move quietly through the courthouse, determined to get in and out quickly, and without being seen. There's an unexpected but very welcome lack of fighters around; I guess most of them are still in Southwold, revelling in the chaos. I can picture them all in the middle of the carnage, just like a bloody lower league rugby team on tour, drunk on violence, smashing the place up, stealing food and weapons, bragging to each other about their best kills . . . fucking morons.

I leave the radio on a desk in the courtroom. It should be okay there – Anderson's bound to be around here somewhere and he'll know what to do with it. I've left radios here before and—

'You okay, Danny?'

I turn, startled, my heart sinking. Hinchcliffe's standing right behind me and my stomach knots with nerves. I was hoping I'd got away with it, but this sly bastard never misses a trick. This was the exactly what I was hoping to avoid: me alone with Hinchcliffe. Much as I want to bolt for the door and disappear, I can't.

All I can do as he beckons me through to his room is follow. 'You did good in Southwold,' he says as we walk.

'Thanks,' I answer. I'm not sure what else I'm supposed to say. It didn't feel good.

'We need to keep showing these people who's in charge, you know?'

'If you say so.' I don't want to risk disagreeing with Hinchcliffe, but what happened in Southwold has really got under my skin. I never expected him to let John Warner have carte blanche to run the place, but his reaction today was extreme.

Hinchcliffe sits down on the corner of his unmade bed and looks up at me. The atmosphere is unbearable. He may be many things but he's certainly not stupid, and he's probably already worked out what I'm thinking. I want to run, but he keeps staring at me and I can't move.

'You still look sick.'

'I am sick. Haven't felt well for days, weeks maybe.'

'Are you eating enough? Want me to get you more food?'

'I'm not eating anything.'

He shakes his head. 'You have to eat, Danny. Look, if you're really that bad, get yourself over to the factory and have a word with Rona Scott.'

'Thanks, I will,' I answer, although I know I probably won't. The last thing I want to do is to submit myself to an examination from Rona Scott. She's the closest thing Hinchcliffe has to a doctor. When she's not working on the Unchanged kids in the factory, it's her job to keep his fighters patched up and ready for battle. She's not interested in people like me.

'You've had a rough week, what with the Unchanged and now Southwold,' Hinchcliffe says suddenly. The tone of his voice is different; it takes me by surprise. 'I know I ask a lot of you sometimes, mate. It can't have been easy with those Unchanged – I don't know how you do it, I really don't. Christ, just the thought of them makes my skin crawl, even after all this time. But that last catch, Danny – you tracked them, trapped them, stayed with them until we were ready to move in . . . That takes guts.'

'Just doing what you asked me to,' I say quietly. Truth is, I didn't have any choice.

'Listen, mate, I don't think I'll need you for the next couple of days. Get some rest. Sort yourself out.'

I hate it when Hinchcliffe's pleasant to me. This isn't like him – he never gives, only takes. I pause and wait for the catch, and when he doesn't say anything, I begrudgingly acknowledge him. 'Thanks.'

I still don't feel able to move. His piercing gaze makes me feel like my feet are nailed to the floor and he knows it. The fucker probably enjoys it.

'Something on your mind?'

'Nothing.'

'Come on, I know you better than that. Tell me what you're thinking.'

How honest am I prepared to be? I sense he wants me to talk openly, but if I'm too critical he's likely to react badly and I don't think I can take a beating today. On the other hand, he's not going to let me go until I tell him what's wrong.

'Honest answer?'

'Honest answer.'

'I don't understand why you did what you did in Southwold. Fair enough if you've got a problem with Warner, but the rest of them . . . ?'

'It needed doing.'

'Did it need to be so brutal?'

'I think so. They needed to know what's what.'

'There's a world of difference between sending a message and what your fighters did today.'

'I knew that was what was bothering you.'

'So why did you ask?'

'Just wanted to see if you'd got the guts to tell me,' he says. 'I thought you would. Not many people would have the balls. You and me, Danny, we've got a lot in common.'

'Have we?'

'When it comes down to it,' he continues, 'we both want the same thing. We both want an end to all the bullshit and fighting and we want an easy life. We're just going about it in very different ways.'

'You want an end to the fighting? Really? That's not what I saw. The Unchanged are gone and all you're doing is looking for someone else to batter instead. We don't *have* to fight any more. I think you want to.'

'That's not how it is.'

'Well, that's how it looks.'

'I know you're happy to bury your head in the sand and keep yourself to yourself, but I'm not prepared to do that. In this world you can either sit back and wait for events to overtake you, or you can go out there and make things happen now, on your terms. That's what I'm doing.'

'That's what you're doing when you're ordering the people in Southwold to be beaten to death? When you've got your fighters burning buildings to the ground?'

'The people in Southwold had a choice; the ones who didn't resist are on their way here now and if they're useful, they'll be okay. The rest are dead. You've got to remember, everything is built on aggression now, Danny. We're all fighters, whether we like it or not. The only thing that separates us is our individual strength and determination. If you don't stake your claim, someone else will.'

'So where does it end? Last man standing?'

'Possibly.'

'I don't buy it.'

'I know you don't, and I understand that. But we'll have to agree to disagree, because I'm the one in charge. And anyway, even if you don't like the way I do things, you're smart enough to know you'll be okay as long as you stay in line and don't piss me off, aren't you?'

'Suppose . . .' For some reason I can't let go of it. 'But did it really need to be so harsh in Southwold? Couldn't you just have dealt with Warner and let the rest of them be?'

'I had to send a message; if I hadn't, I'd have just been heading back in a few weeks to sort them out again. Someone would have taken Warner's place.'

'But Warner's people were cooperating with each other – surely if you—'

'I like you, Danny,' he interrupts, obviously no longer

interested, 'you're way off the mark sometimes, but you're good to have around. You're not like all those sycophants and arse-lickers. You keep me grounded. You make me laugh.'

'You're welcome,' I mumble quietly, not sure if that was a compliment or not. There's no arguing with Hinchcliffe. Today he reminds me of all those long-gone world leaders who used to start wars in far-off places to *maintain the peace*. It's the same kind of flawed logic as the old Ministry of Defence, which only ever seemed to attack. Feeling a fraction more confident now, and as he's clearly in the mood to talk, I decide to take the bull by the horns and ask the question that's been troubling me recently. 'So now the Unchanged are gone, what happens next?'

'What do you mean?'

'Those fighters of yours this morning . . . all they wanted to do was kill. They were like kids at Christmas. So what happens to them now the enemy's been defeated? Do you think they'll just stop? They're not going to want to go back to being bricklayers or teachers or pub landlords . . .'

'I know that, and they won't have to. There's a new class structure emerging here, and we're at the top. Have you looked outside this compound, Danny? Seen how many people are waiting out there? They're the ones who'll eventually do the work. They'll do anything I tell them, and you know why?'

'Why?'

'The two "f"s.'

'The two "f"s? What's that supposed to mean?'

'Come on, keep up! We've talked about this: food and fear. When I need bricklayers and teachers and the like, they'll be fighting with each other to be the one to help.'

His vision of the future seems ridiculously simplistic to me, but what do I know? 'So what happens when the food runs out?'

'That's not going to happen for a long time,' he answers

quickly. 'We'll see it coming and start planning for it when we need to.'

'How?'

'By the time it's a problem I'll have enough of a workforce to start producing food ourselves, and they'll be hungry enough to do exactly what I tell them. But there's no point making people work for food yet, not while there's still stuff to be scavenged. They're not desperate enough.'

'John Warner was trying to get people farming,' I tell him.

'And was it working?'

'Well, no, but—'

'There you go then. It's too soon.'

I could ask him how he ever plans to farm when all the livestock for miles around Lowestoft is either dead, dying or running wild, and when the soil has been poisoned by radiation . . . but I'm sure he knows that anyway and so I don't bother. Instead I try another tack. 'The batteries in my reading lamp are almost gone,' I start to say before he interrupts, laughing.

'Your reading lamp! Fuck me, Danny, you're turning into an old woman!'

I ignore him and carry on. 'The batteries are going in my reading lamp. What do I do when they die?'

'You come and see me and I get you some more,' he answers quickly. 'Same as always.'

'So what happens when *you* run out?'

'I send people out to find more.'

'And when they can't find any? When we really have used them all up?'

'You have to stop reading at night,' he smirks.

I'm serious, and I keep looking at him, and his grin disappears.

'I know what you're saying, mate, and you do have a valid point. What *do* we do? I don't know how to make batteries and even if I did, I couldn't get my hands on the right chemicals and equipment. But the information's out there somewhere . . .'

'It's just that the way you talk about things makes everything sound a lot easier than it's actually going to be. It's not just reading, it's making food, keeping warm, staying alive . . . Once everything's gone we're really going to struggle to get any of it back again.'

'I never said it was going to be *easy*. Thing is, if I'm too honest with people too soon I'll lose their support and I can't risk that. I need the numbers right now. It's still early days. When we're more established here, then we'll start planning ahead, but right now, all that matters today is today.'

Hinchcliffe always does this: he slips all too easily into spouting bullshit and spin. I suppose it's all bloody politics, and it never changes, even after everything we've all been through. I guess it doesn't matter how high the stakes are; to people like him, position and self-preservation are everything.

'The trick right now,' he says, 'is to let the people who matter think *they're* in control. I give my best fighters everything they want, and the Switchbacks who work hard, they get most of what they need too. Compared to the pathetic lives they used to lead, this is much better. They're free, uninhibited—'

'—for now, maybe.'

'Lighten up,' he says.

'I don't want to lighten up.'

'Things *will* improve, Danny.'

'Will they?'

'Of course they will. We'll get that wind turbine working after the winter. Imagine that: constant power for the whole town again.'

'It'll never happen.'

'Yes it will.'

'No it won't. One of the blades is broken, for Christ's sake. Where are you going to get a replacement from? And how are you going to get it up there? Have you got anyone who knows anything about engineering and mechanics? Got a crane tucked away anywhere? Christ, you've just said you'll be screwed when you run out of batteries.'

'It's all out there somewhere,' he says, starting to sound annoyed, 'and there are bound to be people who used to know about these things. They'll help if I give them food and—'

'And if you hold a gun to their heads.'

'If that's what it takes.'

'I think you've got to get the fundamentals right before you start talking about electricity and shit like that.'

'And is that what John Warner was doing?'

'Maybe,' I admit, wondering if I've gone too far. Now I'm back in Lowestoft again, it seems to me that's exactly what Warner was doing.

'You're wrong,' he says. 'Warner was a thieving bastard who was trying to undermine everything that I've got here.'

'All due respect, I don't think Warner gave a shit what you were doing here.'

'The fucker was interested enough to want to steal from me,' Hinchcliffe snaps, a bit of barely suppressed anger in his voice. He gets up and pours himself a drink, but he doesn't offer me one and that's a sure sign I've pissed him off. How bloody stupid can I get? That's not a good idea.

'Sorry, Hinchcliffe. I didn't mean to talk out of turn.'

He leans against a dusty window, looking out over the divided streets of Lowestoft. 'You're okay. Like I said, Danny, you're not like the others. You're always questioning, and I need that from time to time. Just don't let me catch you talking like this to anyone else. I did what needed to be done, and that's the end of it.'

In for a penny, in for a pound. I'm taking a hell of a risk, but this is as good a time as any . . .

'So what about me?'

'What about you?'

'I don't have any special skills. I can't fight any more. You've kept me onside to hunt out the Unchanged, but now they're gone, what happens to me?'

He's quiet for a moment, maybe thinking how he's going to answer. Then he says, 'You're not going anywhere, mate. You underestimate yourself. You've proved your worth to me again and again over the last few weeks. There's a lot of work still to be done to get this place how I want it, and I'm gonna need people like you.'

I make a mental note to start fucking up more often. 'And you really think you'll be able to do that?'

'Do what?'

'Get this place sorted out? Keep people in line? You think they're just going to keep doing what you tell them to?'

'Yes,' he answers without hesitation. 'They won't have any choice.'

I stand there and stare at him, still unable to move, and now I'm unable to speak as well. This guy's out of his fucking mind, but I'm not going to be the one who tells him. The whole conversation leaves me feeling hollow – what chance has anyone got if people like Hinchcliffe are left in charge?

Hinchcliffe wraps his arm around my shoulder and walks me back towards the exit.

'I know what you need,' he says. 'You're too tense. You need to relax. Go home, get some rest, then come back here at dusk. Meet me out the front.'

He shoves me out of the door and as I walk back through the courthouse building I'm relieved to be away from him, but now nervous as hell. Why the fuck does he want me to come back?

16

Hinchcliffe told me to meet him outside the courthouse, but I think he's stood me up. He's not inside, and I've been out here waiting in the freezing cold for ages now. I thrust my hands deep into my pockets, wishing I was anywhere but here. I would go back to the house, but I think I've pissed him off quite enough for one day. He'll kill me if I'm not here when he's ready for me.

The contrast between Lowestoft and what I saw happening in Southwold is stark. Across the road a group of Switchbacks are unloading supplies from a cart and taking them into the police station barracks, where most of the fighters live. Others are collecting waste and dumping it over the compound walls for the vagrants to plunder. Outside what used to be the library people are working on a rudimentary water supply, to replace the previous one, which fell apart. They've lined up a series of drainpipes and water-butts to collect water from the gutters of buildings, and black plastic taps hang over the lip of a low brick wall for people to fill their containers. Lizzie's dad used to have one of those butts in his garden. I remember the kids used to mess with it, and how they complained about the stagnant stench and the flies and the algae . . . and is this the best we can manage now? Still, if it's bad here by Hinch-cliffe's courthouse, it's a thousand times worse on the other side of the barricades.

Just outside the south gate, on the approach to the bridge, there's an old man who lives in an ambulance. I pass him going to or from the house. He's clearly not a fighter – he can barely stand – but he seems able to switch on an angry, violent façade at will, using it as a deterrent to anyone who approaches him. He's well known round here, and Hinchcliffe's fighters laugh at him and take the piss, often taunting him for the sport of it, trying to get him to react and bite back. He collects rocks and chucks them at anyone who gets too close. Fucker almost got me today. His ambulance is useless – it's just a battered wreck with a blown engine and only a single wheel remaining – but it seems to symbolise everything that's wrong here. All around this place people have taken things which used to matter and turned them into nothing. I've stayed here because this place looked like my best option, but I think it's time to reconsider. The longer the violence here continues, the further we seem to regress.

'What d'you want?' Curtis asks as he thunders out through the courthouse door, knocking into me.

'I'm supposed to be meeting Hinchcliffe.'

'He's not here.'

'I know that, I—'

'Factory,' he says, shoving me out of the way.

Bloody typical. I start walking and my legs nearly give way. They've stiffened in the cold, but it's a relief to be moving. My whole body aches and my face is completely numb with cold.

It's not far from the courthouse to the factory, but I always get distracted when I come this way, imagining what this place was like before the war . . . all those seaside shops selling worthless tat, pandering to the hordes of holidaymakers – it's hard now to believe this was once a destination of choice. Lowestoft has all the usual high street chain stores, the supermarkets, banks, estate agents, doctors' surgeries, solicitors' offices, but they're all just shells now, their unlit signs the only indication of what they used to be. Now these wildly different buildings all look the same, dark and uninviting. They've long been stripped of anything of worth and now their inhabitants stare hopelessly out from the shadows. I put my head down and keep moving.

'You seen Hinchcliffe?' I ask a remarkably fresh-faced fighter who's on guard duty at the checkpoint at the end of the road into the factory. He's buried in blankets and slumped down on a chair inside what looks like half a garden shed. He's hardly guarding, and hardly threatening. It's no surprise really; no one in their right mind would want to come here. Apart from some of the more vicious kids (who'd kill you soon as look at you), there's nothing here worth taking.

'He's up with Wilson,' the guard answers. 'He said you'd probably turn up.'

The fact that Hinchcliffe's with Wilson, his chief kid-wrangler, is a relief: it means he's at the opposite end of the factory complex to where Rona Scott does whatever she does to the Unchanged kids. I can see flickering lights in the distance and I wrap my coat around me even tighter as the wind whips up off the sea and blasts through the gaps between buildings. Eventually I reach a set of metal gates behind which the useful kids are kept. There's another guard here – an irritating jobsworth who takes himself too ser-iously. He blocks my way through and when I tell him I'm supposed to be meeting Hinchcliffe he glares at me, then dis-appears. He's only gone for a couple of minutes, then he grudgingly lets me pass.

Hinchcliffe's waiting for me in a small courtyard that's surrounded on three sides by squat, metal-walled box-shaped buildings which were probably industrial units, or lock-ups or something similar. The roofs of the buildings are covered with curls of razor wire.

'Forgot about you, mate,' Hinchcliffe says, and that's as good an apology as I'm going to get. 'I was just checking the stock.'

'The stock?'

'The kids,' he explains. 'I've been thinking more about what we were saying earlier.'

'And?' I press hopefully.

'And maybe you're right. Maybe I'm not looking as far forward as I should be.'

'So what's that got to do with the kids?'

'Everything, you dumb fuck! No kids, no future.'

'That doesn't bode well, does it? All the kids I've seen since the war started have either been Unchanged or wild bloody animals.'

'You lost kids in the fighting didn't you?'

'Three,' I answer.

'One like us?'

'My little girl.'

'Where is she now?'

'Dead, I expect. Last time I saw her she was running towards the base of a bloody mushroom cloud, looking for more Unchanged to kill.'

'Look at this,' he says, gesturing to a narrow window in the front of the nearest metal building. Something's written in chalk on the door – it's hard to make out, but eventually I decipher it as 'BOY 5–7'. Is that a serial number or an age range? I bend down to look through the window.

It takes my eyes a couple of seconds to adjust to the negligible light levels inside and I start, 'What am I supposed to be looking at—?'

Something smashes against the glass. It's a young boy, and he hits the strengthened window so hard that he bounces off and crashes back down onto the floor. He immediately picks himself up again and starts hammering on the window, scratching at it with his fingers, trying to claw his way out and get to me. He moves with the same speed and animal-like agility that Ellis had, before I lost her. He's completely feral. His blue eyes lock onto mine and, after a few seconds, he stops struggling. As soon as he realises I'm not

Unchanged he slopes back into the corner, dejected. I keep watching him, unable to look away.

Hinchcliffe shines a torch around. Christ, the room the kid's being held in is like an animal's cage. There are puddles of what I guess is piss on the floor, chunks of half-chewed food lying around, smears of shit like tyre tracks . . .

'This one like your daughter?'

'Just the same.'

'Thought so. Now come over here.'

I follow him across the square patch of tarmac towards another, similar-sized building, almost directly opposite. The writing on the door of this unit says 'BOY 10–12'. I'm hesitant to get too close to the glass this time, but Hinchcliffe shoves me forward. I tense up, expecting another kid to hurl itself at me and when it doesn't happen I start to relax. I can't see any movement at all through the window.

'Is there anything in here?'

'Over there in the corner,' Hinchcliffe says, shining his torch towards the far end of the squalid rectangular space. Then I see it: a figure slumped up against the wall. It's another boy, older than the first. He stands perfectly still, staring back at me, but not reacting. 'The older ones are starting to show more control,' Hinchcliffe explains. 'Show them one of the Unchanged and they'll still pull its fucking arms out of its sockets, but when they're not fighting, they're more lucid than they were. The older they get, the more control over their urges they have.'

'What point are you making?' I ask, not taking my eyes off the child.

'That maybe the kids can be rehabilitated. That there might still be hope for them. It was pure instinct that made them fight the Unchanged with as much ferocity as they did. Now the Unchanged are gone, we might be able to straighten them out again.'

'You reckon?'

He leads me away from the cells.

'I'm convinced these kids are as wild as they are because they've just lived through the worst of the war. When things calm down again, so will they. We'll teach them how to be human again, how to control themselves.'

'Be human?' I laugh. 'What, human like your fighters? Christ, Hinchcliffe, hardly the best role models for them! Anyway, these children have spent the last year killing. Do you really think you're going to be able to make them stop?'

'What use are they to us if we can't?'

'So what are you suggesting? Are you going to keep all newborns locked up until they've grown out of their viciousness?'

I think he's confused being controlled with being catatonic, but I don't want to risk antagonising him any more. It says something when his idea of progress is producing a kid which doesn't immediately want to kill everything in the immediate vicinity. These children are hardwired to fight now: they've had a year of running wild and their immature, pre-pubescent brains either don't know or don't want to know anything else.

'It's been less than twelve months,' he continues. 'We'll keep studying the ones we've got here. My guess is that newborns won't be like this, because they won't have lived through the fighting that these kids have. It might be that we end up with a missed generation or two, but there's nothing anyone can do about that.'

The guard lets us back out through the gate and we carry on down the road.

'So what about the other end of the factory?' I ask, stupidly prolonging a conversation I never wanted to have. I realise I still don't know why Hinchcliffe wanted to see me.

'What about it?'

'What have you got going on there – is it the reverse of all this? Have you got Rona Scott provoking Unchanged kids until they fight back?'

'Something like that – but it's not so much about making them fight as it is getting them to be like us.'

'I don't understand.'

'They've got to be able to survive, and to hold their own.' Hinchcliffe increases his speed past the furthest end of the complex to a wide footpath which runs parallel with the seawall. The last light of day is beginning to fade.

I don't think I've been out here before. To my left is a sheer drop of several yards down onto another walkway, and beyond that the remains of an abandoned holiday park. There are numerous equally spaced rectangular slabs of concrete visible through the overgrowth and weeds where caravans used to stand, looking eerily like oversized graves. It's an uncomfortable place, silent but for our footsteps and the sea battering the rocks on the other side of the wall to my right.

'There's so much I need to know the answers to, Danny,' he explains as I catch him up, 'things you probably haven't even considered. For a start, what do we do if any of the women give birth to Unchanged kids? A kid's just a kid; that's got to be the position we get to. It'll get easier over time.'

'Will it?'

'Rona Scott thinks so. She says when there's absolutely nothing left but us, they won't know any different. We still don't know why we are like we are, and we probably never will. We don't know if what happened was because of some physical change, or a virus or germ, or even something we saw on TV. Thing is, kids who are inherently Unchanged are going to have to adapt and become like us to survive – either that, or they'll be killed.'

I don't respond. I've thought about this myself, too much, if anything. Months ago, back when I was looking for Ellis, I saw a pregnant woman, and ever since then I've wondered what would happen to a newborn child. What if the kid's born and the mother's gut instinct – that same raw, undeniable gut instinct which made me kill hundreds of Unchanged – tells her to kill her own newborn child? I've had nightmare visions of people crowding around the birth, trying to work out if the baby's like us or like them, trying to decide whether they should keep it alive or drown it in the river. Or worse still, people fighting with each other to be the one who kills an Unchanged child . . . I've even imagined delivery rooms with a dividing line drawn down the middle, and medical equipment on one side, weapons on the other.

I try to bite my lip and stop myself, but I can't help speaking out again. I wish I could ignore what's happening and switch off, but the memory of what happened to all three of my own children keeps me asking questions and searching for answers I know I'll probably never find. 'It's a paradox, isn't it?'

'What is?'

'What you're talking about. You're saying we have to straighten out our kids and corrupt the Unchanged. Isn't there a danger you'll just end up breaking all of them? Aren't you just going to end up with generation after generation of fuck-ups? Kids that can't fight, can't think, can't even function . . . ?'

Hinchcliffe just looks at me and grunts, and I think I've gone too far again.

'Sorry,' I apologise quickly, remembering who I'm talking to, 'I shouldn't have said anything.'

'Yes you should,' he says, surprising me. 'You should keep challenging like this. I told you, no one else has got the balls to do it. You see things differently to the rest of them.'

'I'm not trying to be difficult, I'm just—'

'You're just saying what you think, and that's a good thing. You might turn out to be right about everything, but for the record, I don't think you are. Thing is, there's no way of knowing yet. The world these kids will end up inheriting will be completely different to anything we've experienced, different to what we're seeing now, even. Until then, the only thing we can do is explore every possibility and cover all eventualities.'

'That's a tall order. How are you planning to do that?' I'm really struggling to keep up with Hinchcliffe's fast pace now and I'm relieved when he finally stops walking.

He turns around and grins. It scares the shit out of me when he looks at me like that. 'Now we're getting somewhere,' he says. 'It's like everything else. It all boils down to supply and demand.'

17

My afternoon with Hinchcliffe is clearly far from over. His speed increases again as we continue further along the seawall and I'm left dragging behind, panting hard and drenched with sweat. I look back the way we've just come and see that we've travelled a surprising distance away from the centre of town. The walk back to the house is going to take for ever.

'You're far too tense, Danny,' he says, waiting for me to catch up again. 'I know exactly what you need – help you get rid of some of that pent-up frustration.'

'All I need is some sleep. I'll be okay in the morning.'

'You've been saying that for weeks.'

I notice there are several buildings up ahead, barely visible in the increasing darkness until now. Hinchcliffe pauses to light a cigarette. He flicks the match over the wall, blows out smoke, then carries on, leading me away from the ocean now and up a steep, muddy pathway. As we get closer, I see that there are dull lights flickering in the windows of one of the buildings. It's hard to make out much detail, but it looks like one of those ten-a-penny seafront hotels you always used to find in places like this. It's painted a grubby powdery blue and there's a lopsided signpost at this end of the short front yard with two truncated lengths of chain hanging down where the building's name would once have hung. There's a guard standing just inside the door – Joe Chandra, one of Hinchcliffe's most prized fighters. He's an ugly-looking bastard, like a comic-book villain, with burns covering almost exactly half of his face. I haven't seen him around in a while; I guess I'd assumed he was dead. So what's Hinchcliffe got him posted all the way out here for? My heart's pounding suddenly, and this time it's not because of the effort of the walk.

'What is this place, Hinchcliffe?'

'The solution to a couple of problems,' he replies, giving little away.

'What problems?'

'Regardless of what they turn out to be, we need people to keep having kids. People need food, and they have a need to procreate. So here they can fuck and be fucked for food. Sounds like some kind of screwed-up charity drive, eh?' He laughs at his own joke.

I'm so taken aback by what I'm hearing that I don't realise I've followed him into the building until we've already passed Chandra at the door and gone right inside. The air indoors smells stale.

It's quiet and Hinchcliffe's voice echoes off the walls. 'Like it or not, mate, kids are going to become a valuable commodity. I'm just trying to cover all the bases and keep control of the stock. Most people are only interested in staying alive, and they'll do whatever it takes to achieve that. The women I've got here are willing to get pregnant for food; the men are more than willing to try and get them pregnant . . .'

'So which is it? A brothel or a sperm bank?'

'Both, I suppose!' he laughs, filling the building with his noise. 'It's hardly a love shack, if that's what you mean, but it does the trick.'

'There are no queues at the door. You'd have thought—'

'Times have changed, mate. *We've changed*. Romance and relationships have gone right out of fashion since we all started killing each other, but people still need to fuck.'

'But where is everyone?'

'I'm being selective. You didn't know about this place until now, and I tell you more than I tell most. You have to detach yourself from what used to matter now, Danny.

These are business decisions. Doesn't mean you can't enjoy your work, though!'

'How far have we fallen if sex has just become a business decision?' I ask as we climb a twisting staircase which smells of damp. Thin curtains have been draped over the windows and the faint yellow light comes from infrequently spaced oil lamps.

'Oh come on, don't get all soft on me,' he groans. 'People have been selling sex since the year dot. You have to face facts – this is how things have to be for now, and that's why I've been selective with the people I've allowed to get involved in this so far. Better that a woman gets pregnant by someone who can still fight than by one of the wasters drifting around out there outside the compound. If I started advertising this place there'd be a queue of underclass men outside the door twenty-four seven, desperate to sow their pathetic seed for a quick thrill and a half-decent meal. It's tough, and it's not fair, but for now this is how it has to be.'

'I don't think it's right.'

'To be honest, mate,' he says, stopping at the end of a gloomy landing, 'I don't give a fuck. I didn't bring you here because I wanted your blessing.'

'So why did you bring me?'

'Christ, why do you think?'

'I—'

'You're not the strongest, Danny, but you've got brains, and I know you can fight when you have to. You've already fathered one kid like us.'

He grabs my arm and pulls me further down the corridor.

'But I—'

'You can come here any time you want,' he tells me, pushing me towards an open door. Light spills across the landing. 'The women leave their doors open when they're ready. Everyone's a winner here, you know. I give them double rations if they get pregnant – or I would do if any of the useless cows had actually managed it.'

My brain's struggling to catch up with what's happening, and my body is numb and unresponsive. I just stand there, staring into the hotel room, remembering the last time I was in a place like this. I remember looking for Lizzie, and I wish she was here today. The memory of her face fills me with pain. Despite everything that happened between us, what we both became, there's a part of me that still clings on to what we used to have, and the family we made together. Hinchcliffe shoves me forward again and I make a desperate, instinctive grab for either side of the door frame, not wanting to go through.

'I'll see you later, Danny,' he says, taking a few steps back, then standing and watching me. 'Enjoy yourself, son.'

I've no choice but to do what he says. I step into the light.

18

Inside the room there's a woman sitting on a double bed with her back to me. I'm fucking terrified. If I didn't know Hinchcliffe's bound to be waiting around outside I'd run for it, but he'll want to be sure I've done what he told me to do.

I can't do this – I can't remember the last time I felt anything like sexual desire. I can't remember masturbating since the war began, or even wanting to. I can't even re-member the last time I had an erection – probably with Liz, before the Change split us up . . . I don't want to share my body with anyone now, much less with someone I don't know . . .

The woman on the bed looks wearily over her shoulder. All I can think is, *How many times has she already done this today?*

'You coming in?' she grunts. Her voice is flat and un-emotional.

I take another hesitant step forward.

'Shut the bloody door then.'

'Sorry,' I mumble, and turn to push it closed. I lean against the door and breathe deeply, trying to hide my nerves. When I finally turn around the woman has stood up, but the light's behind her and I can't actually see her face from here. I wonder what she looks like, an unexpected thought that takes me by surprise. She's looking me up and down and I have no idea what she's thinking – I'm suddenly acutely aware of how I must look. I rarely wash any more – not many people do, without running water, or heat, or, too often, privacy. I hack off my hair and shave my beard when I can't stand it any longer, and I can't remember the last time I brushed my teeth . . . No matter, this isn't a mating ritual, this is purely

146

functional. How I look and feel is completely unimportant. But I still don't know if I can go through with it . . .

This horrible silent stand-off continues for what feels like for ever, and I'm on the brink of backing out of the room and taking my chances with Hinchcliffe when she finally speaks. 'You healthy?'

'Pretty much.'

'What's that supposed to mean?'

What should I tell her? That I cough my guts up first thing every morning? That the skin on my back and neck is burned from the bombs? That sometimes there's blood when I piss? If I go into graphic detail, will that put her off me? I don't. 'I'm okay.'

'You had kids before?'

'Three. You?'

'This isn't a date. Your kids, what were they?'

'Two boys and a girl.'

'No, *what* were they?'

I finally realise what she's asking. 'My girl was like us.' I have to block out the names and faces of my dead children if I'm going to get through this. 'The boys were Unchanged.'

She nods and thinks carefully about what I've just told her, as if it's going to make a difference. Then, with a sigh, she unzips her baggy trousers and lets them drop down to her ankles. It's incredibly unfeminine. She kicks them away and lies back down on the bed. The fine detail of her face is still hidden by the shadows but I can see her a little more clearly now. She seems strangely expressionless, and it's hard to place her age. Her long limbs are bony, and her skin is covered in cuts and bruises and for a second I remember how long Liz used to spend each day on looking good – all the creams and lotions, waxing her legs and armpits, shaving her bikini line, hunting down every rogue hair with tweezers . . . My eyes are involuntarily drawn to the top of this woman's legs and her unkempt bush of wiry pubic hair. Since everything changed, we've all become strangely sexless, old and young, male and female alike. How we look is unimportant; keeping warm and staying alive is all that matters. Back in the day, men and women had frustratingly different sexual drives, desires which rarely coincided. Now no one's bothered one way or another. It is obviously as much an ordeal for this woman as it is for me.

'Get on with it,' she says, looking up at the ceiling, not at me. I nervously start to undress, kicking off my boots, taking off my coat and pulling down my trousers. Without really think-ing I start to remove some of the layers of clothing I'm wearing, but she stops me. 'No need for that. Just get it done.'

I didn't think I could feel much more awkward, but I was wrong. Half-naked, I climb onto the bed and kneel next to her on the mattress. I'm hideously embarrassed, my heart's racing, and I'm barely able to think straight. I'm far too nervous even to reach across and touch her. My pathetic flaccid cock hangs down between my legs, shrivelled up to virtually nothing by the bitter cold and the grim indignity of the situation. I can't get hard – maybe erectile dysfunction will save me tonight? I try to remember all the things I used to think about to get myself aroused, but it's having the opposite effect: each image or buried memory I dredge up from the past hurts too much—

It's obviously not the first time this woman has been faced with someone like me. She reaches up and cups my balls with her hand, and though she doesn't speak, she barely even moves, just the touch of her skin against mine is enough and my cock finally starts to stiffen. She gently runs her fingertips down the length of my shaft, touching me more tenderly than anyone's touched me in almost a year, and my head's clear now and there's a sudden burning, almost insatiable need low in my gut . . .

I pull myself astride the woman and force myself into her. It's hard and dry, then warm, and though it hurts for a second as my foreskin snags, it gets easier as I start to move. I'm not thinking about what I'm doing, or the woman; I don't give a damn about what she thinks, or feels, I just keep banging away, harder and harder still, my bollocks slapping against the inside of her thighs, my hands gripping the headboard, and then it happens—

—a split-second pause filled with something which used to matter, and then I feel myself empty into her and I groan with the effort and, panting hard, drop down on top of her. Our bodies are finally close, my head next to hers, but she shoves her hands up under my chest and pushes me away. I roll over onto my back as she slides out from under me and we lie there in silence, side by side, until, without warning, the most brutal and unforgiving wave of post-ejaculation regret I've ever experienced comes crashing over me. I turn my head to one side and finally look into the woman's face, and I'm filled with shame and remorse. She just stares up at the ceiling, waiting for me to leave.

'Go,' she says, and I do it without a word. I virtually fall off the bed in my haste, scooping up my clothes and my boots from the floor and stumbling to the door. My cock is still dribbling thick, sticky strings of warm fluid as I pull on my torn boxers, and I'm struggling to hold onto everything as I yank the door open and crash out onto the landing. Finally I slump against the wall, still only half-dressed and already freezing cold, but not giving a damn. I'm content to let the darkness of the musty hotel swallow me up.

After a few moments I look around, half-expecting Hinchcliffe to be there, nodding his approval and giving me marks out of ten, but I'm alone.

I sit down on the dank, threadbare carpet and dress myself. I feel humiliated; defiled. If I could stay in these shadows for ever, I think I would.

The shame and regret mutates into anger, then the anger turns to guilt. I can't understand how I'm feeling, but every new thought just adds to the confusion. Do I feel so bad because I've been unfaithful to Lizzie? Am I really feeling remorse because I've just fucked someone other than my dead, *Unchanged* ex-partner? *Fucked* – no, wrong word: that wasn't even fucking. Hinchcliffe had it right: it was a business transaction, a way to keep him happy, and for that woman in there – Christ, I don't even know her name – to earn herself extra rations. This is what we've been reduced to. This is the pinnacle of Hinchcliffe's vision for the future.

Now I start trying to rationalise what I've just done, making excuses, looking for reasons why it doesn't matter: my irradiated sperm's probably useless, and even if it isn't, that woman's body has most likely been too damaged. After nuclear bombings or accidents – Hiroshima, Chernobyl, Three Mile Island, Fukushima – there were hugely increased numbers of stillborns, cancers and deformities . . .

Who the hell am I trying to fool? I pick myself up and slowly stagger back down the stairs, my mind filled with memories of sex before the war that I'd tried so hard to keep buried. Now I can't stop remembering the last time Lizzie and I were together. We were both terrified of what was happening outside our home, but came together spontaneously, instinctively. We made love to each other to make ourselves and each other feel wanted and protected. In spite of everything that was going on in the world, the feelings we shared that night were as intense as they ever had been.

And now I push my way out into the freezing cold night, thinking about the kids, about Ellis, Josh and Ed, remembering when each of them was born. and all the good times we had together before the bad . . .

What have I become?

Sex used to be something which transported us out of the daily grind, took us somewhere else. It was something which transcended all the bullshit; it connected Lizzie and me on every level imaginable. And now I've turned something as precious as that into something as brutal and insensitive as everything else . . .

I feel like I've just lost something I'll never get back. Like Hinchcliffe's just taken what was left of my soul.

19

I'm finally back at the house, but all I want to do is turn around and go back into Lowestoft and kill Hinchcliffe. *Fucking bastard.* I kick my pile of books across the living room and they hit the wall with a momentarily satisfying noise, but then all I'm left with is silence.

What the fuck have I become?

Since Hinchcliffe found out what I can do I've been allowed to stand on the outskirts of this vile, fucked-up ruin of a world and observe. I've just about managed to cope with what I've seen because of the distance I've been able to put between me and everything else, but what I did today – what Hinchcliffe made me do – has dragged me down to the lowest possible level and it hurts. He's stripped away everything, and now there's nothing left.

Fuck this: I'm getting out. First thing in the morning I'll leave. I'll take my chances on my own. I'll pack my stuff tonight and help myself to one of the cars by the railway station at first light. I've got plenty of supplies hoarded here; I'll load them up and get as far away from Lowestoft as I can. I don't need anyone else – more to the point, I don't *want* anyone else. Maybe I'll go to the deadlands around the bombed cities. Even a slow death from the radiation fall-out will be better than this.

I try to make myself eat something, but tonight more than ever the thought of food makes my stomach churn. I manage just a few mouthfuls. Fortunately, the beer Hinchcliffe gave me goes down easier. The gas makes me belch, but the alcohol is taking the slightest edge off my anger. I finish the first can and immediately start another, but I'm not even halfway through before I'm running outside and throwing up on the driveway.

When I'm done I drag myself back inside and slump into my chair. I struggle with cold, unresponsive fingers to open the ringpull on my third can. When I put it down on the table, the beer fizzes over the rim. I strap on my miner's lamp and pick up the first book on my pile. I'm tired and it's hard to focus, but still I stare at the cover: a man and a woman locked together in a passionate embrace that's a million miles from what I endured earlier today. The man is strong and powerful, ruggedly clean-shaven, with short, slicked-back black hair, and the woman he's holding is full-figured, her tight clothing accentuating every curve, her painted lips whispering a promise . . . and the light starts to flicker and fade (didn't get those damn batteries from Hinchcliffe, did I?) and I rip off the head-light and throw the damn thing across the room in frustration, quickly followed by the book.

I turn my attention back to the beer, which is still making me belch, but it must be having an effect, because now I can't stop thinking about my kids. Usually I try to stop myself, but tonight I'm desperate not to forget. It's been a long, long time since I've been drunk like this. Now I feel like I'm floating above my chair, looking back down and watching myself below, and I don't like what I see. I'm like a bloody prisoner of war, all curved spine, bulging eyes, spindly arms and legs and scarred skin . . . I keep looking around, half-expecting to see Ellis standing there, the way she used to appear at the side of our bed when she couldn't sleep, looking all wide-eyed and vulnerable. I keep waiting to hear Ed arguing with Josh, or playing his crappy music too loud, or switching the TV in his room on again after I'd told him to turn it off. My kids were annoying little fuckers at times, but I miss them.

Hinchcliffe's vision of the future is terrifying me and I don't *want* to be responsible for bringing another life into this world. I imagine my own kids trying to survive in this foul place – but what if the new one's born Unchanged? I can just picture Hinchcliffe, backing them into a corner, leering at them, screaming at them to fight, or, if they won't, locking them away and trying to break them . . . What if they're too feral to control. Or it's twins, one Unchanged and one like us? Would they fight in the womb? No, that's just fucking ridiculous. Now I know I'm pissed.

And I'm starting to feel really sick – my mouth's watering like I'm going to throw up again. I'll sit still for a while until the nausea passes, then I'll start packing my stuff. Whatever happens, I'm leaving this godforsaken place tomorrow.

20

My head is fucking killing me – it feels like someone's split my skull in two with an axe – and Rufus is pounding on the door again. Why can't he just leave me alone? I moved out from the centre of town so I didn't have to put up with this much bullshit, but it hasn't stopped certain people from spending most of their time out here hassling me. Fuckers. Jesus, it's not even light yet – couldn't he at least have waited until morning? He can fuck off; whatever he wants, I'm not interested. I'll wait until he goes, then pack up and get out of here. I'd be gone already if I hadn't been so fucking stupid and started drinking.

He's a persistent bugger, I'll give him that. Now he's banging on the living room window. I screw my eyes shut and try to swallow down the cough that's building up in my chest so the noise doesn't give me away. Jesus, I feel bad: my guts are more sensitive than ever and my head's about to explode. There's a welcome moment of silence, then the noise changes again – he's moved to the side door, shaking the handle and rattling the chains I use to secure it after the vagrant woman broke in. Maybe it's not Rufus, maybe it's another one of those useless underclass fuckers, trying to get in and steal from me. Bastards.

It's no good. I've got to move.

I reluctantly get up from my chair and immediately lurch to the right, reeling from the after-effects of the booze. I stoop down, feeling faint, and grab the heavy wrench I keep by the front door for dealing with unwelcome visitors like this. I just about manage to stand upright again when another coughing fit hits me, hard. Whoever's outside knows I'm here now. When the coughing subsides I angrily yank the front door open and run down the side of the house, the wrench held high, ready to attack or defend myself, but the combination of the freezing cold temperature and shock immediately sobers me up and stops me in my tracks. Standing in front of me is Peter Sutton, the bastard who stalked me around Southwold.

'How in hell's name did you find me?'

He turns at the sound of my voice and starts walking towards me, his hands raised in supplication, and I lift the wrench again and block his way. That fucker's not coming anywhere near me.

'I guessed you had some connection with those fighters who turned up in Southwold yesterday morning.'

'They were nothing to do with me.'

'I didn't say they were, but you turned up, then they did. It seemed a pretty safe bet that it was more than just coincidence.'

'So what is this, then – revenge?'

'No, nothing like that.'

'That still doesn't explain how you found me.'

'I just went into town and asked for Rufus.'

'But I'm not—'

'I know who you are *now*, Danny McCoyne – here's a tip for you, if you're going to use a false name, don't use the name of someone who actually exists. I asked for Rufus at the barricades and was introduced to your friend. He seems like a decent enough bloke, but you might want to have a word with him about his loose tongue. I described you to him. "Ah, you're looking for Danny McCoyne," he says, and so here I am, Danny, and here you are too.'

'And Rufus told you where I was just like that?'

'Pretty much,' he answers. 'He didn't need to say a lot – he told me where the estate was and said you were the only one here. I just started knocking on windows and doors until I found you. Wasn't that hard really.'

'There are hundreds of houses here,' I say, still a bit bemused.

'I know, and I've been here for bloody ages – but yours is the only house with a fresh puddle of vomit on the drive, so I thought there was a good chance you might have something to do with it.' Sutton's breath billows in clouds around his face and we're both shaking with cold. There's been a heavy frost overnight and everything glistens with ice, white-blue in the first light of dawn.

'Okay,' I say, 'so you found me. Well done. Now what the fuck do you want?'

'Can we talk inside?'

'Why?'

'Because I'm bloody cold and this is bloody important.'

He's insistent if nothing else, I'll give him that, but the fact he won't talk outside the house just increases my unease.

'It's out here or nothing.' My hand starts to feel like it's freezing to the wrench.

'Remember that lorry? The one you said you didn't see?'

'What about it?'

'Want to know where it came from?'

'Not really.'

'That's what I figured, but I'm sure your boss will.'

'My boss?'

'Whoever sent you to Southwold – Hinchcliffe, is it? Come on, Danny, stop playing games. This is *important*.'

Maybe he does having something worth listening to. Could someone else be behind those lorries – another John Warner perhaps? I need a piss, and the bitter cold out here is making it worse. Oh, what the hell . . . Sutton is obviously no fighter. One step out of line and a smack around the head with the wrench'll finish him off. That'll solve all our problems. Against my better judgement, I decide to let him in.

'You've got five minutes,' I warn him.

'Thank you,' he says, scurrying past me to get into the warm.

I gesture with the wrench for him to go through to the living room. 'Try anything and I'll kill you,' I say hospitably.

'I won't, I swear. I don't want any trouble.'

I follow him into the house, watching his every move. 'Okay then, talk.'

He paces the room, and when he starts, he sounds like he's choosing his words carefully. 'I guess your boss assumed those supplies came from him. Did he find out who was supplying Warner?'

'Hinchcliffe's not the investigative type. So do you know?'

'Not yet, but I need to find out.'

'Why?'

'Look, you're the only other person like me I've found in months,' he says. His teeth are still chattering. 'You're the only person I think I can trust.'

'You're not making any sense – for fuck's sake, Sutton, stop beating around the bush and just *tell* me.'

He pauses ominously, then says, 'Those supplies you saw weren't from Lowestoft.'

'Where then?'

'Come with me and I'll show you.'

21

Sutton has a car with a quarter-tank of fuel. He says he got it after the fighting in Southwold. He's obviously no slouch; he says he got away from the centre of the town as soon as he heard the first of Hinchcliffe's fighters arrive and hid in the outskirts until they'd cleared out again. If that's true then he's been a damn sight more alert than I have recently. He drove up to within a couple of streets of the house this morning and in my alcoholic daze I didn't hear a bloody thing. He could have been *anyone*. I shudder at my narrow escape.

Sutton's car is a fairly decent high-end model, but like everything else in this brave new world it's seen better days. It's full of rubbish and the upholstery is slashed. And no matter how smooth the ride might once have been, the surface of the road we're travelling over today is so rough that the best suspension in the world couldn't make this a comfortable journey. Sutton drives straight over a pothole and the sudden lurching of the car makes my stomach heave. I swallow down bile and try to concentrate on the music he's playing. The fact that like me he still listens to music is a good sign, I guess – he tells me it helps calm his nerves – but it's doing nothing for mine this morning; it just makes my head hurt even more.

'It must be because of the smoke from the bombs,' he says suddenly. He's talked nervously for most of the journey without saying anything of any substance. I still don't fully know why I'm here, but I keep telling myself it was worth agreeing because there's the slightest chance he'll show me something worth seeing before I leave Lowestoft for ever –

another place like Southwold, perhaps, or John Warner's mysterious benefactor? Fact is, I need a way out, and this might just be it.

'What's because of the smoke?'

'The drop in temperature. All the snow and ice.'

'It's the middle of winter.'

'I know, but it's not usually this bad, is it?'

'There are fewer people around than this time last year, mate. Fewer cars, and no factories, hospitals or schools, so no emissions or exhausts. Think of all the fumes which aren't being belched up into the atmosphere any more.'

Sutton glances across at me and nods enthusiastically, and something about the expression on his face makes alarm bells start to ring again. I'd put his sudden change of mood down to relief that I'd agreed to come with him, but I'm wondering now if I've made a huge mistake and he really is the psycho I'd first feared. I start silently plotting my escape. When he next slows the car down I'll try and get out. I'll roll away along the ground like they used to in all those action movies, then I'll work out where the hell I am and try to get back to Lowestoft. And if Sutton dares turn up on my doorstep again, I'll introduce his face to my wrench, then dump his useless body. No one will miss him.

'Be interesting to see what happens to the environment now, won't it?' he says.

'Will it?'

'I think so: you've got all that contamination on one hand, and the fact that a huge number of people are dead on the other. Will they cancel each other out? Who knows, Danny McCoyne – maybe genocide will turn out to have been a blessing in disguise!' He laughs manically, loud enough to drown out the music for a moment, and I want out of here.

I know where we are now: we passed through Wrentham and we're turning right at the junction where I turned left for Southwold yesterday. After another mile or so I see something at the side of the road which distracts me temporarily.

I've been here before. There was a vicious battle here; Llewellyn bragged about it once. He said it was like something out of the movies. He was with a group of ex-soldiers who'd been cornered by some Unchanged military. They were massively outnumbered, he'd said (although I'm sure he was exaggerating), but twenty or so of them had dug in and managed to hold off their attackers for hours on end. In frustration the Unchanged commander had requested air cover, and hearing the bombers approaching, Llewellyn had ordered his fighters to attack and then, as the bombs began to fall, they fled – leaving the Unchanged to bear the brunt of their own munitions. And once the air strike was over, Llewellyn's people returned to finish them off. I'm sure he embellished the story with more than a liberal sprinkling of bullshit, but there's no disputing the fact that something huge did happen here. When I first saw this place, the cratered ground was blackened by fire and still covered with the remains of the dead, and the tangled blades of a downed helicopter were sticking up into the air like the legs of a dead spider. Today it looks almost completely different. It's all overgrown, and in a couple of years' time, no one will know that anything ever happened here. It'll just look like part of the natural landscape.

'Not far now,' Sutton says suddenly, and I silently curse myself for becoming distracted. I go over the route we've followed again so that I can get back to Lowestoft on my own if I need to. Out of the corner of my eye I notice Sutton is watching me. 'You've got to believe me, McCoyne,' he says, his voice now serious again, no doubt picking up on my unease. 'What I'm going to show you is *important*.'

'You keep telling me that,' I reply, sliding my left hand into my inside jacket pocket until the tips of my outstretched fingers are resting on the hilt of one of my fighting knives. 'But you still haven't given me any details and I'm starting to think this was a bad idea.'

'It's hard to explain.'

'Try.'

'It's *difficult*. I'm not sure how you'll react, or what you'll think.'

What's he hiding? Is *he* behind the stolen supplies? Is it worse than that?

'You're not making me feel any better about this . . .'

'I swear when we're finished you can just walk away if you want and you'll never see me again. But I don't think you will.'

'What makes you so sure?'

'Because you're like me,' he says again. He's starting to sound like a broken record.

He takes a sudden hard right turn off the road, driving through an open metal gate and out along a narrow gravel track. The front of the car clatters through a deep ice-filled dip, then rattles over a cattle grid and I have to concentrate again just to stop myself from throwing up.

'We're here,' he says, slowing down and steering around the curve of the track towards a motley collection of ramshackle farm buildings that from here look completely deserted. There's blackened fire damage visible around the edges of some of the windows and doors. We drive through a large yard full of iced-over furrows and puddles. Bizarrely, Sutton has to slow down to allow a cow to wander across in front of us. It's alone, and as starved as every other animal I've seen recently. When it looks around and sees us it panics and its hooves skid in the icy mud as it tries to change direction. For a moment it looks like it's got that mad cow disease they used to talk about all the time. I realise it's the first cow I've seen in months.

'Don't see many of them here any more,' Sutton says, echoing my own thoughts, watching me watching the animal. 'Quite a few survived, but I doubt they'll last the winter. The Brutes drove most of them away.'

'Brutes? I thought the Brutes were all dead.'

'As good as.'

'But why would Brutes be here?'

'Because they knew.'

'Knew what?'

Sutton doesn't answer. He drives the car into a dark, open-ended barn and stops it deep in the shadows, parking next to a filthy, beaten-up delivery van. There's a faded picture of a woman's face on its side, advertising something you can't get any more which probably wasn't that important anyway. I stare into the face, still as beautiful and perfect as the women on the covers of the books I read.

Sutton switches off the engine and the sudden silence is unsettling. 'The Brutes knew what we were doing here,' he explains as he opens his door and gets out. 'Don't ask me how, but they did.'

Now I really am starting to get worried.

'So what are we here for? Is this where the lorries are from, or . . . ?'

'No, nothing like that,' he says, leaning back against the car. 'This isn't about John Warner's supplies. Sorry, Danny, I've not been completely honest with you.'

'Fuck it,' I shout at him, 'I *knew* I shouldn't have come here. Either give me the keys or take me back to Lowestoft.'

'You've come this far,' he replies, obviously having no intention of doing either, 'so you might as well see now – this is important, I swear – I've not lied about that. What I'm going to show you changes *everything*.' And with that he walks away as if suddenly revitalised, moving at speed. Shit, what exactly are my options? *Kill him?* I don't know if I could, not now. *Make a run for it?* I'm so hungover, I wouldn't get far. Oh, what the hell . . . even though I'm sick, I'm armed, and I'm still probably stronger than he is. I'm here; I might as well see what he's been blathering on about.

Sutton beckons me to follow him along a track that leads away from the farm buildings, climbing steeply, then snaking away across frosted dead grassland. I let him build up a decent head start, figuring that a little distance between us will give me more of a chance of getting away if I need to. I'm distracted by a sudden noise; there's movement way over to my left. I grab one of my knives, ready to defend myself against an attack, then freeze – Jesus, it's a Brute. My heart starts thumping at the prospect of having to fight. Months ago I'd have relished any conflict, but not today, and definitely not against one of our own. Most of these poor bastards were driven out of their minds by the intensity of their Hate during the war. Killing's all they know now, it's all they have left. And now that there are no Unchanged here, apart from the odd emaciated cow, we've suddenly become an obvious target.

This Brute is old, and female. She's several hundred yards away, and she swaggers slowly towards me like a drunk, as if she's unable to move in a straight line. She's far removed from the strong and vicious fighter she must once have been; now she's just a grotesque physical wreck. I realise as she gets closer that she's completely naked, her dirty mottled flesh almost blue with cold, and she's covered with dirt and countless cuts and abrasions. There are traces of blood around her mouth. Her heavy, pendulous breasts swing from side to side with every clumsy, lumbering movement, and loose flesh hangs from her arms and her gut. She looks like she's wearing a dirty, oversized skin-coloured coat. Poor bitch. She's probably starving.

'Sorry,' Sutton says, scrambling back down the rise, 'I should have warned you about that one. She's usually wandering around here somewhere. Bloody strong, she is, but slow. You'll easily outrun her if she gives you any trouble. Don't know how she keeps going after all this time. Sheer bloodymindedness, I guess.'

He stands and looks at the barely human woman in the distance with an expression on his face which seems to almost approximate pity. I'm surprised by his reaction. Most people, me included, wouldn't give a dying Brute a second thought. Christ, I've seen people spit-roast them and carve up their carcases before now. It's all meat, they say as they shove their fellow human beings on the fire.

Concentrate, I tell myself. *You're getting distracted. This could still be a trap.*

The Brute's speed is negligible, but she's still a very real threat. Sutton nudges me to start moving again then scampers back up the steep bank to the meandering track. Still holding my knife (and telling myself repeatedly that I *will* use it if he crosses me), I follow him. The gradient's steeper than it looks and the ground beneath my feet is increasingly uneven. I climb the hill like an old man, bent over double and pushing down on my knees to keep myself moving forward. Sutton has to wait for me at the top. I stop to catch my breath and look down over the other side. There's a crumbling low-roofed red-brick building at the edge of the track a little further ahead. What is this, his bloody holiday cottage?

'Almost there now,' Sutton says and, before he can move away again, I grab his arm.

'You'd better not be fucking with me,' I warn him.

He shakes his head, pulls himself free and walks on.

'I'll kill you if you try anything,' I shout after him.

'No, you won't,' he shouts back as he disappears into the ruin of the bungalow.

Is this safe? I'm not convinced. The exterior walls might still be standing at the moment, but they look like they'd fall down if anyone leant hard enough against them. The mortar between the damp, moss-covered bricks is powdery. The furthest corner of the little house has been overwhelmed by ivy, brambles and other crawling weeds.

Sutton leans back out of the building. 'This is it, McCoyne. In here.'

22

'Are you sure this is safe?' I ask as I tentatively follow him inside. It's surprisingly light in here – there's still some semblance of a roof overhead, but in places the remains of rotten rafters stretch up into the air, leaving nothing but empty sky above us. Sutton kicks his way through the debris towards a rotten wooden door frame (no door, just a frame) midway along the single remaining interior dividing wall.

It's pitch-black on the other side and I stop, refusing to go any further. 'Whatever you've got in there, just bring it out into the open. This place is about to collapse.'

'It's a lot stronger than it looks. I used to work in construction and I've checked it all out. Anyway, most of the building's buried.'

His assurances don't make me feel much better, but I follow him through into the darkness and grab onto the back of his coat with one hand, my knife still held ready in the other.

'Careful here,' he says, dragging his feet along the ground, inching forward slowly until he suddenly drops down a few inches. I reach out to steady him but he's okay. 'Staircase,' he tells me. 'Five steps down.'

I follow blind down the steep, narrow stairs, my shoulders brushing against walls which have suddenly closed in on either side. At the bottom of the steps Sutton stops and I walk into the back of him. I can't see a damn thing. He gently manoeuvres me until I'm standing next to him in a narrow alcove.

'What is this place?' I ask, whispering. I'm worried that if I speak too loud I'll cause a cave-in.

'Just give me a second . . .' He drags one of his feet along the ground again and although I can't see anything, I can hear something heavy scraping along the floor. I stretch my arms out in front of me and feel my way along a cold, damp wall until the surface under my fingertips changes from brick to metal. I stop and feel back to the point where the change occurs and I run my fingers down an uneven edge to something that feels like a hinge. Another door?

Sutton unexpectedly pushes me out of the way again and I stagger back a couple of paces. I'm all tensed up now, ready for him if he comes for me. My eyes are adjusting to the dark a little and I can just about make out his shape as he bends down to pick something up. Is it a weapon of some kind? If he wanted to kill me (and I don't know why he would) then surely he'd have done it back at the house and spared us both this bloody daytrip to the farm? I think it's a length of metal pipe—

Sutton lifts it up and bangs it against the door three times and the sound of metal on metal reverberates loudly around this small enclosed space, filling my aching head.

'What the hell are you doing?' I shout, but he stops me.

'Shh,' he says, and leans forward to listen. The silence when the noise finally fades is all-consuming. Is he crazy? Nothing happens for an age and I'm about to turn and get out of there when I hear something: a steady *thump, thump, thump*, coming from the other side of the wall. Bloody hell, there's someone in there. I don't have a chance to ask anything because Sutton starts banging again, five times, and this time I stay silent and wait. Then I hear five knocks back in quick reply.

'Sutton, what—?'

'Shh,' he hisses at me again. He rests a hand on my shoulder and this time I allow him the familiarity. We wait, and eventually we hear a single knock coming from the other side. He hits the door once more with the metal pipe, then carefully drops it down and shuffles back out of the way.

'Who is it?' I ask, and when he doesn't answer, 'Sutton, who's in there?'

There's more noise now: metal scraping on metal, the sounds of bolts and latches being undone. At last, with a groan and the high-pitched squeak of stiff hinges, the door slowly opens inwards. There's light in there, faint, artificial light, and it's visible only because everything else is so dark.

Sutton stops and positions himself directly between me and the door. His face is slightly illuminated now and I can see his eyes behind the lenses of his glasses, searching my face and trying to gauge my reaction. He's suddenly anxious again, like he was when he arrived at the house first thing this morning. Christ alone knows what he's got himself mixed up with here. He looks over his shoulder, then back at me again.

I try to push past him but he's fast and he blocks me.

'Just be calm and be patient,' he whispers ominously. 'I told you: this changes everything.'

'Spare me the bullshit, you overdramatic prick,' I say. I'm losing patience with all this melodramatic crap. Sick of all the waiting, I push forward again, and this time he stands aside to let me through. I find myself in the middle of a room no more than a couple of yards square. It's much more solid and secure-looking than the rest of this place might suggest, and there are a load of empty boxes and crates scattered around. The light comes from a single oil lamp resting on a wooden trestle table on the other side of the room. From the very little I can make out, this looks like a bunker of some kind – a remnant from the Second World War, perhaps? A forgotten relic of the Cold War, from those times when paranoid government departments and local councils drew up pointless plans, stupid contingencies for running the charred remains of the country from numerous ill-equipped underground sites like this one, out in the middle of nowhere. For a moment I'm gone, transfixed by my bizarre surroundings, staring at the pale grey walls mottled with damp and remembering a time when it was countries, superpowers, which fought each other, not individuals . . .

The door we came through slams shut behind me and

I spin around quickly. And then I see him. There's an Unchanged man, and he's aiming a rifle straight into my face. In spite of everything that's happened, the unexpected sight of one of them is too much to stand and I draw my knife and run towards him with an instinctive speed and ferocity that surprises even me, knocking the barrel of the gun away and lunging at him, completely focused on smashing his head in and leaving him lying dead at my feet.

'McCoyne, don't—!'

Sutton throws himself at me, slamming me against the wall, and as I slide down to the floor I'm immediately trying to scramble back onto my feet. The Unchanged man stands over me, his rifle pointing down into my face, ready to fire.

'Thought you said he was okay,' he says to Sutton, his voice filled with nervous anger.

'He is okay,' Sutton says, helping me up, but keeping me at a distance. I try to lunge for the Unchanged again, but Sutton anticipates my movements and pushes me back against the wall. 'Control yourself,' he warns.

'Unchanged, Sutton? What the fuck are you doing?'

Before he can answer, the door opposite the one we came in through opens and the Unchanged man appears. Both of them are desperately thin, their tired faces looking drawn and hollow. Their pale skin is covered with sores. How long have they been hiding down here?

'Who the hell's this?' the second Unchanged asks.

'It's okay, Parker,' Sutton tells him, 'he's with me.'

'Fucker went for me,' the first one scowls, his rifle still just inches from my face.

'That was my fault. I didn't tell him about you – I didn't want to risk it until I'd got him down here.'

Sutton's still pushing me back and as I start to relax slightly I feel him loosen his grip. The initial shock's fading and my self-control is beginning to return. *Don't lose your head*, I tell myself. I need to stay calm, stay in control, then get the fuck back to Lowestoft and tell Hinchcliffe about this place.

'What's going on?' I ask. Sutton takes a cautious step away from me and the first Unchanged man panics again. He pushes me back, jabbing the barrel of the gun hard into my chest. I raise my hands.

'Don't,' Sutton says, trying to move the Unchanged away. 'If he was going to kill you he'd have done it by now, believe me. Like I said, it was just the shock of seeing you. He had no idea.'

'So why is he here?' the one called Parker asks, not taking his eyes off me. The other Unchanged stands his ground, refusing to lower his weapon.

'You know why,' Sutton answers. 'I told you I needed help. I can't do this on my own any more. McCoyne was my only option. Without him we're all screwed.'

'You should have warned us.'

'You should have warned *me*,' I say, wincing as the rifle roughly probes my delicate gut.

'I knew,' the gunman tells Parker, clearly enjoying the discomfort he's causing me.

'I had to keep it quiet in case things didn't work out,' Sutton continues. 'Dean needed to know because I knew it'd be him who opened the door and I didn't want him panicking and shooting us both. It was the only way. I didn't want the others to get concerned.'

'Others?' I interrupt, feeling my skin prickling with unease. 'There are *others*?'

Sutton finally manages to get the armed man to lower his rifle. I'm still thinking about killing these evil bastards, but my self-control is continuing to return. Like Sutton said, it was the shock of finding myself face to face with these people that made me react so immediately, so viciously. I know I'd be stupid to try anything: I'm outnumbered and they're armed, and at this moment I don't know whether Sutton would fight with me or against me.

'Get rid of him,' Parker says. 'You shouldn't have brought him here, Pete.'

Sutton stands in the very centre of the room, separating me from the Unchanged like a referee at a boxing match.

'I had to bring him; you know I did. We talked about this.'

'What the hell are you doing?' I demand, ignoring their inconsequential conversation. 'If Hinchcliffe or anyone else finds out what's down here, they'll kill you as well as these two.'

'If it wasn't for Pete we'd be dead anyway,' Dean, the gunman, says.

I don't react. It's one thing finding myself shut underground with two Unchanged scum; actually acknowledging either of them is another matter altogether.

'Do you really think I'm that stupid?' Sutton sighs. 'Do you think I'd let any of them know about this place?'

'You told me.'

'Yes, but you're different to the rest of them, I keep telling you. You're like me. You can help these people. I can't do this on my own any more.'

'Do what? I don't understand – I'm not going to help Unchanged, and neither should you. Just kill them and walk away . . .'

'I can't.'

'But they're just *Unchanged*, Sutton – probably the last of their kind. Things are hard enough up there without all of this.'

'Looks like he's going to be a real help,' Parker sighs sarcastically, leaning back against the wall and staring straight at me. 'Bad move bringing him here. We should kill him.'

'You couldn't do it,' I spit at him. 'And that's why you're down here and I'm up there.'

'I'll do it,' Dean says menacingly, raising the rifle and taking a step forward.

I lunge to defend myself, but Sutton blocks me, wedging himself between us again. He now has me on one side and the barrel of the rifle on the other. With surprising calm and self-assurance, he pushes us both away to our respective corners.

'And how will that help anyone?' he asks, his voice terse,

clearly not impressed. 'It's that kind of bullshit which got us all into this mess. Like I said, Dean, I didn't have any choice. You know how hard this is getting. I can't do everything on my own any more, and if I can't do it, we're all history.'

I grab Sutton's shoulder and turn him around to face me. 'Will you just tell me what's going on?'

He gestures for Parker to open the door opposite the entrance we came through.

Parker's still hesitant.

'Don't,' Dean says, the rifle still raised.

'It's okay,' Sutton calmly replies, 'he'd have killed you by now if he was going to. He's like me. Just give him a little time to get used to the situation.'

'Keep him under control then,' Dean orders nervously, 'because I'll shoot you both if I have to.'

Parker rests his hands on the door, then pauses again.

'You're completely sure about this, Pete?'

Sutton looks seriously at him and nods. 'We don't have any choice.'

Parker opens the door. It's heavy, like a safe door, and he needs to use all his weight to push it fully open. He blocks my way forward and I recoil when I accidentally brush against him. Sutton squeezes between us and Parker reluctantly moves to one side to let him through. I feel the barrel of the rifle resting between my shoulder blades.

'Keep yourself under control, Danny,' Sutton whispers as I follow him. 'Don't do anything stupid.'

We enter another room and although the lighting's marginally better, the shape of the space is very different and I'm still not able to see much. I can just about make out that this is some kind of long, sloping corridor. Sutton slows down and grabs my arm again. He's obviously expecting me to react to something, and as my eyes become used to the low light I see that there are more Unchanged in here, four of them, huddled at the furthest end of the corridor. They're leaning up against the walls and I stare at each one of them as I pass. They look like famine victims from old news reports, with limbs like sticks. Two of them are too weak to even lift their heads, but one has enough strength left to glare at me, a mix of hate and horror on her face. The fourth scuttles away along the floor, hurriedly moving back in the direction from which we've just come, trying to get out of my way. These are broken, empty people. Do they know what I am? I know I should be killing them, or at least finding a way to get someone here to do it for me, and the fact I'm doing neither is adding to the nausea I'm already feeling. These pathetic fuckers make me feel physically sick.

'I don't understand,' I say to Sutton, keeping my voice low, still conscious of the rifle aimed at my back. 'Why? Why risk so much for a handful of Unchanged? Why risk so much for *any* Unchanged? You should have killed them.'

We reach the end of the corridor, and it's just me and Sutton now; Dean and Parker have stopped following, but they're still watching us closely. A lamp hanging on the wall illuminates another metal door.

Sutton sighs and takes off his glasses and rubs his eyes. 'Sometimes you don't have any choice. Sometimes decisions are made for you. Things happen, and you just have to deal with them as best you can. The right option isn't always the easiest one to take.'

I'm still trying to decipher this bullshit when he leans forward and opens the next door. He gently pushes it and it swings open wide, revealing another, much larger space that's filled with light. For a few blissfully ignorant seconds I'm distracted, trying to work out why there's such a vast construction as this buried deep under a farmer's field in Suffolk, and the full enormity of what I'm seeing doesn't immediately hit home.

And then it does, and I can hardly stand.

This place is *full* of people. I can see their faces and hear their voices and smell them and— *Christ!* There must be more than twenty Unchanged in here!

23

Sutton leads me deeper into the large room and I'm struggling to cope with what I'm seeing. For a couple of
seconds all I can make out is an unholy mass of people filling
the space in front of me, and it's almost too much to process.
I've only managed to take a few steps forward when my
dazed and confused brain switches back into gear and the
full implications of what's around us hits home. I take hold
of Sutton's arm, spin him around and slam him back against
the nearest wall. I focus all my attention on him, but I'm
aware of terrified Unchanged scattering all around us, flee-
ing like cockroaches about to be crushed under a boot. Do
they know what I am? They're all watching me, desperately
trying not to let me catch them staring at us. With frightening ease Sutton shifts his balance and reverses our positions
and now *I'm* the one up against the wall. I feel my strength
drain away as a wave of sickness washes over me.

Sutton pushes me through another doorway, grabbing a
lamp as we disappear into the darkness.

Disorientated, I lose my footing and stumble.

Sutton shuts the door and I look up and suddenly I'm
aware of figures all around me. I lunge for the nearest one,
and it collapses under my weight. It's a bloody mannequin.
We're in a room full of fucking shop window dummies.
None of this makes any sense!

I slump down to the floor, my pulse pounding, sweat
pouring off me, trying to work out how I'm going to get
back out and kill those fuckers on the other side of the door.
'What the fuck's going on here, Sutton?' I demand, panting.

He stands over me, looking down at me, and behind the

thick lenses of his glasses, his eyes dart anxiously as he stares at me. 'You're really not well, are you?'

'Don't change the subject. What's going on?' I ask again. 'It's okay.'

'Okay? How can it *possibly* be okay?'

He stares at me again, trying to work out what I'm thinking. Truth is, even I don't even know what I'm thinking right now. Finding so many Unchanged like this has left me with a gut full of bitter, conflicting emotions. I know I should have killed them already, but I don't know if I could do it – I don't know if I have the strength, right now . . . and there are too many of them. I wish someone else had found them and that they could do it for me. They need to be killed, I know that – for months I've been telling myself that the sooner the last Unchanged has been wiped off the face of the planet, the sooner this pointless bloody war will finally be over. I was starting to think it had already ended.

'Sorry about the bullshit about Southwold's supplies,' Sutton says, his voice echoing around the room. 'You'd never have come if I'd told you about this.'

'Damn fucking right I wouldn't have come. For crying out loud, what were you thinking?'

'I said you were like me, didn't I? I know you won't hurt these people. I knew the moment I saw you—'

'Being with these people will bring you nothing but grief,' I tell him. 'You should get rid of them now – and if you can't do that, you should just walk away and not come back.'

'I can't do that,' he says. 'And I think you're wrong. Just let me explain—'

'There's nothing to explain.'

'It's not what you think.'

I try to stand but I can't get up. Another crippling wave of nausea is making it almost impossible for me to move. I think it must be a combination of hangover, nerves, and the airless, sweaty stench of this badly ventilated and over-crowded hideout. My head's thumping.

Sutton helps me to my feet and I lean back against the wall.

'What is this place?' I ask him, looking around at the emotionless painted faces of the mannequins which surround us. Some of them are dressed in old-fashioned army uniforms.

'A nuclear bunker,' he tells me. 'It was operational until the end of the Cold War, then they decommissioned it and turned it into a tourist attraction. Hence the dummies.'

His words just bounce off me. I should probably ask him a load more questions, but my brain is still struggling to make sense of any of this. Stupidly, all I can think right now is how much I hate Hinchcliffe. If it hadn't been for him, then I wouldn't have gone to Southwold, and if I hadn't been in Southwold, I wouldn't have met Peter Sutton, and if I hadn't met Sutton, I wouldn't know anything about this damn place, or the Unchanged hiding down here. Thinking about Hinchcliffe makes me remember what he forced me to do with that woman yesterday afternoon . . . and then part of me starts wondering whether I should just stay down here in the dark and never put my head above ground again. Nothing makes sense any more. Whenever I think I'm starting to come to terms with the way this dysfunctional new world works, something happens that leaves me feeling as confused and disorientated as I did when I killed Lizzie's dad Harry. So here I am, right back to square one again. Life feels like a game of Snakes and Ladders, but without any ladders.

Sutton waits, then cautiously edges nearer. 'I told you, this place changes everything.'

'And I told you, you were an overdramatic prick. This changes *nothing*.'

'Well, it's changed everything for me,' he says. 'Before I found these people I was lost.'

'You've lost your fucking mind, that's about all.'

'I knew you'd feel this way at first, but Danny, just stop and think for a minute—'

'Think about what? About the fact that you're a traitor? About what Hinchcliffe's going to do to you when he finds out about this place?'

'No, I want you to think about yourself, about what you've had to do over the last year. Think about how much you've lost—'

'And how much I've gained.'

'Have you gained anything?'

'My freedom. This time last year I was at a dead end.'

'And things are better for you today because—?' He waits for me to answer, and the silence is deafening. 'You're alone, your health's deteriorating, you're living by yourself in a freezing cold house on an otherwise empty housing estate . . . it doesn't look so great to me.'

'Are things any better for you?'

'Not really,' he answers. 'Truth be told, life's shit for all of us now, you, me, these Unchanged. Killing them won't make any difference.'

'That's not the point.'

'There's something else I want you to see,' he says, supporting my weight and gently leading me back towards the door. More Unchanged scatter when it opens. Their wiry limbs and sudden movements make them look unnervingly insect-like. We go back out into the main area of this part of the bunker. Some sections of the odd-shaped space are dimly illuminated, other corners remain shrouded in darkness. The walls that I can see are covered in old photographs, maps and other paraphernalia, which make the room look smaller than it actually is.

'Just look at them, Danny,' he says, shuffling me around and gesturing over to where a group of them are sitting at a table, watching us nervously. 'These people didn't do anything wrong. They didn't deserve any of what happened to them.'

'Neither did I. Neither did you. This war wasn't anyone's fault, it just happened.'

'But the fact that the war's dragged on? That *is* our fault. We have to stop the fighting.'

'The fighting will end when all the Unchanged are gone.'

'Do you really still believe that?'

'Yes,' I answer quickly, even though I don't. It's an instinctive reaction. Sometimes I think I say these things just because I'm used to saying them, like I've been conditioned to react. 'You know as well as I do that we were all forced into this. We were forced to take sides and fight.'

'And maybe that's where we're still going wrong,' he says, starting to sound suspiciously like the people I heard talking way back in the summer, just before I lost my daughter for ever and half the country disappeared in a white-hot nuclear haze. 'Look at what happened in Southwold,' he continues unnecessarily.

'But this just isn't *right*. You shouldn't be doing this.'

'Not helping these people wouldn't be right either.'

One of the Unchanged closest to me shuffles their legs suddenly, and I almost overreact at this completely innocent movement.

'But you're not helping them, are you? Can't you see that? All you're doing is delaying the inevitable. They'll have to leave here eventually, and the second they do, they'll be killed. Christ alone knows how you've managed to keep them alive down here for so long anyway.'

He shushes me, trying to make me keep my voice down, but I'm past caring.

'I did it because I had to,' he says. 'Come on, Danny, these people have got nothing to do with the fighting. They're just like you and me. You've got more in common with them than with Hinchcliffe and his fighters.'

There's no point arguing; this deluded idiot isn't going to listen. I look around this dank, claustrophobic bunker in disbelief. I've risked and lost everything to help wipe these bastards out, and all the time Peter fucking Sutton was sheltering them – *protecting them*. I'm filled with anger, and now all I want to do is kill the lot of them, Sutton included . . . but I know I won't. I don't even know if I can. I've killed hundreds of refugees like this, but I'm out-numbered, and I'm in no fit state to fight today. Or am I just making excuses? I watch an Unchanged man sitting on the edge of a thin mattress on the floor, holding a woman close, comforting her. Though they're both skeletal – they look pretty close to death – the way they are together reminds me of how I used to hold Lizzie, back before all of this began.

Don't be such a fucking idiot: you're nothing like them, and you had no choice. You did what you had to do. They are the enemy.

But is that really true? Did I have a choice?

'Just tell me why,' I say, surprising myself by asking the question I'd been thinking out loud. I'm hoping Sutton will say something profound which will help make sense of this sudden madness.

'I'll show you,' he answers, beckoning me to follow him deeper into the bunker. As he gently pushes past an elderly Unchanged woman he acknowledges her by name, as if she matters. He takes me down another short corridor and into a large, L-shaped space. We have to step over and around even more people to get to whatever he's trying to show me. One man is badly burned, his face left heavily scarred, but his wounds are clean and have obviously been treated.

'See that?' Sutton asks.

'See what?'

'The kids. Right over on the far side, there, can you see? There're a couple of kids playing.'

I follow the line of his gaze and quickly spot the children, and for a few seconds I'm transfixed. They're *playing*. These are the first kids I've seen since the start of the war who aren't fighting or screaming, or throwing themselves at me and attacking me, or standing swaying in a dark corner in a catatonic haze . . . these children are actually *playing*, the way they used to. They're laughing and talking and inter-acting with each other. They're pushing each other around and picking themselves back up and . . . and it's hard to come to terms with what I'm seeing. This behaviour – once so normal, so innocent – is now strange and unnatural. It's hard to believe that even now, even after being buried underground in this cold, dank armpit of a place for God knows how long, they're still managing to find something positive in this dire, hopeless situation. For the briefest of moments I almost feel a sense of regret. How many people like this have I killed?

FOCUS!

'What about them?' I ask.

'See the older girl with the boy on her knee? Sitting just over from the others?'

I immediately spot who he's talking about: a girl is sitting separated slightly from the rest of the young group, in the soft circle of light coming from another lamp. She is holding a toddler. She looks like an underage mum, probably in her late teens, and he's no older than two years old, three at the most. He sits on her knee and she holds him tight, her arms wrapped around him as she gently bounces him up and down. She probably doesn't even realise she's doing it; it's an instinctive, settling, protecting movement.

'That boy,' he says, his voice suddenly lower and the tone noticeably different, 'is my grandson.'

'Your grandson? But how—?'

He moves me away, turning me around so I'm not staring, but I can't help looking back.

'Please, don't make it obvious,' he whispers. 'They don't know. None of them know.'

'But— I don't understand. How?'

'I don't know what it was like for you, Danny, but I had my doubts about the war from the very beginning. I kept fighting because I thought I had to, because I thought I had to choose a side, and if I didn't kill them, they'd kill me. But I didn't get swept up on the wave of it all like everybody else did. I started to wonder whether there really was a difference between us at all, or whether the Hate and the Change were just the results of some massive, manufactured social paranoia.'

'You think? After all that's happened?'

'Why not? How many people did you know who were actually religious? There used to be thousands of religions, with barely a shred of evidence between the lot of them, all of them the product of overactive imaginations, superstition and fear. People used to kill each other because they believed in different versions of stories which could never be proved or disproved. They used to let themselves die because some book said they shouldn't have blood transfusions, or they cut their hair a certain way, or grew their hair out, or cut off their foreskins or abstained from sex . . . None of the divisions between them were a million miles from what happened with the Hate, were they? They were all intangible, inexplicable and completely pointless.'

I don't bother to reply; this isn't the time for theological debate. If there ever was a god, he's long since packed his bags and moved on.

'After a few weeks,' he continues more calmly, rant over, 'I ended up back around the area where I used to live, where what was left of my family still were. That was where I fell in with Simon Penkridge and Selena, and they helped me learn how to hold the Hate. It was a logical progression for me: it felt natural.'

'But you didn't get sent into the cities?' I didn't see how he could have avoided it.

'Like I said, I didn't buy into the fighting like everyone else – I got out before it was too late. I don't know, maybe people like you and me have got some predetermined setting that's different to the rest. I reckon more people could have learned to hold the Hate if they'd stopped fighting long enough – well, maybe not the worst of the fighters, but the rest of them.'

'The underclass?'

'Yes: those people who only fight when they absolutely have to, not because they *want* to. The problem is, most people like that have been crushed or killed, until all we're left with are dumb feral bastards like this chap Hinchcliffe and his crew. You and me, Danny, we can see beyond the battle; we can look towards other things, bigger things . . .'

I do agree with him, to an extent, but right now all I'm trying to do is look beyond being trapped in this bunker. Regardless of anything Sutton might say (and he hasn't actually said a lot so far), I want out of here. I don't *need* any of this: it's just another dangerous and unnecessary complication I could do without. I've only been here a few minutes and already I feel like I'm caught between Sutton trying to pull me in one direction and Hinchcliffe in the other, and if I don't do something about it fast I'll be ripped straight down the middle.

'I found an Unchanged camp—' Sutton is still talking, 'and I was scavenging food from them. I watched them from a distance for days, scared to get too close. I didn't trust myself – I didn't know what I'd do, how I'd react when I got near. All I did know was that there were faces there I recognised, people who used to be friends, men and women I used to see in the street . . . and then I saw Jodie with little Andrew.'

'Andrew?'

He looks back across the shelter. 'My grandson. Jodie was my daughter-in-law. My son, her husband, was long gone, dead, or maybe lost fighting somewhere. Those two were both Unchanged and eventually they were picked up by the military. They were being evacuated to one of the refugee camps when their convoy was attacked. I'd been following them because I didn't know what else to do. Jodie was killed, but some of the others managed to get away and they took Andrew with them. I waited until I was completely sure I could control myself and not attack them the moment I was with them, then I went in. I helped them, found them a hiding place. Only a few of them know what I am. Parker and Dean, a couple of others.'

'What about the rest of them?'

'They think I'm like them – they think I'm one of the Unchanged who can fake the Hate.'

'And what about me?'

'They'll assume you're the same.'

The very notion of being thought Unchanged stirs up some deep-rooted emotion inside me. It's an uncomfortable, disproportionate reaction that's hard to keep swallowed down. It's even more difficult to suppress my feelings when I start to wonder if they might be right: is that what we really both are?

'So how did you end up here?' I ask, suddenly desperate for a distraction.

'Long story . . . maybe I'll have time to tell you one day. Believe it or not, I reckon this is probably the safest part of the country, geographically, that is. And when I found this bunker—'

'How did you find it?'

'I had a friend who used to visit decommissioned bunkers – weird hobby, who knew it would turn out to be so useful? I remembered him telling me about a few places down this neck of the woods.'

'Very convenient.'

'Well that's how it is.' He shrugs.

'So if it's your grandson you're worried about,' I ask, 'why not just get him out of here and leave the rest of this lot behind?'

He leads me over to a quieter part of the room. 'You're the only person who knows about Andrew – I never saw him that often and he was barely a year old when the war started. He hardly knew me.'

'But you haven't answered my question.'

'Apart from the fact he'll never survive anywhere else, I don't think I'd be any good for him. I'm not getting any younger, and I was a crap parent first time round – once he'd grown up my own son didn't want anything to do with me.'

'And are these people going to be any better?'

'Take a look around you, Danny – just look at them. Look at how they talk to each other, how they interact. Listen to them: it's a million miles removed from what we're seeing in places like Lowestoft. This is how the world used to be – *this* is what we lost because of the fighting.'

'Bullshit.'

'Is it? You saw what happened in Southwold. That's as good as it's going to get up there. And do you really think it's ever going to stop? Look at what's happening: the human race is regressing – it's like some kind of de-evolution. Take the Brutes. You saw that poor bitch by the farm, didn't you? They're incapable of functioning any more. The kids are the same – you must know how wild they've become?'

I don't bother telling him about the things I've seen.

'And the fighters,' he continues, 'for Christ's sake, they're in charge now. People have stopped *thinking*: violence has taken the place of discussions, negotiations. There's no such thing as compromise any more, and day by day what's left of civilisation is becoming less and less civilised. Where's it going to end? Those stupid fuckers ruling the roost are never going to relinquish the power they've suddenly been given, are they? Things are going to get far, far worse before they get any better.'

'So? There's nothing anyone can do about it. How is keeping a bunker full of Unchanged alive going to make any difference?'

'Don't you see? These people are *constant*. They're normal. It's us who're the freaks. At first this was all about keeping Andrew safe, but I've come to realise that these people here are all that's left of the human race. We've just got to hope there comes a time when they'll be able to go back above ground and start again.'

Fuck! Sutton has truly lost the plot. 'Are you out of your fucking mind? You've got to face facts: these people are history. You're right: all we've got left now are cunts like Hinchcliffe and places like Lowestoft.'

'You're wrong,' he protests. 'Help me keep them safe, Danny. All's not yet lost.'

I'm not listening to any more of this bullshit. 'All *is* lost,' I tell him as I shove him out of the way and try to find my way back to the exit. I can't take any more of this today. Has Sutton been driven crazy by months of fighting? Whatever's behind this madness, it's not my problem. I'm going to do exactly what I promised myself I'd do last night – I'm going to leave Lowestoft and get away from everything and everybody. I sidestep the man and woman I was watching earlier; they're lying together, their bodies still locked in an embrace, and all I can think about suddenly is being shut in that damn hotel room yesterday and that rough, loveless sex and how empty and vile it made me feel . . . The only person I want to be with now is me. I don't need anyone else. Maybe I'll go and tell Hinchcliffe about this place, then leave them all to fight out their futures between them.

I'm desperate to get away. I turn to go through the door into the corridor and walk straight into Joseph Mallon, coming the other way.

24

'Danny?' Joseph Mallon says, his voice trembling with uncertainty and surprise. 'Danny McCoyne, is that really you?'

'Joseph?'

Is it him, or have I finally lost my mind? Am I so sick I've started hallucinating now? His voice is unmistakable, but he looks literally half the man he used to be. His face, broad and beaming when he held me captive in the convent, is now distressingly gaunt. His cheeks are sunken and hollow, the whites of his eyes are as yellow as his teeth. He wears a grubby woollen jumper several sizes too large which hangs off his shrunken frame.

'I thought you were dead.'

'I thought *you* were dead,' I answer, slumping back against the wall in disbelief. This can't be happening. I feel like I'm about to pass out: my hands and feet are suddenly numb and heavy, my fingertips are tingling, my eyes not focusing properly . . . surely I *must* be hallucinating.

'You two know each other?' Sutton asks, chasing after me, sounding as shocked as I am. Mallon stares at me, his rasping breathing sounding uncomfortably erratic. He's in worse shape than me. He grabs my hand and shakes it furiously, grinning like a madman.

'Did you know about this?' I ask Sutton. I look straight at him, demanding an explanation, but he doesn't answer. I can't tell whether he's genuinely shocked, or if he orchestrated this whole situation just to try and keep me down here.

'I had no idea—'

'What happened to you, Danny?' Mallon says as he looks me up and down. 'You look like shit, man.' I don't have chance to respond before he speaks again, turning to talk to Sutton this time. 'Danny was one of the ones I told you about, back in the city, with Sahota.'

'But how did you—?' I'm unable to finish my question. I'm not even sure what it is I'm trying to ask. He might look like a shadow of the man he once was, but Mallon is still infinitely more composed than I am. He's acting like he's found a long-lost friend, not someone he kept locked in a cell for days on end, chained to a piss-soaked bed – someone who wanted to kill him. I focus on that thought for a second: yes, there's still a part of me that thinks I should do it.

'Back at the convent,' he begins, in that instantly familiar, rich accent, 'there was a lot of bullshit flying about.' He looks at Sutton. 'I told you about Sahota, the guy pulling the strings there? I figured out what he was, what he was all about, and how he was training up people like Danny here for some crazy last crusade. I knew he was bad news, but I didn't let on. I acted dumb and played along with it because I didn't have any choice – I knew he'd kill me if I stepped out of line. He gave me food and he kept me safe from all the chaos outside, so I put up with it, but I knew it wouldn't last, and I was ready. The moment he packed up and disappeared, I knew something bad was coming.'

'Wait,' I interrupt, 'he *disappeared*?'

'It was like someone flicked a switch, Danny. One minute he's sitting in his office, giving out his orders, the next he's loading up a car, clearing out the supplies, getting his people together and getting the hell out of there. And just before they left, they killed everyone else – except me of course. Luckily, I was one step ahead of the game. I locked myself in your old room, as it happens: hid under the bed and waited there until I was sure they'd all gone.'

'But the bomb . . . how did you get away?'

'I guess you could call it a combination of good luck and

common sense,' he answers. 'The area around the convent was empty – there wasn't a single person left there but me. Then, next day, crack of dawn, everything goes crazy. I hear fighting, then there's this bloody great noise and the army starts racing away from the middle of town. Didn't take a genius to work out that the shit was about to hit the fan big time. Sahota's people had left a couple of cars behind and I'd got one of them ready, so I hauled arse and joined the convoy out of the city. I saw the explosion in the distance, but I was far enough away by then. I dug in with the military until they were attacked. Me and a couple of others managed to get away, and that was when we ran into Peter here and his people. Because he's like you he was able to keep up all the bullshit and pretence and keep us hidden. And now here we are, several months and several stops further down the line. And here you are too. Jesus Christ, Danny McCoyne, it's good to see you! I can't believe it's you!'

I can't believe it's him either. I try again to make sense of everything I've heard today, to unweave the stories Mallon and Sutton have told me. I'm looking for a logical explanation as to why I'm down here in a bunker buried under a farm with a bunch of foul Unchanged. But I can't. It's as impossible as it sounds. And yet my overriding emotion right now, stronger even than anything I feel for Joseph Mallon or the Unchanged? It's *anger*, at Hinchcliffe and Sutton. And now, if what Mallon's just said is true, then that anger spreads to Sahota too, because after dispatching me and many others into the city to sacrifice ourselves in the name of the Cause, he turned tail and ran. Cowardly fucker.

'I need help to look after these people,' Sutton says. I look into his face but in the half-light his expression is impossible to read. Is he genuine, or is he just another manipulative shyster, out to exploit me, just like everyone else? 'This is their only chance. This is *our* only chance.'

'You shouldn't have brought me here.'

'Yes I should – please stay, Danny, I need your help. I can't do this on my own any more.'

'Can't do what exactly? You keep saying that.'

'I can't provide for all these people by myself. I was working in Southwold to try and get food and water, but there wasn't enough and—'

The penny drops.

'So that's it? That's why you really wanted me here? You think because of my connections with Hinchcliffe I'll be able to sort everything out for you, keep you stocked up with supplies? *Fuck off*, Sutton. Go and hijack one of those lorries you saw in Southwold.'

'No, it's nothing like that,' he back-pedals quickly, 'I didn't even know you *were* connected to Hinchcliffe – if I had, then maybe I wouldn't have brought you here.'

'I wish you bloody hadn't.'

'Take a look around you,' he says, his voice intentionally louder, as if he's wanting to be heard now. 'These people deserve more than this.'

'Not my responsibility.'

'Yes it is,' he shouts, loud enough to fill the whole shelter and stop all other conversations dead. 'It's *our* responsibility.'

I shake my head with despair. What do I have to do to make this dumb fucker understand?

'It is not *my* responsibility,' I shout back equally loudly, then lower my voice again. 'I'm not interested. What's to stop me bringing Hinchcliffe's fighters here and ending this bullshit today?'

'You won't do that, Danny,' Mallon says. 'I know you're better than that. I know what kind of a man you are. I saw it—'

'You saw nothing.'

'Yes I did: back at the convent, I saw a man who still had his priorities straight, even after all that had happened. You were still thinking about your family when all that everyone else like you wanted to do was kill. Tell me, did you ever find your daughter?'

'What was left of her.'

'Sorry, man. Was she—?'

I shake my head, but I can't bring myself to explain. It hurts too much. I look deep into Mallon's dark eyes, and I wish with every fibre of my being that I'd never met him or Sutton. But then, I remind myself, without Mallon I'd never have been able to get back into the city and I'd never have found Ellis and shared those last few moments with Lizzie. They'd have died together in the bomb blast, and I'd have been none the wiser. Strange how important, in retrospect, those last few seconds we had together were. I think about them every day. Lizzie gave up everything she had left for Ellis, and the memories of what happened to her and what my daughter became still fill me with unbearable pain.

I can't take this.

I can't *do* it.

I push past both of them, making a run for the exit. Mallon tries to hold me back, but I shrug him off and keep moving.

25

The cold air outside hits my chest like a hammer blow, but I keep moving. I run back towards the farm, but I've scarcely made it to the top of the rise before I'm doubled-over with pain, coughing so violently I can hardly breathe. I'm making so much noise that the solitary cow bolts for cover again. I make it back to the buildings, stumbling down the slope, and in a brief gap between painful convulsions I manage to spit out a lump of green phlegm against a wall and suck in a much-needed lungful of air. I watch it as it slowly drips to the ground. My spit is red-brown and streaked with blood, and there's a foul metallic aftertaste in my mouth. Fuck – what's happening to me? I'm falling apart, physically and mentally. I slump back against the wall of the burned-out farmhouse, too weak to stand alone, sobbing with the pain. Christ, it hurts.

Peter Sutton slowly approaches. I wish he'd fuck off and leave me alone but I'm too tired to fight or argue.

'I'm sorry,' he says, pathetically. 'There was no other way.'

'You should never have brought me here,' I tell him again. I'm still wheezing badly.

'I didn't know what else to do. I'm desperate, Danny. I didn't have any choice. When I saw you in Southwold and realised you were like me . . .'

I slide further down the wall and land hard on my back-side on the ice-cold dirt.

'You *did* have a choice – you still do. You can just walk away from this place right now and not look back. Just forget about them.'

'And is that what you're going to do?'

'That's exactly what I'm going to do,' I tell him, pausing mid-sentence to clutch my chest as another wave of cramping pain takes hold. It's snowing hard now, and I can feel my face and hands starting to freeze.

'You know I can't do that,' he says, standing over me and looking down. He helps me sit up straight again.

'Why not? What the fuck is stopping you? Why not just leave them down there to starve to death? It'll be easier on them in the long run – better than being forced out into the open and killed, and that's what's going to happen eventually. They can't stay down there for ever.'

'Those people down there are more human than most of what's up here.'

'Then maybe it's time to redefine "human".'

He crouches down in front of me as I gasp for breath. The cramps have returned yet again and I'm shivering now, freezing cold. Sutton continues to watch me, but I can't read his expression – I can barely even focus on his face through the snow.

'You're in a bad way. Listen, there's a doctor here – one of the women back there, Tracy, she used to be a GP. She might be able to do something to help you.'

'You think I'm going to let one of the Unchanged touch me? Jesus Christ!'

'Come on, rise above this, Danny. I really need your help.'

'The best way I can help is to bring Hinchcliffe here and finish this today.'

'You won't do that, I know you won't. I understand why you're feeling this way, and I've listened to everything you said, but you know as well as I do that I can't just abandon these people. I can't give up on my own flesh and blood . . .'

I have to try and make him see . . . 'After I met Mallon,' I explain, speaking slowly, trying to conserve energy, 'I went into one of their refugee camps. We were sent there to kill, but I was looking for my family. I needed to find out what had happened to my daughter. I knew she was like us.'

He looks confused. 'But if she was like us—?'

'I knew her mother would have done everything she could to try and keep the kids together. I managed to track her down, and I was right. She had Ellis drugged and tied up.'

There's an awkward silence. He's knows there's no happy ending to my story because of the comment I made to Mallon earlier – and because there are no happy endings any more.

'I tried to take her with me, get her out of the city, but it was impossible. She wasn't my little girl any more. There was nothing left of her but Hate. Christ, Peter, you should have seen her – she didn't even know me. I was trying to get her to safety, but she wouldn't stop fighting. The city was tearing itself apart all around us and all she wanted was to keep killing. I managed to get us just out of range of the bomb blast, but even then, even after that, after all we'd been through, she just carried on fighting. Her Hate wasn't like the Hate that made you and me fight, it was a thousand times worse than that. It had poisoned her to the core.'

'So where is she now?'

'Dead, probably.'

'And why are you telling me this?'

At last I manage to drag myself back up onto my feet, though my legs feel heavy. 'You need to understand that you're not helping anybody by doing this. I've come to a conclusion, and I think you need to do the same: this world is dying. It's sick to the core, and there's no hope left. You and me, we'll grow old and die, or we'll get ourselves killed, and in the end there will only be people like Hinchcliffe, his fighters and the worst of the children left. And if you'd seen the things I'd seen, then you'd know that your grandson back there doesn't stand a chance – none of the kids do, and without kids, there's no future. You should just block the bunker door and bury the lot of them. Now get me back to Lowestoft.'

I hawk up another gobbet of phlegm and clear my throat, then take a few slow, painful steps, After a minute I stop again. He's not following. Every extra movement takes ten times the effort it should, but I slowly turn back around.

'I think you're wrong,' he says.

'Well, I know I'm right.'

'Just answer one question for me, Danny. Why did you bother?'

'What?'

'Looking for your daughter and wife . . . why did you bother?'

'Because I didn't know what Ellis had become. Because I had this fucking stupid idea in my head that she'd be just as I left her and we'd stay fighting side by side together until the war was over. I thought some kind of normality might eventually return, but it won't. The world is dead.'

'Not yet it isn't.'

'Jesus, Peter, my own *daughter* didn't even recognise me.'

'You said you had other kids. What happened to them?'

'Ellis killed them.'

'How many?'

'Two boys.'

'Both Unchanged?'

'Yes.' I carry on walking back to the car.

He carries on talking. 'So tell me,' he shouts after me, 'knowing what you know now, if I'd taken you down into that bunker today and you'd seen that one of your Unchanged sons had survived, would you still be turning your back on them?'

26

Sutton is true to his word and drives me back to the house. He leaves me there with barely any protest, although he does start to talk about how I can find him again if I change my mind. I tell him not to bother; I don't want to see him again, and if I do, I'll kill him. I tell him I'll have to tell Hinchcliffe, but he laughs. He says it doesn't make any difference because the bunker's secure – unless Hinchcliffe's got a few oxyacetylene burners or a tank lying around, no one's getting in, and the Unchanged aren't about to come out.

But the house isn't where I need to be. I hang around there for a couple of hours, trying to pull myself together, hoping that the constant thumping in my head will stop and I'll start to feel better. I've been telling myself it's just the after-effects of the beer from last night, or the food I'd eaten yesterday, or the dog the day before that, or whatever I'd done the previous day or last week, but I know it's not.

This is serious: I can't go on like this. I'm getting worse every day.

I'm back inside the compound now, walking towards Hinchcliffe's factory, about to do something I should have done a long time ago: admit that I need help.

The snow's stopped and it's pissing down with rain now, which is just adding to the fucking misery. The late afternoon sky is filled with black clouds. The guard on the approach road recognises me and lets me through. Other than him I see only one more guard, standing just inside the entrance at the end of the factory where the Unchanged kids are held, sheltering from the rain. I'm scared and I bottle it, walking straight past towards the enormous useless wind turbine which towers over everything. It's a symbol of what this place once was, and what it'll never be again: the ultimate physical manifestation of all Hinchcliffe's bullshit.

It's no good. I can't put this off any longer.

I walk back the other way, and this time the guard in the doorway sees me and yells at me to either 'get over here or fuck off'. He's wrapped up against the bitter cold, wearing so many layers that he looks grossly overweight. His mouth is hidden by a scarf and his upturned collar and he has ski goggles covering his eyes. He has a rifle slung over his shoulder. I presume it's there to stop escapees, rather than to prevent anyone breaking in.

'What do you want?' he demands, his voice muffled.

'Rona Scott,' I answer. 'I need to see her.'

'Says who?'

'Says Hinchcliffe.'

He lifts up his goggles and eyes me up and down, then he pulls his scarf down a couple of inches, just enough to clear his mouth, making it easier to speak. 'I've seen you before, haven't I?'

'Have you?'

'Yeah . . . Ain't you the one what finds the Unchanged?'

'That's me,' I answer quickly, desperate to get out of the cold. It's raining even harder now, and the water is bouncing back up off the pavement. 'Look, is the doctor here? I really need to see her.'

He stops to think again. This guy's not the smartest, and that's probably why he drew the short straw and ended up being posted out here on his own. I can't tell whether he's trying to psych me out with these long, silent pauses, or if he's just slow. I reach inside my coat and he reacts to my sudden movement by swinging his rifle around.

'Don't,' I tell him, raising my hands to show I don't want any trouble. When he relaxes I take out a can of drink from my pocket, hoping to speed up this painfully drawn-out encounter with a little bribery. He half-heartedly tries to remain impassive and hard, but I can see a sudden glint in his eye. He's like a kid looking in a toy shop window.

'Inside,' he says as he takes the can from me. He glances from side to side before moving out of the way to let me pass. As if anyone else has followed me out here on a day like this. Fucking idiot.

The building is oppressively quiet, save for a few muffled sounds in the distance, and it's no warmer indoors than out. I've never made it this far in before. This end of the complex looks like it was mostly office space. I'm in an open-plan reception area which has been turned into a checkpoint by Hinchcliffe's guard. It reminds me of the reception desk back at the council offices where I used to work. There are a couple of rooms filled with rubbish leading off from here, and a wide staircase which goes up to the first floor. Another door opens into a long, dark corridor which I presume leads into the rest of the factory. Curious, I walk towards it and try to peer in through a porthole-shaped safety-glass window.

'Not that way,' the guard says, making me jump.

'Where then?'

There's no response, but he looks at me expectantly. I dig down into the pockets of my coat again and this time I bring out a packet of sweets. I picked them up before I came out, thinking they might be useful.

'This is all I've got,' I tell him, talking to him like I used to talk to my children. 'Where's the doctor?'

He points up the stairs.

'There's a load of offices up there and she's in one of them. First or second floor, don't know which.'

'Thanks for your help,' I say sarcastically as I chuck him his sweets.

I'm dripping wet and exhausted. I start to climb up the metal steps, my boots clanging noisily, filling the building with noise. At the top of the first flight of stairs is an open door and, beyond it, another narrow corridor with three doors along one side and one at the far end. Fortunately there are long, rectangular windows in each of the doors which allow me to see inside. Rona Scott is sitting in the first room, slouched in a chair, staring straight ahead. This must have been a meeting room once, though the only furniture is a long grey desk covered with stuff. I pause before trying to attract her attention, feeling undeniably nervous. Wait— she's talking – is someone in there with her?

Rona Scott looks exhausted. Her face is flustered, her cheeks blood red, and she's smoking a cigarette, flicking ash onto the dirty terracotta-coloured carpet. I've spoken to her (rather, she's spoken *at* me) on a few occasions before today, and I'm not relishing the prospect of having to talk to her now. She's a foul-tempered woman at the best of times. I'm tempted to turn around now and go back to the house, rather than face her, but she suddenly gets up, moving unexpectedly quickly, and I step back, trying to keep out of sight but still be able to see her through the glass. From my new position I can see that the room is actually double-length, and the far end is in almost total darkness. There's a concertina-like folding wall across the middle which has been left half-open. Dr Scott strides purposefully through the gap and disappears out of view.

'Do something, you useless little prick!' she yells at some-one unseen, her bellowing voice muffled but still clearly audible even through the closed door. 'For fuck's sake, come on!'

The hostility in her voice is unnerving, and I actually start to edge back towards the stairs before telling myself to get a grip. She reappears again and mooches through the clutter on the table. She picks something up – looks like an open glass jar – then moves back into the shadows.

'You know you want it,' I hear her shout. 'Come on, react! Don't just sit there, you pathetic piece of shit!'

She walks back this way, the jar held out in front of her, then she looks around. *Damn, she's seen me!* I try to get out of the way, but it's too late, there's no backing out now.

She angrily yanks the door open. 'What the fuck do you want?'

'Sorry,' I stammer, immediately on the back foot, 'I didn't mean to disturb you . . .'

'Yes you did,' she bawls at me. 'No one ever comes here unless they don't have any choice. You didn't come here by accident, so you *did* mean to disturb me.'

'Hinchcliffe said I should—'

'You McCoyne?'

'Yes, I—'

'He said you'd probably turn up at some point. Give me a couple of minutes and I'll be with you.'

When she stops talking I become aware of a faint whimpering noise coming from elsewhere in the room. Dr Scott moves away from the door and I follow her inside. At the far end, strapped to a chair by ropes tied across her tiny torso and around her ankles and wrists, is an Unchanged child. It's one of the kids from the council depot nest we cleared out earlier this week, I'm sure it is. When she sees that someone else is in the room, she starts moaning in fear, tugging at her restraints to try and get free, but the effort's too much and she soon gives up and slumps forward sobbing, letting her bonds take her weight. Her long greasy hair is hanging down and covering her dirty face. Poor little sod. What the hell has Rona Scott been doing to her?

'Interesting,' Dr Scott says, watching both the girl and me, her eyes flicking between us.

'What is?'

'The way she reacted when you appeared,' she says.

'She recognises me, that's all. I helped catch her.'

'I just need one of these little cunts to show a bit of backbone and start fighting. Get Hinchcliffe off my back for a while. It wasn't so bad when Thacker was in charge.

Hinchcliffe's got no patience. He wants results or he wants them dead.'

The little girl, shaking with cold, cries out again. In a sudden fit of rage that takes both me and the child by surprise, the doctor spins around and hurls the glass jar at her. It hits the wall just above her head and explodes, showering her with sharp shards of glass and sticky globules of food.

'Jesus, what the fuck are you doing?' I shout, forgetting myself.

Dr Scott leans back and looks at me disapprovingly. 'Looks like someone's been spending too much time around these things.'

'It's not that; I just—'

She's not interested. She runs towards the girl again, grabs her shoulders and yells into her face and the child screams back at the top of her voice. She's tied tight, but still straining to get away. 'That's better,' Scott says, taunting the kid, slapping her cheek. 'Now that's more like it.' She turns her back on the still screaming child and looks at me. 'Right, this way.'

She shoves me out of the room and locks the door. The little girl's cries are muffled, but not blocked out completely. She stops in the middle of the corridor, preventing me from going any further, waiting expectantly. I realise what she's waiting for and reach into my inside pocket and pull out a half-full packet of cigarettes. I've been holding onto these for a while. She studies the packet for a moment, checks how many smokes are inside, then grunts her approval and heads for the staircase.

We climb another flight of steps up to the second floor, which looks identical in layout to the first, and she takes me into the room at the far end of the corridor. It's twice as big as any of the others and there's a wide window on one wall which gives Dr Scott a virtually uninterrupted view out across Hinchcliffe's compound. On the opposite wall, a smaller window overlooks the sea. Driving rain clatters constantly against the glass. There's more light in here than in any other part of the building I've been in so far, but that's not a good thing. This is Rona Scott's personal surgery-cum-living quarters, and I'd have preferred not to be able to see anything.

'Over there,' she grunts at me, pointing across the room, and I pick my way through the rubbish which covers the floor. There are unpleasant stains and used swabs and dressings everywhere, crusted hard and brown. Discarded bandages lie around the place looking like gruesome paper-chain decorations. This place makes me realise just how much the role of a doctor (if Rona Scott ever really was a doctor) has changed. They're no longer concerned with the ongoing wellbeing and general health of their patients; now they're here just to patch people up and keep them fighting as hard as possible for as long as they can. As with any war, countless numbers of people have suffered horrific injuries over the last year. Fortunately for them, most of them died on the battlefield, or later, more slowly, as a result of radiation sickness, infection or malnutrition. Doctors like Rona Scott are rarely bothered by people like me, and it shows. This surgery might have the faintest smell of antiseptic, but it has all the dignity and class of some back-street chop-shop.

Dr Scott walks over to where I'm standing, drops her cigarette and stubs it out on the carpet. I've never been this close to her before, and I pray I never am again. Her breath is foul and she looks as if she's been personally collecting samples of all the diseases and conditions she might still have to treat. The bottom of one of her ear lobes is missing; it's been patched up with sticking plaster, but both the plaster and the ear are still covered in blood. I find myself hoping that little girl downstairs was responsible for the injury.

'Right, make it quick. What's wrong with you?'

'Where do I start?'

'What hurts most?'

'Everything hurts,' I answer honestly. 'No appetite, lost a load of weight, fucking awful cough, sometimes there's blood when I piss . . .'

'You look bad.'

'Thanks.'

She picks up a torch and shines it into my eyes, sighing with effort every time she moves. I don't know whether she's as unfit as I feel, or whether she just resents every second of time she's wasting on me. Is she like this with everyone? Is it because I'm not a battle-scared soldier, or one of Hinchcliffe's precious fighters?

'Strip to the waist,' she orders and I immediately do as I'm told. I'm starting to shiver even before I'm done. I catch a glimpse of myself in a full-length mirror in the corner and I have to look twice to be sure it's really me. I stare at my skeletal reflection. Christ, I can see every individual rib. I'm pigeon-chested. My chest goes in instead of out, like it used to . . .

'Stand still,' she says, but I can't stop shaking. She peels off her filthy fingerless woollen gloves and starts touching me and I instinctively recoil from her unforgiving, icy fingers. She roughly pushes and prods at my skin, working her way around my kidneys and belly with the bedside manner of a butcher working in an abattoir. I wince when she jabs her fingers into me, just below my ribcage, then wince again when she pinches my gut. Is she actually doing anything, or just using me for stress relief? Finally she unearths a stethoscope from under a pile of papers and used dressings on a window ledge and presses it against various different parts of my back and front. Examination over, she tells me to get dressed.

'Well?' I ask as I quickly pull my clothes back on again.

'Not a lot to say really.'

'So what's wrong with me?'

She groans and plumps herself down onto a chair which creaks with surprise under her sudden weight. She rummages around on top of a desk and fishes out a half-smoked cigarette, then spends a few seconds picking dirt off the filter before lighting up. The bitch is doing this on purpose, I'm sure of it: she's enjoying tormenting me by dragging this out unnecessarily. She's probably heard what I can do with the Hate and now she's showing me who's in charge.

'Were you close to any of the bombs?' she eventually asks.

'Which bombs?' I answer stupidly.

'*The* bombs. Remember? Great big fuck-off explosions? Bright light? Mushroom clouds?'

'I was about ten miles from one of them. Might have been further. Why?'

'Don't suppose it matters, really, but it almost certainly didn't help. We've probably all had enough of a dose by now. How long were you exposed for?'

'Exposed?'

'How long were you out there?'

'I don't know. I passed out for a while. I was picked up on the motorway, but I don't know how long.'

'Wouldn't have made much difference anyway,' she says, drawing on her cigarette and looking past me at the rain running down the window. 'No doubt we'll all end up going the same way in the end. Christ, they threw enough of that shit up into the atmosphere to do us all in.'

'So what's wrong with me?' I ask again, although I think I've finally managed to work out the answer. I think I probably knew it before I came here; I just didn't want to accept it.

'Cancer,' she finally says, before adding a disclaimer: 'probably.'

For a second all I can think about is the way she said 'probably', as if we're still in the old world and she's covering her back in case she's made a misdiagnosis and I sue. The

fact she's just confirmed my worst fear goes almost unnoticed at first, but then it slowly starts to sink in. *Cancer.*

'Where?'

'What?'

'The cancer, where is it?'

'I'd do an MRI scan, but the power's down,' she says
sarcastically. 'Hard to say for certain,' she finally answers.
'You've definitely got something big in your gut, probably
in your stomach too, but there are bound to be more. Those
are secondaries, I think, but I'm no expert. Truth is you're
probably riddled with it by now.'

I stare at her, my mouth hanging open, knowing what I
want to ask next but not knowing if I can.

She looks up at me, makes fleeting eye contact, then
looks away again, anticipating the question that's inevitably
coming.

At last I manage to mumble, 'How long?'

Dr Scott takes another drag before answering. 'Don't
know,' she says finally. 'No accurate way of telling any
more – could be weeks, could be months, maybe a year at
the absolute outside if you're lucky.'

'If I'm *lucky?*'

'Figure of speech.'

'But isn't there anything you can do?'

'Like what? The National Health Service is falling apart at
the seams, in case you hadn't noticed. There are no spare
beds anywhere. Come to think of it, there are no beds . . .'

'There must be *something.*'

'You know the score, McCoyne! You've been around here
long enough to know what it's like. There probably used to
be a cure, or some surgical procedure that might have given
you a little more time, but things have changed. If there was
a drug, your chances of finding a good enough supply now
are pretty much zero, and even if you did, it'd probably be
contaminated. On top of that, you wouldn't know how to
administer it. There's no point wasting the little time you've

got left worrying about it, if you ask me. And you did ask me, so I think you should listen.'

'But there must be *something*—' I say again.

She shakes her head. 'Only thing you can do,' she starts to say, giving me hope for the briefest of moments, 'is take control and finish it sooner rather than later. Save yourself the pain.'

'You're joking.' My brain is completely failing to process what I'm being told. 'Tell me you're joking.'

She looks at me with disdain, then gets up and walks towards the door. She holds it open and waits for me to leave. 'Do I look like I'm joking? When was the last time you heard me laughing? When was the last time you heard anyone laughing? Tell you what, here's a good one for you: find yourself a gun and shove it in your mouth. Take one bullet tonight before bedtime. Caution, may cause headaches and drowsiness . . .'

Her insensitive comment goes unanswered. Suddenly the room is painfully quiet, the only noise the rain as it continues to hammer against the windows.

'Just go,' she says. 'There's nothing I can do for you. There's nothing anyone can do: all you've got to do is live with it till you die from it.'

27

I'm on the edge of the empty estate, almost back at the house. The thought of being shut away in the dark makes my heart sink, but it's the only place I've got left to go. I don't remember how I got here – I don't even remember leaving the factory.

Take a couple of days off, Hinchcliffe told me. Relax and sort yourself out, he said. What a fucking joke: *relax*? Since when has anyone been able to relax in this vile, fucked-up world? And as for sorting myself out? Jesus, that's equally impossible. In the space of a day everything has become infinitely more complicated – and yet I suppose it's immeasurably simpler at the same time. I've got more to think about, but less time to do it. My mind flits constantly as I walk through the torrential rain, never settling on any one thing long enough to give me time to work anything out. If I'm not thinking about the fact that I'm dying, I'm thinking about Peter Sutton, Joseph Mallon and the crowd of Unchanged buried underground, and if I'm not thinking about them, I'm thinking about the little girl strapped to the chair in Rona Scott's bloody torture chamber. Poor little cow, I can't get her out of my head. And if I'm not thinking about her, I'm thinking about my own kids, and that's never a good sign. But there's one main thought I keep coming back to: *I am dying of cancer.*

If this had happened to me in my old life, I'd be panicking now, and so would everyone else. I'd be thinking about the kids and Lizzie, checking whether I'd got any insurance cover, avoiding all the difficult but necessary practical conversations that Liz would want to be having with me about the future I wasn't going to have . . . But today there's no panic and no noise, just a strange, uneasy calm: an empty black hole where my life used to be. I knew I wasn't well, nothing the doctor said came as a great surprise, but at least there was still an element of doubt; I could still think I might wake up tomorrow feeling better.

But that's gone now, and the only thing I know for sure is that I'm well and truly fucked.

There was a guy at work who got cancer. We all had half a day off for his funeral. The crematorium was packed – there were hundreds of people there, all affected by that one death. Christ, no one will even notice when I go; when I die my body will just be left to rot. No one gives a shit about me personally; they all just take what they need from me, then dump me.

I trudge slowly through the estate, soaked to the skin, and now I start laughing to myself at the bloody irony of it all. I've survived the war, God knows how many attacks, battles big and small, a gas chamber, bombings, even a nuclear blast, just so my own body can kill me.

I remember Adam, the crippled fighter I spent a few days with last summer, when the war was close to reaching its peak and the killing still felt brave and righteous. I often think about him: he was in constant pain, barely able to move without help, and all he wanted to do was fight. In spite of his physical limitations, the only thing that mattered to him was wiping out the last of the Unchanged before they could get to him. But it's not his determination or his aggression I remember most, it was his attitude to death. I sat with him as his body shut itself down and I listened to him still talking about the next fight and the next kill as if he was going to go on for ever. He was like an animal, blissfully unaware of his own mortality, living for each moment, not wallowing in self-pity and waiting for his life to reach its inevitably anti-climactic ending.

But I am almost the exact opposite of Adam: he felt free,

uninhibited, while I feel trapped. His death meant nothing to him; mine is all I can think about. I'm already consumed by it; I'm doomed to spend my last days, weeks, months (if I'm *lucky*) wondering how many more times I'll wake up and see the sun rise, how many more times I'll fall asleep, how many more fights I'll have or avoid, how many books I'll read, how many more times I'll go to certain places or see certain people . . .

I'm boxed into a corner, with Hinchcliffe on one side and Peter Sutton on the other, and I have realised that I have to do something about this, or take Rona Scott's advice and finish things right now. Last night I was on the verge of packing up and getting out of here for good; now? Christ, I wish I had.

There's a light up ahead: someone with a torch is coming towards me. They've a coat over their head, but I can tell by their height and the way they're moving that it's Rufus. What the fuck does he want now? Why can't everyone just fuck off and leave me alone? There's always someone looking for me, and they all want something. None of them ever want to do anything for me. Well, they can all go to hell. I've got nothing left to give.

'Danny,' he yells as he flags me down, his voice sounding even more tense and unsure than usual, 'thank God I found you. Hinchcliffe wants to see you.'

'Hinchcliffe can fuck off,' I tell him, pushing past and continuing on towards the house. Rufus scurries after me, again overtaking and getting in my way, desperately trying to stop me. 'Where have you been?'

'Leave me alone, Rufus.'

'But I've been looking for you all day.'

'And now you've found me.'

'You have to come . . .'

'I don't *have* to do anything,' I tell him. 'You can tell Hinchcliffe to go fuck himself. I'm through running around after him. I quit.'

'No, Danny,' he says, beginning to sob, 'you can't. *Please.* If I go back without you again he'll kill me.'

'Then don't go back. Make a stand. Let someone else deal with him.'

'But I've never seen him like this before. Please, Danny, you've got to come.'

Decision time: how much longer do I keep putting up with all this crap? I don't enjoy seeing Rufus like this, but at least he's still got a choice. My hand has been forced.

'Listen,' I tell him, a hand on either shoulder, standing him upright and looking into his face, 'I'm not going back. I'm finished with this place, I'm finished with Hinchcliffe. I'm going to pack my stuff and get out of here, and if you've got any sense, I think you should do the same.'

He stands there looking at me pathetically, dumbstruck and terrified. 'You can't—? I can't—'

What he does next is up to him, but my mind's made up. 'Yes you can, Rufus. Hinchcliffe is an evil cunt and the only hold he's got over you is fear. Don't go back. Walk out of here tonight and find somewhere else. That's what I'm doing.'

'But there is nowhere else. I—'

'Good luck, mate. I hope everything works out for you.' With that I force myself to sidestep him. When I look back I see he's still standing in the pouring rain in the middle of the street, just watching me go.

28

I know I've made a rod for my own back, but that's just how it is. Once Rufus plucks up the courage to go back and face Hinchcliffe (and I know he will – he'll be too scared not to, and he doesn't have the strength to walk away from this place), then the shit will hit the fan. Hinchcliffe'll probably send Llewellyn or one of the others out here to find me. I know I'm doing the right thing, but I've managed to put myself under a whole load of pressure I didn't need. But you have to go with your gut feeling, I guess, even when your gut is apparently stuffed full of tumours.

The day has evaporated and it's late now, but I force myself to keep working, packing up as much stuff as I can carry before word filters down to Hinchcliffe that I'm no longer playing ball and the fucker explodes. My plan, such as it is, is to get as much together as I can, then maybe move it to another house nearby, just to get it away from here. Then I'll get myself a car, and once I've done that, I'm gone. Goodbye, Hinchcliffe, goodbye Lowestoft, and goodbye Rufus too. I feel bad for him, but he has to make a stand too. He doesn't even have to fight, just walk.

Once I've packed everything except for the food under the floorboards I head upstairs to check if there's anything of any worth left in the bedrooms. I've only used the living room and kitchen, so the upstairs rooms are just as the previous occupants left them. That freaks me out: I'm stepping back in time into a dust-covered reminder of the pre-war world. It's like the people who lived here just got up one morning and never came back – that's probably exactly what happened. There's a pile of washing still waiting to be put away on the end of an unmade double bed, and a boardgame abandoned on a kid's bedroom floor, the last game never finished. I try not to look at the pictures of the people who lived here that decorate the walls; I can't help but think their eyes are following me as I walk around what's left of their home.

The only things I keep up here are a few weapons: a pistol, a handful of bullets and a grenade, which I hid in the empty water tank. The grenade's a souvenir from the final battle in my home town. Julia gave it to me before I—

What was that? Shit – a *car?* I run to the front bedroom window and look down, but though I can hear it, I can't yet see it – until it screeches around the corner at the end of the road and overshoots the house, then the driver slams on the brakes and reverses back, wheels skidding on the icy road. Fuck, it's Hinchcliffe himself! What's he doing here? He must be extremely pissed off to have dragged himself out of the courthouse. I stand to the side of the window and press myself back against the wall, trying to work out how I'm going to get out of the house without him seeing me. Rufus gets out of the car, but he tries to hang back. Hinchcliffe's obviously having none of it: he's grabbed the poor little shit and is marching up the drive. Now he's kicking the front door.

'Open up, McCoyne,' he screams through the letter box. 'Open this fucking door right now!'

What the fuck do I do now? I'm too scared to go down to him, but I'm too scared not to. I could try the attic, but I don't know if there's a ladder to get up and even if there is, I'd just be backing myself into a corner. Downstairs I hear the door begin to splinter as Hinchcliffe boots it again. What the hell did Rufus say to him? I know I told him to stand up for himself – is that what he's done? Or has he betrayed me so that Hinchcliffe would go easy on him? My fear suddenly increases massively: what if Hinchcliffe had me followed earlier? What if he knows about Peter Sutton and the

Unchanged? Worse still, what if I was wrong about Sutton? What if he's double-crossed me and told Hinchcliffe *I'm* the one harbouring Unchanged to get himself off the hook?

'Open this fucking door, McCoyne!' Hinchcliffe yells again, shaking Rufus like a dog.

I guess my best option is to get out through the rear of the house. I'll come back later and fetch my stuff. I check around the edge of the window frame again. There's only Hinchcliffe and Rufus here, no other fighters, so I could hide in any one of the hundreds of other empty houses around this estate and they'd be none the wiser.

On the street below, poor old Rufus tries to make a run for it, but Hinchcliffe's having none of it and kicks his legs out from under him. Rufus crashes down on his back on the driveway with a heavy thump and a horrible yelp of pain. Hinchcliffe kicks him in the kidneys, screaming at him that he's not going anywhere until they've found me, then he takes another run at the door.

I've got to move fast – but I'm not even halfway down the stairs when the door flies open, finally giving way under the force of Hinchcliffe's boot. I try to turn back, but I trip and land on my backside on the bottom step as splinters of broken wood and shards of glass go flying in all directions around me.

'McCoyne,' he yells when he sees me, 'where the fuck have you been?'

'Upstairs. I was asleep,' I tell him, trying to lie my way out of trouble. 'I'm sick.'

I can't tell whether or not he believes me, but he turns back and grabs hold of Rufus and hauls him into the house. Rufus stares at me with a petrified expression on his face. He's been badly beaten; his right eye is swollen shut and there's blood running down his chin. At least he's managing to hold my gaze, and that's a good sign, I hope. I don't think he'd be able to look at me if he'd told Hinchcliffe what I said earlier. Poor bastard's no good at handling situations like this.

'Where have you been?' Hinchcliffe asks again.

'I already told you, asleep upstairs.'

'No, earlier. I sent Rufus to find you and you weren't here.'

'When?' I ask, deliberately acting dumb, hoping he'll give me some details to help flesh out my story. 'I'm not well. I had a few drinks and I took some stuff to help me sleep . . .'

Hinchcliffe glares at me, the shadows and darkness making his face look uncomfortably angular and fierce, accentuating his anger.

'What time was that?'

'What?'

'You heard me.'

'I don't bloody know – I don't wear a watch. It was dark and—'

'What about earlier? Where were you this afternoon?'

'I went to see Rona Scott.'

'I know about that, she told me. I'm talking about before then.'

I can't risk telling him anything. 'I don't know – look, Hinchcliffe, I'm sorry if I wasn't around. Did Dr Scott tell you what she told me? That I'm dying? I've just been walking around, trying to get my head together so I could—'

'We're all dying,' he interrupts. 'Now stop pissing around and tell me where you were when the plane flew over.'

'*Plane*? What plane?' What the hell is he talking about now? The skies are empty; they have been for months. Even the birds are dying out. The last thing I saw flying was the missile carrying the warhead which destroyed my home town. I don't feel any less nervous now, but suddenly the pressure is fractionally reduced. Is this the reason he's come out here? Unless he thinks I was flying this plane (which would be impossible), then maybe I'm not the real focus of his fury tonight.

'Just before midday,' he says slowly, spitting each word at me, 'a plane flew over the town.'

'And you think I've got something to do with it?'

'Don't be so fucking stupid,' he snaps, confirming my suspicions, 'of course I don't think that! I don't know what the fuck you do out here on your own, but I do know you're not flying fucking aeroplanes.'

'What then?'

Frustrated, Hinchcliffe turns his back on me and kicks what's left of the door shut. Rufus flinches at the noise, then shuffles further away, trying to move deeper into the house and hoping neither of us will notice. I start to feel marginally more confident; it seems I'm not the problem here. Someone else has pissed him off.

'*I* run this place,' he says, turning around and advancing towards me menacingly, pointing his finger into my face.

I take a step back to get out of his way and trip and fall onto the stairs again. I've never seen him like this before: so incensed he's barely able to keep himself together. I need to watch my step here and choose my next words carefully – I don't want to say anything to push him over the edge.

'I know you run Lowestoft – everyone here knows it.'

'Yes, but those fuckers up there don't,' he yells, jabbing his finger skywards.

'Yes, but—'

'But *nothing*. I need to keep control here. I need to know exactly what's going on. I can't have people doing things that I can't control, you understand?'

I'm not sure I do. 'So what, did they just fly over? Just happen to come across the town by chance?'

He massages his temples. 'No, they flew circuits, put on a proper fucking show. They might have found us by chance, but they definitely checked everything out properly before they left.'

'So what type of plane was it?'

'What?' he asks, confused.

'What type of plane? Military? A jet or bomber?'

He shakes his head again. 'No, nothing like that.'

'What then?'

'Just a little plane. Two- or four-seater, something like that.'

'So what's the problem? Someone probably just got lucky, managed to get a plane up and—'

'What's the problem?' he screams at me, storming forward again, now so close that I can feel his hot booze-tinged breath on my face. 'What's the problem? The fucking problem is that they're doing something I can't – I can't allow anyone to have that kind of advantage over me!'

'A little plane? Is that really such an advantage?'

'Well, if you'd been here like you should have been, McCoyne, you'd have seen the effect it had. *That's* what I'm talking about. When that plane flew over, every single fucker in Lowestoft stopped what they were doing and looked up at it. My fighters, the underclass . . . every single fucking one of them.'

'Yes, but a two-seater plane . . . Come on, what are they going to do?'

'Nothing right now, but it's what they *could* do that's important. They've got one plane today. They could have two tomorrow. They could train pilots and have a whole bloody fleet up in the air before we know it. And now they know we're here they'll be back. They could drop bombs on us and there'd be nothing we could do.'

'But that's not likely to happen, is it? Like I said, it's probably just someone who got lucky—'

'I know that and you know that, McCoyne, but the hundreds of dumb bastards lining the streets of this town don't.'

'So hunt them out – try and get whoever it was onside.'

For a moment he's quiet. He leans back against the wall and runs his fingers through his hair, then massages his temples. I'm sure he's already thought of that – he's probably already sent his fighters out there hunting down the plane and its pilot. And if and when he finds them, I know he'll leave them with no choice but to work with him.

'Thing is,' he says, sounding marginally calmer again, 'seeing people flying around affects what the people here think about me. They know I don't have any planes, so they automatically assume those bastards up there are superior. This is eroding my authority, putting unnecessary strain on the control I've got here. I can't let that happen, you understand?'

'Yes, but—'

He holds up his hand and stops me talking. 'And there's also the very real possibility that they *might* attack from the skies. What would I do then? Have people standing on rooftops chucking stones back at them if they fly low enough?'

'The chances of them attacking are remote . . .'

'How do you know that? And anyway, a chance is a chance. It gives them a tactical advantage and we have got to do something about it.'

'*We?*' I say stupidly.

Hinchcliffe glares at me again, then starts pacing around the living room. Rufus scuttles out of the way as he moves towards him, but Hinchcliffe's spotted the wrench I leave lying around for self-defence. He picks it up and starts swinging it from hand to hand, getting a feel for its weight.

'Here's what's going to happen,' he announces. 'I'm sending Llewellyn and a few others out at first light to find those bastards. Llewellyn reckons he's worked out where they're likely to have come from. He'll find them and either bring them back to me or get rid of them. And you're going with them.'

'Me? Why?'

'Don't pretend you don't fucking know: same reason I always send you. You're so fucking insignificant no one gives you a second glance. You can assess the situation better than most. And if you can't assess it, you can at least spy on the fuckers and tell me what's going on.'

'But I'm *sick*.'

'So? I'm not asking you to run a fucking marathon.'

I try to think of a valid reason that'll make him change his mind, but I can't. 'Okay,' I say, desperate to pacify him, though I'm already trying to think of ways to get away from this mess once and for all.

He starts walking back towards the door and after a moment's hesitation Rufus follows in his footsteps, obviously unsure what to do next. Clumsy bastard knocks another stack of books over and walks into Hinchcliffe when he stops suddenly.

'Sorry, Hinchcliffe,' he mumbles pathetically, cowering back. Hinchcliffe ignores him and slowly turns back around to face me.

'Where were you, Danny?'

'What?'

'When the plane flew over, where were you? You still haven't told me.'

'I don't know when that was. Like I said, I'm sick. I went for a walk to try and clear my head, and when I got back I went to see your doctor.'

'Does it affect your hearing?'

'What?'

'This "sickness" of yours, makes you deaf, does it?'

'No.'

'So how comes you didn't hear anything? They were circling Lowestoft for almost an hour, maybe even longer. How could you not have heard it?'

'I don't know – how am I supposed to answer that? I've had things on my mind. I don't know when it happened – I could have been asleep, or down by the beach . . .'

'It's all a bit fucking *convenient*, isn't it?' He stares at me, unblinking. Does he know more than he's letting on?

'Is it?' My pulse is racing, but I hold his gaze.

He finally breaks eye contact and looks away, and the relief is immense. 'No, probably not.'

'What, then? What are you saying?'

'You talk the talk, Danny, but do you really understand how important this might be?'

'You've just explained.'

'So you understand that it's crucial for me to keep control of this place?'

'Yes.'

'So why weren't you here?'

'You *told me* to take some time off. You *said* you didn't need me.' I'm beginning to get aggravated now.

'I thought you were smarter than that.'

'What?'

'I might have told you I didn't have anything I needed you to do for a couple of days, but I didn't say you could go away on a fucking holiday, did I?'

'I didn't go on holiday, I just—'

He holds up his hand (and my wrench) again to silence me. Arrogant bastard.

'In future you'll be here exactly when I want you to be. Understand?'

'Have I ever not been? Have I ever—?'

'I need to know who I can trust, Danny. You let me down today. Llewellyn could have been on his way by now – if you'd been there, he could have followed the damn plane out of town. Now we've given them a head start and they could be anywhere.'

'They're *flying*, Hinchcliffe. They could be anywhere anyway.'

He takes another couple of steps closer and I freeze.

Keep your fucking mouth shut, you idiot, I scream to myself.

'When you get back with Llewellyn,' he seethes, 'you're going to collect up all your shit from this house and find somewhere to stay in the middle of town, closer to the courthouse.'

'But—'

'I'm not asking, I'm telling.'

'What difference does it make?' I protest, desperate not to give up my privacy, remembering too late that I'm not planning on hanging around. Hinchcliffe moves closer still and I immediately shut up, regretting my outburst. Then, with a grunt of sudden, unexpected anger, he spins around and smashes the wrench into Rufus' face. Rufus immediately drops to the ground and I stare at him, stunned. He lies on his back, arms and legs still moving, his face covered with blood, whimpering through broken teeth. Hinchcliffe leans down and smacks him in the head again, finishing him off. He stands up, one foot either side of the now motionless body, and thrusts the bloody wrench at me.

'Don't ever give me any reason not to trust you again. I don't know where the fuck you were today, but from now on you do exactly what you're told. You don't ask questions, you just do what I tell you. Understand?'

'I understand,' I say quietly, looking down at the battered body of my friend.

'Get the stuff you need together. We're heading back into town. And don't *ever* fuck with me again, Danny, because you *will* regret it.'

29

This is my worst nightmare. I'm in the back of an armour-plated van with Llewellyn and three other fighters, and I'm scared shitless. Llewellyn's never trusted me; I'm pretty sure he's been waiting for a chance to get me away from Lowestoft on my own. There's something different about the way he's behaving towards me today, and the longer this journey lasts, the more convinced I am that he persuaded Hinchcliffe I should be part of this pointless expedition so he could get rid of me. Fucker's going to kill me and concoct some bullshit story to explain to Hinchcliffe why his little pet is dead.

The four members of my armed guard talk to each other in secretive whispers, deliberately excluding me, but I'm used to that – I've felt like an outsider the whole time I've been in Lowestoft. No matter how I look at it, I've got a foot in neither camp: I'm not a fighter, nor am I underclass, not like the rest of them. But I'm not Unchanged either. I'm just an unwanted mixed-breed outcast. Today my paranoia has been ramped up by several hundred per cent, but whatever their intentions, I won't know for sure what Llewellyn and his little gang are planning until they make their move. I'm hoping that wherever we end up, I'll be able to find a way to give them the slip; what I do after I've broken cover is anyone's guess. I don't suppose it matters any more: I'm not eating, hardly drinking . . . I'll just find a rock to crawl under and sit it out. I can't waste any more time thinking about it – I might not have any time left.

Llewellyn is sitting up front next to the driver, Ben Healey. In the back with me are Chandra, the disfigured guard I saw outside Hinchcliffe's hotel breeding centre, and Swales, a cocky young bastard I've had little contact with before now. They've been hand-picked for their aggression and strength.

We're in radio contact with Hinchcliffe, but communications with Lowestoft have been brief and infrequent. I'm not going to risk saying anything, but they surely must realise we're never going to find that plane today – Christ, it could have come from anywhere, overseas, even. No one knows for sure what's happening in other countries (it's hard enough finding out what's going on here), but I'm guessing everywhere else must be in as dire a state as us. The fact remains: looking for the plane and its pilot is going to be like looking for a needle in a pile of a thousand massive haystacks. What if it came from somewhere on the other side of the huge radioactive scar which now stretches much of the length of the country? There's no point saying anything to Llewellyn; he's never going to listen to me. Instead he'll just concentrate on his impossible task without question – if Hinchcliffe told these morons to kill themselves I think most of them probably would . . . but it's more likely they're going to kill me.

Llewellyn glances over his shoulder and makes eye contact with me and my blood runs cold. The bastard's enjoying this; he can't wait to be shot of me. The longer I'm around, the more he resents the fact that I'm useful to Hinchcliffe. Fighters can be replaced, but me . . . I'm unique, unfortunately, and Llewellyn doesn't like it.

I peer out of the wire-mesh covered window and see that we've entered the outskirts of what used to be the city of Norwich. It's a lifeless place now, nothing more than a desolate shell. It obviously wasn't big enough to warrant being nuked, but over the last few months it's been systematically stripped clean, first by Thacker, then Hinchcliffe. It's too large to be governed effectively, and it's not as geographically well placed as the port of Lowestoft, so it's been abandoned, left to decay.

A sudden sharp crackle of static comes from the radio. Llewellyn grabs it quickly and talks; though I strain to hear what he's saying, it's impossible. He turns around and looks back at me again, and his expression says more than a thousand words ever could. He looks on edge, nervous almost. Now I'm certain that he's going to try and get rid of me – but why now? And why all the way out here?

I'm stuck in this van until we stop moving. *Keep to the plan*, I tell myself repeatedly. *Wait until they let you out, then fight, keep fighting, and if and when you get the chance, run like fuck.*

30

The van grinds to a sudden juddering halt alongside a ruined department store. The front wall has collapsed, spilling rubble out onto the street and leaving every level of the building open to the elements. We're parked up on the pavement, hidden by a mountain of fallen masonry, well out of sight. Over the way there's a road sign pointing back towards Lowestoft and, for the first time ever, I almost wish I was back there. Anywhere but here.

'Out,' Llewellyn orders from the front seat and Chandra grabs my arm. I panic and try to fight him off, but he's stronger than me and all my struggling does is encourage his mate Swales to grab hold of my other arm. Llewellyn runs around to the back of the van and yanks the door open, and between them they frogmarch me out onto the street, almost carrying me as if I'm made of paper. Llewellyn has a pistol in his hand and I don't doubt for a second that he'll use it. I force myself not to fight, but to swallow down the Hate, keeping control, just like I did even when I was neck-deep in vile Unchanged. I did it yesterday, and I can do it now. The element of surprise is all I have left. I have to bide my time and catch these bastards off-guard.

'Llewellyn, I—'

'Don't talk, just fucking move,' he says, throwing my rucksack at me, then shoving me hard between the shoulder blades. 'We don't have long. You're an unnecessary complication, McCoyne.'

What the hell did he mean by that? I try to ask, but no one's listening. With Llewellyn behind me, Healey in front and the other two on either side, they've got me boxed in. I don't understand why they needed to bring me all this way just to put a bullet in my head . . . They're marching at a speed I find difficult to match, but Llewellyn keeps pushing me in the back whenever I slow down. He's helpful like that. For the first time in weeks, I want to fight back, but all the anger and aggression I used to have, the fury and the rage that used to burn inside me, is gone now. There's nothing left. Before today there was always a way out, but I can't see one now. My only option is to try and break free and run, though I know I don't have either the strength or the speed to outrun even one of these men, let alone all of them. This time I'm truly fucked.

We stop at a traffic island and Healey consults a folded-up map, checking our location against what's left of our surroundings. 'Not far now,' he says, and I am filled with the same cloying sense of dread as when I was being led blindfolded through the convent with Joseph Mallon. And now, just for a single dangerous second, I'm distracted, thinking about him again. I almost envy him and the rest of the Unchanged, buried in their bunker, isolated from the alien world above them. Maybe some of what Peter Sutton said yesterday was right: they're safe, I'm screwed. Who's the most sensible now?

'You nervous, McCoyne?' Llewellyn says, breaking rank and catching my eye. I try to play it cool, but I fail completely and my terror must be obvious. His face remains passive and unemotional at first, but then he can't help himself and he breaks into a wide, sadistic smile. He's actually enjoying this. Evil motherfucker. 'Do you think we're going to find any aeroplanes today?' he sneers. Chandra sniggers and tightens his grip on my arm when I try to react. This isn't right. If they knew how sick I was would they let me go? Maybe I can persuade them to free me because I'll probably be dead soon anyway and no one will know any different. It's not like I'm going to go back to Lowestoft and tell Hinchcliffe what they've done . . .

Who the hell am I kidding? Do I really expect hard fuckers like this to show any compassion? I don't even bother trying to fight. I'm saving my energy so I can make my final break for freedom when the right moment comes. And by the look of things, that's not going to be long. We duck down through a hole in a chain-link fence, then cross a patch of scrubland. My nerves increase with every step until I blurt out, 'Whatever you're going to do to me, just fucking do it!'

Llewellyn looks at me, puzzled. 'And what makes you think we're going to do anything to you? You're paranoid, mate.' Then he turns to Healey. 'This it?' he asks.

Healey nods, Chandra lets go of me and I try to run, but they're too damn fast. Llewellyn shoots out his arm, grabs me and pulls me back into line.

'Don't,' he warns ominously.

The area of town we've reached seems to have suffered slightly less damage; most of the buildings around us are still largely intact. Following some predetermined plan, my four-man guard suddenly disperses. Healey and Swales go one way, Chandra stops walking and takes a radio out from his backpack. Llewellyn still has hold of me and he keeps me moving forward. I try to prise his fingers off my arm, but he's having none of it. He tightens his grip.

'Just do it,' I beg pathetically, 'please—'

'Pull yourself together, you miserable dick,' he says as he drags me towards a wide-fronted Gothic-looking building. What the hell is this place? It's too big to be a church – was it some kind of school? Or a prison, or some other public office, before the war?

He pulls opens the arch-shaped, white wooden door, looks around, then pushes me inside. He shuts it behind us and finally lets me go. 'Listen, I'm not going to kill you. I've got better things to do today.'

'Then why did you—?'

'You shouldn't even be here. Fucking Hinchcliffe. Don't know why he sent you out with us.'

It takes my eyes a few seconds to become accustomed to the light indoors. We're standing in the entrance hall of some kind of museum. It has the unmistakable air of the past about it; a bubble of the old, old world, trapped here in the rubble of the new.

'What are we doing here?'

'It's funny how things work out sometimes,' Llewellyn says conversationally, although from where I'm standing there's nothing funny about it at all. 'You never know what you're going to find around the corner these days.'

I follow him up several flights of a wide, marbled stair-case, my legs weak with effort, to the second storey of the building, past glass cabinets filled with remnants of long-dead people and long-lost things. This place is remarkably ornate, and remarkably well preserved, and I find myself remembering a time when there was more to life than just hunting and killing and fighting to stay alive. There's some damage here (there's some damage everywhere), but many of the paintings, statues and displays remain virtually untouched. None of this is important now; what's happened to us all has made who we used to be completely irrelevant. No one's interested in art, nor in any other aspect of the world before the war. It's strange to think that you could be the owner of an original Picasso, or a Burne-Jones, or a Titian, but it wouldn't matter a damn because no one would trade it for food. It's bizarre to think that all the paint-covered canvases around the world which used to command almost unimaginable prices are worth less in real terms now than a single can of beans.

I'm allowing myself to become distracted by my surroundings, and I can't afford to be. Llewellyn's radio crackles again and he holds it up to his ear. He take a few steps away from me as he speaks, and a tinny voice bursts from the loudspeaker. I can't make out what it's saying, but Llewellyn seems to understand perfectly.

'We're ready out here. Healey's on the ground for you. We'll be waiting in the museum.'

'What's this all about?' I ask. I'm now genuinely curious. 'Why are we here?'

'You'll see,' he says, enjoying making me squirm. 'You've got about fifteen minutes to wait. Have a wander around, but don't try and get out because Healey's guarding the door downstairs and I've told him to break your legs if you try anything.' He laughs. 'Relax and enjoy the exhibits! Soak up the atmosphere . . .'

Fifteen minutes feels like fifteen hours. Llewellyn continues to watch me, until eventually something distracts him outside, when his expression immediately changes and he becomes more serious. He beckons me over and I stand beside him in front of a floor-to-ceiling window and look down over the overgrown grass slope we walked across to get here.

'Your friend Hinchcliffe,' he finally says, 'isn't quite as smart and all-powerful as he thinks he is.'

'He's not my friend,' is my immediate reaction.

'Figure of speech. You know what I mean.' He seems about to tell me more when there's another ugly burst of noise from the radio. 'Got it,' he says after listening to another indecipherable transmission. He calls down to Healey, whose on the ground below us, and Healey looks up. 'They're here,' he tells him.

'Who's here?' I ask, confused.

'I fucking hate Hinchcliffe,' Llewellyn says. 'I know it's not about who you like or don't like any more, but I fucking hate him, with his stupid long hair and his fucking attitude.'

'So why have you stuck by him?'

'Same reason you have: like it or not, the bastard has influence and he's hard as nails. It's better to have him onside than end up fighting against him.'

'And is that what you're planning, some kind of rebellion? An uprising in Lowestoft?'

'It's not about what *I'm* planning, but you're not a million miles off the mark.'

'What then?'

Llewellyn looks as if he's about to answer, but then he stops and stares out of the window into the distance, then he presses his ear against the glass, then taps it with his finger.

For a few seconds I hear nothing, and I'm starting to wonder if my hearing is as screwed as the rest of my knackered body, but then I gradually become aware of a low rumbling noise. It quickly gets louder, and it's soon so deep and so loud that the window starts to rattle and shake in its frame. And then I see a tank appear, belching black exhaust fumes into the air as it bulldozes its way across the grassland, caterpillar tracks churning the ground, and stops directly below us. There's a crudely painted red and white circular insignia on its front and its side. I've seen those markings before . . .

I look up again and see that the tank was just the first of several vehicles now moving towards the museum in convoy. Christ, what is this? Most of the advancing machines are clearly military, although there are several civilian cars and bikes here too, bulked up with improvised armour plating and other defences, and they're all decorated with the same red and white concentric circles as the lorries I saw in Southwold. Nestled right in the middle are two heavily armoured troop carriers. Where the hell did this lot come from? The traffic fans out, leaving a space for the first troop carrier to drive closer to the museum. It stops a short distance from the entrance, brakes hissing.

'Bang on time.'

'Llewellyn, what is this?'

'You ever heard that expression, keep your friends close and your enemies closer?'

'Yes, but—'

'Well, get ready to meet your friends. Word to the wise, McCoyne: doesn't matter who you are or what you can do. These days all that matters is keeping onside with the fuckers who've got the most muscle and the biggest guns, and that's this lot. This is just the advance party.'

The door of the troop carrier slides open and somewhere between ten and fifteen figures quickly emerge, all of them wearing similarly coloured clothing – a very basic, improvised uniform of sorts. The troops form a loose protective guard of two roughly parallel lines which stretch from the vehicle right up to the door of the museum. A number of other people follow them out of the transport and walk through the gap that's opened up between them. I see two men, then a woman, then a small, white-haired man who walks with a stick . . .

'Who are they?' I ask.

'See the old guy?' Llewellyn says, with something approximating pride and genuine emotion in his voice. 'That's Chris Ankin.'

I can't believe what I'm hearing. 'Chris Ankin? *The* Chris Ankin?'

'Mind your Ps and Qs,' he says as he tugs my arm and leads me back down the stairs. 'Prime Minister, President, Commander-in-Chief, Sir, Your Highness . . . call him what you like, he's the boss man now.'

31

Llewellyn and Chandra are whisked away and Healey returns to the van. I'm left alone with Swales, who seems almost as bemused by events as I am. I'm beginning to get the distinct impression he's here just to make up the numbers. We watch from a ground-floor window as the new arrivals quickly set up camp. Some build fires and erect temporary shelters; others are dispatched into what's left of Norwich, presumably to look for fuel and supplies and anything else of value. They're working *together*, and there's no hint of aggression or any pecking order.

Swales notices a queue forming outside a mess tent. He heads straight for it and I follow him. We're given a little food without question – some kind of bland, rice-based paste and a few thin biscuits, and a mug of coffee – and then left to our own devices again. It's not great tasting, but it's not half-cooked dog either, and I manage to swallow a few mouthfuls. We sit on a bench in a sheltered alcove just outside the museum building, out of the way of everyone else, but still close enough to watch whatever's going on. It's funny, less than an hour ago Swales was definitely one of 'them', but now we're thick as thieves, comfortable in each other's company because there's someone new in town and neither of us have any immediate desire to mix with these strangers.

There's controlled activity all around us still as these people, whoever they are, establish their makeshift base. Each person is carrying out their allotted task without question or complaint, people who were obviously fighters working alongside people who obviously weren't . . . it's a pale imitation, but it's almost like things used to be. This is like what I saw in Southwold, albeit on a much grander scale. So what's the connection? Are they all stealing from Hinchcliffe?

'You gonna eat that?' Swales says, nudging me with his elbow and nodding at my practically untouched food.

'You want it?'

He snatches the plate and starts scooping up the rice paste with clumsy fingers, smearing nearly as much of it over his face as he manages to get into his mouth.

'Good?'

'Good,' he answers, wolfing down a biscuit. 'I'll eat anything, me,' he continues, showering me with crumbs.

'So I can see.'

Swales obviously isn't the sharpest tool in the box, but his strength and size (and no doubt his track record and ongoing appetite for violence) have helped him become one of Hinchcliffe's 'élite'. He's strong, impressionable and, I expect, easily manipulated – perfect fighter fodder.

'So what do you reckon to all this then?' he asks.

That's a surprisingly difficult question to answer. These days something happens every few minutes which skews my perspective on everything again – everything feels fluid; nothing sits still.

'Depends what "all this" is, doesn't it?'

'Don't get you.'

'Well, first I thought we were out plane-spotting, then I thought Llewellyn was going to kill me, and now I'm sitting having lunch with half an army. I'll be honest with you, Swales, I don't have a fucking clue what's going on any more.'

'I got told nothing. Llewellyn said he'd got a job for me, that's all. Didn't know nothing about all this.'

'So what do you think about it all?'

Swales has a naïveté and innocence which may well prove to be his undoing. He talks candidly, barely even thinking about what he's saying. Still, that probably makes him more honest and reliable than most of the backstabbing bastards Hinchcliffe surrounds himself with. 'Got to be a good thing, ain't it? This is like things used to be.'

'I guess.'

He pauses to eat, and when his second plate's almost clear, he says, 'You know what I used to do for a job, mate? I used to flip burgers, 'cause that was the only job I could find. There's plenty about the old times I miss—'

'But not flipping burgers?'

'Definitely *not* flipping burgers!' He laughs. 'I miss me mum and me brother, even though he turned out to be one of *them*. I miss me mates . . . Don't get me wrong, I wouldn't go back for any money, but I wouldn't say I'm happy with the way everything is, you know?'

'Like what?'

'Like the fighting. You do it 'cause you have to, but that don't make it right. You can't just kick back and relax like you used to, you've always got to be on the lookout. Llewellyn says you got to stay one step ahead of everybody else, 'cause the one bloke you're not watching is the one who'll creep up behind you and kill you.'

'And what do you think about that? Is he right?'

'Suppose. I'm just tired of it, is all. But what's happening here, what that Chris Ankin bloke's doing, that sounds like a better option to me. Llewellyn says Ankin's gonna see all of us right in the end.'

Poor bastard, he really does believe everything he's told. But then again, I think to myself as I look around this place, maybe I'm the one who's wrong? He may have been a long way from the front line of battle, but more than anyone else Ankin has been in control from the start. He's not like Hinchcliffe – Hinchcliffe was just someone who just happened to be in the right place at the right time and took advantage of what he found to force himself into power. Ankin is different – and to have kept control for so long through so much, he must have done the right thing by his people. There's a world of difference between the organised uniformed people here and Hinchcliffe's army of a couple of hundred individual fighters. Johannson, Thacker and many others have proved how tenuous positions of power have become, and yet this weak-looking old politician has outlasted them all.

Maybe Peter Sutton was wrong and our species *can* take a step back from the abyss? Who the hell am I kidding? I'll believe it when I see it. 'It'll take more than this lot to make everything right again,' I mutter.

'But that's the best part,' Swales says excitedly, 'there *is* more than this lot. That's what Llewellyn reckons, anyway. He says there's thousands more of them on the way to Norwich. Thousands of them!'

32

An unexpectedly comfortable night's sleep on the floor in a quiet corner of the museum is rudely interrupted at first light. Despite the fact that the first thing I see is Llewellyn's scowling face glaring down at me, I immediately feel different today. Optimism is too strong a word, but there's no denying that, unexpectedly, things are looking more hopeful this morning than they have done in months. The illusion doesn't last long when I start coughing my guts up and I remember what Rona Scott told me. If really this does turn out to be the dawn of a brave new world, I'm probably not going to get to see very much of it.

Llewellyn is chaperoning me this morning. I manage to get outside to take a piss in the half-inch of snow that's fallen overnight, but before I've even finished shaking myself dry he's already dragging me back indoors. He seems uncharacteristically anxious as he herds me into a busy room on the ground floor of the museum and tells me to sit down and shut up. I don't have to wait long to find out why.

In a week which has been crammed with bizarre events, this takes the cake. The last few days in particular have been unbelievably surreal, like a crazy, barely controlled chain reaction, and it feels like the more I try to shut myself off and pull away from the madness, the worse it gets. Being forced to contribute to Hinchcliffe's fucked-up breeding programme was bad enough, but even that paled into insignificance alongside the unspeakable things that Peter Sutton showed me underground. In the space of a couple of days I've been told I'm dying; I've watched Rufus, the closest thing I had to a friend, killed in front of me for no reason

233

other than Hinchcliffe's spite, and I've convinced myself I was going to be executed . . . and now this?

Here I am, in a dusty museum café, sitting across a table from Chris Ankin. *The* Chris Ankin, the very same ex-government official who broadcast that message I heard so long ago: the call to arms for all us fighters who, until he dared to speak out, had felt persecuted and alone. This is the man whose face I saw on a computer screen in the back of a van when my life changed direction again; the man who, by word of mouth alone, managed to coordinate an invisible army which marched into Unchanged settlements and stirred them up so much that they imploded and tore themselves apart. *That* Chris Ankin, the closest thing to a true leader we've had. Until now I'd never actually stopped to think about how much I owe this man, but without his words I'd have been alone, completely unprepared for the onset of war. Without his planning and foresight I'd never have made it back into the city, I'd never have learned to hold the Hate, and, most importantly, I would never have shared those last few precious minutes with Lizzie and Ellis.

It seems that whenever I cross paths with Ankin, everything changes. And today that makes me feel very nervous. Why is he here, and why does he suddenly want to talk to me?

As usual I'm like a fifth wheel, and the longer I have to wait, the worse I feel. Right now Ankin is busy talking to someone: a clean-shaven, relatively smartly dressed man. It's strange; I look around at the people who arrived here with Ankin and in some ways it's almost as if I'm looking at another race, another species, even. Without realising I'm doing it I make a pathetic attempt to straighten my long, straggly hair with the tips of my fingers, as if it's going to make a difference. These people are far better organised than anyone else I've seen since the war ended; they're better fed, and fitter too. Most of them are wearing something resembling a uniform, they are regimented and controlled, they have a clear command structure which appears to work, with clearly defined jobs to do. They might be amateurish and ill-disciplined compared with the military powers before the war, but they're so much more capable than anyone else I've come across since the bombs were dropped. I thought that what I'd seen in Lowestoft was as close to civilisation as we were ever going to get, but these people are on another level altogether. I remember the ragtag armies I used to watch in TV footage from African and Middle Eastern conflicts a lifetime time ago: the warlord-ruled militias which used to butcher, rape and pillage their way through the starving nomadic populations. Incredibly, these people here look *less* aggressive, though they're armed to the teeth, and each person here (me included) has probably been involved in more atrocities than all of those so-called freedom fighters put together, but now they're calm and in complete control.

The man talking to Ankin stands up and disappears, and Ankin finally turns his attention to me. I feel my pulse quicken.

'Danny McCoyne,' he says. 'Llewellyn's told me a lot about you.'

'Has he?' I reply quickly, silently hoping that the bit he *hasn't* heard about me includes the time I recently spent underground with more than thirty Unchanged and didn't kill them.

'He says you're a useful man to have around.'

'Does he? He's got a strange way of showing it. I thought he was going to kill me yesterday.'

Ankin smiles broadly. 'We all have to keep our cards close to our chest these days, Danny. Your friend Hinchcliffe wouldn't have taken it well if he knew Llewellyn was working for me.'

'You don't know the half of it,' I tell him. 'And by the way, in spite of what you might have heard, Hinchcliffe's definitely no friend of mine.'

'But you know him well.'

'Better than most, I suppose. Not through choice.'

'I understand that – bit of an awkward character, by all accounts.'

'Bit of a cunt, actually.'

'Quite. Anyway, back to you. I'm sure you've got more than a few questions you'd like to ask about what you've seen.' He smiles at me – a glimpse of an obviously fake and well-rehearsed politician's smile from way back – and he studies my face intently. The power of his stare and his undeniably authoritarian presence is such that everything else seems to fade away and lose focus until it feels like we're the only people left in the room.

'I'd like to know where you came from, and where you've been – why's it taken you so long to get here?'

He thinks before answering, still staring at me, still smiling. 'Tell me, Danny,' he finally says, leaning forward and, again like an old-time politician, avoiding answering my question by asking another of his own, 'how much do you know about this strange new world of ours?'

'Not a lot. I know some of what's happening around Lowestoft, not much else.'

'And that's about as much as I'd expect. Don't you think it's strange how much things have changed over the last year or so? I'm guessing that this time last year you were probably stuck in a rut like most of the rest of us, just going through the motions, getting through life as best you could, one day at a time.'

How right he is . . .

'And now you can do pretty much what you want, when you want, can't you? Your priorities have completely changed, of course, and you have to work harder to get the basics like food and water and such stuff, but you're your own master now. You're less restricted and held back than you used to be.'

Apart from the spectre of Hinchcliffe which looms over

me constantly, he's right again. But he's not telling me anything I don't already know.

'But there's an obvious paradox here, isn't there?' he announces.

'Is there?'

'Yes. Your world's suddenly got a lot smaller, hasn't it? A year ago you could switch on your TV or go online and you could find out in seconds what was happening pretty much anywhere around the world. You could send an email or pick up the phone and talk instantly to people in other countries.'

'And now we only know what's happening immediately around us,' I interrupt, anticipating what I think he's going to say next. 'Anything could be happening elsewhere, but if we can't see it or hear it and we can't walk there or drive to it, we probably wouldn't ever know anything about it. All the borders and barriers have been broken down, but we can't get close enough to them to get over to the other side.'

'Exactly,' he says, leaning back in his chair, wagging his finger at me. 'Llewellyn was right about you: you really do get it!'

That makes me feel uneasy again. I've forgotten how I'm supposed to respond to compliments – these days, on the very rare occasions someone says something positive about you, it's inevitably followed by either a request for help or an attempt on your life. I'm hoping Ankin's going to ask me to help him, because if things get heavy around here, I'm fucked.

'What point are you making?' I ask.

'Tell me how you got here,' he replies, still managing to avoid my questions.

'What, how I got to Norwich?' I say stupidly. He shakes his head.

'No, how you got through the war. How you managed to survive for this long.'

'Just did what I had to, I guess. I just kept fighting.'

'There are plenty of people who just kept fighting, and most of them are dead. What makes you any different?'

'Luck of the draw,' I answer, not sure I want to give anything else away.

'I don't believe you. There's got to be more to it than that. Look at what happened to the Brutes – now that's the result of just fighting, and you're clearly no Brute, Danny.'

'I caught a few breaks, had some close calls . . .'

Ankin's clearly growing tired of my bullshit. 'Llewellyn says you can hold the Hate.'

'For what it's worth,' I answer. 'Not much call for it these days, now the Unchanged are gone.'

'True, but having that ability says something about the kind of person you are. It shows that you're less impulsive than most, that you've got self-control and willpower. Tell me, Danny, where did you learn to do it?'

'Came across a guy called Sahota. Or rather, he came across me.'

'Ahh, Sahota! I had a feeling you were one of his.'

'One of his?'

'From his "re-education" programmes.'

'Is that what he called them?'

'So you were sent into one of the refugee camps?'

My mind suddenly fills with unwanted memories of those nightmare days last summer. 'I've never been through anything like it before,' I tell him. 'It was incredible . . . horrific . . .'

'But you did it,' he says, 'and you survived it. No matter how bad an ordeal it was, you managed to get through it and come out the other side, and in relatively decent shape too, considering what happened. Seems to me, Danny, that if you managed to get out of that almighty mess in one piece, then Llewellyn's right, you're definitely someone worth having onside.'

His smooth talk is really starting to unnerve me.

'Look, just cut the crap. What do you want?'

Ankin grins at me, and yet again avoids answering the question. 'We were just talking about how much the world's changed, and how it feels like everything's become smaller and more confined. Our needs and priorities have changed too. As a race I think we've reached a pivotal point in our development and—'

'Spare me the bullshit and get to the point.'

He sighs. 'I think we've reached a make-or-break moment. You told me that all you know now is Lowestoft. Well, let me broaden your horizons a little. When the enemy refugee camps imploded, then exploded, much of the country became uninhabitable. Virtually every major city centre was destroyed, most of them completely vaporised, some by us, some by them. As you'd expect, the radiation and pollution has spread since then, even more people have died, and even more of the land has been contaminated. I've been trying to coordinate what's left, and ascertain how much of the country is actually still inhabitable.'

'And how much is that?'

'Less than you might have thought. It's pretty much just the extremities now: apart from Edinburgh and Glasgow, much of Scotland escaped the worst of it, and parts of North Wales are clear too. Cornwall and some parts of Devon are liveable, but pretty much everything else, from Leeds and Manchester down all the way to the south coast, is dead. Now all that might not be as big a problem as it sounds, because as you've probably noticed, there aren't that many of us left alive. There's no way of knowing exactly how many, but our best estimations are a million at most, and maybe only half that number. So what I'm trying to do is unify the remaining population and bring it together.'

'Good luck with that.' I laugh, not even bothering to try and hide my scepticism. 'You'd be the first person in history to manage it.'

He ignores me and continues, 'The radiation makes travel difficult at best, and getting cross-country is nigh on impossible. You either need to fly, go the long way around, or choose one of the less polluted regions and move through it damn fast. Sahota's actually over on the west coast as we speak, negotiating with the Welsh.'

'Negotiating with the Welsh! Bloody hell, it all sounds a bit tribal.'

'And that's exactly how things will be if we don't do something about it right now. Someone needs to make a stand, try to bring some order to what's left before we lose complete control, and that's why I'm here. London and the South-East is dead, but where we are now, from the outer-most edge of the East Midlands across to the east coast, and from Hull right down to Cambridge, is one of the largest inhabitable areas remaining. We're in control of most of it now.'

'Try telling that to Hinchcliffe.'

'Exactly, and that's my problem. We've known about him for a while and until now we've been happy to let him get on with what he's been doing. He's managed to build up quite a little empire for himself.'

'He has, and he's not about to let anyone come in and take it over. You do realise that, don't you?'

'Of course I do, and I wouldn't expect any different. A man in his position is naturally going to want to protect his investment, not give up power – but I didn't actually say anything about taking over. The best option for all concerned would be to get him onside.'

'I can tell you now, that's never going to happen. Hinchcliffe's not much of a team player.'

'I do get that impression. Ultimately it'll be his decision. It's true that people like him don't tend to give a damn about anyone or anything else. I'm not naïve, Danny; I do know what I'm dealing with here.'

'Are you sure?' I ask, thinking he's actually got no bloody idea quite how mad Hinchcliffe is.

'We used to call them dictators,' Ankin says with a wry

laugh. 'But my focus is the people, not Hinchcliffe. I gather there are a lot of people in and around Lowestoft who need help. We are thousands strong, with more firepower than—'

'I know you used to be in government, but that doesn't mean anything now. I know exactly how Hinchcliffe will react when you turn up. He's only out for himself, and he won't *ever* recognise any authority but his own. You turn up and you'll just be walking straight into a fight to the death, no matter how many soldiers or guns you've got.'

'You're probably right,' Ankin says nonchalantly, 'but like I said, Hinchcliffe isn't the only person trying to carve out a place in the history books for himself. We have dealt successfully with situations like this before. At any rate we have to start somewhere, and we have to make a stand.'

History books – now there's a quaint, old-fashioned notion. People don't bother with *any* books these days, much less those which are concerned with our redundant lives before the war. Ankin just told me he wasn't naïve, but I can't help wondering if he really does appreciate how deep-rooted the damage inflicted on the population as a whole has been. I look at him across the table. His face is frustratingly difficult to read.

'Was that your plane that flew over Lowestoft?'

'Yes.'

'And what exactly was the point of that?'

'Threefold, I suppose. First, it was a signal for Llewellyn – and his excuse, if you like – to come to Norwich and rendezvous with us. We've had to carefully coordinate our arrival here.'

'Coordinate with whom?'

'Llewellyn for a start, and various other people too. The plane was the easiest way of letting him know it was time. Second, I wanted to stir up the people of Lowestoft, get them thinking. I thought a fly-past by a small unarmed plane would be enough of a distraction to make them ask questions, but not enough for them to misconstrue it as a threat. I didn't want to bring out the big guns, not just yet.'

'And the third reason?'

'To get Hinchcliffe thinking too.'

'You certainly managed that. Fucker was livid – he killed my friend just because you got him all riled up.'

'That really wasn't my intention. I just wanted him to realise he's not the only one left with any influence around here.'

'He's the only one with any influence in Lowestoft.'

'That's true, at the moment, and say what you like about him, he's managed to turn the town into the largest and most established community we've yet come across.'

'It's hardly a community,' I mutter, 'more like several thousand people who happen to be in the same place. It's nothing more.'

'Okay, wrong choice of word, perhaps: settlement, then – but whatever you want to call it, he's managed to keep a lot of people in order.'

'The fighters are scared of him, and everyone else is scared of the fighters, that's all.'

'And what about you?'

'I'd be lying if I said I wasn't scared of what Hinchcliffe might do. I've seen him in action. He genuinely doesn't give a shit about anyone else, and he'll do whatever he thinks he needs to to make his point. He always says everything boils down to the two Fs – food and fear.'

'I don't necessarily agree with that, but I know where he's coming from.'

'So how come you know so much about Lowestoft?'

'We've had people in and around the place for a while. Llewellyn risked a hell of a lot for us, and there were several others. Do you know Neil Casey?'

'I thought he was dead,' I tell him, remembering the day I spent grave-digging, desperately trying to see if one of the bodies I was helping to bury was Hinchcliffe's missing foot-soldier.

'He wasn't this morning.' Ankin chuckles to himself. 'Last time I spoke to him he was still very much alive.'

'Hinchcliffe sent me to look for him in Southwold. Was that place your doing too?'

'Southwold was initially down to John Warner, nothing to do with us, but I'd been talking to John for some time. We shared a lot of ideals, and we were doing what we could to help. He was definitely on the right track.'

'And I assume you know what happened there?'

For a moment the politician's bland face changes and he looks grim. 'What Hinchcliffe did in Southwold was unforgivable. We were hoping to use the place as a staging post instead of here. It was a difficult one to call, and I got it wrong. I didn't intend John and his people to get dragged in like that. Hinchcliffe was obviously under the impression that Southwold was a threat.'

'He saw it as a threat to his authority, nothing more than that.' No point saying anything about the part I played in Warner's downfall. Even though Hinchcliffe manoeuvred me, I do feel partially responsible for what happened.

'The thing is, Danny,' he continues, the tone in his voice suddenly changing, 'what Hinchcliffe's doing won't last. He's going to run out of supplies and ideas eventually, then he's screwed.'

'I know. I've tried talking to him about it.'

'And when people like Hinchcliffe realise their number's up, they never go quietly. But what happens next in Lowestoft is crucial, and we can't afford to fail. We're in danger of losing so much of what we used to have, you know? All that knowledge, technology and experience . . . it's too important just to throw it all away. We'll end up living in caves again.'

'So what exactly are you planning – and more important, why are you talking to me?'

'Believe it or not, I didn't know anything about you until we arrived here – you're a bit of an unexpected bonus, Danny. You're someone who's had unprecedented access to Hinchcliffe. You know how he thinks and how he works. Long and short? I want your help – because, in answer to your first question, as soon as all my people are in position, we're heading for Lowestoft. Thousands of people are suffering there, and I've got a duty to try and help them.'

'And what about Hinchcliffe?'

'Well that's the million-dollar question, isn't it? We'd been planning to infiltrate and get rid of him—'

'—which is what he did to Thacker, the guy who was in charge before him.'

'I know.'

'But if you do that, you'll be operating down at his level, and that makes you no better than him.'

'I'm well aware of that too, and it was a price I was willing to pay to get rid of him – but it doesn't have to be that way now.'

'Why not?'

'Because we're going to give Hinchcliffe a choice, make him think he's still in control. Who knows, if he plays ball with us, he still could be.'

'And what if he tells you to fuck off?'

'Then that's up to him. Like I said, we're going to give him a choice. He can let us in to help strengthen and support the town—'

'Or?' I press when Ankin pauses.

'—or he can get out and leave running the place to me and my people.'

'That's never going to happen.'

'It will if we handle him right. And that's why I'm so pleased that Llewellyn introduced me to you.' He pauses ominously, but I already know what's coming next. 'I want you to go back into Lowestoft and make sure Hinchcliffe is aware of all his options. Make him see the bigger picture.'

244

'No way! You're out of your fucking mind if you think I'm going to be the one to go back there to tell him to pack his bags and get out!'

'No, no,' Ankin says, holding up his hands defensively, 'that's not what I'm asking at all. I want you to go back there as someone who knows him, not as a messenger from me. Just tell him about us – give him chance to get used to the idea before we arrive. Come on, Danny, can't you see how much easier that'll be? I've got thousands of people waiting to march into Lowestoft, and when they see us, most of the people who are already there will immediately switch sides. It'll be Hinchcliffe and a few hundred fighters against everybody else, and they won't stand a chance if it comes to a pitched battle. So let's you and me do all we can to try and stop that battle from ever starting, okay?'

33

I've been kept under close watch since my meeting with Ankin first thing this morning. I was taken into a small office on the first floor of the museum under the pretence of waiting to see the main man again a few hours ago, but the longer I've been left here, the more obvious it's become that this is just a holding cell. It's getting dark now, and I don't think they're going to let me out until it's time to go back to Lowestoft. The door's not locked, but every time I look out I see people swarming around on the landing, usually Chandra or Swales taking it in turn to keep watch.

Llewellyn says that Ankin is expecting to rendezvous with thousands more of his people outside Lowestoft, and from what I've already seen I've no doubt it'll happen. As soon as they're in position, Llewellyn said, Ankin is also expecting me to trot off into town and explain to Hinchcliffe that he needs to step aside and let someone else take over the town. Like fuck. Hinchcliffe's not going to play ball and neither am I. I'm getting out of here.

My body clock is ticking fast and I can't afford to waste any more time. My days are numbered, and I really couldn't give a damn about any of these people and their stupid, pointless power struggles. It's exactly the same bullshit politics I used to try and avoid getting tangled up in at work, but here the stakes are immeasurably higher. Except for me. My fate is already sealed. Nothing any of them do will make any difference to me now, so why should I care? What does it matter to me who's left running Lowestoft or the whole damn country for that matter? Sitting here alone in the dark over the last couple of hours I've reached an important conclusion: I'm not going to waste the little time I have left on anyone else – Hinchcliffe, Ankin, Llewellyn, Peter Sutton, Joseph Mallon . . . fuck the lot of them. I don't care where I end up, I'm just going to get as far away from everyone and everything else as I possibly can.

I've waited hours for a chance to make my move, and now it's time. Both Chandra and Swales have gone and the landing is clear. Shivering with cold, I fasten up my coat and swing my rucksack onto my shoulders. I carefully push the door open just a crack, suddenly feeling like a character in one of those old spy movies I'd forgotten about until now. When I'm sure the corridor outside is empty, I take a few tentative steps out of the room then stop and listen. I can hear a myriad of muffled noises coming from outside and the floors below, but up here it's silent and I keep going.

A sudden movement out of the corner of my eye makes me freeze. At the end of the short landing, where this stunted corridor opens out into the main part of the museum viewing area, a lone boot is sticking out from behind a wall. I creep closer until I'm near enough to peer around the corner, and I see that it's Swales. The dumb bastard is fast asleep on guard duty. Other than him there's no-one else on the rest of this level. It's almost dark – the only illumination coming from the very last light of day seeping in through grimy glass panels in the ceiling high above my head. I stick close to the wall, clinging to the shadows, and cautiously edge along, aiming for the staircase I climbed with Llewellyn when we first got here. I'll go down to the ground floor then try to find another way out. Hardly any of these people know me, so it shouldn't be too hard to slip past them. Hinchcliffe always says I have a face that's easy to forget but that doesn't stop me feeling like the centre of attention. There's bound to be a window I can climb through somewhere. Failing that, there'll be emergency exits and fire escapes I can use. If I can retrace my steps through the dead streets of Norwich, I'll be able to find somewhere to shelter and hide until it's safe. Ankin's march into Lowestoft is going to happen with or without me so, by this time tomorrow, this ruin of a city should be deserted again. If I stay off the roads and vary my route, I'll be as hard to find as Ankin's damn aeroplane.

I reach the top of the stairs and peer down over the ornately carved balustrade. I can hear voices below, but it's hard to be sure exactly where they're coming from. I take a few, hesitant steps down, then stop to listen again. The voices are moving away and getting quieter. I think my way is clear. I start moving again, almost down to the first floor now, concentrating on trying to get to—

'Where the fuck d'you think you're going?'

The wide staircase makes the voice sound directionless and it's impossible to see much in the gloom. I look around me and see nothing and no-one, but then the thump of heavily booted feet thundering down the steps after me makes me look up. Shit, it's Healey, Llewellyn's driver. I try to make a run for it but he's faster than me and he anticipates my movements. He stretches out his long, muscular arm and grabs my rucksack. I try to slip out of it, figuring I'll be faster without it anyway, but he yanks me back before I can get my arms out of the straps and I fall backwards, the back of my head cracking against the marble stairs.

'Llewellyn!' Healey shouts, his voice filling the building. 'Get up here!'

He starts dragging me back up. His strength is immense and he pulls me up the stairs like I'm a rag doll. I kick my legs and try to grab hold of the hand rail but everything's happening too fast and I can barely get back up onto my feet. Llewellyn pounds up the stairs towards me, emerging from the darkness like a wild animal charging, face full of fury and rage.

'Who was on guard?' he yells as he thunders past me, grabbing one of my bag straps and helping Healey haul me up.

'Swales,' Healey immediately answers, not about to take any of the flack.

We reach the top of the stairs and I finally get my feet back down and stand up straight. Llewellyn lets go but Healey keeps hold of me and throws me back towards my cell. Swales lumbers towards us, a panicked expression on his still half-asleep face.

'Sorry, Llewellyn,' he starts to say, 'I couldn't help it. I didn't mean to—'

Llewellyn doesn't let him finish his sentence. He punches him in the mouth – a short, sharp, stinging jab – and then, when he hits the deck, he starts repeatedly kicking him in the belly, sending him sliding further back across the floor each time his boot makes contact.

'You useless fucker,' he screams at him as the pounding continues. 'They'll have our bollocks if he gets away.'

Healey pushes me back into the office again and slams the door shut. I try to open it but he's holding it from the other side. I can hear Llewellyn yelling orders, but his words are drowned out by the noise of someone dragging furniture across the landing to block me in. When the noise finally stops I can hear him again.

'Go get Ankin. He needs to talk to this freak and put the little bastard straight.'

34

I'm trapped. I've been over every inch of this damn room and the only way out is the door I came through, now blocked by some immovable piece of furniture, and the window, which is bolted shut. In desperation, I grab the fire extinguisher, which is the heaviest thing I can find, and throw it at the glass, which shatters, filling the room with noise and allowing the bitter wind to gust in. The already low temperature plummets. I knock out the last shards of glass and lean out, but I'm too high up and it's a sheer drop onto concrete. There aren't even any drainpipes or ledges I could use to help me climb down.

I turn back to the door at the sound of voices and fast-approaching footsteps. I've got my knife ready this time and I'm gripping it tightly. It's my life, what's left of it, and now I'm ready to fight. The office door is yanked open and Chris Ankin storms in. I flinch away from the bright lamp he's carrying. As my eyes adjust I catch a glimpse of Llewellyn and several others crowded outside before the door's slammed shut again. The harsh illumination makes Ankin's weathered face look severe and intense. He's much older than me, and physically smaller, but the sheer force of his entrance makes me cower back until I can't get any further away.

'Put that bloody knife down, you useless fucker,' he spits at me. So, no more smooth talk then. He puts the lamp down on the edge of a desk, then leans on his walking stick and glares across the room at me, breathing hard. 'I don't think you quite understand,' he says, pointing at me accusingly. 'Or perhaps I did not make myself completely clear earlier: whether you like it or not, you are going back to Lowestoft, and you are going to deliver my message to Hinchcliffe.'

All that smarmy vote-winning pretence has been dropped now, and for the first time I'm seeing the real Chris Ankin. I've never been good at dealing with people in positions of authority, and I feel as anxious now as I do when I'm with Hinchcliffe. But there's an important difference here that I'm quick to remember: Ankin has no hold over me. He needs me more than I need him. I'm a dead man walking, and what happens in Lowestoft is of no consequence to me any more.

'Why exactly should I help you?' I ask him. 'What are you going to do if I don't do what you say? Kill me?'

He moves towards me again menacingly. 'Here's my position, McCoyne,' he says, virtually spitting out each word. '*Everything* hinges on us getting into Lowestoft and keeping the structure of the town intact. You'll help because I've told you you'll help, and if I have to march you in there with a loaded gun held to your head, then that's what I'll do.'

This isn't the way I wanted it to be, but so be it. I have nothing left – no family, no friends, no life, no possessions that matter . . . and I just can't be bothered arguing any more. The harder I try and fight, the more I lose. 'Okay,' I say, 'kill me now then.'

'What?'

'I won't do it, Ankin. I'm tired of fuckers like you pushing me around, telling me what to do. You're going to have to kill me, because I'm not going back to Lowestoft.'

'Don't be so bloody stupid,' he says. 'What's that going to achieve?'

'Absolutely nothing – which is exactly what me talking to Hinchcliffe is going to achieve. I've tried to make you understand that the man is a complete fucking *psychopath*. There is not a hope in hell that he's going to shuffle off into the background and let you take over everything he's built up in Lowestoft.'

Ankin's a sensible man, I'm sure of it – regardless of the games he plays, and the outdated political interests he still nurtures, I know he's no fool. He looks straight at me and I can see him silently weighing up his limited options. He's in a crap position to try and bargain with me, and even though he has no idea how hopeless my personal situation really is, I think he knows it.

'Hinchcliffe relies on you, doesn't he?'

'He's a nasty, resourceful bastard who doesn't rely on anyone. He uses people, that's all – and if I'm not around, he'll just find someone else.'

'You think? That's not the impression I get from Llewellyn. He seems to think you're different. Tell me, how long have you been there?'

'A few months.'

'And how did you come to Hinchcliffe's attention?'

'I led him to some Unchanged nests, helped him to hunt them out.'

'So you've been pretty valuable to him?'

'I wouldn't go that far – and definitely not now the Unchanged are all gone.'

'But he obviously still needs you, otherwise he wouldn't have sent you out here with Llewellyn. No offence, but you're not the strongest-looking fighter I've ever seen.'

'None taken.'

'Look,' he says, sounding weary, 'I'm going to lay things on the line for you. You're going back into Lowestoft tomorrow, whether you like it or not.'

'Like fuck I am—'

'You don't have any choice. Like I said, taking the town is of paramount importance.'

'Spare me the rhetoric. I won't go.'

'You will: this is bigger than you and me, Danny, much bigger.'

He starts pacing the small room, running his fingers through his shock of white hair, and he's obviously seething with anger and frustration. But the strangest thing is that, suddenly, I feel nothing – no fear or apprehension . . . absolutely nothing. But I'm still curious. Something still doesn't ring true.

'I don't get it.'

'Don't get what?' he says.

'I don't get why you reckon you need Lowestoft so badly – it's just a modest little town, for crying out loud. Why not just move on to the next place?'

Ankin walks to the broken window. It's dark outside now; I doubt he can see much. But still he stares out for an uncomfortably long time.

'Okay,' he finally says, 'I'll level with you. Everything I told you earlier? I didn't give you the full picture.'

I wonder what the hell he's going to say next. He's got no reinforcements, perhaps? That there's an even bigger army out there hunting *him* down?

'It's the politician in me,' he says quietly. 'I can't help trying to give everything the right spin, get my point across – it's hard to break the habits of a lifetime, you know?'

'Try.'

He sits down on the edge of the desk. 'Things are worse than I implied. I just didn't want to put too much pressure on you at once.'

'Worse? How could things possibly be any worse?'

He sighs deeply, then starts, 'Sahota's not negotiating in Wales. Last I heard, he was fighting to get a foothold in the north of the country. We haven't had any contact from him for a while.'

'How long?'

'About three months.'

'*Jesus.*'

'I told you that Devon and Cornwall were probably liveable, but the fact is the contamination's so bad we haven't even been able to get down there. We don't hold out much hope of anyone being left alive there now. You know how it all happened: the refugee camps drew people into the cities, and where the Unchanged went—'

'—we followed.'

'Exactly. Most of our people were drawn inland, towards the fighting. In Scotland, Glasgow and Edinburgh were taken out, two bombs within an hour of each other, and the cumulative effect of that was devastating – most of the country's uninhabitable now. In fact, the only parts of Scotland we think might be habitable are the bits where no one lived in the first place – and if there is anyone left, they're going to have a hell of a job living through the winter.'

I'm trying to process his words. 'So you're telling me the whole country is dead?'

'I'm saying that this area is far more important than I originally led you to believe.'

'You're saying that this is it?' Now I'm beginning to see why he's in such a state.

He pauses before answering, 'Pretty much. There were a few other towns, but not any more – it's all so fragile, Danny; all it takes is a few cracks to show and they fall apart.'

'*Bloody hell!*'

'So you can understand why I need to get into Lowestoft, can't you? It's the largest centre of population there is.'

'On this side of the country?' I'm still hoping I didn't quite understand.

'No, in the whole bloody country.'

'Fuck me. You're not joking, are you? Lowestoft . . .'

'I'm pretty sure there are more people left alive than there are just in Lowestoft, but they're scattered over massive areas. There's nowhere else like Lowestoft; it's probably the biggest concentration of people left alive, and that makes it unique. And anyone who's left out on their own over the next few months is going to find it bloody hard to survive without regular food supplies. It's going to be an extreme winter because of the bombs—'

'But if you're as well supported as you say you are, why not just take Hinchcliffe out and take the damn place by force?' I ask, rubbing my head.

'It's an option, and I haven't ruled it out, but it wouldn't necessarily be as easy as it sounds. First of all, Hinchcliffe and his fighters will do all they can to protect themselves. Second, remove him, and some other tough bastard will just rise up and take his place. If we go in mob-handed from the word go there's a real danger we could bring the whole damn place crashing down around us. Then what? Having you here has given us an unexpected opportunity to try to negotiate, break this cycle of violence. We all need Lowestoft intact – we need the people to survive, the buildings to survive, Hinchcliffe's food stocks to survive—'

I break in: 'He won't tell you where the food is – no one knows but him.'

'I'm sure he won't, but that just further underlines my point. This is our very last chance.' Ankin's words have become a bit of a blur; I'm struggling to come to terms with the fact that the run-down little seaside town on the east coast, the place I've been trapped for the last few months, is now the most important place in the country – maybe even the new capital.

'So what about you?' I ask him. 'Why are you here now?'

'We've been on the road for most of the time – we were originally based near Hull, but that wasn't an ideal location; the pollution levels up there became too dangerous. And with the numbers of people we've been trying to coordinate, it just became impractical. We needed to find somewhere safer and more central, and that's Lowestoft.'

'So that's your real reason for coming here, is it? You're a king without a kingdom.'

'It's really not, although I can see how you could look at it like that. The fact is, it's less about the kingdom and more about the subjects. We need *numbers* if we're to get this country functioning again, if we're going to be able to salvage anything from the ruins of what we've all lost. We can criticise his methods, but Hinchcliffe's managed to do just that – but from everything I've heard, he's only interested in feathering his own nest, and everyone else can go to hell.'

'That's pretty much it.'

Ankin looks down at his boots, all the bullshit and spin suddenly knocked out of him. He looks defeated. 'We *have* to do this, Danny. This might look like a minor skirmish in comparison to the things we've all seen and done over the last year, like two tribes scrapping over a strip of land, but it isn't, it's so much more than that. Everything I'm hearing tells me Lowestoft can't continue to survive the way it is, and at the same time my people can't survive without Lowestoft. If we don't make this happen, then this country will die. This is our very last chance. The pressure's not just on your shoulders, but you can make a crucial difference here. You're in a unique position to help stop our slide back into anarchy.'

'I think you might be too late.'

'Well, I don't, and while there's breath in my body and even the slightest of chances, I'm going to do everything I can to make it happen.'

I have to give him his due, he's good, and I'm almost buying into his story, but it's all irrelevant to me now: everything I ever cared about is gone and nothing matters.

But Ankin has one more card to play. 'I assume you don't owe Hinchcliffe anything,' he says, his voice flat and unemotional now, 'so what could I do to make you help me?'

'There's nothing,' I say, truthfully. 'All I have now is time, and I'm rapidly running out of that. I just want to spend the days or weeks I've got left on my own, no more fighting, no more bullshit politics and exploitation, no pressure . . . No offence, Ankin, but you can fight your own battle with Hinchcliffe tomorrow.'

I turn to walk away, wanting to end this pointless conversation, but a gust of cold air hits me and before I know it I'm doubled over, coughing my guts up. I manage to turn away and avoid the embarrassment of showering Ankin with bloody spittle.

'You don't sound so good,' he says when I finally stop. 'Come to mention it, you don't look so good either.'

'I'm sick.'

'You don't say. Been suffering long?'

'Since the bombs.'

'What, some sort of cancer is it?'

'That's what I'm told.'

'And what are you doing about it?'

I collapse into the chair, panting hard. When I get my breath back I reply, 'What can I do? "Live with it till you die from it", that's the advice the doctor gave me.'

'Must frustrate you though, knowing that before all this happened, there might have been some drugs you could have taken, or something else you could have done?'

'It breaks my fucking heart. It's this bloody war that's made me sick.'

'I agree, and that just reinforces everything I've been trying to say to you. It's so important we finish the work we've started here, try to put what's left of this broken country back together. I don't suppose medical care is very high up on Hinchcliffe's list of priorities, is it?'

'He doesn't give a shit unless he's the one who's hurting.'

Ankin watches me as I cough again, then wipe my mouth. I instinctively hide the smear of blood on the back of my hand.

'This country needs you, Danny.'

'Well, I don't need it.'

'Look, I'm not promising anything, but I could have a word with a few people we've got here with us. Most of my medics are elsewhere right now, but we do have a doctor on site. He won't be able to operate, or come up with a miracle cure or anything like that, but I'm guessing you're probably well past that stage anyway. But he might be able to make the time you've got left a little easier.'

'Are you bribing me?'

He grins. 'I suppose I am – but it's a genuine offer, Danny: you help me, and I'll help you.'

'And you think your people *can* help me?'

'I'll be honest with you: I doubt we can save you, but I'm pretty sure we can make things a little easier – either give you a while longer, or make the wait a little shorter, whichever you choose. You interested?'

'Not really.'

'Come on, Danny,' he says, his frustration clear, 'just talk to Hinchcliffe for me. They say he listens to you.'

'Hinchcliffe doesn't listen to *anyone*.'

'You underestimate yourself.'

'No, you overestimate me.'

'That's not what I'm hearing. Look, there's nothing you can do or say to change the fact that we're marching on Lowestoft tomorrow, and that includes you. Go on ahead and talk to him for me, pave the way for us, and I'll guarantee your safety.'

'And how are you going to do that?'

'Leave it with me. Llewellyn will travel with you; he'll get you in and he'll get you out again, and after that the time you have left is your own, I promise. A few more hours, one meeting with Hinchcliffe, then I swear you're free to go.'

35

I t's pitch-black, the middle of the night, and rain is coming in through the broken window when Llewellyn barges in and hauls me up onto my feet. He doesn't say a word as he pushes me downstairs and shoves me out through the museum's main entrance. He leads me through the muddy quagmire outside.

'Time for your check-up,' he says, then he pushes me into the back of a long red and white lorry and slams and locks the door behind me.

It's as dark inside the lorry as it is out. As I work my way by touch along its length, looking for another way out, I realise it's some kind of medical vehicle, laid out like a makeshift mobile surgery, maybe one of those blood dona- tion units which used to come to the council offices back home every so often. I used to give blood just for the free cup of tea and an hour off work.

I'm drenched and shivering. The windows are all welded shut, and there's no other obvious way out other than a skylight above me. Groaning with effort, I manage to drag a metal box across the floor, but it's not high enough, and the tips of my fingers barely reach the ceiling. I'm looking around for something else to stand on when the door flies open again and I look around to see a balding, willowy man climbing into the unit, using the handrail to both support himself and haul himself up. He looks at me with a mix of bewilderment and disinterest, then calmly closes the door again and hangs his lamp from a hook on the ceiling.

'Danny McCoyne?' he asks as he removes a scarf and two

outdoor jackets, then puts on a heavily stained white overcoat.

'Yes.'

'Sit down please, Mr McCoyne, and do stop trying to escape. There's really no need. I'm actually trying to help you. It's bad enough that I have to come here at this hour, so let's not make things any harder than they need be, hm?'

I am taken aback for a moment by being called Mr McCoyne for the first time in as long as I can remember. I obviously have no other option, so I do as he says.

He takes off his half-moon glasses which have steamed up, and cleans them on his grubby lapel. Something about his manner, the way he carries himself, suggests he's well educated. In comparison to Rona Scott, who is a brutal butcher, he's a bloody angel. I visualise this man standing amidst the carnage on the battlefield, carefully dissecting Unchanged rather than just hacking them apart like everyone else.

'Mr Ankin has asked me to have a look and see if there's anything we can do for you. How long have you been sick?'

I think for a moment, then admit, 'I don't know when it started; it's only over the last few weeks that things have got really bad.'

He nods thoughtfully, then carries out a physical examination. He does pretty much the same things Rona Scott did, but he makes me feel like a patient, not a slab of meat, and after he's checked my pulse, listened to my heart and looked into my eyes, he asks me about allergies and medication – all the other questions doctors used to ask, back in the day. I'm feeling nervous suddenly, and without thinking I start asking questions back, making pointless small talk to calm myself down.

'Have you been with Ankin long?'

'Several months.'

'And where have you been based?'

'In this unit, mostly,' he answers as he prods and pokes at my gut with freezing-cold, elegant fingers.

'Have you seen much of the rest of the country?'

'Too much,' he says. He's obviously in no mood to chat.

'Ankin was telling me about Hull. Were you there?'

'For a while, until the fighting.'

'What fighting? Ankin said—'

'Look, I know you're anxious, Mr McCoyne, but I'm trying to work, so I would be grateful if you would be quiet and stop asking questions.'

The doctor shoves his hand down the neck of his jumper and pulls out a bunch of keys on a chain. He studies them carefully, holding each one up to the light, then picks one and unlocks a metal cabinet. He mooches through the clinking glass bottles and phials that fill the shelves before selecting one. He peers at its label through glasses which are now perched perilously close to the end of his nose.

'You're obviously very important to Mr Ankin,' he says, rejecting one bottle and picking up another. He laughs wryly. 'They don't just dish this stuff out to every Tom, Dick or Harry these days – do you have any idea how many people are walking around out there in the same kind of condition as you are?'

'I don't know how many people are walking around out there full stop,' I answer quickly.

'Fewer than you'd expect,' he says. 'Now I'm no expert, but I've seen an abnormal level of cancers and deaths from—'

'Wait a second, go back a step: what do you mean, you're no expert?'

He finally settles on a third bottle half-filled with clear liquid and draws a syringeful from it.

'I'm no expert, but I'm no idiot either – the truth is, there aren't any experts left. This time last year I was researching genetics at Birmingham University, cutting up fruit flies, writing papers and delivering lectures to students who couldn't have been any less interested if they'd tried. I'd originally planned to go into general medicine – I did my degree, got the basic training out of the way – then I changed my mind and my specialism. So no, I'm not a complete novice, Mr McCoyne, if that's what you're worried about. But you know how these things have a habit of turning out: since the war started I've spent most of my time patching up soldiers so they can keep fighting – I suppose you'd call it learning on the job. It makes a change to be asked to do something different.'

'But you do know what you're doing?'

'I know enough. Listen, I may not be an oncologist, but you're not going to find anyone better to help you today. Anyway, no one's forcing you to have this treatment. Just leave if you want to, and we'll say no more about it. I would offer to get you a second opinion, but mine's the only opinion left!' He chuckles to himself.

I don't see the funny side myself. 'It's okay. Just do it.'

'You're a lucky boy,' he says, as he checks there are no air bubbles in the syringe.

'I don't feel lucky. What is that stuff, anyway?'

'Steroids; the drugs'll keep you going for a while longer – won't do anything to fight the disease, but they'll mask the symptoms for a time.'

'How long?'

'A day, maybe two.'

There's a lull in the conversation as I peel back various layers of sodden clothing to expose the top of my right arm. 'And what about me?'

'What about you?'

'How long do you think I've got left?'

I've asked the question before I've realised what I'm saying, and I immediately wish I could rewind time and retract it. It's too late. He looks down at me again and frowns, then returns his attention to preparing the drugs for injection.

'Bear in mind,' he says, hunting for a swab and a clean

dressing, 'that I don't have any medical notes for you – not that anyone has any notes any more. So my estimations could be way out. This is based purely on my gut instinct, and several other recent cases I've seen, nothing else, and you also have to remember that we're going into the coldest part of winter, and I doubt any of us are eating properly, so we're all going to be more susceptible to—'

'I understand all of that,' I interrupt. 'Just tell me what you think.'

'I'm afraid I don't think you have long, Mr McCoyne. I don't think you have long at all. From what I can see, it looks pretty well advanced.'

He shoves the needle into my skin, but I don't feel a thing. He drops the syringe into a plastic bin, then picks up another. He grips the same arm tight, then injects me again. This time it hurts.

'What the hell's that? Jesus, how much of that stuff are you putting into me?'

'Not steroids this time,' he says, his voice beginning to fade. 'This one's a special request from Messrs Ankin and Llewellyn.'

36

'm moving . . . being thrown from side to side . . . I open
my eyes a bit and find myself in the front passenger seat of
a van – might be the same one which brought me to
Norwich. Llewellyn's sitting next to me. I pretend to still be
asleep while I try and work out what's going on. Now I'm
more awake I realise I feel less ill than usual – could it be
that the drugs Ankin's doctor gave me are actually having
a positive effect? I certainly feel a little stronger – and that
makes me realise how sick I really am. A pothole in the road
causes the van to lurch, I hit my head against the window
and sit up. Llewellyn looks across and sees that I'm awake.

'Fuck me, you took your time coming round,' he says. 'I
was starting to get worried. Thought Ankin's quack had
given you an overdose.'

Overdose? *Injections*. It starts coming back to me. I sit up
and try to rub my eyes, but as I do so I realise my wrist hurts
and my hand is yanked back when I try to lift it. Fuckers
have handcuffed me to the van door. 'What's this for?'

'It's just a precaution,' Llewellyn says. 'I didn't want you
doing a runner on me. Now shut up, wake up and get ready.'

'Why, where are we?'

'About five miles out of Lowestoft.'

I sit up quick in panic and look around. He's right: we're
on the A146 heading back towards Lowestoft, and we're
not alone. There are several vehicles ahead of us, and many
more behind: Ankin's army, all easily identified by the
circular red and white insignia painted on each of them.
The crude designs vary in size and shape from machine to

machine, but their simple aim is achieved – these markings clearly differentiate them from us.

'So what's the plan?' I ask. 'I assume there is a plan.'

'Ankin's troops are already in place,' Llewellyn explains, 'split between the north and south roads into town.'

'Already?'

'They're on the outskirts. There're thousands of them by all accounts, drawing the crowds away from Hinchcliffe's compound. It's called tactics, you see, McCoyne. These people are smart, and well tooled. They'll get the locals onside, and that'll leave just Hinchcliffe and the rest of his men for Ankin and us to deal with. I'll get you in, and while you're talking to Hinchcliffe, I'll be telling the others what's going on.'

'And what exactly am I supposed to be telling him?'

'Christ, you're bloody naïve, aren't you? It doesn't matter. Ankin doesn't give a shit what you say, and we all know exactly what Hinchcliffe's reaction's going to be.'

'So why are we even bothering?'

'To keep him busy – to distract him from what's actually happening.'

'You mean I'm just a decoy?' So much for all that 'Hinchcliffe listens to you' crap. Fucking politicians!

'That's about it.'

'*Shit!* Forget it – I won't do it.'

'Listen, mate, you're handcuffed to this van and we're not stopping until we're outside Hinchcliffe's front door. I'm delivering you personally. You don't have a lot of choice. Do what you've got to do, and if you behave yourself and Hinchcliffe doesn't do you in, I'll come back and get you out of there.'

'You bastard! I'll tell him what's happening – I'll tell him what you did.'

'Do you think I care? Hinchcliffe will be finished before nightfall, and you too, if you're not careful.'

'And what about Curtis and the rest of them? You reckon

they're all going to swap sides just like that, just because you tell them to?'

'Well, that's up to them, isn't it? But wouldn't you? Let's face it, with Ankin and all this lot on one side, and a shit like Hinchcliffe standing on his own on the other, there's no contest, is there?'

I'm not about to admit he has a point.

37

The A46 splits and we head south, down towards the bottom edge of Lowestoft, passing close to the housing estate where I've been living. The van is still surrounded by Ankin's vehicles, with a tank leading the way. Just over a mile to go now.

We're soon passing through the familiar shanty-town on the edge of Lowestoft, but it's a very different scene to what I've seen here before: more of Ankin's troops are busy forming a blockade on the A12 where the first of the underclass hordes are gathered. I understand that this is just one section of Ankin's so-called army, but there are far fewer of them than I'd imagined. I've been picturing endless columns of uniformed soldiers, armed to the teeth and backed up by huge amounts of firepower. The reality is unsettling: there are just hundreds where I expected to see thousands, two or three tanks where I expected to see twenty or thirty, and one small aeroplane . . .

'Where's everybody else?'

'I think this *is* everybody else,' Llewellyn replies under his breath, sounding as surprised as me.

I can see several ranks of these so-called soldiers blocking the road ahead. Each of them is carrying a makeshift riot shield. Coming the other way are the first of the underclass, and I watch a bizarre range of reactions taking place wherever the two sides collide. Some people are staying in their shelters, apparently too frightened to move, while others are grabbing whatever they can use as weapons, determined to protect themselves at all costs from these perceived invaders. I can see some are capitulating immediately, while others have started to fight like they've just uncovered an Unchanged nest. The vehicle leading the convoy begins to slow.

'What the fuck?' Llewellyn mumbles, as shocked by what he's seeing as I am.

We're about two-thirds of a mile from the compound now, just on the edge of the bulk of the underclass settlements. The convoy stops well behind the line of shield-bearing 'soldiers' and I sit up in my seat to try and get a better view of what's happening. I'm not sure I should have bothered: all over the place I can see that same range of reactions: some people are throwing themselves at the feet of Ankin's troops as if they're their saviours, about to pluck them up and whisk them away from the unending hell their lives have become, while others are attacking the invaders. I wonder if they're driven by some deranged desire to defend what little they have here because it's all they have left. Deeper in, people are beginning to turn against each other now; rifts are appearing as some want to fight and some want to surrender. There's no consensus and it's all turning into one unholy mess.

Llewellyn stops just short of the soldiers. Ankin's transporter, running behind us, has stopped too and I can see one of Ankin's lackeys running towards the van. Llewellyn opens the door and leans out to speak to him.

'What the fuck's going on?' he demands but the man just tell him to keep moving.

'The rest of us will hold position here until this has died down and we've had word that McCoyne's inside,' he says. 'Ankin says we'll start our advance in about an hour. Same goes for the columns waiting by the north gates.'

Columns? Christ, that's an overly ambitious term to be using if what's going on here is any indication. From where I'm sitting, there doesn't look to be much of a difference between Ankin's people moving one way and the ever-increasing crowds of underclass coming the other. In fact, other than the colour of their shirts the similarities are frightening.

The lackey disappears quickly and Llewellyn slams the door. Conversation over.

'Well?'

He doesn't answer me, just swerves around the back of the vehicle in front and carries on down the road. He blasts the horn as we approach the human blockade and a ragged split appears. We accelerate and drive through, narrowly avoiding a bunch of desperate underclass running the other way. A lump of concrete smashes against the window I'm staring out through, and I jump back in shock, thankful the glass is protected by a layer of heavy-duty wire mesh.

The last half-mile to the compound is easier. Looks like word of the approaching army hasn't yet reached the population, so most of them are going about their business (or lack of business) as normal, and they barely bat an eyelid as we drive past. It's early; I guess most of them are still in their shelters, delaying the start of yet another godawful day for as long as they can. Ahead of us I can see a group of scavengers, picking their way through a mountain of frost-covered refuse – an unplanned landfill site where a children's play area used to be – looking for scraps of food among the putrid rubbish. Others crowd around fires. Almost all of them ignore us.

We eventually reach the south gate across the bridge. Llewellyn glances across at me, then blasts the horn. A pair of eyes appear at a wire-mesh observation slot. They disappear again quickly and the gate is opened.

'Don't fuck this up,' he tells me. 'All you have to do is keep him busy. I'll give you an hour. And get this straight, freak: if you try anything stupid, I'll kill you. Ankin says you want out of here, so just do as you've been told and your freedom's yours.'

I don't respond – I barely even hear him, partially because I'm too scared to care, but also because something's not right here. The centre of Lowestoft feels different this morning. Though I'm sure there are more fighters on the streets than usual, and some of the Switchbacks are unexpectedly armed, the place is otherwise empty. Llewellyn tosses a set of keys over to me as we near the centre of the compound, but I drop them in the footwell and have to contort myself to reach them. Eventually I manage to unlock the handcuffs and for a moment I consider making a run for it, until in the wing mirror I catch a glimpse of a mob of people in the street behind us. There are even more of them ahead of us, on either side of the road. But Llewellyn appears oblivious.

'I'm going to leave you just short of the courthouse, okay?' Llewellyn says. 'Just keep him occupied. Do what you've been told and you'll be okay, understand?'

'I understand.'

He throws the van sharp right. 'We both want the same thing, McCoyne: we both want shot of Hinchcliffe. But I swear, if you—' He stops talking abruptly.

The road ahead is blocked, and I can see some familiar faces among the fighters advancing towards us. They surround the van and Curtis, Llewellyn's deputy, hammers on the glass.

Llewellyn winds his window down.

'Hinchcliffe wants to see both of you,' he says. Llewellyn looks across at me, a hint of nervousness in his eyes.

'Doesn't change anything; just makes things a little more complicated,' he mutters. 'I'll square things with this lot, you go in there and feed him as much bullshit as you can.'

Before I can argue he's out of the van and Curtis is opening my door and pulling me out.

Llewellyn tries to speak to Curtis. 'We need to talk.'

'Not interested. Get moving.'

'But, Curtis—'

'If you've got a problem, tell Hinchcliffe.'

Llewellyn starts to struggle, but he stops when the stunted

barrel of a shotgun is shoved into his ribs. We're led towards the courthouse, surrounded by a phalanx of fighters.

'Good morning,' someone shouts, and I look up to see Hinchcliffe standing on the roof of the courthouse. 'Bring them straight up here, boys,' he orders. 'I've been looking forward to this.'

38

We're escorted quickly through the building. Llewellyn is in front, marching with an arrogance which belies the nerves I know he must be feeling. The place is almost completely deserted, no one in the corridors or the usually busy courtroom hub. As we walk through Hinchcliffe's personal quarters most of the fighters drop away; in spite of everything, there are some places that are still sacrosanct. No matter what happens, Hinchcliffe's ivory tower remains intact. His rooms are in as bad a state as ever, looking like a particularly rebellious teenage boy's bedroom. There's a woman lying sprawled out on the floor. I only notice her when she yelps with pain when Curtis treads on her outstretched hand. She looks drugged; her face is blank – another private extension of Hinchcliffe's foul breeding programme, no doubt.

We go past the conference room, through another door I haven't entered before, to a dark staircase. I climb the first flight, Llewellyn right in front of me, turn through a hundred and eighty degrees to a shorter second flight. A final door leads us to a flat roof, where Hinchcliffe is waiting for us. Curtis doesn't stay, and now I have only Hinchcliffe and Llewellyn for company. Hinchcliffe pushes the door shut.

The roof is completely clear but for a deckchair and a pile of supplies. An empty beer can is blown across the asphalt by a gust of wind. It's damn cold up here, and it's starting to snow again. Llewellyn starts jabbering like a nervous kid, but KC is not listening. He walks away from us both, then he stops and turns back to face us.

'Find the plane?' he asks casually.

'I—' I start to answer, trying to come up with something, anything, to buy me a little time.

'Not you,' he interrupts. He points directly at Llewellyn. 'You.'

'Listen, Hinchcliffe,' Llewellyn begins, 'I just—'

'Wait a second,' he says, cutting across him, 'before you start, do me a favour and spare me the bullshit, okay? Honesty only on my rooftop, right?' He winks at me like a psychotic, old-school serial killer playing with his victims, taunting them before going in for the kill. Crazy bastard. He takes a sudden step forward and I take half a step back, not sure how much space there is between me and the edge of the roof.

'Hinchcliffe, you really need to listen,' Llewellyn says again.

'Do I? And why would that be, Llewellyn?'

His once-loyal fighter swallows hard and anxiously shifts his weight from foot to foot.

'There's an army coming,' he says, quickly changing his story to try and dig himself out of the hell-sized abyss he's suddenly gazing down into. 'Look, there was nothing I could do, mate. They found us and—'

I'd like to have heard the rest of his lies, but Llewellyn isn't even allowed to get to the end of his sentence, let alone to the punchline: out of the blue, Hinchcliffe drops his shoulder and charges into him, sending him flying over the edge of the roof. There's a moment of complete silence – everything, everywhere, stops suddenly – then I hear him hit the ground. There's no need to look, but I don't have any choice. Hinchcliffe puts one hand around my shoulder, grabs hold of my arm with his other hand and pushes me towards the edge. Below us, Llewellyn's body lies impaled on a spiked metal railing. The legs are dangling down and the head's cracked open on the concrete like an egg. 'Nasty,' Hinchcliffe says. Bastard.

Right now I don't give a shit about Llewellyn; I'm far

more concerned about what Hinchcliffe's going to do next. His hold tightens; for a moment I start to struggle, then I stop. What's the point? He's far stronger than I am, and there's nothing I can do – but if I am going down, I will try and take this fucker with me. He moves a hand to the back of my neck and pushes my head further forward until I'm leaning right over.

'Hinchcliffe—' I start, though I've absolutely no idea what I'm trying to say, but he suddenly pulls me back, spins me around, pushes me away and starts laughing.

'What the fu—?'

'Just playing with you!'

'What—?' I stagger away from him, trying to put maximum distance between us.

'Don't worry, mate,' he says, 'I know the score.'

'Do you?' Fuck, I wish I did. I'm still backing away, and he follows me towards the door which leads back down into the building.

'I knew that fucker was up to something,' he explains. 'I'd had my suspicions for a while, but all that business with the plane really sealed it for me. Did he think I was fucking stupid? Llewellyn was a hard bastard, and he had his uses, but he wasn't nearly as smart as he liked to think he was. I can't believe he really believed I'd buy all that bullshit about piling a few mates into a van and driving off to find that fucking aeroplane – give me some fucking credit. That was one of the reasons I sent you along: to screw things up for him, complicate whatever his crazy plan was.'

'*One* of the reasons?'

'Yeah. I knew there was a good chance you'd end up back here again, then you'd help me fill in the blanks. Our pal Llewellyn and whoever he was working for, they're not the only people indulging in the odd spot of subterfuge and double-crossing.' He's grinning like a maniac at his own cleverness. 'When I sent you lot out the other day, I sent Curtis after you. He followed you into Norwich, stuck around long enough to see this bloody army that's supposed to be coming, then came back and told me all about it.'

'But what he saw was only *part* of the army,' I stutter. 'There are reinforcements coming too, thousands of them.'

'And you believe that?'

'Why shouldn't I?'

'Because I've seen them, Danny. I've got people out there watching. They've told you thousands, but there are just a few hundred of them loitering at either end of town. Ask yourself, if they were as all-powerful and all-conquering as they'd have you believe, wouldn't they have conquered us already?'

'I suppose, but—'

'It's all fucking spin, mate. They're trying to make themselves look more impressive than they actually are. Who's behind all this?'

'Remember Chris Ankin?'

'Chris who?'

'He used to be in the government.'

Hinchcliffe thinks for a second, then his face lights up. 'Ah, I've got him. Work and Pensions, wasn't he? A fucking mouthpiece in a grey pinstripe suit, all talk and no bollocks. Pathetic. Thing about people like that,' he continues, 'is that you should never believe *anything* they tell you. There's always a hidden agenda.'

'Ankin was the one who spread the messages though, remember? The one who coordinated the attacks on the cities.'

'There you go, my point exactly: he's got you completely suckered in. And I thought you were smarter than that, Danny boy. Nobody really coordinated those attacks; they occurred naturally. What happened in the cities was inevitable, and only someone who'd either got something to prove or something to hide would try and take credit for them.'

He might have a point, but that's not important right now. 'Hinchcliffe, they're marching on Lowestoft.'

Hinchcliffe walks over to his deckchair in the centre of the roof. He sits down, picks up a pair of binoculars from beside the chair and starts scanning the horizon. 'So do you think should I be worried?'

'What kind of a question is that? Of course you should be fucking worried! Have you not been listening to anything I said? There's a fucking army marching on Lowestoft and they want you out – doesn't matter how big it is, it's a fucking army!'

He continues to stare into the distance, now looking in the direction from which Llewellyn and I approached a short while ago. Even from up here I can see signs of activity in the streets around the compound.

'Are they well armed?'

'They've got more than you have. Tanks and all sorts . . .'

'Probably not got a lot of ammo though.'

'So? A tank's a tank: they'll drive straight through the gates, Hinchcliffe!'

'And what's been the reaction of the good folk of Lowestoft so far?'

'Some were trying to fight, some just keeping out of the way – I guess most of them will just do whatever they're told to do. You know the score, Hinchcliffe – it's like Llewellyn used to say, always keep in with the bloke with the biggest gun.'

'So why here? That's the thing I don't understand. Why are they so interested in Lowestoft?' he asks. He genuinely has no idea; well, I hadn't worked it out either, so maybe it's not that surprising. 'Surely someone who's as powerful as this Ankin guy claims to be could take their pick of any-where, so why here? Are they just trying to prove a point?'

'They're here because this place is all that's left. Ankin reckons this is the pretty much the population centre of the country now.'

For a few seconds Hinchcliffe is quiet. He has a bemused expression on his face and I can see he's trying to come to terms with what I've just told him.

'Fuck me . . .'

'That's what I said when he told me, but I think it's true, Hinchcliffe: everywhere else is dead.'

'So why did you come back here, Danny? It's out of the frying pan into the fire for you, isn't it?'

'Because they made me,' is my immediate answer, 'and when I refused, the bastards drugged me and chained me up inside a van. I didn't have any choice. Believe me, I'd rather be anywhere but here.'

He looks puzzled. 'Strange. Why go to all that effort?'

'Because I'm supposed to be a decoy. I was supposed to keep you busy while Llewellyn spread the word around town that you were under attack.'

'And he thought that was going to work?' He starts laughing again. 'Bloody hell, mate, Llewellyn was even more of a fucking idiot than I thought. My fighters might be hard as nails, but they'll run like everybody else if their necks are on the line.'

'I tried to tell him. I said you wouldn't listen.' I'm numb with cold and I desperately want to get off this roof, but Hinchcliffe hasn't finished with me yet.

'Tell me, Danny,' he says after a moment, 'what would you do? If you were standing here in my shoes right now, what would you do?'

'For a start, I would never be in your shoes,' I answer quickly. There's no point being anything other than honest with him now. 'I'm not *like* you. It's stupid bastards like you who caused all this mess in the first place.'

'Now, now,' he says, remaining unsettlingly calm, 'no need for name-calling.'

'I'm through with fighting, and I'm through with you, Hinchcliffe. I'd have turned my back on this place and all the grief that goes with it a long time ago if I'd thought things would have been any better elsewhere. For a while this was somewhere I thought I could base myself, a place to rebuild my life after months of fighting and running, but I was wrong. And if I really was in your position right now, then I'd be seriously thinking about slipping out through the back door and letting Ankin get on with it.'

Hinchcliffe nods thoughtfully. 'So you think I should give up control of Lowestoft, just like that?'

'I don't know – to be honest, I don't really care. The way I see it, the whole world has been destroyed by this war, Hinchcliffe. I don't know if this place might still be the beginning of something new or whether it's the very end of everything, but either way, it's not looking good.' I'm freezing, and Hinchcliffe won't listen to anything I've got to say, so there's no point wasting my breath. I walk over to the door and I'm about to open it when he speaks again.

'You've met this Ankin,' he says, heaving himself out of his deckchair. 'Tell me, Danny, do you think things would be any different if he was in charge here?'

'I can't answer that – and what does it matter?'

I reach down for the handle again, but he grabs my wrist and won't let go. 'Don't,' he says. 'You're staying with me, Danny. I still need you.'

39

The longer Hinchcliffe does nothing, the more likely it is that Ankin will be forced to make a move – maybe that's what he's hoping. Hinchcliffe's tactics – if any of what's happening now is actually planned – are almost unfathomable. As I can't get out of the building, I head back up onto the roof of the courthouse again and use the binoculars he's left up there to scan the streets below. They're virtually deserted; most of Hinchcliffe's fighters have been ordered to congregate around this building, or sent to guard the gates and the food stores. There're about a hundred of them downstairs, armed with every last weapon they can lay their hands on. Is he really planning to defend his territory like this, with sticks and stones against tanks and guns?

There's a quiet buzzing sound which steadily increases in volume, and now I can see Ankin's plane approaching quickly from the general direction of Norwich. It's no doubt here to spy for Ankin, and to whip the crowds around town into a nervous frenzy, and there's no doubt that'll work. The noise coming from the fighters below me begins to grow louder and more fractious: these men want to fight, but what can they do when their enemy is a couple of thousand feet out of reach above them?

I feel too exposed up here, so I go to look for Hinchcliffe. I can hear his voice, echoing through the otherwise empty corridors as he barks orders at his fighters, sending groups off in different directions. I peer outside the main entrance and there he is, right out in front of the building, coordinating the chaos.

A car screeches around the corner and pulls up in front of

the courthouse. Curtis gets out. 'The whole fucking place is surrounded,' he says, and though Hinchcliffe says nothing, plenty of other questions come from elsewhere in the crowd.

'Surrounded by what?'

'How many are there?'

'Someone said tanks – have those fuckers got tanks?'

'Should have stuck with Llewellyn—'

'Defend the positions I've told you to defend,' Hinchcliffe says, his voice suddenly louder than the rest, 'the food stocks, the gates, this building.'

'What's the fucking point?' someone stupidly asks. 'We're outnumbered. There's ten times as many people on the other side of the barrier, and that's before—'

The fighter doesn't get a chance to finish making his point; Curtis has already dragged him out of the crowd and now he's attacking him with his machete. The fighter is taken by surprise; he drops to the ground and raises his arm to protect himself, but Curtis keeps chopping down, slicing into his flesh until he's virtually removed the man's arm. Then he rams his boot onto the man's chest to keep him down and starts to hack at his head and neck. I melt back into the shadows and disappear into a room just off the main entrance. There's a big window there and I watch as a range of reactions spreads through the fighters with lightning speed. Someone jumps Curtis, smacking him across the back of the legs with a metal bar and dropping him to his knees, then someone else goes for Curtis' attacker. Another fighter wades through the crowd to get to Curtis' car, until someone cuts him off and tries to take the car for themselves. Others turn and run for cover . . .

Hinchcliffe has made his way unnoticed back into the courthouse and as the chaos outside spreads like a bush fire, quickly increasing in ferocity, he shuts and bolts the door behind him. I hold my breath and stay perfectly still, listening to his footsteps moving along the corridor outside this room, until I'm sure he's gone.

It's time to get out of here – I'm sure this is my last chance. I need to get to the house, get whatever I can, then leave here and never look back.

40

A broken sign hanging from the ceiling points towards a fire exit hidden behind an untidy stack of boxes and crates, most of them empty. I push my way through the rubbish until I can force the door open. I'm desperate to disappear before Hinchcliffe comes looking for me, or the sudden violence outside escalates even further. I follow the metal railings around the side of the courthouse, shuddering as I pass Llewellyn's impaled corpse, but as I run through the massive puddle of blood that's bled out of his body I don't give the stupid fucker a second glance. I pause at the back of the building to make sure no one's about, then I sprint away, feeling hugely thankful for the steroids Ankin's doctor pumped me full of earlier today. If I hadn't been drugged up to the eyeballs, I'd never have been able to run like this. No doubt I'll pay for it later, when the effects wear off, but right now it doesn't matter.

I follow the main road towards the south gate, keeping the ocean to my left, but another sudden swell of trouble in a side-street forces me to change direction. The red-brick shopping centre is one of the sites where Hinchcliffe stockpiles food and supplies, and right now it's in the process of being ransacked. Fighters are scrambling through debris, desperate to get their hands on whatever they can, but as they fight their way back out into the open a gang of Switchbacks are there, attacking them. They corner one fighter laden with cans, who manages to batter one of them away until three more of them take him down. Their blades are flashing in the early morning light; their bludgeons are pounding him into a pulp. Men still loyal to Hinchcliffe try for a while to stop the looting, but they're soon overcome and either battered into submission or forced to switch sides. I glimpse inside one of the food buildings through an open door as I run past; it's virtually empty now. Has everything already been taken, or was there never anything there to begin with?

Lowestoft is falling apart around me. Until now the spectre of Hinchcliffe has loomed large, and everyone has been in his shadow, too afraid to do anything that might risk incurring his wrath. But his dominance has been challenged without even a single shot being fired, before his fighters in the compound and Ankin's army outside the town have even traded a single blow. The ease with which everything is fragmenting is terrifying. It's almost as if Ankin intended it to happen this way . . .

Another left turn leads me back towards the coast and the main road again. The streets are filling with activity; word of what's happening has spread with lightning speed. Everyone I see looks uniformly panicked, and scared, with no idea what they should do. I can see some barricading themselves into the buildings where they live, trying to block up any doors and windows which are still accessible from outside. Others are preparing to defend themselves.

Depressingly, most have resorted to violence and hate, the language of the moment. Small mobs are appearing on street corners, armed with clubs and blades and whatever else they can find. Some of these groups of people merge into larger gangs; others turn on each other in sudden, desperate fights over territory and weapons.

At last: I can finally see the south gate up ahead, but I'm obviously not the only person wanting to escape. There's already a large crowd there. A couple of fighters still loyal to Hinchcliffe are trying to push them back into the compound, but there are others doing the exact opposite, trying to get the gate open. A couple of the more athletic are scrambling up the sides of the lorries which form the barrier and are throwing themselves over.

A fight breaks out in the middle of the crowd in front of the gate: one fighter, a young, aggressive bastard I've taken a beating from before now, is warding off several men with a pistol and a knife. He's gesturing desperately towards the metal barrier, but his words are being drowned out by increasing levels of noise coming from the other side. He lashes out at the one-legged guard who can't get away, slashing a line across his chest with the tip of his blade, then starts firing his pistol. He kills two more and wounds a third by throwing it at someone's head when he's out of ammunition. The gunshots are enough to force people to scatter momentarily, and the brief distraction gives him enough time to get the access door in the gate open and get out. Fighters race to the barrier and close the door almost immediately, but it's too late: I can see the young fighter running down the road with his arms held high in surrender.

And coming towards him, heading for the heart of Lowestoft, is one of Ankin's tanks. Behind the tank, for as far as I can see, the road is filled with more people and vehicles.

Inside the compound the crowd is reacting with increased anger and fear, and another fight erupts which spreads rapidly.

I desperately need to find another way out of town. If Ankin's this close, and if he has anything like the manpower he's boasted of having, then the entire compound must surely be surrounded by now. I double back on myself and run away from the ever-expanding riot, heading towards Hinchcliffe and the courthouse again. I'm seriously lacking anything resembling a coherent plan of action. In the space of just a few minutes the streets have begun to fill with even more chaos and confusion as wanton violence floods the entire compound.

I've run out of options. All the major routes north and south are blocked now, and everything to the west will be impassable before long as the panic and rioting increases. The beach is the only sensible route left to take. It'll take me much longer to get away, but it's a much less obvious route out of here, and I'm counting on fewer people trying to come this way. Providing the tides are kind and the violence here is confined to the square quarter-mile around Hinchcliffe's base, I should be able to follow the shingle and sand until I'm level with the housing estate.

Happier now I've got a plan, I turn and head for the ocean. My body's still fooled into thinking it's healthy, and I'm pretty sure I can keep running at this pace if I don't push too hard.

The noise of the waves is increasing steadily as I approach the sea, but then I become aware of another, even louder noise. Ankin's plane again? I look up, and stop dead in my tracks at the sight of an actual helicopter, flying low and fast towards the town centre. For a second I'm transfixed as I watch the machine piercing the dark grey clouds, tail lights blinking through the gloom. It's been so long since I've seen anything like this . . .

And now it's directly over the centre of Lowestoft, flying this way, and though my brain is screaming at me that whoever's flying the chopper isn't interested in me, or even capable of attack, common sense has gone out of the window and now I'm running like I think the pilot's about to machine-gun me down.

And it looks like everyone else feels the same, because the arrival of the helicopter has whipped the crowds behind me into a frenzy, herding many of them in this direction. Fuck, are we being *rounded up*? I've almost reached the beach now, but there are other people swarming nearby and with the threat of attacks from the air it's suddenly a dangerously exposed place to be. I need an alternative.

I look around, and then I see it: an isolated place where I can shelter until the chaos dies down; a place where no fucker in their right mind would go.

I put my head down and start sprinting towards Hinchcliffe's factory.

41

The place is deserted, Hinchcliffe's guards long gone. This vast, featureless building looks ugly as hell in the late morning gloom. I head straight for the entrance I used when I saw Rona Scott, but I'm disorientated and end up at the wrong end of the site, outside the metal industrial units Hinchcliffe showed me. The doors of several of the small buildings are open and for a moment I panic, thinking I'm about to be surrounded by a pack of feral kids working together like starving hyenas. Then the helicopter flies off towards the other end of the compound, and as the noise of its engine finally fades I realise this place is silent; everyone's left.

I peer into the unit I saw before and see I was almost right. The children are long gone, probably released by the kid-wrangler, except for one. It's the older boy I saw with Hinchcliffe. He's sitting in the corner of his cell, covering his head.

'Get out of here,' I shout at him. 'Run!'

But the kid doesn't move – he doesn't even react. He's catatonic. I know I can't waste any more time here. Now I know where I am, I turn around and make for the entrance I used to get to Rona Scott's surgery, figuring that's as good a place as any to shelter. The main door has been left unlocked and I close it behind me when I slip into the building. I stop for a moment and lean up against it, panting hard and listening for sounds of movement. I'm conscious that my own racket is filling this otherwise empty place.

I'm unsurprised to find the guard's station in the reception area has been abandoned. The desk is empty, and behind it I find a dirty sleeping bag lying among crushed drinks cans and food wrappers. When I spot an empty liquor bottle the scavenger in me takes over and I quickly check through the mess, but the only things I find of any value are a pathetically weak long-handled torch, some scraps of clothing, and half of the packet of sweets I used to bribe the guard the other day. Looks like he was rationing himself. Poor sod didn't get to finish them before either duty called or he fled.

I shout out, just in case I'm not alone, 'Hello – is anybody there?' I'm relieved when no one answers – the last thing I want is to be trapped here with Rona Scott, or any of Hinchcliffe's other cronies. Then I hear something, like a scurrying noise, somewhere in the building. I keep still as I try to work out what it is, but I lose track of it when Ankin's helicopter flies overhead again. It was probably just rats. Vermin hide in places like this, away from the bulk of the population but still close enough to hunt for scraps. Back in town, rodents are hunted for food – it's as if our places at the lower end of the food chain have become interchangeable.

This place will have to do. With a little luck I can hide out here until either things blow over or, more likely, come to a head when Ankin's army breaches the gates. I can bide my time, then get out of town along the beach as I'd originally planned.

I retrace my steps to Rona Scott's room where she confirmed my death sentence. That was a few days ago – Christ, that all? A few days? So much has happened that it feels like a lifetime ago. And that thought makes each step take ten times the effort. How much closer am I to my inevitable end? Is this what it's going to be like from now on, constantly wondering how long I have left?

The room is dark, the closed blinds letting in virtually no light, and to my intense relief the doctor's not here. I go inside, open the blinds a little and start going through the clutter on the table, looking for food, but I stop when I hear muffled shouting in the far distance, followed by gunfire and a high-pitched scream. Sounds like a lynch mob catching up with its target. Then I jump in shock when I realise the little girl I saw here last time is still here, still strapped to her seat. She's sitting bolt upright, staring at me in abject terror.

I approach her cautiously. The last thing I want is for her to panic, start screaming, or do anything that might let people know I'm here. 'I'm not going to hurt you,' I tell her, and even though she probably doesn't believe me, I mean it. But she doesn't react – she's too scared even to move. She doesn't even flinch as I kneel down in front of her. 'You need to go,' I tell her. 'There are people outside who'll hurt you. When you get out there, just run . . .'

I touch her wrist to undo the first of the bindings, and she still doesn't move, not even when I brush against her skin. She's as cold as the room we're in. I look into her face again: her eyes are still focused on a point far in the distance. I shake her shoulder and wave my hand in front of her face, but it's no use. She's been dead for a while.

Upstairs, Rona Scott's 'surgery' is also empty. I have a quick search around, looking for anything like the steroids Ankin's doctor gave me, but I know I'm wasting my time. I find a bottle of paracetamol tablets, two-thirds full, and I shove it into my coat pocket; I'll take a couple if the pain gets too bad – but then again, if the pain gets that bad maybe I'll just take the whole damn lot.

From the window up here I can see virtually all the way to the very heart of Hinchcliffe's compound. The helicopter is buzzing overhead. I think the south gate is open now. There's a crowd on this side of the barrier trying to get out, and an army on the other side trying to get in, their numbers swollen by huge waves of underclass looking for food or vengeance or both. The same thing's surely happening at the other end of town, and at any other potential access points. I stand and watch as the people of Lowestoft collide head-on and tear themselves apart.

Is this what happened in Hull? And in all those other

places where I'm sure similar communities must have sprung up around the country? And was Lowestoft really the last of them? If Ankin's right, and this is the only place left, then the chain reaction that's spreading through this town now really is the beginning of the end of everything.

42

From the window I can see the streets are filled with constant, frantic movement now, and I wonder where in all that chaos out there is Hinchcliffe. The overwhelming uncertainty consuming this place and my own frustrating inability to do anything is affecting my concept of time: I don't know if I've been here for one hour or four. It's icy-cold in this building, and outside rain is falling. Everything looks relentlessly grey and my head is pounding. Are the effects of the drugs fading already?

I'm staring at a street fight in the distance, numb to the bloody violence, when there's a series of sudden bright flashes around Hinchcliffe's courthouse. Explosions? I think I can see flames in the windows now. Looks like the police station, where he barracked his fighters, is also under attack; a flood of people are running from the scene, but they've barely got away before they collide with an equally large surge of people coming from the opposite direction. What the hell's going on? As I keep watching, several of Ankin's tanks roll slowly towards the burning courthouse, converging on it from different directions.

The centre of Lowestoft is a bloody war zone. There are thousands of people there now, far more than there were originally, the cumulative effect of Ankin's invading army and the hordes of underclass all descending on the place at the same time. There are other buildings on fire too; before long the whole town will be in flames.

I need to move. The fighting is still a distraction at the moment, but it's only a matter of time before they come looking around here. I should act now, take advantage of Ankin's drugs before they completely wear off.

I have one last quick search around the doctor's surgery, then head back down to the guard station. I'm about to leave, but I stop myself. This building is huge and relatively inaccessible and, more importantly, most people were too scared to come here. Knowing that, wouldn't this have been a perfect store? I decide I can afford a few minutes to scout around; apart from anything else I need to try and eat now, while I'm feeling relatively normal, cram my body with as much nutrition as I possibly can. It scares me to think about how I'm going to feel again when the drugs wear off.

Opposite the main door is the entrance to a long, dark corridor. I grab the torch I found – the light's poor, but it's heavy enough to make a decent club – and set off. There's a second door, at the far end of the corridor, and when I peer through the port-hole window I find myself looking out over a vast hangar-like space. There are large clear panels in the corrugated metal ceiling which let in some light, but it's hard to make out much detail. The door's stiff and it sticks at first, but at last I manage to shove it open – and immediately stop and cover my mouth, trying to stop myself gagging at the appalling, immediately recognisable stench. It's the un-mistakable stink of death.

There's a raised metal gantry three feet up running around the edge of this cavernous room. I walk along it slowly, my footsteps echoing around the building. There's a mass of industrial pipe-work hanging down which obscures much of my view, and for a second I wonder whether this was another of those gas-chamber killing sites from the begin-ning of the war. I stop walking and, just for a second, I think I can hear something in here with me, a quiet scrambling sound, over on the far side, echoing off the walls. The vermin I heard when I first arrived here, perhaps? The combination of the dead flesh I can smell and the fact that so few people ever came to this place would make this a prime site for a nest of rats or other scavengers. It's weird. In spite of everything that's happened to me recently, and all that's going on less than a mile away in the centre of Lowestoft, the idea of stumbling blind into a horde of starving rodents is more frightening than anything else.

As I get further I go into the room there's more light, so I jog along the gantry to get out of the shadows.

Bizarre. At the far end of this open space the floor has been divided up with metal barriers into a number of pens, maybe as many as twenty altogether. It looks like a cattle market. But I'm sure Hinchcliffe told me this place was originally used to process seafood . . .

Then I remember what he was using this factory for, and even though I don't want to look, I climb down to check the nearest of the pens. I feel sick to my stomach, and it's not just because of the smell.

The pens created by the metal dividers are approximately six feet square. The floor of the one closest to me is covered with what looks like hay and scraps of clothing, but otherwise it's empty. In the one next to it, however, there's something else. It's odd-shaped, and it's hard to make out what it is until I lean over the railings. I immediately wish I hadn't. Lying slumped in the corner of the cage with its back to me, one arm stretched up and shackled by the wrist to the highest of the metal rungs, is the emaciated body of an Unchanged child. It's so badly decayed I can't estimate either its sex or its age. And there are more of them. As I start walking again I see there are bodies in most of the pens. A lot of them are just bony husks, but a few clearly died more recently and are less decayed.

There's a yard-wide pathway running right down the middle and I follow it, looking from side to side and struggling to come to terms with what I see around me. I've seen more horrific sights in the last year than I ever thought possible – images I still see when I close my eyes each night – but I've never come across anything like this before.

Regardless of the fact that these children were, as far as I can tell, Unchanged, the wanton cruelty that they've been subjected to in this place is unimaginable. For a second I think about Hinchcliffe again, and I hope that fucker is burning alive in his courthouse palace right now. To have tried to turn a couple of children and have failed is one thing. To just have killed them would have been understandable in the circumstances. But this? Hinchcliffe and Rona Scott must have derived some sick, sadistic pleasure from this appalling torture. Evil fuckers.

I crouch down and look between the metal rungs into another pen where there's a small boy about the age my youngest son was before he was killed. For a moment I think he might still be alive and I shine the miserable light from my torch into his face and bang it against the railings to try and get a reaction from him. Nothing happens and I realise I was wrong. I stare at the corpse a while longer. The boy was probably older than he looks; his limbs are long, but his body's shrunken by decay. His arms and legs weren't chained – couldn't he have at least tried to get away? Maybe he knew it would have been futile . . . or maybe he no longer had the strength. I shine the torch around the pen and see that there are chains in here after all. Then I look at his withered right wrist and I realise his shrunken hand just slipped out from his shackles.

In every subsequent pen I pass, I see something horrific. I thought that nothing could hurt like this any more, but I was wrong. I'm really struggling to comprehend what I'm seeing. In one cage is the body of a girl, ten or eleven years old, perhaps, and her chains have been wrapped around her neck several times. Did someone do this to her, or did she do it to herself?

Is this the great victory we've been fighting for? Am I *responsible* for it? I helped bring many of these children here, so what happened to them must be my fault, at least partly. But what was the alternative? If they hadn't died here, they'd have died somewhere else. A year ago people were flying around the world, sending probes out into space, eradicating diseases, firing atoms around underground tunnels to find out how the universe was created . . . and look at us now. If Lowestoft truly is the last best hope for this country, and if this kind of atrocity is at its very heart, then what hope do we have? This was Hinchcliffe's great plan for the future – is Chris Ankin's vision any different?

I stagger back across the pathway and collide with a barrier; the racket of metal on metal takes for ever to fade away into silence. I know I should keep moving, but I'm unable to look away from the pen I've just disturbed, where two bodies have been chained by their necks diagonally opposite each other. For a moment I'm struggling to work out why they were being doubled up, then I realise their rotting bodies are covered in scratches, bruises, even what looks like bite marks. *Fuck* . . . these kids had been forced to fight each other to the death, like dogs or cockerels. Hinchcliffe has been using them for sport . . .

There's another sudden noise, much closer this time, and far too loud for a rat. I spin around quickly, but I can't see anything. 'Who's there?' I cry out, figuring it'll either be one of Hinchcliffe's fighters or Ankin's soldiers, and trying to work out my story, but no one answers. The noise comes again, even closer: a frantic shuffling and scurrying as something does its best not to be seen. Then there's the faintest chink of metal on metal, like chains being rattled. I look around, but I still can't see anything— *Wait!* There, in the far corner of the cage behind the one I'm standing right in front of—

I clumsily climb over the barriers to get closer, almost falling when one of my boots gets tangled up, and my sudden movement unleashes a wave of panic in the shadows. And now I can see it: one of the children is still alive!

An Unchanged boy tries to climb out of his pen and into another, but there's a chain wrapped around his ankle. He's terrified, and he's yanking at the chain, trying to free himself, but he's too weak and he falls down onto his face, yelping with pain when he hits the ground. He's backing away from me as I climb into his pen, pushing himself along the floor until he can go no further back. He's about the same age as my son Edward was. He's barely clothed and blue with cold. And he's in much worse physical condition than I am.

'Don't fight,' I tell him softly. 'I won't hurt you.'

He just stares at me. He's too afraid even to blink, and I don't know what to do. Every time I move he flinches. I climb back out of his pen and into another to put some space between us. I'm hoping he'll see that I'm not going to kill him.

'Are there any more of you?' I ask.

The boy doesn't answer. Now I'm looking at him, his face looks familiar. He's the lad from the last Unchanged nest I helped clear out, I'm sure he is. I lean forward and he spits at me, and now I know I'm right.

'Are there any more of you?' I ask again. I give him a few seconds to answer, but he remains silent. I wait a moment longer, but I can't afford to waste any more time here. I climb back over the barriers until I reach the walkway. This catatonic kid is lost anyway; there's nothing I can do for him.

'Wait,' says a quiet voice says from behind me.

When I turn back I see that he's at the front of his cage now, leaning against the barrier, but I keep walking. I'm determined to get away from Lowestoft, and everyone and everything in it.

'Please,' he says, 'let us out.'

I keep moving, but when he rattles his chains against the barrier in protest I turn back again. 'Shush,' I say to him, 'they'll hear you if you—'

I shut up when I realise he's not the one making the noise; it's coming from another pen on the same side of the walkway, a little further back. And now I can see another

Unchanged child looking up at me: a little girl, her small round face ghostly pale. She wearing nothing but a grubby ripped T-shirt several sizes too big, and she's standing on tiptoes, trying to look at me over the top of the metal divide. When I take a step towards her she takes several panicked steps back, almost tripping over her own chained feet.

'You're the one who told them where we were,' the boy says accusingly, his voice now stronger.

'What?'

'We were hiding, and you told them where we were. It's all your fault.'

'I had to do it,' I say without thinking, then I curse myself – what the hell am I apologising for? Why the fuck am I explaining myself to one of the Unchanged?

'No, you didn't. They wouldn't have found us if you hadn't told them. It's your fault.'

Arrogant little bastard. The way he's shouting now reminds me of the way I used to argue with Ed. I start walking again, and the girl starts to cry.

'Let us out,' the boy demands, but I ignore him and keep going.

Then I stop again, because now my head is suddenly full of stupid, dangerous thoughts. He's right, isn't he? It *is* my fault they're here. But what else could I have done? It was them or me, and these days you have to look after yourself 'cause no other fucker's going to help. Anyway, they'd have had to come out of their shelter eventually – all I did was make things happen faster than they would otherwise have done. I'm saving them pain in the long run – or at least I would have, if they hadn't ended up in here.

'Please!' he shouts as I try and walk on, but this time I stop because I know I'm wrong. No matter how I try to justify what I did, these kids are only in the position they are today because of me. It doesn't matter what they are or what I am or what we're supposed to do to each other; I can't just leave them to die here. Lowestoft is burning around us, for

Christ's sake. Well, maybe I *can* leave them, but the point is, I realise, I don't want to. The very least they deserve is a chance, no matter how slight. I can't deny them that.

I walk back towards the little girl and check her chains. They're held with a padlock.

'Don't hurt her,' the boy shouts as the girl squirms to get away. 'I'll get you if you hurt her.'

'I'm not going to hurt anyone,' I answer, testing the strength of the lock and the clasp around her bony ankle. 'I'll be back. I'll see what I can do.'

The noise of battle outside is increasing in volume, even through the walls of this huge place. I can hear occasional bangs and screams, the helicopter flying overhead, guns and shells being fired, and the constant noise of engines. I try to block it all from my mind as I look for something with which to free the children. All I need to do, I tell myself, is let them go.

In the furthest corner of this dreadful place I find a blood-stained workbench that's covered in lengths of chains, discarded locks, bits of bone, small teeth and other less easily identifiable things. There's a huge bunch of keys hanging on a metal hoop on the wall, but there are far too many to go through and I can't waste time checking each one of them. Instead I opt for a set of long-handled bolt-cutters leaning up the side of the bench. I head back to the pens and the girl screams as I advance towards her with the bolt-cutters held high. Her helpless sobbing is heartbreaking.

'For fuck's sake! I'm not going to hurt you,' I tell her, desperate for her to understand. 'Look—' I climb over to the boy, and he too recoils from me, but I'm stronger than him and I drag him back across the floor until he's close enough for me to get the cutters to the padlock. It takes a moment to manoeuvre the jaws in place, and a second more to snap the loop of the padlock. The chains fall to the ground with a rattle.

The boy removes his shackles, then he clambers out of the pen after me. He's clumsy and stiff, his muscles wasted away after being restricted for so long, but he's determined to follow me.

This time when I approach the girl she's a little quieter, still sobbing, but not screaming any more. I carefully ease the blade of the cutters over the loop of her padlock, then press down hard. It takes more effort this time, and I can feel my own energy levels really starting to fade now, but eventually the lock gives way. I unravel her chains and then, when she can't get over the barrier, I reach down and lift her up. There's nothing to her, absolutely no weight at all. She holds on to me, her tiny arms tight around my shoulders, her legs wrapped around my waist. I try to put her down, but I can't; she won't let go.

I'm immediately reminded of how it used to feel when I held Ellis and the boys, hugging them close to me, hearing their breathing, reacting to their every movement . . .

Put the fucking kid down and get out of here, I tell myself firmly.

I try to lower her, but she still won't let go, and when another loud explosion rocks the building, she grips me even tighter, her fingers digging into my back.

Put the fucking kid down!

This time I peel her off me, prising off her fingers and unravelling her legs then putting her down and backing up to put some distance between us. She just stands there, looking up at me, not saying anything but asking a thousand questions with those huge, innocent eyes.

At last she whispers, 'Where's Charlie?'

'Who's Charlie?'

'Charlie,' she says. 'You *know*, Charlotte. She came here with us.'

I imagine she's talking about the dead girl upstairs. I find I can't tell her the truth. 'She's already gone,' I lie, 'and now you need to do the same. Get out of here. There's trouble coming.'

'Where?' the boy asks, shivering. He's dressing himself in the rags he's stripped from another child's corpse.

'What?'

'Where do we go?'

'How am I supposed to know? Just stay away from the town. Get onto the beach and follow it south as far as you can.'

'Which way's south?'

'That way,' I tell him, pointing. I start backing away from them both again.

'But the people out there,' he continues, his voice unsure, 'the Haters . . . they'll find us, won't they? They'll kill us . . .'

The girl starts to cry again, and I struggle to shut the noise out. What do these children think I am? I spent a couple of days in their shelter with them, but surely they must know I'm not like them? Then again, they also know I'm not acting like any of the other people they've seen since they've been here, so what the hell are they supposed to think?

'Can't you take us back?' the girl asks, her voice barely audible. Her bottom lip quivers and tears roll down her cheeks.

'Back where?'

'Back to where we were before. With Sally and Mr Greene, where all those cones and traffic signs were.'

She's talking about the storage depot where I found them. 'You can't go back there,' I answer quickly, not thinking about the effect my words will have on her. 'That place is gone now, and all the people who were there are gone too.'

And now her tiny body is juddering as she sobs.

'You got any food?' the boy asks. 'I'm *really* hungry.'

I check my bag and my pockets, but all I find is the half-finished packet of sweets, which I hand over.

'My daddy says—' the girl begins.

'—that you shouldn't take sweets from strangers,' I say, finishing her sentence for her, immediately slipping back into parent mode, even after all this time. 'And your daddy was right. But things are a bit different now, aren't they?'

She doesn't answer, too busy cramming several of the

sweets into her mouth. Strings of sticky dribble are running down her chin. This is probably the first thing these kids have eaten in days. The roar of another engine outside snaps me out of my dangerous malaise and I start jogging towards the nearest door.

'You can't leave us,' the boy shouts after me.

'Yes I can.'

'But they'll kill us—'

'It's probably for the best.' I know I should just keep moving and not look back again, but I can't. Standing behind me, their mouths full of sugar, their faces streaked with blood and dirt and who knows what, are two kids, two normal, everyday kids, behaving like normal, rational human beings, not like the hundreds of blood-crazed mad bastards fighting to the death outside this place. They're kids like the children in the family I used to be a part of, before the Hate came and tore everything apart and left my world in ruins. They're not like the barely controlled, feral creatures Hinchcliffe held captive elsewhere on this site. This completely helpless boy and girl deserve better than this – but what else can I do? They're dead already. The second they're outside this place they'll be torn to pieces . . .

My head fills with images of them being attacked by a pack of people like me, being ripped apart, just because they're not like us. It's inevitable – it's just the way the world is now – but the idea of them being hunted down and killed suddenly feels completely abhorrent.

There is an answer. It's obvious, but I don't want to accept it.

'Please,' the boy says hopefully, his eyes scanning my face, desperately searching for even the faintest flicker of hope, 'just help us to get away.'

'Okay,' I say, cursing my stupidity as soon as I've spoken. 'I'll take you somewhere there are other people like you.'

43

I find a van parked up in an open space next to a roller-shutter door, the keys still in the ignition and I open up the back and try to get the kids inside but neither of them will move. They're staring at the metal cage bolted to the wall and I realise this is the same van, the one they brought me and these kids back in after the nest had been cleared out. No doubt they're remembering the last time they travelled in it, just like I am. It's a worn-out, unreliable old vehicle but, in the absence of anything else, for now it'll have to do.

'Get in,' I tell them, gently pushing the girl forward, but still she doesn't move.

The boy reaches out to take her hand and I ask him, 'What's your name, son?'

After a moment he replies, 'Jake.'

I crouch down and say, 'And what about you?'

She looks at me with big, terrified eyes and at last she whispers, 'Chloë.'

'Listen, Chloë, we don't have a lot of time. There's a lot of fighting going on outside, so we need to get away fast. I know you're scared, but if you don't get into the van, you're not going to make it, do you understand? You don't have to get into the cage, just into the van.' I have to bite my tongue to stop myself from shouting, *Just get in the fucking van!*

Chloë looks at Jake, who scowls as he thinks about what I just said, then he nods and they allow me to help them into the back. I shut them in, then head over towards the roller-shutter door, but there's another bloody padlock. I fetch the bolt-cutters, and it eventually gives, but not without an unexpected amount of effort. I'm soaked with sweat now, and I can feel the sickness returning almost by the minute.

The engine starts on the third try. I will the fuel gauge to keep moving as I watch it climb, but it barely reaches a quarter-full. Still, that should be enough to get us out of Lowestoft and clear of the fighting. Then it's just a question of finding Peter Sutton and the Unchanged bunker, where I can dump the kids and then, *finally*, disappear. I try to visualise the route to the bunker – the roads are long, straight and featureless around here. One wrong turn and I could end up back in the centre of Lowestoft before I've even realised I'm going the wrong way.

'Hold on,' I shout to the kids as I turn the van around and pull away. I can see them in the rear-view mirror, huddled together in the corner. They're obviously freezing cold, and absolutely terrified, but at least they're free of Rona Scott's nightmare torture factory. 'Keep your heads down,' I call to them. 'Don't let anyone see you, okay?'

'Where are we going?' Jake asks as I steer through the open door and onto the road, out into the grey light of day.

'There's a place I know – someone took me there a few days ago. There are people like you there.'

'Like the old place?' Chloë asks.

'Better than that,' I tell her.

The engine splutters and almost dies, and I remember how unreliable this heap of a van is. I drive away from the factory, accelerating hard, then just as suddenly I slam on the brakes. *Fuck.*

'What's the matter?' Jake asks, sounding nervous again.

'Nothing,' I lie. 'Just trying to decide which way's best.' Truth is, I didn't think this through; there is no 'best way' out of here. Heading north around the top of the compound would probably be easiest, but that's taking us in completely the wrong direction. The best option – the only real option, I guess – is to head south, try to get out over the bridge. For a fraction of a second I consider dumping the kids altogether, and for another fraction I wonder about trying to run along the beach with them, but I know both these choices are useless too.

It's no good: all I can do is start driving and hope for the best. I accelerate off again, and for the first few yards it's pretty easy. The roads are still swarming with people, but they're more interested in surviving than anything I might be doing. *All I need to do is get over the bridge*, I keep telling myself. *Once I'm on the other side of the water everything will be easier.*

The massive rush of people and vehicles I saw coming across the bridge and through the gate earlier is more like a slow trickle now. There are people running along the streets like sheep, some moving towards the burning courthouse, others trying to get out of town. The air is filled with drifting smoke and the figures on the road move to either side as I drive towards them. It's less than half a mile to the gate; a couple of minutes and we'll be out of here.

I swerve around a fight which has spilled out of a building, and when I look back in my mirror I see that Jake has his face pressed against the glass.

'Get your fucking head down!' I scream at him. He does as I say, but it's too late, he's been seen. There's the slightest delay – perhaps they're unable to process the bizarre reality of an Unchanged child in the middle of the crumbling chaos of Lowestoft – but then I have to brake hard to avoid colliding with some kind of armoured vehicle coming the other way, the engine almost dies and a horde of people begin throwing themselves at the sides of the van. They're hammering against it, trying to rip open the doors as I gun the engine, and I barely manage to keep the vehicle on the road. At least the children have crouched back down and covered their heads in terror.

I finally manage to get some speed on as I round the bend in the road, and now I can see the bridge ahead of me. The gates are open, but there's a heavy military presence here.

Looks like Ankin's troops are blocking the way in and out of town. I guess they're doing all they can to keep the trouble contained. I can already see several of them moving towards me, their weapons raised.

'Stay down!' I yell again at the kids. *This is it.* I grit my teeth, sit bolt upright in my seat, grip the steering wheel so tight my wrists ache and jam my foot down on the accelerator pedal. Through the windscreen I see sudden, frantic movement as we hurtle towards the troops, and they dive away in either direction as I smash through them. Shots ring out and a hail of bullets thuds into the side of the van. The back window shatters, showering Jake and Chloë with glass.

'Who's shooting?' Jake asks. He crawls along the length of the van then gets up and hangs over the seat next to me, blocking my view behind.

'Get out of the *fucking* way,' I scream at him, trying to push him away, while still keeping control. I shove him hard out of the way and in the suddenly clear rear-view mirror I see headlamps behind us. The fuckers are following.

'Someone's coming,' Chloë wails, looking out through a bullet hole. 'I can see motorbikes.'

She's right: there are two bikes and a Jeep in pursuit now. We're on the A12, and although it's littered with debris, the road is virtually clear of other traffic. Sticking to it is the safest option right now – if I try and find an alternative route I could end up driving down a road that's blocked, or accidentally doubling back, because I don't know the area that well. I need to keep going until we reach Wrentham; that's not far from the bunker. For now, I've just got to keep moving . . .

The road is straight and empty and the miles flash past quickly. Our pursuers are gaining; I guess that's inevitable, given the dilapidated state of this van. So that's two problems: being caught, obviously, but an even bigger concern is how do I get us in to Sutton's bunker without leading Ankin's soldiers straight to it?

'Are we nearly there?' Chloë shouts at me from the back of the van and her innocent comment strikes an immediately familiar chord.

I instinctively react like I always used to: 'We'll get there when we get there.'

'They're coming,' Jake tells me. 'Drive *faster*.'

'I can't,' I tell him truthfully.

One of the bikes accelerates and within a few seconds it's up alongside us. I try to ram it off the road, but the driver anticipates my clumsy manoeuvre and drops back out of the way and it's me who almost loses control. I clip the kerb, steer hard, but overcompensate, caught out by the camber of the road, and hit the kerb on the other side, allowing the second bike to squeeze through the gap and overtake us. I'm starting to wish I'd stayed hidden in Rona Scott's office rather than starting this foolhardy bloody mission to get us out of Lowestoft.

Here's Wrentham. The Jeep is gaining steadily as we enter the village at speed, sandwiched between the bikes. And now the dumb bastard on the bike ahead of me is regretting being in front. He looks back over his shoulder, trying to work out which way I'm going to go as we race towards the cross-roads, but he chooses the wrong option and takes the South-wold turn as I hang a right, onto the road which leads to the bunker. I shove my foot down hard on the accelerator pedal again to get to maximum speed, to take advantage of this moment of clear road ahead, but the van's really struggling to keep going, and it's just a matter of seconds before both of the bikes are swarming around the back again. Fortunately the road here narrows slightly, and if I weave from side to side there's no way either of them is going to get past.

I catch a glimpse of something through the bare-branched trees, but it's gone again in a heartbeat, and I think I must have been mistaken, but then there's another gap in the hedgerow and I can see the remains of the battlefield I saw when Sutton brought me out here. So I was right: we're close now, very close—

This must be it. I'm sure I can see the outline of the farm buildings up ahead. I swerve hard, blocking one of the bikes which is trying to overtake me again and Chloë cries with pain as she's thrown across the back of the van and her head hits the metal cage. Her piercing scream cuts right through me, but it helps me focus too. It's like when Ellis and Josh used to fight in the back seat of my car.

'Hold on,' I tell them both, as much for my benefit as theirs, and after quickly checking over my shoulder that they're both braced for impact, I let one of the bikes slip past, then slam on the brakes. The first rider races ahead, at first not even noticing I've stopped. The second driver pulls up hard to avoid a collision and loses balance, the bike kicking out from under him. I accelerate again, but this time the engine threatens to stall. I will it to keep going, and our speed finally begins to increase. I steer hard right through the open gateway into the dilapidated farm. There's a few precious seconds of space behind us.

The worn tyres struggle to keep their grip on the icy mud track and the back end swings out violently as I turn and smacks against one of the gateposts. I'm trying to remember the exact layout of the farm as I career towards the collection of dark, empty buildings. I'm desperate to get out of sight before any of our pursuers catch up. Directly ahead now is the derelict cowshed where Peter Sutton left his car when he brought me here. The Jeep has just turned into the farmyard. I drive into the shed, slam on the brakes and kill the engine. Should we run for it? I know we've probably got a minute or two before they find us – maybe I can try and distract them from the kids by telling them who I am, what Ankin sent me to do? No, there isn't time.

'Keep your bloody heads down,' I tell the kids again. I can hear the Jeep approaching. 'Don't move a bloody muscle – if they see either of you, we've all had it.'

I sink down into my seat and keep completely still. I move only my eyes, just enough to watch in the mirrors. Within a few seconds the Jeep's appeared in the muddy yard behind us. It skids to a halt, swiftly followed by the two bikes. With the two bike riders and at least one soldier in the Jeep, probably more . . . the odds aren't looking good. I could try and take them by surprise – drive off, and hope I get enough of a head start that I can find a hideout somewhere, then come back here later once I've lost them – but the chances of achieving that in a clapped-out out van that's low on fuel in a place I don't know? I'm kidding myself if I think that's going to work.

'My head hurts,' Chloë whimpers.

'Shut *up*,' I hiss at her. 'They'll hear you.'

Jake reaches across and covers her mouth with his hand. In the yard behind us, two of Ankin's soldiers get out of the back of the Jeep. I watch the driver gesticulating – probably ordering them away in different directions as they join the two motorcyclists and fan out across the farm. One of them starts walking directly towards our cowshed, no doubt following the fresh tracks we've left in the mud and ice. Moving as carefully as possible, I reach across to the passenger seat and grab the bolt-cutters I brought with me from the factory.

I can hear the soldier approaching, boots crunching louder with every advancing step. It's a woman, her face smeared with the grime of battle, and she's carrying a pistol. She peers into the shed, then edges into the darkness cautiously. Not stupid, then: she's not about to take any chances. She moves slowly, inching ever closer to the back of this still-warm bullet-riddled wreck of a van. For a fraction of a second our eyes seem to meet in the rear-view mirror, but I don't think she's quite sure what she saw. She takes another step forward, then stops and spins around on the spot. The tense silence is interrupted by a single gunshot, the back of her skull explodes out over the back of the van and I hear her dead body slam against the vehicle before she drops to the ground. I can't see anything, but I would guess that there's someone standing on the other side of the farm with a rifle. There's a second shot – I can't see if it hits anyone – then there's a third shot, and I'm pretty sure that one's from another direction entirely. I'm trying to work out what's going on from my pitifully small viewpoint while still keeping low in the driver's seat; I don't want any of Sutton's lot taking me out before they realise who I am and what – *who* – I've brought them.

I can see two soldiers crouched down on my side of the Jeep, using the car for cover. They begin to return fire, single shots, and almost instantly a hail of gunfire ricochets around the farm. It reminds me of a Western gunfight, one of those old Saturday afternoon films I used to watch when I was a kid. Then the windscreen of the Jeep is shattered by a bullet and I only realise the driver was still inside when his now-dead body half-falls out of the door. One of the others runs for cover, but he's shot as he sprints towards this dilapidated shed. The last soldier scrambles up and runs back to the nearest bike. He drags it upright and jumps on, and promptly showers his fallen comrades with mud as he hauls it around in a tight circle and aims at the farmyard gate.

I get out of the van, run round to the back and help the children climb out. Holding Chloë's hand tight in one hand, Jake by the other, I position us just inside the shed door where I can still see out. In the distance, at the highest point of the dirt track before it drops down towards the bunker, a lone figure is frantically waving at me.

'Okay, now we've got to run,' I tell the children, and as we pound across the churned-up farmyard, Jake pulls free and sprints ahead. Now I can see the man waving us on is Dean. Last time I saw him, that rifle was aimed at me.

'Behind you!' he shouts. I turn around and see a man, gaining on me fast. I must have lost track in the confusion; I really didn't think there were any left.

'Keep running and don't stop,' I tell Chloë, shoving her away, and I turn around to try and fend off Ankin's soldier, but I've misjudged his speed and he's on top of me before I can do anything to defend myself. He's got a riot baton, which he swings around and thumps into my gut. The incredible pain immediately makes me fold me in two and I'm flat on my back in the mud before I know what's happened.

He drops down hard on my chest, forcing every scrap of oxygen from my lungs. 'What the fuck are you doing?' he screams into my face. 'They're *Unchanged*, you fucking traitor!'

He's got my arms pinned down with his knees and there's nothing I can do to protect myself when he punches me in the face. He spits in my eye, blinding me for an instant, and I don't see his fist coming until he smacks me in the mouth again. The pain is intense – but all of a sudden the weight lifts and I draw in a shuddering breath. As my eyes come back into focus I realise killing the Unchanged is more important to him than dealing with me; he's sprung up and is about to race after them when, more by luck than judgement, I manage to catch hold of one of his feet in my outstretched hand and he trips and slams down face first into the mud. He's faster and stronger by far than I am and he's back up in seconds. He shakes me off with ease, but spares the time to turn back and boot me in the right kidney for my troubles.

I've been enough of a distraction that Dean's been able to get closer, and now he steps forward and fires into the soldier's face at point-blank range. The corpse drops on top of me, what's left of his dead head smacking hard against mine, and I fight to stay focused and keep breathing through the sudden all-consuming darkness.

44

I sit up quickly, but the pain's too much and I immediately drop back down and my skull cracks against the hard ground. I try to open my eyes, but it's dark, and everything's blurred. Someone's standing over me, looking down – Unchanged – and I instinctively try to get up and fight before I remember what happened and make myself hold the Hate. I try to move again, but I can't: everything hurts too much. Now I can see a bit more. I think, judging by the damp smell in here, that this is the small room at the entrance to the Unchanged bunker. The features of the person looking down at me are slowly becoming more distinct.

'Joseph?' I ask. My voice is hoarse. I feel like I've been run over by a tank.

'Lie still, Danny,' he says. His face might be distressingly haggard, but his voice is still immediately recognisable. He gently rests his hand on my shoulder. 'Tracy's done what she could for you.'

'Tracy?'

'Our doctor. She's cleaned your wounds as best she can, but you're in a bad way. '

I try to get up again, and this time I manage to prop myself up on my elbows. It takes me a while, but at last I manage to shuffle my broken body around until I can lean back against the wall. I lift my hands to my swollen face and pick dry blood from my eyes. I don't know whether it's the beating I've just taken or the drugs finally wearing off – maybe it's a combination of both – but I feel *really* bad. The worst it's been.

I realise there's someone else here – a woman, watching me. Doctor Tracy, I presume.

She mutters, 'If the stupid bastard won't listen, there's nothing I can do to help him,' and storms out of the room.

Joseph acknowledges her, but I ignore her. 'What happened?' I ask him. I have to concentrate really hard to sound out each word.

'We knew *something* was going on out there – what with the planes and helicopters and engines and stuff, so Peter's been staying above ground, keeping a lookout, trying to work out what the hell was going on. And then you showed up here, and all hell broke loose.'

'The children—' I start, 'I had two kids with me—'

'They're safe with the others. Where did you find them, Danny? Are there more?'

'It's a long story that you really don't want to hear,' I answer, catching my breath as a wave of pain washes over me. 'And no, they're the last.'

'I would like to hear that story one day, but not today – today we have big problems to sort out first.'

'Where's Peter?'

Joseph moves to one side, and I see a body on the other side of the room covered by a bloodstained sheet.

'Shit.'

'Poor sod got caught in all that shooting – the bastards got him before Dean could get them.'

He passes me a bottle of water and I swill some around in my mouth and spit it out, trying to clear the blood. I drink a bit, and it wakes my body a little, makes me feel slightly more alive. I try to focus on my surroundings. The boy, Jake, is standing behind Parker in the doorway, watching me.

'What's happening out there, Danny?' Mallon asks quietly.

I look straight at him. 'I didn't tell anyone about you, if that's what you think.'

'I didn't say that.'

'It's nothing you haven't heard before,' I tell him. 'Just the same old, same old.'

'What?'

'You were right you know, back then at the convent. All those things you used to say, about not fighting and making a stand, trying to break the cycle. I thought you were a fucking crank at the time, but you were right.'

'I don't follow,' he says. 'What's that got to do with today?'

'We're imploding,' I say with a sigh. 'What's left of the human race is tearing itself apart out there, and there's nothing anyone can do to stop it. The last army in the country is marching on the last town in the country, and there's probably very little of either of them left by now. It's like you said: every man for himself and woe betide anyone who gets in the way of a strong, determined man.' I stop to cough, shocked at how much it hurts, and when it finally wears off, I add, 'And the thing is, the less there is left to fight for, the higher the stakes get.'

'That still doesn't explain what you're doing out here, or how you came to have these children with you.'

'I made a decision a while back – before I knew about you and this place, even. I decided I'd had enough of fighting, had enough of everything, really. I was trying to get away – the kids were just a complication.'

'I don't believe that.' I can hear the smile in Joseph Mallon's voice.

'Believe what you like – I couldn't leave them out there on their own, so I was just delivering them to you before I fucked off for good. And that's what I'm still planning to do.'

'Well, that might not be so easy. They know where we are now, Danny – they've seen us here. We're well and truly up shit creek, and we've not even got a canoe, let alone a paddle. We need your help.'

Why can't everybody just leave me be? 'Listen,' I start,

'I'm past helping anyone. I'm sick and tired of being used – it just gets me deeper and deeper into the mire, and it never does *anyone* any good. I'm sick, and I'm dying, Joseph, and I just want to be left alone to live out my last few days in peace and quiet. There are enough of you here to be able to look after yourselves.'

'Jesus, Danny, if millions of us were wiped out by your kind, what chance do less than thirty of us have? We can't do anything without help, and now that Peter's gone, it's down to you.'

'You've got no chance at all,' I tell him, keeping my voice low so that Jake doesn't hear.

'We've been down here for months,' Mallon says. 'We're weak and we're tired, and we know damn well that the odds are stacked against us, but we're not going to just give up.'

'You've got weapons and it's chaos up there,' I say. 'You might still have a slight chance.'

'We've got a handful of guns,' he corrects me, 'but we've just used most of our ammunition saving your backside.'

'Then maybe you shouldn't have bothered.'

'Maybe you're right,' he says angrily, 'no, let me rephrase that. We just used up half our ammunition helping Peter Sutton and saving the life of those two kids – but whatever we did, and whoever we did it for, that's academic: we need your help now. We've got hardly any supplies left and we'll starve if we don't—'

'You want supplies?' I interrupt. 'I can tell you where to find supplies, but I'm not—'

'Listen, Danny, those bastards up there are going to come back. Dean says at least one of them got away, and there are dead bodies out there, remember? So whether we like it or not, they'll know we're here somewhere. You think they're just going to forget about us? Forget about you? Even if they can't get into the bunker, they'll be waiting for us when we eventually come out.'

'I'm nothing to them.'

'That's not what Peter said.'

'With all due respect, maybe you shouldn't have listened to everything Peter said.'

'He was a good man; he kept us alive. I trusted him.'

'You call this *living*? Look around, Joseph: this place is not much different to the mass graves I saw outside the gas chambers. You're all just sitting here waiting to die.'

'And what about you?'

'Oh yes, me too. But you'll probably all outlast me. I don't have long left.'

'So why let it end this way? Why don't you do *something* with the little time you have, Danny? After all you came through just to get here – how hard you fought to find your daughter, the things you managed to survive . . . I can't believe you're being so defeatist now, after all you've been through?'

'Sorry if I've let you down,' I snarl, concentrating on another sudden cramping pain in my gut rather than anything Mallon has to say.

'It's not just me, though,' he continues. He's not giving up on the guilt trip any time soon. 'It's the rest of them. It's everyone down here. You're our last chance.'

'That's bullshit.'

'Is it? Way I see it, even if everything else has fallen apart up there, you can still help us. You, me and everyone else down here, we might be all there is left now.'

45

An hour passes, maybe longer, and the pain gradually subsides, but I know the bastard who attacked me above ground has done some serious damage to my already seriously damaged insides. The temporary relief Ankin's doctor's drugs gave me is definitely over; I can feel my body giving up and breaking down by the minute.

The Unchanged have left me alone in here – I don't know whether they're maintaining a respectful distance from the dead and dying (my only company is Peter Sutton's corpse) or if they're just afraid of me – but the door is open and I can hear Joseph addressing the group. Christ alone knows what he's telling them; my guess is he's trying to get them ready to leave, but doesn't the dumb bastard realise what it's like up there now? Surely Sutton must have told him? These people are almost certainly the last Unchanged left alive, and as soon as they put their heads above the surface they'll be hunted down and killed. They might last a few hours or days, maybe even a week if they're lucky, but sooner or later they'll be found and destroyed. Their fates are as certain as mine, poor fuckers. My tired, confused mind fills with nightmare images of the little girl, Chloë, being tracked and killed by my dead daughter Ellis.

The voices are becoming raised, and I try to sit up so I can hear better, but the pain in my gut is too severe and I have to lie back down and stretch out again. I roll over onto my front and gradually manage to lift myself up onto all fours, then use the wall to get myself upright.

It takes me a while, dragging my heavy feet, but by the time I get close to the other end, Joseph's in full flow again.

'We've talked about this.' There's a pleading note in his voice that suggests he's tried this before. 'We knew this day would come eventually.'

'We have to stay down here,' someone protests. 'They'll never find this place.'

'You reckon? They know we're around here somewhere, that's the difference, and they'll keep on looking until they find us. We've all seen what they're like: they won't stop until they've forced us all out into the open and killed us all, because in their misguided minds they still believe it's *them or us*. That's why we need to move from here now, while we've still got a chance, before they come looking.'

'It's suicide.' A woman's voice.

'No, it isn't,' he says, sounding eminently reasonable – he really does have that sort of voice. 'Sitting down here in the dark slowly starving to death? That's suicide. I agree it's not much, but at least we do have *some* chance up there.'

'But where are we supposed to go? They're everywhere.' I think that's the doctor, Tracy. Her voice is full of anger. I'm close enough to see her now, standing opposite Joseph. Her arms are crossed, her body language uncomfortably confrontational. I keep walking, gravity and the incline helping me to move. Almost there now.

'Peter and I discussed that: you are right, but they've been hit almost as hard by this war as we have. Their numbers are massively reduced. Peter had a plan, don't forget. He wanted us to head for the coast, get on a boat and get off the mainland. Doesn't matter where we go after that, we just have to—'

'And where exactly do you think you're going to get a boat from?' I ask, staggering a little until I lean against the door frame for support. I'm dripping with sweat.

Joseph turns around. 'We're on the coast. There'll be something somewhere.'

'You're *hoping*. You're going to need a better plan than that. There's not much left undamaged up there, you know.'

316

'I didn't think there would be.'

'So what are you going to do exactly? Just walk around all the boatyards together until you find something, all of you wearing hats and dark glasses, hoping no one notices you? Get real.'

A ripple of nervous conversation spreads quickly through the group. For the first time I can see them all.

'Why don't you just fuck off,' Tracy says. 'Go back and—'

'We'll manage,' Joseph insists, interrupting, trying to diffuse her anger. 'We have so far.'

'It's thanks to him that Peter's dead,' a badly burned man yells, gesturing at me accusingly.

'It's thanks to Danny these two children are alive, Gary,' Joseph counters.

'There's nothing left of most of the towns around here,' I tell them. For some reason I feel strangely obligated to be honest, to let these poor bastards know exactly what they're going to be dealing with above ground. 'I was told that Lowestoft was the only place left, and that's being torn to pieces as we speak. As far as finding a boat? You'll be lucky to find anything still floating, never mind anything big enough to carry all of you.'

'Peter told me about a couple of places – Oulton Broad, does that sound familiar?'

I know the place he's talking about: it was all about pleasure cruising and family boating holidays before the war. It's close to Lowestoft, but far enough away from the centre of town to have remained relatively ignored. It's weeks since I've been there. 'Okay, so Oulton Broad's a possibility, but even if you managed to find a big enough boat, you've still got a huge problem before you even start looking for sanctuary.'

'And what's that?' Dr Tracy growls.

'Oulton Broad's inland – if you're planning on heading for the sea, you're going to have to sail right through Lowestoft to get there. And in case you weren't paying attention,' I add sarcastically, 'there's a bit of a war going on up there right now.'

'Well, that could work in our favour,' Joseph says optimistically. 'They'll be distracted.'

'You reckon? I'll tell you something, if anyone gets so much as a sniff of just one of you lot, then everything else will be forgotten, all the infighting will stop instantly and you'll be the only targets once again.'

Another frightened murmur spreads quickly through the group. Many of the Unchanged are staring at me now. I make momentary eye contact with Chloë. Perhaps she doesn't fully follow the conversation, but I can tell from the expression on her face that the implications of what she's hearing are clearly understood.

Jake is sitting on a desk and swinging his legs. He points a finger at me. 'I bet he can show us a better place to find a boat,' he says. His voice is quiet to begin with, but he steadily gains confidence. 'He knows where to go,' he tells the others.

'He's already told us he's not interested in helping,' Tracy says.

Jake doesn't care what she thinks.

'Then *make* him do it.'

'We can't.'

'But you *can* show us, can't you?' he says again, looking straight at me. 'We were by the sea when you found us – you must know where the boats are.'

Joseph looks back at me again. 'Well?'

'I know of a couple of places, but you're not listening to me, are you? It's going to be hard enough for any of you to get anywhere near Lowestoft to start with. Then, if by some miracle you do manage to find a boat, there's the little question of getting it going. I don't know anything about boats or engines—'

'But we do,' he interrupts. 'You think we haven't planned for something like this? Do you think we've just been sitting down here twiddling our thumbs, feeling sorry for ourselves and staring into space for weeks on end? We knew this day would come eventually. As good as it was, this place was never going to last. Where's Todd?'

A gangly, awkward-looking bugger with an Einstein-like shock of grey-white hair emerges from the gloom at the back of the group. 'My name's Todd Weston,' he says, stepping over and around people to get closer to the front. 'I know my way around boats. You get me to it, I'll sail it.'

I lean back against the wall and look up at the ceiling. How the hell am I going to get through to these people? 'But do you really think you're just going to trot along to Lowestoft, pick yourselves up a boat and sail it away into the sunset? Did you not hear me? The place isn't full of holidaymakers any more; it's a fucking war zone. There's so much smoke and shit in the air that you can't see the fucking sunset any more, never mind sail away into it.'

'And where exactly is the fighting?' Joseph asks.

'Want me to draw you a bloody map?'

'Don't be facetious. I just want to know if the fighting's near the boatyards,' he says. His voice is annoyingly calm, bordering on patronising.

'I don't know for sure. It seemed to be concentrated in and around the compound in the centre of town from what I saw of it, but—'

'So theoretically we could get in and out again without anyone noticing?'

'Hardly – what are you planning to do, bus people in in coaches?'

'Lose the sarcasm and change your attitude, Danny,' he snaps, his voice suddenly harder. 'We're talking about people's lives here. Stop looking for excuses and try to find a way out – that's what the old Danny McCoyne would have done.'

'Yeah, and the new Danny McCoyne wouldn't bother at all. Look at me, for Christ's sake: I'm a dead man walking.

I'm riddled with cancer, I've just had seven shades of shit kicked out of me and—'

'And you're still going. You're standing here helping, whether you realise it or not. You continually underestimate yourself. Don't forget, Danny, you're the man who managed to find the proverbial needle in the haystack. When the whole country was going to hell in a handbasket around you, you were the one who managed to find his daughter and save her. I don't know of any other man who could have done that. If it wasn't for you, she'd have been—'

'I didn't save her,' I interrupt angrily, doing all I can not to think about Ellis.

'What your daughter became, what happened to her – none of that was your fault. You did all you could, and far more than most. You fought your way into the heart of the biggest bloody battle of all, then managed to get yourself and your girl back out again before it was too late. I don't know anyone else who's done anything near comparable. Peter Sutton was in awe of you, you bloody fool.'

'Then he was the fool, not me.'

'Can't you see, you're our only option, Danny. Without you we're screwed.'

'I'm screwed anyway.'

'I know that, and I'm truly sorry, but what else are you going to do with the time you have left? You're not exactly the kind of man who'll just crawl under a rock and wait there to die, are you? You're better than that, I know it. So go out with a purpose. Give people something to remember you by.'

I know he's playing to his captive audience, but the thing is, there's a part of me that knows he might be right. I *am* different to the rest of the useless brain-dead fucks who inhabit this poisoned, dying country – my problem is I've always struggled to accept responsibility, and I don't see why I should start trying to change things now. Surely it's too late? Joseph looks at me expectantly, and I do all I can to look anywhere else. Tracy glares at me. Parker and Todd are a little less vicious, but no less hopeful. Dean's holding his rifle as if he's about to point it at me to try and force me to help. I look from face to face, and finally find myself looking straight at Chloë and Jake again.

Deep breath. 'Okay, so I'll ask you once more: how do you think you're going to get everyone onto a boat, assuming you can find one, that is.'

'No one said that was what we were planning,' Todd says. 'When Pete, Joseph and I first started talking about this, we ruled that out straight off. We knew that if we had to get away fast, we'd be better bringing the boat to the people, not trying to take the people to the boat.'

'What, here? Are we close to a river or—?'

Todd's shaking his head at me, but it's Joseph who says, 'We were going to split up. Peter, Todd and I were going to find the boat; everyone else was going to head to a pre-arranged point further down the coast and wait for us.'

'What pre-arranged point?'

'We hadn't got that far,' he admits.

'Great.' Every nerve in my body that still feels anything is screaming at me to shut up and get out of here, but there's something screaming equally loud at me not to. As hard as it is for me to accept it, Joseph's right. I think about everything I've seen and been a part of in Lowestoft these last few days, and I know I can't just turn my back on these people. There's more decency and civility here in this cramped bunker than there is in the rest of the country combined – and anyway, I'm just fooling myself if I think I'm going to get far on my own. My body is well and truly fucked. I'm living on borrowed time. My choice now is simple: I can either die alone, or I can try and do the right thing by these Unchanged. The last Unchanged.

There's a hushed, expectant silence throughout the bunker.

'Southwold,' I eventually say.

'What?' Joseph asks, looking confused.

'That's where you need to go. That's your ideal meeting point, ten miles south of Lowestoft. Get everyone down there, then get a boat from one of the yards in town and sail it down the coast. With a little luck you'll find something near the sea. Southwold is a dead place now. It's your best option – probably your only option.'

'So will you help us?'

I pause again. Am I completely sure about this? *Think carefully.* 'I'll do what I can,' I hear myself answer, regretting the words before they've even left my mouth.

'We'll need supplies. We've got nothing.'

'There's a house I was using; it's more than a mile outside Lowestoft. I've got a load of stuff there I'm never going to need. If we're careful we can collect it on the way through to the boatyard.'

'We need to get moving then,' he says. 'Let's clear this place out. We should be ready to leave by morning. We should move fast, while they're still distracted with their bloody in-fighting; before they start looking for those corpses up there.'

46

Though they were better prepared for this day than I'd expected, my unannounced arrival at the bunker and Peter Sutton's subsequent death have forced the Unchanged to drastically alter their plans. We left as dawn broke. Sutton had hidden a delivery van in the cowshed (ready for a day like today) and with that and my van there's enough room for the bulk of the group. Sutton and Parker are driving them down to Southwold, to the lighthouse, if it's still standing. I'm on my way back into Lowestoft in the dead soldiers' Jeep with Todd and Dean. We're going to clear out my stash of supplies, then load the whole lot into the biggest boat we can find that's still seaworthy. And then, if by some miracle we manage to sail through Lowestoft and out the other side, we'll rendezvous with the others at Southwold. I hold out very little hope of ever getting there, and it's becoming increasingly difficult to hide my pessimism.

It's another icy-cold day, and the fact that the windscreen of this Jeep was shot out in the fighting yesterday isn't helping. Not only has there been a severe frost, but everywhere is covered with an inch of snow this morning, the white on the ground making the sky look dirtier than usual. The bodies of Ankin's soldiers were frozen solid when a couple of the men tried to shift them earlier. The snow makes it easy for anyone to follow our tracks, but we don't have any option. Although the three sets of tyre marks all lead in the same direction initially, they split at Wrentham, so with a little luck anyone trying to track our movements will follow the Jeep back towards Lowestoft and leave the others alone.

I'm in constant pain now, but I have to drive. Dean and Todd are in the back of the Jeep, both of them armed and ready to fight if they have to, but hidden under blankets until that moment, because if anyone sees them, we're all dead. I keep telling myself that I must be out of my fucking mind to be a part of this madness. At least the fact that we're in one of Ankin's vehicles with its unsubtle red and white circle markings should make us less conspicuous if we're spotted. Unless Hinchcliffe somehow won yesterday's Battle Royale, that is. If he's still in charge, the paint job instantly makes us a target.

I drive back down the A12 and it's not long before I can see Lowestoft up ahead – not the buildings, just a dark haze where the grey smoke of battle is still drifting up into the sky, and a faint orange glow lighting up the underside of the heavy cloud cover. Is the whole place alight? Is there anything left of the damn town? Even today, months after everything first began to fall apart, after all the endless killing and all the wanton destruction I've witnessed, the sight of the dying town in the near distance makes my cold heart sink like a stone. It might make our mission simpler, but it's all been so fucking pointless. I don't know who fired the first shot yesterday, and I doubt Ankin or Hinchcliffe do either.

I'm planning to turn off shortly, about a mile and a half before we get anywhere near the centre of town, and use the back roads to get into the estate. *Wait.* There's movement on the carriageway up ahead. As I slow down, Dean starts to shuffle nervously under the blanket.

'What's wrong?' he asks.

'Now's not the time to be looking up,' I tell him. 'There are people coming.'

'What kind of people?'

Stupid bloody question! 'What kind do you think?' But who the hell are they? They're as drab as everything else, blending into their surroundings so it's hard to gauge their numbers. Now I'm a bit closer I can see there are perhaps twenty of them, and they're dragging themselves wearily away from Lowestoft. They've got bags and boxes – maybe their few remaining belongings? – and they're moving alone or in pairs, large gaps between them. They don't even look up when I pass, keeping their heads bowed; could be exhaustion or fear, maybe both. They look like refugees – that would make sense, I suppose, as much as anything makes sense today. I imagine the fighting continued after I got away yesterday, so there's probably hardly anything of the town left, and so no point staying there any more. This may well be the beginning of an exodus – or maybe it's the tail end? I wonder if these few people are all that's left.

'Who is it?' Dean asks after I've pulled off the main road and am accelerating again.

'Refugees. As lost as the rest of us.'

The house looks just as I left it, the door that Hinchcliffe kicked in still swinging to and fro in the wind. I reverse down the drive and park next to the side door. There are no footprints in the snow but mine. When I get out and peer in through the living room window it doesn't look like anything's been disturbed – place looks like a fucking bomb site, but it's the same bomb site I left earlier in the week. I check up and down the road again, and once I'm sure it's safe, I open the back of the Jeep and pull the blankets off Dean and Todd.

'In there,' I tell them, pushing them towards the front of the house. 'Move!' I'm terrified that someone's going to see them. I follow them in and walk straight into Todd's back – he and Dean have both stopped dead and are staring into the living room. I push past them to see what's wrong. It's Rufus' body. I forgot about him, poor bastard. I grab my dead friend's ankles and try to drag him out of the way.

'This is the kind of thing you're up against,' I tell them,

struggling to move Rufus, who's frozen to the ground. 'This guy was a friend of mine who fucked up.' I glance up and see them both staring back at me in horror.

'Your friend? But why—?' Todd starts to ask.

'Not me,' I quickly interrupt, putting him straight. 'I didn't do it.'

I don't know if they believe me or not, but it doesn't make any difference. I pick up my sleeping bag that's still draped over the back of my chair where I left it, and use it to cover Rufus up. There's nothing worth salvaging in this room – my books and some of my other belongings are scattered all around the place, and that's where they'll stay now. I don't need them any more. Even if I started reading another book today, I doubt I'll last long enough to finish it. I go through into the kitchen, beckoning the men to follow, and peel up the lino.

I lift up the floorboards, revealing my stash. 'Start with all of this,' I tell them, 'then open the cupboards and take everything. I'm going to have a look upstairs and see if there's anything useful.'

I remove the padlock and chain from the side door so they can load up the Jeep, then throw Dean the keys and leave them to it. I climb the steps to the mausoleum-like rooms on the first floor, heading straight for the water tank where I keep my pathetic weapons cache: a pistol, some ammunition and a grenade.

Last time I was here – last time I was trying to leave Lowestoft – I was working alone, and intending to travel alone. Things are different now: the Unchanged need enough stuff for at least thirty people – bedding, clothes, furniture they can break down for firewood. Everything counts today, so we're going to have to completely empty this place. If we have time we should check a few of the other houses too, make sure we fill the Jeep before we set off for the boatyard.

The noises downstairs have stopped; by the sound of

things they're done loading the Jeep. My body hurts like fuck, every movement an effort, and it's hard to concentrate, but I've been keeping watch from an upstairs window, making sure no one comes snooping around. The people we saw as we were driving back here are a concern; if any of them drift off the main road and end up in this estate we could be in trouble. I lean against the window sill and stare out at the drifting black smoke rising up over what's left of Lowestoft in the distance.

Okay, time to go. Time for one last check around upstairs. I've thrown sheets and duvets down the stairs, and a load of clothes from the chest of drawers. There's a little soap and shampoo left in the bathroom, and a few other things in a mirrored cabinet on the wall. We had one like that in the flat back home. I used to shave in front of it, but the man I see when I look in the mirror today is nothing like the man I used to be. Today I look like the life has been sucked out of me; I'm actually thankful for the mess of hair and the straggly beard, because they're hiding the full extent of my physical deterioration. The longer I look, the more frightened I get. If someone cut me open, I think they'd find more cancer than man now.

I pause to catch my breath in the back bedroom, the child's room with the abandoned boardgame on the floor. I used to avoid coming in here, but things feel different today. It's not much, but I pick up a couple of teddy bears and shove them in my pocket, along with the grenade and gun. I bet that kid Chloë will like them. She deserves to have something like—

'What's going on, Danny?'

I freeze, unable to move a muscle. I'm staring at the wall dead ahead, gripping another toy tightly in my hand. I know that voice. It's calm, composed. Confident. I slowly turn around and there, standing in the doorway in front of me, his clothes glistening with streaks of freshly spilled blood, is Hinchcliffe. My mouth's dry and I can't speak. *How can this be happening?*

'Found two Unchanged downstairs, helping themselves to your stuff. What's that all about? Don't worry, by the way, Danny, I sorted them out for you. Stopped them stealing anything. Killed both of the fuckers dead before they even knew I was watching.'

'I can explain, Hinchcliffe—'

'I doubt you can.'

He takes a step towards me and I move back until I hit the wall and I can't go any further.

'It's not what you think.'

'How would you know? You don't know what I think. I don't know how you think, either. I thought I was starting to understand, but you keep surprising me, Danny McCoyne.'

'Why are you here?'

'Because I knew you'd come back. You're so fucking naïve. You've got no idea, have you?'

'I don't know what you're talking about.'

He walks forward again, and I've got nowhere left to go. He leans over me, an arm on either side of my shoulders, pinning me down without even having to touch me. He checks my pockets, taking my grenade, my pistol, and one of my knives. He digs the tip of the knife into the wall, level with my eye-line, twists the blade around and makes a hole. Plaster dust drifts down and lands on my boot.

He takes the knife out and gesticulates with it as he speaks. 'Why do you think I've kept hold of you for so long, Danny?' he asks. 'Is it because of your dynamic personality? Your sparkling wit? Your remarkable strength?'

Sarcastic bastard.

'Because I'm useful to you? Because I can hold the Hate? Because I can hunt out the Unchanged?'

'Right on all three counts,' he says, 'but you still don't completely get it.'

I can't think straight, and even if I could, I doubt I'd be able to understand what he's talking about. He pushes himself away from the wall and walks away. I have two more knives on me. Should I just try and attack, get this over with? The temptation's strong, but I don't think I can – and even if I did try, Hinchcliffe's always been far more powerful than me. He's just killed two Unchanged men without breaking sweat. I wouldn't stand a chance.

'You, Danny,' he explains, pointing at me with my blade, 'are unique. Didn't you ever wonder why I gave you so many chances?'

'To be honest, I was just relieved you weren't kicking the shit out of me. Anything else was a bonus.'

He laughs and sits down on the end of the narrow bed on one side of this room. He picks up a small metal toy – looks like a musical box – from a bedside table, then puts down my knife and turns the key to wind it up. When he lets it go it starts to play a tune, a lullaby. I can't remember the name of it, but it makes me want to cry.

'The reality, Danny,' he says, talking over the beautiful noise, 'is that you're different. I told you before that I liked the way you could take a step back from everything, remember? You've always been able to look beyond the fighting and see the bigger picture. Most people think you're a useless coward, and to an extent you are, but there's more to you than that.'

'And how is a useless coward supposed to help the all-powerful Hinchcliffe?'

'Simple. You're always looking for the way out. You come at problems from a different perspective, one that no one else sees. We're all focused on the kill, but not you. I came back here for you, Danny, because I knew you'd be trying to get away from the fighting, not running towards it like the rest of them, and I knew you'd end up here again eventually. I'm not stupid, I know how much stuff you've got hidden away here. Christ, I've been giving you extra rations for weeks and I know you've not been eating any of it. It was pretty bloody obvious you'd been stashing it away somewhere, close enough to Lowestoft for you to get to, far enough to avoid any fallout, so to speak.'

'Take everything.'

'I don't want your food, you moron.'

'What then?'

'I want to know where you were going. I knew you'd have a plan to get away, Danny, I just didn't think it would involve Unchanged.'

'It doesn't now you've killed them.'

'For fuck's sake, what else was I going to do? They were *Unchanged*, Danny.'

'They hadn't done anything wrong.'

'They were still breathing, that's wrong in my book.'

'Then maybe you need a new book.'

He gets up fast and charges across the room, slamming into me before I have chance to react, shoving me hard against the wall. His hand is wrapped around my throat. 'Don't push me,' he hisses in my face, tightening his grip. 'I'm really not in the mood. I've had a bad couple of days.'

'It didn't have to be like this.'

'Like what?'

'You could have talked to Ankin. You could have tried to find some common ground.'

'I didn't get the chance – and anyway, the Unchanged *are* our common ground, or at least they were. Now it's just every man for himself. It wouldn't have mattered if I'd talked to Ankin for six bloody months and agreed with him on everything, the end result would have been the same.'

'No, it wouldn't. There was no need for what you did.'

He lets me go and takes a step back. 'What *I* did? You fuckwit, Danny, *I* didn't do anything – and, just for the record, neither did Ankin. Lowestoft is dead today because Ankin's appearance gave people a choice.'

'What do you mean?'

'I watched the whole thing from up on the roof once it kicked off. I always knew there was a chance it was going to happen, and that's why I came down so hard on John Warner in Southwold last week. People always think the grass is greener on the other side, but it's not. You have to take away the temptation. Everywhere you look now, everything is fucked. Word got around that Ankin had surrounded the town and half the people panicked and tried to fight them off, because they thought they were coming in to raid Lowestoft, just like we've raided everywhere else. The other half were throwing themselves on Ankin's mercy. They were thinking these arseholes in their bloody uniforms with their bloody tanks were bringing them some kind of salvation. It was the people themselves who destroyed Lowestoft, not me and not Ankin. Granted, it would have been better if the stupid fucker hadn't turned up like that, but that's how it goes.'

'But I don't understand . . . you just walked away from it all?'

'Walked away from what, exactly? From a few hundred fighters who couldn't take a shit without checking with me first? From a couple of thousand underclass who could barely function? Do you think any of that actually mattered?'

'But what about your breeding plan? The stuff that was going on at the factory? All the food you'd been storing?'

'The stores were almost empty, and the factory was just a remnant from Thacker's day, something to keep Rona Scott entertained and out of my hair. And as for the hotel . . . that was just a way to keep people quiet, keep them occupied. You know, all that stuff you said after you came back from Southwold that time, you were absolutely right: the world is well and truly fucked, and the only thing that matters now is looking after number one. No amount of farming, fucking or fighting is going to change anything. I stayed in Lowestoft because it was my best option, until now at least, but it was never anything worth fighting for. I knew it wouldn't last.'

'What about your fighters?'

'What about them? They can make their own choices. They've got brains . . . some of them, anyway. Those who haven't will just go the way of the Brutes.'

'And what about you? What do you do now?'

'Well, that's the million-dollar question, isn't it? And it depends on you. Like I said, I always knew something like this was probably going happen sooner or later – didn't think it would be quite so fast, though.'

'What do you mean, it depends on *me*? What have *I* got to do with anything?'

'You've got a plan, haven't you? You weren't just show-ing those foul fuckers downstairs around your house, were you? You must have had a damn good reason to risk bring-ing them here.'

'I was giving them the food. I don't need it.'

'Bullshit. Where were they going to take it?'

'How am I supposed to know?'

He shoots out his arm and slams me back against the wall again. 'Pissing me off is *not* a good idea, McCoyne. Tell me what you were planning.'

I can hardly breathe now, and every fibre of my body is screaming in agony. 'I'm not telling you anything – listen, just kill me if it'll make you feel better. I'll be dead soon anyway.'

He screws up his fist and pulls it back and, for a moment, I brace myself. But he doesn't hit me; instead he turns around and kicks the abandoned boardgame across the room in frustration.

'You're probably right,' he says, 'you can't talk if you're dead.'

'I'm not going to talk.' I'm sounding belligerent now.

'You don't have to. I'm getting to know you too well. I can tell when you're lying.'

'Why would I bother lying now? What's the point?'

'Depends how many more Unchanged you're hiding.'

'I'm not hiding any Unchanged – come on, Hinchcliffe—'

'Deny it all you like, I know you're helping more of them.'

'Think what you want.'

'The taller guy downstairs,' he says, 'just before I killed him, I heard him say something about a boat. And something about a guy called Joseph.'

I've got no choice but to try bullshitting my way out of trouble. 'The name means nothing to me. All I know is they were going to try and take a boat from one of the boatyards in town.'

'They'd never have made it.'

'That's what I told them.'

'I still don't believe you.'

'I still don't care.'

He stands across the room and glares at me, and I can see him thinking, working through the options. 'So where is this Joseph?'

'I told you, I've never heard of him.'

'And I told you, I can tell when you're lying. So if the Unchanged were trying to get onto a boat, it's safe to assume this mystery man Joseph and his pals are close to water.'

'Hinchcliffe, there's nothing I can tell you.'

'They're not going to want to travel any further inland, so the coast would have been the best option. And as the bulk of Ankin's forces came from Norwich to the north, I'm guessing they'll have wanted to travel south. Am I getting close now?'

My silence gives him all the answers he needs. He grabs my arm and drags me downstairs.

47

Hinchcliffe knows his way around this place far better than I do. Bastard's clearly had his escape routes planned for some time. He drives the fully loaded Jeep at a frantic speed along back roads I didn't even know existed. He skids frequently on the ice and snow; he's obviously as keen to get away from Lowestoft as I am.

The nauseous panic I've felt since he appeared in the house has finally started to recede. I've spent weeks focusing on myself, every decision made at the potential expense of everyone and everything else. Hinchcliffe is still doing exactly that, but now I find that I can't. I know that the fate of Joseph Mallon and the rest of the Unchanged now rests squarely on my shoulders, and suddenly it matters. Peter Sutton told me they were all that was left of the human race, and I'm starting to think he might be right. If I don't get to Southwold, they're fucked. I might not have the boat we promised them, but this Jeep full of supplies is their lifeline. This food will buy them a little time, and with all that's happening in and around Lowestoft, that time might be enough for them to find another way of getting away. But if I turn up there with Hinchcliffe, they won't have a hope in hell, so I have to get as close as I can, then find some way to get rid of him.

'All this was inevitable,' he says as he swings the Jeep around another corner, just missing hitting a lone vagrant who scrambles for cover. Hinchcliffe doesn't even flinch.

'What are you talking about?'

'The war, them and us . . . the human race has been on a downward spiral ever since the first caveman killed the fucker living in the cave next door because he'd stolen his woman or his dinner.'

'We were better than that,' I mutter. 'It didn't have to be this way.'

'Yes, it did. We're all hardwired to want to survive, and when push comes to shove, we'll do it at the expense of everyone else. I worked in the City, remember? I used to shaft people for a living. When the Change came, the war that followed was inevitable; there was nothing any of us could have done to stop it. We just did what we had to do, you included.'

'We've all played our part, I don't deny that. But trying to rebuild a society based on power and fear? How was that ever going to be anything but a failure?'

'I was never trying to rebuild a society, you idiot. Don't you listen? I was just trying to *survive*. This day has been a long time coming,' he continues, swerving around a round-about the wrong way and rejoining the A12. 'Thing is, Danny, people have *always* been out for themselves, even when they made it look like they were cooperating. Look at this Ankin guy, and all those other politicians you remember: they were elected to serve the people, but all they were doing was making sure their own backsides were comfortable, lining their own nests. All the Hate did was accelerate things; it has helped us all cut through some of the bullshit. Look back and you'll see that *everything*'s always been built on power and fear. Think back to any story you remember from the news before all of this began, and you'll be able to trace it back to someone, somewhere, who wasn't prepared to be fucked over by someone else.'

I don't need to do what he says because I'm sure he's probably right to an extent – but I also think he's wrong, and the fact that a small group of Unchanged have survived this far, and against all the odds, is proof positive. We pass a couple more people, fighter and underclass, I guess, because of their relative sizes, and I notice they all look the same now, pathetically lost, with nothing left to fight for. Hinch-cliffe doesn't even notice them. The bastard truly doesn't give a damn about anyone but himself.

'It can't be as simple as you try and make it sound. Fighting doesn't solve everything.'

'I never said it did,' he says, struggling for a moment to keep control of the Jeep in the slush.

'That's what you're implying.'

'You can get people to do what you want without hitting them.'

'But it's easier if you do hit them? Or just let them *think* they're going to get the shit kicked out of them?'

'Something like that. Look, it's survival of the fittest, that's all I'm saying – and I'm damn sure I'm going to be the one who survives.'

'What for?'

'What kind of a question's that? It's obvious—'

'Is it? Spell it out for me, Hinchcliffe, because I don't get it. If you're the only one left standing after all of this, how exactly will you be feeling? You'll be a lonely fucking despot with nothing to do and no one left to order around. There's a cost to everything, and the more you take, the more you destroy. The last man standing in this world will inherit a fucking empty ruin.'

'You've been spending too much time around Un-changed,' he sneers at me. It's snowing hard again now, a sudden blizzard, and it's blowing in through the broken windscreen, making it hard to see exactly where we are. I'm aware of buildings on either side and I realise we must have reached Wrentham, just past the midpoint between Lowes-toft and Southwold. If I'm going to try and get out of this mess, I need to act fast.

'Just let me go, Hinchcliffe. Keep the Jeep and all the food, just let me go.'

'Why should I?'

'Because I'm dying. I'm not like you; I don't want to fight

any more. I just want to go somewhere quiet, somewhere I'm not going to be surrounded by people taking from me. I've got nothing left to give.'

'My heart bleeds,' he says, clearly not giving a shit. We're approaching the junction in the road now and he brakes hard. He almost loses control of the Jeep again and ends up skidding to a slow stop against the kerb. 'But we both know that's not true, don't we? We need to find this guy Joseph, remember? So which way now?'

'You choose,' I say, determined not to help. We're barely two miles from Southwold, three at the most.

'Interesting,' he mumbles, opening his window and looking down at the road, where the earlier snow has thawed and then frozen again, 'lots of tyre tracks here. I'm guessing this was you earlier?'

I don't bother answering. He drives forward again, following the tracks he can see, and I slump back into my seat with relief. He's taken the wrong route and we're heading towards the bunker now. If he keeps going this way we'll end up back at the farm. I'll make a break for it once we're there. There's a motorbike still lying in the yard, I think, and Peter Sutton's car is probably hidden somewhere nearby. Or maybe I can just trick Hinchcliffe into going inside the bunker, then shut him in? The idea of burying the bastard alive down there is appealing.

'Wait a minute,' he says suddenly, 'this isn't right: this road leads inland. You might have come *from* this direction, but this wasn't the way you were planning to go back, was it, Danny?'

He takes my lack of response as the answer to his question and pulls hard on the handbrake, spinning the Jeep around in the icy slush through one hundred and eighty degrees until we're facing back the way we came. This time when we reach the junction again he looks more carefully at the tracks. My hope that enough fresh snow had fallen to make things less obvious was in vain; he soon spots the wide sets of tracks left by the van and the delivery lorry. The fucker is frustratingly smart. The tone of his voice changes as he accelerates towards Southwold; he sounds excited. He is virtually salivating at the thought of killing Unchanged again.

'How many of them are there?' he asks me. 'There's at least two sets of tracks here, so we must be talking more than five. Ten? Honestly, Danny, you should have known better than anyone that we'd find them eventually.'

'Just leave them alone, Hinchcliffe. Let them be.'

He shoots a quick glance in my direction, letting me know in no uncertain terms what he thinks of that idea. 'You must be sicker than I thought. Leave *Unchanged* alive? For fuck's sake, Danny! I can't believe I'm hearing this.'

He's riled, and I sense an opportunity to distract him – his temper and aggression might yet be his undoing. There's only about a mile and a half to go now, so I need to act fast.

'They're not a threat to you, Hinchcliffe,' I start. 'Just about everybody else worth worrying about is dead – why don't you just get over yourself? Just fuck off and get on with what's left of your own life. Leave the Unchanged alone.'

'Listen to what you're saying, McCoyne,' he growls. 'These are *Unchanged* we're talking about! They were the cause of this whole fucking mess – and *you* want to let them live?'

'What difference does it make?' I ask. 'There's hardly anyone left alive now. Just go your own way.'

'You fucking moron – I should kill you!'

I know where I am now; I can see the snow-covered roofs of the business park where I left the car when Hinchcliffe sent me to Southwold before. If I'm going to do it, I need to do it now.

'I'd rather spend the little time I've got left with the Unchanged than you, Hinchcliffe,' I tell him, deliberately antagonising him now. 'It's fuckers like you who caused this war. At least they're—'

He snaps and lunges across the car at me and I duck under his flailing arms and grab the steering wheel from him, turning it hard right. He tries to shove me back out of the way, but I've caught him off-guard and I won't let go. His balance is off-centre and his reaction is too little, too late. When he finally manages to push me away, he looks out of the windscreen and tries to steer in the opposite direction, but we're going too fast and the ground is covered with ice. The Jeep skids, lifting up onto two wheels, then it flips over. I've already tensed my body and I brace myself as we roll over and over until we stop with a massive jolt as we hit the side of a building. The impact thumps the Jeep back down onto four wheels, my head snaps back on my shoulders with the sudden impact, and there's an immediate sharp, jabbing pain in my right ankle, but at least I stay conscious. Hinchcliffe wasn't wearing a seatbelt and he's thrown forward. His head smacks hard against the steering wheel and there's a sickening crunch. He drops back into his seat, blood pouring down his face.

For a moment I just sit there, numb with the shock of the crash, watching Hinchcliffe and waiting for any sign of movement. He's completely still; I can't see a flicker of life. I unstrap myself and force myself closer, desperate to make sure. I put my ear next to his mouth, terrified he's about to wake up and lunge forward. *Nothing.* No sound. I try to feel for a pulse with numb, ice-cold hands, but I can't feel anything.

This is it.

I'm still alive, and what's left of me is in one piece. The passenger door's buckled and won't open, so I have to scramble out through the broken windscreen. I look back, once, then I start down the road, wishing I could move faster.

It's about a mile to Southwold.

48

I can taste blood in my mouth, and I'm dragging my right foot with every step, but I'm almost there. I follow the intermittent tyre tracks left by the others for as long as I can, then take a shortcut across the very same fields I worked in when I was last here. The ice-cold air numbs the pain a little. The falling snow reminds me of ash drifting down, and I feel a sense of déjà vu, recalling walking along the motorway just after the bomb. I remember lying on my back on the warm, sticky tarmac and watching Ellis as she disappeared alone into the radioactive gloom. The memory of everything I lost that day is enough to keep me moving towards the centre of Southwold. I might still be able to help the rest of the Unchanged get away, but more than that, I don't want to die out here on my own.

I stagger into the village, fading a little more with every step. Everything looks different here today; I'm not even entirely sure this *is* Southwold. The dusting of snow makes everything look featureless, but that's not the real reason for my confusion: the wrecked buildings, destroyed by Hinchcliffe's fighters, peek out through the ice, almost as if they're ashamed to be seen, and the pointless devastation is heartbreaking. The village now looks uninhabitable; I can see row after row of burned houses, and my own disorientation continues until, at last, the distinctive outline of the lighthouse rears up out of the snow ahead of me. It may be one of the only buildings left undamaged. I head straight for it, alternately looking up at its unlit light, then down at the undisturbed snow lying all around me, desperate to find more tyre tracks or footprints. Surely they'll be hiding inside

– no Unchanged with any sense of self-preservation would risk being caught out in the open.

I cross the road and walk past the ruins of the hotel from where John Warner used to run this place. The building has been completely gutted by fire, as have many of the surrounding buildings. There's a snow-covered mound of charred corpses, blackened limbs entwined, in the middle of the village square. The burned faces are staring eternally into space, and I force myself to look away. I want to remember this place as it was when I was last here. John Warner had genuinely good intentions, but he was wasting his time; I realise that now. What's left of my side of the human race is fucked: doomed to repeatedly beat itself into oblivion until there's nothing left of it but ashes and a handful of empty, hollow men like me.

I take a wrong turn and have to double back, following my own footprints until I find the track again. I'm exhausted when I eventually reach the lighthouse and I lean up against the curved outside wall of the building for support, slowly sliding around it until I find the door. I half-step, half-fall inside.

I am relieved to finally be out of the biting wind. The building is as silent as a tomb, and I catch my breath with surprise when I step back and trip over the outstretched arm of a corpse. I look down and, bizarrely, I feel real relief that it's someone like me and not one of the Unchanged. Judging from the stink, not to mention the skin discolouration, this guy's been dead for a while. Probably one of Warner's lookouts, killed by Hinchcliffe's men.

I stagger to the foot of the stairs which spiral up inside the lighthouse and I listen hopefully but all I can hear is my own laboured breathing. Maybe they're hiding at the top of the tower?

'Joseph,' I shout, my voice echoing around the confined space, but though I wait for an answer, none comes.

'Joseph, it's Danny—'

Still nothing.

I start to climb, knowing I have no choice but to check every inch of the building, just to be sure. It's not long before I'm wishing we'd agreed on a meeting place with fewer stairs. I have to stop after every third or fourth step and psych myself up before I can climb higher. I'm craning my neck upwards, searching for movement in the shadows way above me. Where the hell are they?

With each step I take, the more obvious it becomes that Joseph and the others never made it to Southwold. I guess anything could have happened to them once they'd left the bunker. Those tracks in the snow, they could have been made by anybody – this whole area may well have been crawling with people, any one of whom would have killed the Unchanged in a heartbeat, massacring every last one of them before even stopping to question why they were there or how they'd managed to survive for so long.

And if the refugees didn't get them, it's likely that Ankin's troops would have. With hindsight, leaving the bunker now seems like the stupidest, most suicidal of moves . . .

But they had to try: they couldn't just sit there and wait to die, could they? I shout out a couple more times as I continue to climb, my legs trembling with the effort, but each time the only reply comes from my own voice, echoing back at me.

Finally I crawl the last few steps on my hands and knees and reach the top of the lighthouse. I have to use a rail to haul myself upright, and I stand and catch my breath, taking a moment to let my pounding heart calm before I push myself through the door and out onto the observation platform. The wind's freezing, and even stronger up here, and I have to hold on tight just to stay upright. I lean back against the glass which surrounds the huge now-redundant lamp and stare out towards the North Sea. I'm barely able to support my own weight any longer. I'm filled with an overwhelming, crushing sense of disappointment that they're not here.

As I look out into the nothingness of the grey clouds and falling snow I find myself imagining how the Unchanged might have been caught. I picture Joseph, trying hopelessly to reason with Hinchcliffe's Neanderthal fuckers or Ankin's troops, whichever found them first. I picture the little girl – Chloë – trying to run from them, her bare feet crunching through the snow as she's chased down by a pack of the foul bastards . . .

I've had enough.

The more effort I put in, the less I achieve. It's time to stop. I should go back inside, drag up a chair and sit back and watch the sun rise as many more times as I can before I go. No one will disturb me up here – no one will know where I am. More to the point, no one will care.

Is this the moment where my life starts flashing before my eyes? Just for a second I allow myself to drift back and remember things as they used to be before the war: the hell-hole of a flat where I lived with Lizzie and the kids; barely making ends meet on the pittance I earned at my mindless job; the endless arguing, struggling with the kids, and all the grief I used to get from Harry . . . but I'd still rather be there than here today. Christ, I spent so much time focusing on the negatives that I completely missed the positives which were there in abundance: the security within the four walls of our flat, the closeness I had with Lizzie and the children . . . It's an old cliché, but it's so true: you never realise what you've got until you lose it. I remember the war, and the euphoria I felt whenever I ended an Unchanged life – I can't believe that I was actually *thankful* for the Hate, for the freedom I thought it gave me. And now, even though I try hard not to, I find myself thinking about Ellis again, remembering what the Hate did to her, what she became. What it did to all of us . . .

It must be time now.

343

I lean back against the window and look out to sea, numb with cold, weak with effort and hollow with disappointment. I'd go back inside, but I'm too tired to move, and everything's too much effort. Maybe I'll just sit here and—

Wait. What's that? It's probably just the snow, my eyes playing tricks on me, but I thought I just saw something moving down there at street level. I lean forward and look down, though I'm struggling to focus through the blizzard. Then I see it again: a brief flash of movement between two buildings as someone runs from right to left. I shield my eyes and peer out along the seafront, but I can hardly see anything through the white glare. As I follow the line of the promenade, I see *something* – scavengers? Refugees from Lowestoft? Or maybe I'm just hallucinating now? Perhaps that'd be a good thing . . .

I look out towards the remains of the pier, then fix my eyes on the car park, which begins outside its dilapidated frontage and stretches away into the distance. I can see the shapes of several long-abandoned vehicles, and a couple nearer the entrance to the pier which aren't quite as covered in snow. Wait a second—

I lean precariously far out over the edge of the railings, as far as I dare, knowing another few yards won't make a scrap of difference but praying it will. I'm desperate to make out more detail. Through a momentary break in the fast-falling snow I can see it's a van and a lorry, and although I can't distinguish any real level of detail from back here, I'm sure I can make out a woman's face on the side of the lorry. I remember staring at a woman's face on the side of the lorry in the cowshed, just before Peter Sutton showed me the bunker. And that's definitely the van I drove away from Hinchcliffe's factory yesterday.

Jesus Christ, they must have made it – Joseph and the others made it to Southwold! I quickly scan the length of the pier again, this time focusing on the collection of ramshackle wooden buildings on the walkway which stretches out over the ocean. And now I can see them, some sheltering from the blizzard in empty gift shops and cafés, others hanging out over the railings, waiting to catch sight of the boat that's never going to come: the last of the Unchanged.

I make myself move again. I've got to get down there.

Stumbling down the tightly spiralling steps is infinitely easier than climbing up. I curse myself as I trip over the corpse again, then start moving towards the pier, wishing I could go faster but knowing I'm on my last reserves of energy. There's not much time left, either. When I reach the promenade I start the long walk up towards the pier. The bitter wind is knocking me two steps sideways for every step forward I manage, and I'm walking virtually blind, the snow like a dense fog.

But eventually the pier looms large ahead of me, a once proud and grand façade that's now as crumbling and worn as everything else.

'McCoyne,' someone shouts, and I look around for who-ever's yelling.

I can't tell where it came from, or who it was – didn't sound like Joseph; was it Parker, maybe? Or one of the others? The noise of the wind and the waves just adds to the confusion. I stop when I reach the Unchangeds' vehicles and look back to see someone walking towards me – whoever it is, he's clearly struggling – is he injured? I take a couple of steps back towards him, then stop, shocked: it's *Hinchcliffe*.

Now I try to get away, but his hate and fury are driving him on, making him oblivious to his pain. He reaches out and grabs my shoulder, then spins me around and throws me back against the side of the van. The noise echoes through the air like a rifle shot. I can't stop myself bouncing back off the metal straight into his fist and he catches me hard on the chin. I slam back against the van again, then drop to the ground. My face is numb and my head is filled with blinding pain as he picks me up by the collar and lifts me up until our faces are just inches apart. My feet are off the ground, toes barely scraping the slush.

'Hinchcliffe, I—'

'What the hell are you trying to do?' he screams. 'I should kill you right now!'

'That's your answer to everything,' I say, and he throws me back against the van again. This time I drop to my knees and watch him as he comes towards me, drenched with his own blood, fist raised ready to strike again and finish me off. I don't have the strength to defend myself any more. Just let it happen . . .

But he stops himself and says, 'I don't understand – why, Danny? You could've had it all.'

'What, like you?' I manage to spit at him. My mouth is filled with blood. 'We've lost everything, all of us, you stupid bastard, and it's all thanks to people like you. The more you try to take, the more stuff slips through your fingers. Do you not realise that? You started with a whole town and ended up barricaded into one corner of it: a prisoner in your own headquarters. But you've lost that now, and there's nothing left. It's over. It's all gone. Just leave me alone, Hinchcliffe.'

He's still staring down at me, breathing hard. He takes a step back, then runs forward and punches his fist into the side of the van. I slowly pick myself up. My blood is dribbling red into the snow around my feet.

'Just kill me if you're going to,' I say wearily. 'Why don't you just get it over with?'

'Because you're still useful,' he snarls. 'Look around you, Danny. The fact you're here at all just proves my point: there are people still fighting and dying in Lowestoft, but you're safe – *we're* safe. It's like you've been observing the rest of us, only getting involved and getting your hands dirty when you absolutely have to.'

'Or when you forced me to.'

'Look what you achieved—'

'Hinchcliffe, that's just it: I've achieved *nothing*. I've lost everything, just the same as you.'

'But you're the man who walked free from a gas chamber. You've told me stories, about how you talked your way out of Unchanged traps – for Christ's sake, Danny, you were almost right under one of the bombs, but still you managed to get away.'

'Right place, right time,' I mutter, still not understanding what he's getting at.

'It's more than that. It *has* to be. Listen to me, Danny, we can get out of this mess and start again. I know where we can find food, and there's a place—'

'You're out of your fucking mind! You just don't get it, do you? All you know now is fighting. You won't ever change, it doesn't matter where you go or what you do; the end result will always be the same. You don't need me to help you fuck things up again.'

Hinchcliffe turns and as he walks away I can see that he's limping badly, and losing a lot of blood from his left leg.

I push myself off the side of the van and try to slip past, but I've barely taken more than a couple of steps before he lunges for me and I lose my footing and hit the ground. I'm on my back, looking up at him as he draws a machete.

'Maybe you're right,' he starts.

'Leave him alone, you bastard,' another voice shouts, and Parker appears in sight, aiming a rifle directly at Hinchcliffe. Behind him Joseph Mallon is standing in an open doorway.

Hinchcliffe stares at them in disbelief. Unable to suppress his instinctive hatred of the Unchanged he dives at Parker, who scrambles back out of the way. He fires the rifle, but he misses as Hinchcliffe, anticipating, drops to the ground. He's obviously oblivious to any pain because he's on his feet almost immediately, wielding his blade, and Parker's rifle and his severed right arm fall into the snow just a short distance from where I'm lying. Hinchcliffe drags the Unchanged man down and drops onto his stomach, then plunges the machete into his flesh, again and again and again. He's totally consumed with the Hate, everything else temporarily forgotten.

I drag myself back up and push Joseph away. 'Get out of here,' I yell at him, and I shove him back through the door and pull it shut again. I watch him as he watches me through the glass, then he starts to back away, because Hinchcliffe is up again. I catch a brief reflection of him and I spin around to catch him as he throws himself at the door like a vicious animal.

It takes all my remaining strength to hold him back as he hisses, 'Unchanged,' trying to fight his way past me, 'we have to kill them . . .' He tries to throw me to one side, but I've got hold of him and I won't let go. We spin around a full three hundred and sixty degrees together, almost like we're dancing, and he smashes me against the door again. I feel every bone in my body rattle, but still I won't let go.

'Just leave them, Hinchcliffe,' I plead with him, our faces just inches apart.

'Leave them? Are you out of your fucking mind? Listen to yourself! You know this will never be over until they're all dead and—'

'You know as well as I do that this is *never* going to end,' I pant. 'If we're not fighting Unchanged, we're fighting each other. It's like you said: we're on a downward spiral, and this is rock bottom.'

'You're further down than me,' he says, and he lifts up his knee and thuds it into my balls. A wave of nauseating pain shoots through me and I let him go.

Another Unchanged man bursts out through the door and rushes him, hitting Hinchcliffe at speed, and the two of them smack into the side of the delivery lorry. For a second it looks like Hinchcliffe's been overpowered, but his raw aggression and sheer brute strength is remarkable; he pushes the malnourished Unchanged man away with barely any effort, snatches up Parker's rifle by the barrel and beats the man around the head repeatedly with its wooden butt.

'Come on,' a desperate voice whispers in my ear, and Joseph gets his hands under my shoulders, lifts me back up, and drags me towards the pier door.

Hinchcliffe doesn't notice; he's totally focused on the kill, venting all his anger, hatred and frustration on the poor battered bastard who lies dying at his feet.

49

We move quickly through the dilapidated amusement arcade, Joseph supporting me as we stagger between the rows of silent gaming machines, weaving around one-armed bandits and smashed videogames, at a speed I can barely match. He leads me through an open door at the far end of this large, high-ceilinged room onto the pier, where I'm almost blown over by the wind, which is ferocious. The slatted wooden walkway is slippery as grease, the snow and ice turned to slush by the salt spray. Ahead are several narrow buildings, stretching up along the centre of the pier, and a door at the front of the third one along is being held open.

'Get inside,' Joseph says, shoving me into a gift shop; there are still rows of dust-covered souvenirs on the shelves that line the walls. There are Unchanged cowering in every available space, their frightened faces staring back at me wherever I look. They're all desperate for help and reassurance, but I'm in no position to provide either. Some of them are armed, ready to fight, for all the good it'll do them.

'Where are Parker and Charlie?' a man crouching down next to me asks.

Joseph shakes his head and I mutter, 'They didn't stand a chance. None of you do.'

'What the hell happened, Danny?' Joseph asks. 'What about Todd and Dean? The boat?'

'We never made it as far as the boatyard,' I explain. 'Hinchcliffe was waiting for me back at the house – he waited until we'd loaded up the Jeep, then he killed them both while I was out of the way. I didn't know he was going to be there, Joseph, I swear. The fucker caught me out.'

'Who is he?' someone else asks.

'Shit. Peter told me about him,' Joseph says. 'Said he was the worst of the worst.'

'That's about right.'

'But there must be something we can do?'

Tracy, the doctor, gets to her feet. 'I know exactly what we can do,' she says, picking up a bludgeon. 'We kill the fucker.' She has to get past me to get out, but as she tries to push me aside, I try to hold her back.

'Listen,' I start, 'you don't understand—'

'No, *you* don't understand,' she yells at me. 'There are almost thirty of us and just one of him. We have to get out there now and kill him.'

'Then that will make you just as bad as him.'

'So? We have to do this to survive – there's a world of difference between killing just one man to save all of us and all the thousands of innocent deaths that people like him are responsible for.'

'Is there?' I ask.

'Of course there is!'

'So what do you think I am?'

'What?'

'Me and Peter Sutton, how do you think we managed to survive above ground for so long?'

'Peter told us,' she answers; 'he told us he learned how to fake the anger so he could make them think he was like them. He said you were the same. Peter risked *everything* for us.'

'There's no disputing that,' I say, 'but he wasn't completely honest with any of you either.'

There's a ripple of discontent that I should dare to say something negative about Sutton.

'What are you talking about?' she asks after a moment.

'We're like them, not you,' I tell her, 'Peter and I. We're

the Haters, just like Hinchcliffe out there, and all those other bastards who've hounded you and hunted you and made your lives hell for the last year.'

'I don't believe you,' she says, but her eyes drop and she flinches away.

'It's true,' Joseph says. 'I knew Danny from way back and he's right: he was a killer. He learned how to suppress the urge to fight.'

The space around me grows in size and I sense people pushing themselves back against the walls, trying to put the maximum possible distance between us.

'Then as soon as we've finished with this Hinchcliffe, we'll come back for you,' Tracy sneers.

'Probably not worth the effort. I'll be dead soon, anyway.'

'Good.'

I'm about to speak again when someone screams. I turn around and look back along the pier in time to see Hinchcliffe coming this way.

'Thing is,' I tell them, 'whatever it was that caused the divide between us, it doesn't matter now. I don't know *why* it happened – I doubt any of us ever will. All that matters is what happens next. We've got to abandon all this "us or them" bullshit, because *we're* all that's left of the human race. You can either put a stop to the killing today, or keep going at it until we're all dead.'

'Which part of this don't you understand, you fucking moron,' Tracy snarls. 'If we don't kill him, he'll kill us!'

Hinchcliffe is checking each of the wooden buildings in turn, kicking down doors in his rabid hunt for the Unchanged.

'The first person I killed,' I tell all of them, shouting to make myself heard over their nervous voices and the sound of the wind battering this exposed shack, 'was my father-in-law. And do you know why I did it? You want to know what made me kill Harry, and the hundreds of other people I went on to kill after him? I killed them all because I thought that if I didn't, they'd kill me. Do you understand that? People like *me* killed people like *you* because we thought we had to do it before *you* killed *us*. Does that make any sense? It doesn't to me – almost a year further on, I still don't understand why. But does it sound familiar? It should, because you're saying exactly the same thing now: kill him before he kills us.'

'That's the way it has to be,' Tracy says, and my empty heart sinks because I know she's right.

The door at the other end of this narrow building flies open and Gary, the badly scarred man, rushes out into the open. He's armed with a length of metal tubing. He runs back towards Hinchcliffe to try and head him off, but the poor naïve bastard is still shackled with the uncertainty of being Unchanged and instead of immediately attacking, he stops short and wildly swings at Hinchcliffe, who deflects one glancing blow then catches the end of the pipe as it comes towards him again. Even as badly injured as he is, he has more strength than this single starving Unchanged. They're both holding grimly onto the metal tubing, one at either end, but Hinchcliffe uses his greater weight to swing Gary around into the railings that run along the edge of the pier. He screams in agony and drops to his knees, and before anyone else can react, Hinchcliffe is laying into him, beating him to a bloody pulp with ferocious speed, then lifting up his battered frame and pushing it over the side of the pier into the freezing waves below.

'Get them out of here, Joseph,' I yell as panic spreads quickly through the group, and he immediately starts herding the surviving Unchanged out through the door at the far end of this narrow space and back down the pier, moving them along the other side of the wooden buildings. I check around for the children and see a woman is carrying Peter Sutton's grandson in her arms, and someone else has got Chloë on their back. Then I see the boy Jake's head deep in the middle of the throng.

'Keep moving and keep safe,' I yell after them. They're all that's left now.

I exit through the other door. Hinchcliffe's staggering towards this building and I block his way forward, trying to buy them a little time. He stops and rocks back on his heels. He's panting hard.

'Just let them go, Hinchcliffe,' I tell him again, though I know my words will have little if any effect. 'What difference does it make to you whether they live or die? There are so few of them left – there are so few of *us* left. Just let them go—'

'You know I can't do that,' he says, lurching closer to me, 'and you shouldn't be able to either.'

He clumsily tries to sidestep me, but I move too, and he just slumps against me, exhausted, his sudden weight almost knocking me over. He tries to push past, but I won't let go.

'Are you scared of them?' I ask. 'Do you think a few starved Unchanged are that much of a threat to you? Christ, Hinchcliffe, some of them are just *kids*.'

'It makes no difference,' he growls.

'Just walk away – I'll come with you. We'll go wherever you want, start again somewhere, like you said. Let's just end this today.'

'I'll end it, Danny, and I don't need your help any more.'

'But can't you see? The fighting is the *cause* of all of this, not the solution—'

Hinchcliffe grabs me and flips me over, slamming me down onto my back and winding me. I can hardly breathe. As he starts to walk away I roll over and reach out to try and catch him, but I'm too slow and I watch helplessly as he strides down the pier. I crawl over to the handrail and use it to drag myself back up onto my feet as Hinchcliffe pulls my pistol from his pocket. He starts firing indiscriminately at the Unchanged and the first two shots go nowhere, but the third hits one of them in the leg and a woman collapses with a shrill scream. As if inspired by her pain he surges towards her, and though she's still alive when he reaches her, she's dead within seconds, finished off by the remaining bullets and a volley of savage kicks to the side of her head.

In the chaos the Unchanged have split up. Though most of them are continuing to move back towards the shore, others have panicked and are running towards the end of the pier. Hinchcliffe is heading after them, half-staggering, half-sprinting. It's almost unbelievable, how he's managing to find the energy to keep moving. He tackles the closest of them, an elderly man with long wispy white hair, and pulls his legs out from under him. He smashes the old man's face repeatedly into the metal base of an observation point, continuing long after he's dead, until the head is a misshapen lump of gore, scarcely recognisable as human.

The Unchanged woman was right: Hinchcliffe will never stop. He has to die. I grab a stubby blade from my belt – the last weapon I have – and move towards him. As I drag myself along the railings I skirt massive holes in the decking, huge chunks that look like they've been bitten away by some enormous creature. I can hear the pier creaking and groaning beneath me, as if the metal struts are straining to hold us up now. Maybe they are.

By the time I've managed to make it across, Hinchcliffe is attacking another man, smothering his screaming face with his hand. He's distracted enough by the intensity of the kill that he doesn't notice me until I throw myself at him. He lets go of the man's corpse and turns on me, using his bulk to force me back into the furthest corner of the pier. He grabs me around the throat, then tightens his grip. My feet slip in the slush and I can't get a grip. I can hardly breathe. I try to stab him but he's too fast, despite his injuries. He catches my wrist and smacks it down against the railings. The knife drops.

His eyes lock onto mine. 'I've had enough of you, Danny McCoyne, you useless cunt. You're worse than they are.'

'I'm *the same* as them,' I gasp. 'We *both* are.'

He shoves me back, an expression of utter contempt on his hate-filled, blood-streaked face, and he raises his fist, but my eyes focus on something happening behind him and he sees that I'm distracted and looks back over his shoulder.

The Unchanged are returning. A group of four of them are advancing towards him, led by Tracy, the doctor. She's brandishing her bludgeon, holding it up high, ready to strike.

Hinchcliffe drops me to the ground, immediately dismissed, and he turns and throws himself at them, growling in his Hate-fuelled frenzy.

Tracy lashes out, but he ducks under her weapon and grabs the man beside her instead, catching him completely off-guard. He twists the man's outstretched arm around and forces the knife he's carrying up into his own gut. Tracy spins around and smacks the bludgeon down across his back, and Hinchcliffe drops to his knees. Another man comes at him with a block of wood and the two of them rain down a barrage of blows, but still he keeps fighting – the fucker's on his knees, but he won't give up.

Blood is pouring from Hinchcliffe's gashed skin, matting his long filthy hair. He tries to stand, pulling himself up onto one foot, but before he can get fully upright the fourth Unchanged comes at him and plunges a serrated blade deep into his belly. He drops onto his back, his skull cracking against the deck, and this time he doesn't move.

I lean back against the edge of the pier, too exhausted to do anything. The three remaining Unchanged stand over Hinchcliffe's corpse, then turn to face me.

'Now you,' Tracy says.

'Just leave me. I helped you.'

'You're one of them, McCoyne, and as long as there are any of your kind left alive, we're all still in danger.'

'You're wrong. It's over now.'

'It will be once you're dead.'

The three of them come at me like a pack, with a speed

and anger I can't match. I try to squirm past, but one of them trips me up, rolls me over onto my back and stamps his boot into my groin.

'Kill him,' another one of them shouts, yelling into the wind, '*finish* it!'

I try to get up, but I'm kicked straight back down again and I land on top of Hinchcliffe's bloody corpse. His eyes flicker open. I can't believe the bastard is still alive.

'You were wrong,' he says, gurgling blood, his voice barely audible. 'You should have listened to me—'

'Fucker's got a grenade!' Tracy shouts.

Rough hands grab me under my shoulders and drag me off Hinchcliffe and I'm dropped on my back again. I manage to turn my head, and I see that Hinchcliffe has the grenade he took from me earlier. One of the Unchanged tries to prise it out of his hands, but it's too late; the pin's out. Someone stamps on his wrist and his fingers instinctively open, letting it go, and as I watch, it rattles along the walkway. The Unchanged scatter, running past me screaming, but it's too late; there's nothing they can do. They can't—

EPILOGUE

They dragged those bodies they could find from the surf beneath the collapsed pier. A few were injured, but most of them were dead; one was dying. They carried the dying man to safety and hid him in an empty building, and made him as comfortable and warm as they could; there was nothing more they could do for him than that.

They stayed there for more than half a day. Danny McCoyne briefly regained consciousness when they started to move and drifted in and out of darkness for a couple of minutes, just long enough time to know that the Unchanged were carrying him. He could hear the snow crunching beneath their feet – or was it shingle? He looked up, and between flashes of brightness, he saw a face he recognised.

The man put a reassuring hand on his shoulder and spoke to him. 'Not long now, Danny. Almost there.'

The next time Danny McCoyne woke for longer than a couple of minutes, almost two days had passed and the whole world felt like it was moving, rolling beneath him. He felt the same hand on the same shoulder, gently shaking him awake this time. He tried to sit up, but he couldn't. He had no strength left.

When Joseph saw that he was awake, he called for help and two men wrapped Danny up in blankets and carried him outside. The brightness hurt his eyes and his vision was blurred, but he could see and feel enough to realise that they were at sea. They set him down in a deckchair, and Joseph sat next to him.

Danny looked around and, very slowly, his eyes began to

adjust to the daylight. At first all he could see was the grey sky above and the blue-green water around them, but soon he could make out distant browns and blacks too as the world slowly began to come into focus. He was looking back towards the land and the blackened, smouldering ruins of yet another dead town.

'We've been out here for the best part of two days,' Joseph said quietly. 'A few of us found this boat just outside Southwold and managed to get it going. I just wanted you to know that we made it. Thought you'd like to see what you did before you—'

He didn't need to finish his sentence; Danny knew what he was avoiding saying. Joseph was right, he didn't have long – he was surprised he was still here at all. Or maybe he was dead already? He didn't think that was the case; he could still feel his body running down. Some bits of him ached; other parts he couldn't feel at all. He hurt less than he had before, but he knew that wasn't a good thing, not in this case.

The boat turned slowly through the water. The hazy yellow sun was right above them now, just about visible through the wispy cloud cover. It hurt Danny's eyes, but it was too beautiful not to look at.

'This is what's left of Felixstowe, I think,' Joseph said. 'We've stopped a few times to look for supplies, but every place we've tried has been pretty much the same as this. Everywhere is dead. Not a soul left alive. Oh, we found your Jeep before we left Southwold, got all the supplies you brought with you. Quite a hoard you had there, Danny.'

Joseph waited for a response, but none came.

'We're going to keep heading down this way. My guess – my hope, maybe – is that if we can get south of what's left of London, we might find somewhere, Kent, maybe. Dungeness, perhaps.'

'Isle of Wight,' Danny managed to say, his weak voice sounding like someone else's. 'It's supposed to be nice there.'

'I'll bear that in mind,' Joseph said.

Danny didn't say anything else. He just sat back and listened to the normality of the moment: the waves lapping against the bow of the boat, the engine chugging contentedly, people talking, kids playing . . .

'You still here, Danny?' Joseph asked, startling him. 'I was hoping you were going to stay with us a while longer.'

'Don't know if I can.'

He rested his hand on Danny's arm. 'You should try. You deserve it. You did a good thing, you know.'

'I did more bad things than good. We all did.' He turned his head slowly and looked across the deck of the boat. He saw people standing out in the open, surveying the dead town they were approaching. Just a couple of days ago, they'd been trapped underground with little realistic prospect of ever seeing daylight again. He watched Chloë playing with Peter Sutton's grandson. They were both bundled up in as many layers of clothing as they could comfortably wear. At the bow of the boat, a man and a woman stood together, locked in a passionate embrace. The wind was blowing the woman's hair, the two of them looking like characters from some film.

'You want a drink?'

'No. Save it,' Danny murmured.

'You should try and have something.'

'No point. Just want to rest now.' He closed his eyes, the brightness finally too much to stand. In the darkness he remembered the people he'd lost. He wished that Lizzie and their three children were on this boat now instead of him. Or maybe here with him . . .

A few seconds passed. Or had it been minutes? The dead town seemed closer than when he'd last looked.

'You still with us, friend?'

Danny's eyes flickered open again. 'Very tired, Joseph.'

Joseph wrapped another blanket around his shoulders and Danny let his head loll forward, but he snapped it back again quickly when he heard a child yelp with pain. The noise startled him, made him panic—

'Don't worry, it's nothing,' Joseph said, sensing his dying friend's unease. 'It's just kids being kids, that's all.'

Danny watched as a woman separated Jake and Chloë. They were bickering over half a can of drink.

'She stole it off me,' Jake protested. He yanked Chloë's hair, then grabbed the can from her and knocked the rest of it back in one gulp.

'That was mine!' Chloë screamed, lunging for him again. 'I'll get you for that,' she sobbed.

Danny, exhausted, let his eyes flicker shut.

THE END

ACKNOWLEDGEMENTS

Sincere thanks to all those who've helped make the *Hater* series what it has become: both those who've read and enjoyed the books (okay, maybe *enjoyed* isn't the right word), and those involved with the publication of the series (especially Brendan Deneen and all at Thomas Dunne Books in New York, and all at Gollancz in London).

Particular thanks to John Schoenfelder and Jo Fletcher, without whom (a) these books might never have happened, and (b) the overall story wouldn't have been half the story it eventually became.

Thanks to my friends and family, especially Lisa and the girls. Ladies, without you all I'd probably have plenty of cash and loads of spare time, but I'd also be bored, lonely and completely uninspired. I may be becoming a grumpy old man and I might not say it often enough, but you are my world and I love you all.

Finally, thanks to my late father-in-law, John Tipper, and my mother-in-law Betty, for introducing me to Lowestoft and the surrounding area. Thanks also to whoever it was who once casually said to me, 'I bet it's easy thinking about the end of the world when you're staying with the mother-in-law,' and set me on the path to writing *Them or Us*!